High Riding Heart

Blaze of Change

Book 2

Purr-
Welcome back to
the moose Ranch!
Enjoy the new adventures!
- Kathryn Bartow

Kathryn Bartow

Blaze of Change
Copyright © 2019 by Kathryn Bartow

This book was printed in the United States of America.

ISBN13: 978-1-949570-76-2 (Paperback)
ISBN13: 978-1-949570-77-9 (eBook)

Library of Congress Control Number:

BOX OFFICE MEDIA CREATIVES
42 Broadway, New York, NY 10004
info@boxofficebrand.com

To my readers:

I Thank you for choosing to read the continuing story of the Moore Ranch. All the characters, locations and activities, their names, descriptions and content are fictional. Any resemblance to actual persons living or dead, events or locales are entirely coincidental.

CONTENTS

If
What is ahead of you
Scares you,
And
What is behind you
Hurts you,
Then
Look above you
He will never fail to help you.

"God, Hope and Faith... mix in good family a few Prayers and you will prevail at every hardship and challenge."

-- Sara Moore Barnes

Part 1
Revenge

Cecelia Lang, one of the Detectives from Carnon that was involved in the Murder Investigation of Wes Grant on the night of the Brandon Rodeo was in fact hiding her own intentions and agenda all the while Russell Barnes was accused of committing the crime and had been held in the County Jail. Kent Harrison and Nick Borden from the Brandon Police Department uncovered her plot and intentions against Wes and proved during the Court Trial that she had pre-meditated plans and ambitions, therefore resulting in Russell's aquittal. John Moore purchased the Rodeo Stock of the Barnes Rodeo Company ensuring the payment of legal fees owed to Sara's brother Mark Bloom for his representation of Russell. When the 'dust settled' from the trial, Russell hired on to the Moore Ranch; he and Sara married a year later.

****

In her hands she held fast to the article in the *Brandon Times* dated two years earlier reporting the release of Russell Barnes; she also held the wedding photograph of Russell and Sara Moore. Though no one was present to hear her words, Cecelia Lang looked at the barren walls of the cabin and spoke with certainty; "I'm going to make you... little missy, you will rue the day you asked your brother to help that slimeball Barnes... and you..." She brought the newspaper article to the forefront; "You... when I get through with you you are gonna know what hurt really is. You think this is over? Not a chance... not by a long shot!"

Reaching for the glass of whiskey she had poured from the last bottle of her father's private reserve, Cece turned toward the deeply inset fireplace centered on the north wall of the cabin. Resting her attention on the dusty photograph of her father standing next to her with the 12 point Buck she had skillfully hunted in the heavy Thanksgiving snow just days after her twenty-first birthday. Uncle Sy had captured the 'Kodak moment' of her claiming the kill on what unbeknownst to them all would be their last hunting trip together. Raising her glass to the photograph she quickly drank the whiskey in one swallow. Slamming the emptied glass on the table beside her she knew she was ready… a sly smile creased the corners of her mouth, her eyes in a partial squint, as she picked up the handgun from the coffee table that awaited her retrieval. Stroking the barrel, she paused… finally … she had two years in jail to work this out… the sense of satisfaction consumed her. As she returned the gun to the previous position on the aged woodwork, the sight of her father's gun next to the rope, knives and duct tape arranged neatly in the center of the stout handcrafted tabletop challenged the level of euphoria and intoxication of the whiskey. Years of abuse from her father as he taught her to properly clean guns and reload bullets had left the scarring in the hand worked surface she now slowly traced with her right hand fingertips; her slight smile and sigh acknowledged the memories were among the happiest she had with him.

Cecelia's heart raced with anticipation; she would begin tomorrow. It was to her advantage that the media had not yet disclosed the information as to her release from the Carnon County Correctional Center; no time for the Moore Ranch to prepare for what Cecelia Lang had planned.

"Well Pops, guess I'll set in your chair and wait. Got any advice for me? I know, I've thought of everything." Lowering into the chair, she placed both hands on the worn leather armrests. Rubbing the leather forward and back, she sighed heavily. With a renewed smirk; Cecelia Lang poured another glass of whiskey.

*****

Sitting in the captain's chair at the kitchen table; newspaper layed out flat before him, John Moore smiled at his wife of 55 years as she poured his second cup of coffee. "Well, do you still think getting into the

Rodeo business was nonsensical? My dear, just look at the 'life' around us here, this ranch has had the two best money-making years that I can ever recall. Guess it helps that Michael has taken over the hard work and has even learned how to aquire venues. Folks from all over want our stock at their Rodeos, Why..." "Hold on there John," Mary sat beside him and placed her left hand on his right arm, leaned to him and kissed him gently on his cheek; "Yes, Michael is doing a fine job with *your* adventure. He's a young man now, with dreams and a future he needs to decide for himself. If you recall, after the Wes Grant Murder Trial he seemed interested in Detective work. I think he would be a fine Law Officer." Smiling as she stood up slowly removing her hand from his arm, he noticed a firmness in her voice. "John, we have to let *him* choose what he wants. Ranching is in his blood and he loves it, the cattle herd is flourishing, Sara has managed the horses and Russell... well, he truly has been a surprise." "Mary, if anyone knows that, it's me. If I had just trusted Sara..." "Don't go there John... you had to learn for yourself the man that Russell is... I for one am relieved that it all turned out." Mary leaned over and kissed John on the top of his head and then ran her fingers through his thinning hair. John returned to the paper; lifting it out of the glare of the swag ceiling light over the table.

"Oh no!" John slammed the paper back on the table. Mary was startled by the vehemence of John's outburst. "What was that for?" She had returned to the sink and was placing the cleaned dishes in the strainer. "Cecelia Lang has been released from the Carnon County Correctional Center." Mary dropped a glass, as it shattered on the floor she was unable to move aside as she stood locked in place at hearing his words. John looked up from the paper "Don't move... Stand right there... I'll get the broom."

Michael had been dilegently going over the receipts from the Centerton Rodeo when the sound of the breaking glass diverted his attention to the voices in the kitchen. He had been in a deep concentration of the report with no concern as to his grandparents yet he now found himself straining to hear the reason for the interuption. "Gram? You okay?" "Yes, dear. Just dropped a glass. Your grandfather is cleaning it up" "Ok... just checking!"

The resounding tones of the antique hall clock chimed 8 am. Michael looked to the wall where the massive work of handcarved Black Walnut boasted the filigree of horses and cattle; above the clock face the livestock brand of the Moore Ranch had been deeply burned into the wood. The sideways diamond shape surrounding the outlined -M-; the emblem of a heritage held true through generations of an honorable family. Watching the carved horsehead chain weights reposition as the bull on the pendulum slowly swayed in perfected rhythm, the chimes of the hour rang as Michael marveled at the vision he imagined of his great great grandfather presenting it as a gift to Belle Moore; the original matriarch of the ranch the day they lifted the arciform over the entrance road effectuating the inception of the Moore Ranch Legacy.

Returning his thoughts back to the present and with a quick second 'look over' of the papers and figures before him, he knew with certainty the ledger was correct. The large brown leather chair slid easily back away from the oak desk. Michael propelled the chair backward with his feet while rubbing the arms of the chair his father and past patriachs of the ranch had sat in while overseeing the accounts of business. As if he could feel the presence of those fine men, he took a moment to gaze at the wall where the family photos of yesteryear as well as recent photos from the wedding of his mother to Russell Barnes were proudly displayed. Russell had refused them taking memories of his father Samuel from the wall, he knew that Sara loved Samuel even after his death and would not discount that in his marriage to her. Samuel was a Moore and Russell stated many times he wished he had been able to know the man as a rancher and as a father. Michael knew that Russell had no intention of replacing the father he loved, he was now his mother's husband. Michael had an affection for the man that brought 'life' back to her and proved to be a fine mentor in the Rodeo business. He placed the papers in the file folder as he stood up slowly taking in a heavy breath, he smiled as he exhaled on the walk to the file drawer already opened for receipt of the paperwork. He then retrieved the piece of his father's neckerchief he carried with him; gave it a squeeze: "Another good Rodeo Dad, another good Rodeo." Closing the drawer and then placing the tattered cloth to his heart, with a small sigh he then replaced it to his pocket.

John was at her side with the dustpan and old sweep broom even before he had finished his behest to her. "Are you alright?" "Yes, guess it just startled me, I didn't realize it had been that long already." Mary had feared the return of Cecelia Lang. She was unpredictable and dangerous. Combine that with a revengeful woman and the only result Mary could see was not good. Not good for Russell and certainly not good for Sara. She had hoped her fears had remained masked. "Not long enough in my book! She should have seen a lengthier sentence if you ask me!" There was no hesitation in his expression of opinion.

"When was she released?" Mary had sat in the side chair of the table, a slight shake in her voice. "10 days ago." "And they're just now letting people know? What kind of paper is this? There are a lot of folks that will take great concern to this!" She pulled the paper from John and began reading the article. "Oh, John… we have to tell Sara…" "And Russell too" The elder Moores held hands; each in their own mind invisioning the responses to the announcement.

"Tell mom and Russell what? Gram, are there any of your blueberry muffins left?" Michael was across the kitchen, reaching for the muffin tin on the counter; "Oh good… one left just for me!"

"Come sit by me dear, I'll get the butter for your muffin" "Thanks Gram. MMMM… these are the best you've ever made!" "You say that everytime!" "You know why?" "No, but I'm sure you are going to tell me!" She smiled at her grandson and then winked at John. "Cuz if I tell you they are your best then you just have to try again to do better! That way you just keep making them aso I can keep eating them!" "Oh, you think that's it, do you!? Well if you want it to be then it is. You are a silly boy at heart sometimes and I sure do love you and love that you love my muffins!" Gram teasingly pinched Michael's cheeks then kissed the top of his head and laughed as she retreived the butter dish from the counter and set it on the table next to his plate. Returning to the chair she had been in, she reached for John's hand and bowed her head. Michael missed the glance between his grandparents in their silent communication.

"Michael, Cecelia Lang has been released." Six words spoken by his grandfather and then silence. Michael's hand dropped to the table still holding the muffin.

Sara entered the kitchen " I absolutely never tire of this… Seeing the two of you hand in hand… The love here is so deep. I am so Blessed to be a part of this family, Good Morning Michael, you're up and about early today!" Sara reached in the cupboard for her favorite coffee mug; the hand made clay art project Michael had made for her when he was eight years old. He had made one for both his parents. In the 'Barrister' book case by the television the mug he had made for Samuel set next to a photo of Micheal and Samuel at the art show with his first place blue ribbon for 'Most Humorous'.

"Get your coffee dear and come sit with us." Sara noticed the uneasy tone of Mary's voice. "Sara, you know that even with Samuel gone, you are a daughter to me, and Russell, well, all I can say is…" "Oh goodness Mary, she knows… Just tell her would you!" "Tell me what?" Mary looked at John, then to the newspaper still on the table and then slowly reached her left hand out to Sara. Sara lowered her mug to the table; "What is it Mary? You've got me worried now" "Cecelia Lang has been released."

Sara slowly released the hold on the coffee cup, raised her arms from her elbows and rested her head in her hands. Without lifting her head she spoke; "When?" "10 days ago." John interjected himself back into the conversation. Still with face hidden so as to not reveal the concern overtaking her; "Russell left for the Co-Op meeting early this morning, oh God, I'm sure he knows by now. This is going to be a living Hell for him." In one motion she raised her head, lowered her arms and regripped the coffe mug. As she drew a long sip of coffee Sara accepted the extended hand of the beloved mother of her deceased husband, she looked into Mary's tearful eyes... eyes that Sara had seen weep for dying calves, tear joyfully at the birthing of a foal, smile in pride as Michael grew through the years ... the eyes of a heart broken mother when she buried her son... and the eyes of acceptance when Sara married Russell. Now, she saw something not usual for the undaunted grande dame of the family... Fright.

Michael stood behind Sara and placed his hands on her shoulders. "Sure hope it's not too much to ask... but... when I brought the horses in for feeding this morning, Capp's got a half decent cut on his left forearm. Have not a clue where he'd got himself tangled. I'll take the tractor and some tools out and check the fence line. That's all I can figure that he could have done. Would you look at it Mom? I put furacin[1] on it and left him in his stall. "I'll help you get the fencing tools and look at him while you're out." Sara was glad to have a diversion from the Celcelia Lang news.

"Good to the last drop! Isn't that the slogan these days?" Sara had risen from her chair and stood now at the sink. "Excuse us... please, another day in the life of the rancher is well on it's way. Fence fixing and horse healing shall not be interupted by the likes of one Cecelia Lang!" "Sara, we'll let Russell know you're in the barn when he gets back." The concern in John's voice was not unnoticed by both Sara and Mary. "Go on now... help Michael get the tools gathered... we'll see you when you get back in." "Come on Hank, you too Baron... Michael will want his side-kicks out there with him" All three laughed at the elation of the Border Collies as they quickly ran past the kitchen table and stood waiting at the back door. Sara reached down to pat each of the dogs. "You are really a couple of clowns, you know that don't you?" She opened the door and the race to Michael began. Laughing, Sara tried to keep up with the dogs knowing it would be to no avail.

---

1 Nitrofurizone –Furicin--is a water soluble based anti bacterial oitntment or spray for wound care

Winded, Sara met Michael in the barnyard. "Hey Speedy...I was going to help you!" Sara smiled as she looked upon her grown son. So much like his father; Sara knew with certainty that Samuel was proud of the man standing before her. She felt the familiar touch on her shoulder. Looking to the Heavens she placed her right hand to her heart.

"I'll be at least two hours out there, think I'll use the chain saw and cut up that old tree in the back corner that fell during the winter. It still baffles me that Capp got cut out there. Just doesn't make sense. Not that high on his leg. I put him out with the colts last night, none of them would hurt "Uncle Capp"! Besides... Mom? Mom.. where are you?" Startled out of her thoughts Sara regained her composure. "Good idea... your grandfather has been complaining about it for weeks! Be careful... I'll have lunch for you when you get in. I Love you!" "I love you too, Mom. You ok?" " Yes, just the news this morning. We'll deal with it if the need arises. Let's just hope all the worry is for nothing. I'll get the gate..." Sara reached her hand to wave as Michael passed her on his way through the corrals toward the Red Pasture.

Observing mother and son, Cecelia Lang remained hidden in the hay loft of the aged horse barn. She could hear the conversation regarding the injury on the gelding's leg and that he would be out there a while. This fit right into her plans. Snickering to herself she said "Have fun at the fenceline... that's not where he got cut." She held the smaller of the two hunting knives that had been removed from her belt for the purpose of the wound distraction in her left hand as she rubbed the blood off with loose hay. When she could no longer hear the tractor she checked to make sure that Sara was approaching the barn. Her visual attention fixed on Sara; Cece reached with her right hand and opened the snap of the knife case, returning it quickly. She re snapped the flap without a double check to insure the knife was safely restrained.

Sara opened the barn door unaware that Cecelia Lang was stealthily making her way toward her. The larger of her knives held tightly in attack position.

Cecelia did not know that her smaller knife lay in the hay where she had been hiding.

"Well, Capp, looks like we need a little time in the cross ties. Michael has concerns as to your leg wound. Sure hope you won't need a Vet, our Miss Katy won't be home on break from Ohio State for another few weeks!" Approaching Capp in the end stall, Sara held the halter in her left hand as she reached to the stall latch with her right. A nicker from the horse paused her motion.

She felt a knife point in her back.

"Don't scream. Don't say a word. Ain't nobody gonna hear you anyway."

Sara knew that voice. Cecelia Lang.

Sara started to speak, the pain in her back intensified. "That's a good girl... keep quiet. Hurting you... right now anyway... that's not in the plan." With the realization that this woman had every intent to harm her, Sara braced herself for a fight. A fight for her life.

Sara lifted her heel and waited for Cecelia to shift her weight. At the moment she did so, Sara stepped her heel onto the toes of her assailant with such force that the pressure of the knife released from her back and Sara had time to step sideways; no longer positioned between the stall door and Cecelia. She dodged a thrust of the knife aimed at her throat. Falling back against a stall door, Sara quickly regained her footing and turned toward the tackroom. A much needed reserve of adrenelin fueled by her trepidation surged through her as she ran through the aisle of the barn.

Cecelia grabbed a lasso rope hanging on another stall and with the precision of a seasoned roper had the loop ready at the hondo[2] knot.

---

2   The Hondo knot is used to form the loop the lasso or lariat slides easily through to tighten the loop

She picked up the halter that Sara had dropped when she fell against the stall door and flung it toward her target; the well thrown loop caught Sara's feet as she jumped over the halter.

Sara tucked her arms in anticipation of the fall to the ground in hope of being able to roll out of the fall. "Got you... you bitch... now maybe you'll listen to me." Cecelia approached Sara as she was rolling over and when she was close enough, Sara bent her legs and kicked her assaulter in the mid section pushing her away. Cecelia let go of the rope and with the taughtness gone, Sara escaped the bind. Grabbing the stall wall, she was able to pull herself back to her feet; resuming her quest for the door. The pain in her right ankle slowed her gait and she could feel blood on her left hand. No time to be concerned. Afraid to look back, Sara limped with as much speed as she could attain. Cecelia was close behind her and by the sound of her pounding boots on the barn floor, she could easily overtake her.

"Not so fast...You're not going to get your way this time! This time you are going to be the one to lose everything! You and that scum husband of yours."

One well aimed punch centered in Sara's back and Cecelia Lang had succeeded in knocking down her prey. Now all she had to do was get her out of there without being discovered. "You are a tough one... better take precautions" She retreived the lasso that lay on the barn aisle floor just a few feet from the door. Noticing a triple loop of fence wire hanging on a nail above them Cecelia spoke aloud, "What luck I am having today! Sure as hell is better than duct tape! Too bad it's smoothe wire, 'barbed' would have suited me just fine."

Sara was unaware of the conversation.

Satisfied that the restraints were secured, Cecelia stood up to look upon the bound woman she blamed for the travesty that had become her life. "This is definetely my time, my time to show all these rats this cat means business!"

The length of rope left over worked as a pulling handle; easing the strain of the lifeless body weight. Dragging Sara toward the tree line knowing soon they would be hidden safely in the overgrowth, Cecelia felt the rise of triumph. Her plan was working.

Regaining conciousness Sara realized her hands were bound tightly with the fence wire. Neglecting the intesity of the restriction, she knew she would have to get back up on her feet if there was to be any hope of escaping her captor. Scrambling the ground she attempted to interupt the pull Cecelia had on the rope that was tied under her arms and around her upper chest. Sara knew she only had one chance… she hoped her arms were long enough and still had the strength… "Please God, help me!"

Hearing Sara's faint voice, Cecelia's stride was paused. "Not going to happen… you are mine now!" Sara swung her arms back in aim of Cecelia's legs hoping to knock her down. Estimating the intention, Cecelia flipped the rope and Sara was flung face down into the ground. Sara screamed her last plea before darkness once again.

****

Michael reached the far end of the pasture and turned the tractor against the hillside. Satisfied it would remain stationary, he stopped the motor and set the brake. He looked over at the fallen tree and realized it was much more massive than it had appeared when looking at it from a distance. "Well….. Mountain Man… this is going to be a bit more of a challenge! Are we up for it? Absolutely! Good thing I brought the big chainsaw… gonna need all the help and horsepower I can get!" Reaching for the tools Michael could hear Capp whinneying. Looking toward the barn Michael again found himself talking aloud, "Sorry, Capp… Mom must think you need to stay confined or she would have let you out. Mom knows best!" He turned back to the wagon of tools. Michael's laughter was halted when he again heard his horse only this time the tone was different. The intensity of the tone caught Michael's attention, as he turned back around to see the barn and ranch house, a movement in the woods off to the right caught his

13

eye. Capp had a pleading in his whinney. Straining his focus on the movement on the right, Michael heard his mother scream. Hank and Baron barked a response to Capp and then turned to Michael. "Yup... let's go boys! Now!"

There wasn't time to start the tractor and Michael knew he could run faster and not have to open the gates. The chainsaw landed beside the other tools when Michael tossed it behind him as he began to run. "I'm coming Mom! I'm coming" With the swiftness of a deer he ran down the hillside, lept the fences and stood where he had last seen her. "Mom!!!!!! Where are you?" The dogs announced their arrival at the barn and soon had their noses to the ground following an unfamiliar scent.

"John? Is that Michael? Do I hear the dogs? I didn't hear the tractor come back, what do you suppose is wrong?" "Sit tight Mary, I'll go out to the barn and see what's up." "I'll pause the movie... just love this new video thing where you can pause." "Yes, all these newfangled things, what will they come up with next?"

John was on his way out the back door when he saw Michael running behind the barn. A quick glance to the Red Pasture to see the tractor still there and to hear the urgency in his grandson's voice; elevated concern for Sara as she had been in the barn tending to Capp.

"Michael......Michael.... What's wrong? Where is your mother?"

"I don't know. That's just it! She isn't here. Gramp, she isn't here. She's gone. I think someone took her. Gramp, we gotta find her."

"Whoa... what did you say? Someone took her?"

"Capp was making all sorts of weird sounds and it caught my attention and when I looked over this way I saw something or someone in the woods. I ran down the hill and Mom is nowhere. Is she in the house with you?"

"No, Michael, she isn't. Maybe she's in the barn… maybe she scared a wild animal out of it and that is what you saw."

"Gramp, she didn't come out when I yelled for her."

"We best go in and check to see and check on Capp too." He hoped he had not conveyed to his grandson his concerns for Sara's safety, Cecelia Lang was back in the area and John didn't trust her.

"Mom? You in here?" The carriage doors were open as they entered. Michael could see the halter on the aisle floor and the trail of blood when he looked toward Capp's stall. "Gramp!!!! Look!!"

Both men ran to the halter. Michael picked it up, held it to his chest and as Capp whinneyed again he felt dazed as he walked to his horse. "Oh Capp… where is she? What happened? Gramp… Mom never even got to Capp… the same medicine is on him that I put there. He was trying to tell me something was wrong." "Good thing you listened or we might not have known until it was too late. She can't be far, you and the dogs start searching the woods, I'll go in and call Kent Harrison, he'll get the police out here right away. We're going to find her Michael… we're going to find her and she will be alright." "But Gramp… the blood…." John placed his right hand on Michael's left arm. "As tough as she is… it might not be hers." "You are right… she always thinks positively… we have to now as well." Michael grabbed his rifle out of the saddle scabbard tied to his father's saddle that was gifted to him on his thirteenth birthday. To himself he said, "Think positive… yeah, I positively think I'm gonna shoot the sonavabitch that took her!"

Hank and Baron were at the tree line waiting for Michael. The three wheel ATV had trouble starting and Michael's frustration escalated. "Darn you… not now… start… please! I have to find her!" He had nearly given up hope after several unsuccessful attempts when the engine coughed and finally remained running. "Time to ride! I'm coming boys… to the woods!" With the ATV in high gear Michael drove past the running dogs and was soon traversing the hillside behind the barn. "Thanks Gramp for making me take that safety course… and you had your doubts…" Holding the rifle in his left hand, Micheal stood and raised his left arm straight up in the air. "Right on! We're ridin'now!" Returning to the seat he manuevered down the embankment and across the rocks in the creek and saw a piece of his mother's shirt on the ground as he climbed the other side. "Boys! Look!" Hank and Baron sniffed the fabric and in a single movement both dogs turned to the right off the trail in pursuit of the scent.

"Brandon Police…." John Moore did not wait for the completion of Mrs. Harrison's salutation.

"Mrs. Harrison, this is John Moore out here on…"

"I know where you are … you sound like there is a problem"

"There is, you have to send help out here right away! Sara is missing… I think she's been kidnapped!"

"Whoa… kidnapped? Tell me what happened." As John relayed the course of happeneings, she put the phone on 'speaker' so the officers in the station could hear as well. He had not finished when Detectives Kent Harrison and Nick Borden waved to her indicating they were on their way.

"Mr Moore… slow down… Kent and Nick are on their way and they have four officers with them as well. Stay in your house. Be mindful of any unusual activity in or around the house, do you know where Michael is?"

"He and the dogs are in the woods looking for Sara. He's on the three wheeler."

"Mr. Moore, does he…"

John interupted her, "Yes, he has a rifle."

"Damn" Her voice trailed off as she finished the word. Sgt. Blakeman entered the reception area of the station to see the concerned look on her face. Raising his eyebrows and with a look seeking an explanation for her concern, he opened both hands in an outward movement. His attention turned to the phone as she again spoke.

"Mr. Moore..... please..... Stay put. The men will be there soon. Give Mary my prayers."

"Thank you, I just can't sit here and do nothing when she could be hurt or even..."

"Stop... right there... You have to stay focused. Let us do our job Mr. Moore, please."

"I can hear the sirens coming down the road. Thank you. I will let you go now."

"Mr. Moore... be careful." She heard the click of the disconnection.

"What is going on?" Sgt. Blakeman had leaned over Mrs. Harrison's desk trying to see the information she had written down of the conversation with John Moore.

"There's trouble out at the Moore Ranch. Sara is missing, they think she was kidnapped."

Simultaneously and in an alarmed tone; "Cecelia!"

"I'm going too... Get someone to sit at my desk." Sgt. Blakeman was out the front door before she could answer or refuse him his command.

*****

17

Russell leaned back in his chair while listening to Paul Jennings' monitone voice. It was hard to keep attention to the meeting and he realized that Don Harbor, sitting on his right was nearly asleep. "You don't get to nap if I don't!" Russell nudged Don under the table with his foot. Looking away from Paul he grinned as he spoke to the aged manager of transportation. Startled, the portly man was at full attention to the amusement of the others sitting around the table.

"Ahem!" In an attempt to regain control of the meeting, Paul fisted the table to bring the focus of the members back to him.

"Now, we have to discuss the feed mixer business. It really is time to think about replacing the old verticle feed mixer, the repairs are getting out of hand. Any opinions?" "I've done a bit of research on the new horizontal mixers and their efficiency ratings. Looks favorable. We can even mix feeds with high concentrations of molasses with the paddle style and we all know the fancy horse people like to treat their horses with sweet feed. If we want to keep up with the market we're going to have to improve our systems." Russell had stood as he spoke enabling him a clear view of each man sitting at the table. "Think about it, many of the ranchers in the area have 'lotted' off parcels and the moderate horse operations have moved in to our area. We still have a major market of big ranch spreads but it appears as though the trend is aiming at the smaller ranch and smaller herds of livestock. We need to compete with the tack shops and even the hardware stores that are selling the shiny pre bagged specialty feeds from national companies. We have the ability to draw a lot of business revenue just by pampering the smaller operations. With that being said, I think we might also consider delivery service as well."

"Now hold on there, this is a Co-op for the ranchers that belong here. We've been self sufficient for more years than you've been around this area, what makes you think you can tell us what we need to do to keep in business?" Steven Blane interupted Russell, projecting a definite ire in his tone. The Blane Family Ranch had been the founding contributor to the Co-op. Each year the Blane family sponsored 4-H and FFA[3] participants at the County Fair by providing the stall and pen bedding for their animals.

Steven Blane personally sponsored the Fair King and Queen contests.

"I understand your concern, and with all due respect to your family and to the Co-op, I recommend that we purchase a Horizontal Paddle mixer in order to fulfill the current needs of the community and to incorporate a delivery service to enhance…"

"Stop right there… you're not making sense, if we were to deliver to them… why would they need to come in and buy anything else? Seems to me we'll be losing sales not gaining them!"

Russell turned to Steven and smiled. "Steven, if we pamper them with delivery of the large items, and include small items in the delivery if they know of them ahead of time, then they as the customer will feel a sense of loyalty to return the compliment so to say. They will come in to the store for items they might have been able to buy elsewhere, but will prefer to patronize the company that takes care of them. These are a whole new breed of folks, women that can't lift big bags of feed… granted they can get those big saddles up on their horse, but to lift feed bags, they want someone else to do that for them. Customer Service… We have to provide Customer Service on their terms in order to hold them."

"He's got a good point, Steven." Usually quiet during the meetings and abstaining from conversation, Don's speaking up in agreement with Russell brought an instant silence in the room. "Russell, that pretty wife of yours is heavily involved with the horseback riders in the area, perhaps you could consult with her…"

---

3   F F A The Future Farmers of America is an organization for youth in preparation for agricultural careers.

Halting Don in mid sentence, Jimmy Blane ran into the door and then opened it, out of breath and still holding onto the doorknob, trying to keep it from swinging out of his grasp he caught his breath, "Mr. Barnes... you gotta get home... something about Sara... the police station called and said you need to get home!"

Russell turned from his chair and put his left hand on Jimmy's shoulder. "Catch your breath... now what did you just say?" "You gotta get home, the cops called... something about your wife!"

As Russell fled through the doorway he heard Don say; "I make a motion we buy a horizontal..." Russell was out of hearing distance and did not know that the motions to buy the mixer and implement his ideas on delivery service were made and passed. All he knew was he had to get home.

The radio in his truck skipped on and off as he drove irratically through the ruts in the 'old wash board' road that he had decided to take as a shortcut to the Moore Ranch. The road was seldom used because of the condition of it but there was no other choice in his mind that today his F150 would be navigating it at a high rate of speed.

Slowing down for the cattle guard[4] the radio came back on at the moment the newsman began his report.

"In local news, the two year sentence of Cecelia Lang in the pre meditated attempted murder during the Wes Grant trial that headlined as the Russell Barnes Self Defense Murder Trial is now up. Lang has been released and said to have returned to Carnon." The radio went off again.

Russell stared at the dashboard of the truck in wanting disbelief of what he had just heard. An automatic response of both hands slamming

---

4   Cattle Guard   a series of grids over a pit extending side to side in a roadway spaced as to prevent loose livestock from crossing thus eliminating the need for a gate in a fence line.

onto the steering wheel resulted in the blare of the horn which in turn brought him out of the stuporous daze befallen to him. Renewed with an even more vehement need to get to the ranch as he pushed the accellerator to the floor board of the truck, he could hear sirens off to the north heading toward Highway 9.

Speeding through the right turn onto the ranch road, Russell held steadfast to the lurching of the truck as the rear left panel barely missed careening into the arch post. He saw the Police cars parked at the barn as he aimed for the walk way to the house. The dust from the sudden stop of the truck in the driveway had not settled as Russell ran with great swiftness and then lept the porch steps. With barely enough time for the door latch to release, he threw open the aging ingress of the homestead. Clutching the short wall of the laundry room, his back arched as he attempted to halt the forward motion of his body.

"Russell!"

"Mary! What is happening" I got told to get home right away and on the way here I heard that Cecelia Lang is out of the Carnon Correctional joint and I heard sirens..."

Mary had placed her left arm over his back and her right on his right shoulder. "Sit... don't argue just yet, sit." "Mary?" "I know, I know... Michael is out..."

Mary had not finished her sentence when Detectives Nick Borden and Kent Harrison entered through the still opened back door.

"It was open..." "Come in... tell us what you think. Tell us you've found Sara!"

"Found Sara???? What is going on???? Kent, talk to me, please!!

"We got the call from Mr. Moore regarding..."

Russell interupted the Detective, "John called the Police? What for? Where is Sara?"

"You know what, I think we will make better use of time if I fill you in on the way out to the barn. We have a team of experts with us for finding even the most remotely valuble clues and evidence that I have all confidence is waiting for us out there as that was the last place that Sara was known to be."

"You really think she was kidnapped don't you? I heard on the radio today that Cecelia Lang is on the loose again. Oh, God.... Noooooooooooooo."

"Russell... we're here to do a job. I understand this is difficult for you..." Kent had not finished his sentence when they heard a voice in the loft. "Hey... up here, think we've got something you need to see Detective Harrison!" In perfect assimilation, the two men moved toward the straight ladder step leading to the upper level of the barn. Kent reached his hand to Russell to steady the feared man as he stepped off the top rung and into the haymow. "You ok? You don't have to see this if you..." "I need to Kent, I need to." "Man, I hope I find someone to love someday the way you love Sara..." "You will... it took me years... be patient. Right now, you and I need to find out what is up here your team is so interested in."

"Over here! I found a knife!" Kent gloved his hand and reached for the weapon. "Watch your step! There's blood... oh God, there's blood!" "Russell, I am sure you remember Matt Brewer. He has transferred here from Carnon for good now and as he is now certified as a Forensic Investigator, we are really glad to have him with us. Who would have thought his first case over here would be related to his last one in Carnon!" Russell reached his right arm and held out his hand to Matt. Grasping firmly in response to the laudation, Matt smiled as he nodded his head. "It's good to be here. I have spent two years interning in East Dale and ready to take on Brandon. I hear Nick Borden and Callie McGregor are making it official in October!" "We sure are!

Hope you can make it to the wedding." Nick had joined them in the hay loft. "Wouldn't miss it!" Matt offered his right hand to Nick as he topped the ladder and with his left arm, he placed it behind Nick in a 'man hug' position.

Returning his attention to the evidence, Matt commented to the group of men awaiting his report. "That knife you are holding has very little blood on it and look at this..." He leaned in to point specifically to the blade. "...These hairs are really short and dark. Sara has light hair. Didn't you say that Capp had a cut on his leg and that is why Sara was out in the barn? I'm speculating that our suspect Cecelia purposefully cut Capp's leg in such a way as to give probable cause being the fence line. That would get Michael out away from the barn and Sara into it. Cece hid up here and didn't realize that she dropped this knife."

"Makes sense, Matt. Good catch. But what about the blood downstairs in the aisle way? If she left the knife up here..." As soon as he said it, Kent realized that there was likely another knife or weapon and Cecelia still had it. Matt held out his hand to retrieve the weapon as Kent handed it to him. "We'll test this blood to verify if it is human or not. The lab already has a few samples from down stairs." "Samples? Like more than one?" "Yes, had to get several, hoping to find just who all it belongs to. Blood tells a serious story for us. We've collected 3 boxes of articles to take to the lab for prints, DNA and blood. Hope you don't mind." "Not at all! You do what you need... take what you need... if it helps find her!!!!" Russell's voice faltered as he spoke and even though he tried to hide the trembling of his hands, he knew the men around him understood his fears and did not comment or condemn his actions. "I'm so relieved that not only do we have the toughest team of men working to find her but you are my friends as well. You love her too. Thank you. Thank you everyone for all you are doing." Russell could no longer hold back his tears. Kent placed his right arm over Russell's left shoulder, "We're going to get her back, I promise. Now, let's head back downstairs and get the searching started. After you Russell..." In respect for Russell, each man made his way down the ladder without speaking.

Bruce Netty stumbled into the barn exhausted from running back to the barn from the trail he had found leading into the woods. "You gotta see…" "Catch your breath son, what did you find?" "Pieces of a shirt. Here…" As he handed the pink cloth to Nick, Russell fell to his knees. "Sara had on her favorite Marshall Tucker Band tee shirt this morning. The bottom of it is pink." Kent reached down and put his right hand on Russell's left shoulder. Facing his friend, he knelt down. "We're going to find her. She is the toughest woman I know. We're going to find her."

"We have to. Kent, we just have to." The four men were momentarily silenced as each had images in their minds of what could possibly transpire in the hours and possibly even days that lay ahead.

"Take us to where you found the strips of her shirt." "This way…" Being young and referred to as "The Rookie", Bruce knew he had the opportunity to prove himself valuable to the Department with this case and he had every intention to do so. "There are three-wheeler tracks out the side door, you think she's…"

"Those are Michael's, he and the dogs are out there somewhere already ahead of you." Approaching the men as he entered the barn, John Moore spoke slowly; "The Remington isn't in his saddle scabbard… I don't think he will hesitate to use it so you men had best get to finding him before this bad situation gets even worse. Russell, you might want this…" John handed him the Winchester shotgun he kept behind the seat of his truck. "I'm too old, I can't help out there… go… get our girl… use this if you have to." "John…" "Go…"

"Hold up Russell, you need to stand this one down, sorry… I know you want to go, but you just can't. You're too close emotionally and that only ends up wrong. You won't be any good to Sara if you compromise us doing our job. This is what we are trained for. Please, I do not want to have to restrain you. Stay here at the ranch we will notify you the minute we know anything. Besides, after all you have been through to clear your good name and gain the trust of everyone, I can't let you risk that if this gets ugly…" "I can't do that Kent, I …" "You have to. I have to insist." "The boys…" "Boys? You didn't mention anyone other than Michael…" "Those three are always together, my best assumption is they are here … he would have seen to it." "Those darn hooligans… Michael was already in the woods when we got here. The others may be as well. I am not sure just how I am going to rein them in, but I have to for everyone's safety and assurance of the outcome of this that we all want. Believe me, I am not happy at all that they are in the woods and I don't want to have to worry about you as well."

John put his arm over Russell, "Come on, you heard the detective. I know you want to go, believe me, I know… but… perhaps it's for the best." "It's not 'for the best', she's my wife… I should be there for her." "Be waiting for her when she returns, she will want that." "Oh, John…" "I know Russell, I know" "It's just wrong…" "I know." The elder placed his left hand on Russell's back hoping to reassure him.

They stood for several minutes listening to the men as they devised their plans to rescue Sara. Russell turned to John with a downtrodden sigh; "I hate this." "I do too. I'm so sorry."

Kent was glad to see that the all-terrain vehicles had arrived quickly after he had made the call to the station. "Horses would slow us down, glad we have these!"

Slowing just slightly as they passed the men standing at the ATVs, Brent and Charles rode towards the woods. "Not these horses Detective Borden… we'll help don't you worry!" "Mr. Thomms… You boys be careful! Hey! Come back… you can use a 'walkie'…!" Charles set his horse into a sliding stop, spun around and retrieved the walkie-talkie and was back in a lope beside Brent as if all in one movement. Out of earshot of the four men, Brent 'fisted' Charles' arm as they galloped to the trail. "Show off!" "Yup!" she is a good mare! Gotta strut her stuff!"

"Darn it, Borden, those kids should not be out there!" "All due respect sir, how did you plan to restrain them on horseback?" "I just told Barnes he couldn't go and you give those 'yahoos' walkies? What's the matter with you?" "They can get eyes in the woods where we can't." "And you think Barnes couldn't do the same? Geez, that is just cruel to the guy… just cruel. Wait until you're married, you are going to see things from his standpoint. Hope you're ready for that." Kent walked toward the four wheel drive truck they would use for the search. As he opened the door, with a glance toward Russell and John he could see the anguish in the body language of the husband wanting with all his love to be a part of the search. Kent shook his head and sighed. Speaking above the sound of the engine, "We'll bring her back, I promise. We'll bring her back." Kent sat in the driver's seat and spoke not a word as Nick entered the vehicle.

"Did you bring a gun? All I have is my .22" "Why of course I did Mr. Thomms, you think my old man Hunter raised a scare-dee cat? Got my pistol right here." Charles tapped the holster on his right side. "Got my knife too… what? Don't look at me like that! I'm pree-pared! Like a good boy scout!" "Yeah, you're a good 'Scout' alright! As long as you are 'scouting out' Marge Pelton! Speaking of Marge, did you call her about this?" "Yeah, she's worried and said that she and Mary will come over to stay with Gram Moore." "Bet they bring their horses, what do you think?" "Yup." "Hey… over there" Charles followed Brent's gaze to see a bent bush branch with blood on the break.

A familiar whistle engulfed the stand of trees. Brent and Charles recognized it immediately as the 'secret whistle' of the 'Three Amigos'. In one voice, "He needs help!" Pushing the horses to a faster gallop they followed the tire tracks of Michael's ATV until at last they found him stuck in the creek bottom.

"You can't go? Then the horses will tow!!! Never underestimate *real* horsepower!" Charles' rope was around the handlebars of the ensnared machine faster than Michael could re seat himself. "Hang on! Put 'er in Neutral! Pop that baby outta there!" Lady backed away from the creek bed and as the rope became taught, the ATV eased out of the mud. Brent dismounted and while taking the rope off the handlebars he began to laugh at the sight of the three friends, two horses and one mudded machine. "We just can't go anywhere and not find some kind of trouble!" "Nope! Makes life fun!" "Get back on that thar mudball and head out to the meadow, we'll take the trail to the old rail bed, they meet over by McGregor's back lot." "Good Plan"

"Boys? You there? Over." Charles threw the walkie talkie to Michael.

"It's Michael, here. Over."

"Where are you? Over."

"The old creek bottom, I got stuck. Charles and Brent pulled me out. They are going to the old rail bed and I'm heading for the meadow. Over."

"Any luck? Over."

"Just a broken bush branch with blood on this trail. Looks like this is the right direction. Over."

"Mrs. Harrison radioed in, there's an old cabin about 2 miles north that Lang's grandfather once owned and maybe her dad too, we're heading that direction over the Ridge, pick up the mine road and hope to find the cabin. Over."
"10-4. Over and Out"
"Over and Out."

******

Roused from her stupor by a sharp pain on her left side, Sara tried to focus through her swollen eyes. "Well hey there 'Mary Sunshine,' welcome back to the land of the living. Not that you have much more of that to do, but I suppose you ought to feel your death, that would just make it all the more better a victory for me." Cecelia stood over Sara's bruised and broken body as she lay on the floor of the cabin. "How...?" "Don't try talking little Missy, I would think it would be rather painful as you knocked the side of your face on that rock pretty hard. Suppose screaming for help will be out of the question too. Such a state you are in! And nobody knows you are here. Pity, I have you all to myself." "They'll find me..." "Don't hold your breath on that one, this cabin supposedly burned down years ago, ain't nobody gonna be coming up this way, not even close."

"They'll find me..." Sara slipped back into unconsciousness.

****

"There it is... the old cabin. I'd heard it had burned." Michael spoke in a near whisper. Hidden in the woods within 200 yards from the cabin, the ATV engines were off and the horses stood securely tied to trees. "Guess your mother did a little Detective work herself on this one! I Sure am going to have to thank her when this is done Detective Harrison." Nick Borden spoke before Kent had a chance. "Thank goodness for her or we might never have looked here." Kent leaned in to speak with only Nick; "Listen, I know you think I was hard on Barnes, but you and I both know his emotional state would render a for certain bad outcome of all this, we just can't take that chance." "I know, you are right, but geez, did you see his face... man, that is a look I don't ever want to see again. It's like he was..."

Charles had been standing off to the side of the group; he turned completely around before returning to the others. "Guys, there's a faint scent of fire in the air... we need to get closer to that cabin!" "Matt and I'll take the front, Nick... you and Bruce take the back. You three... you stay put. This is a police matter and should things go wrong, you should not be a part of it. Do you hear me?" He spoke knowing that the likelihood of them obeying him was very slight. "I mean it. Stay here." Michael glanced at Charles and Brent. No words were needed between them. They knew. "Can't promise you that, Sir. Just can't promise you that." "Your mother does not need you hurt... or worse... we are going to get her. Trust me." Kent Harrison knew that his words fell on deaf ears. All he could do was hope that the young men used good judgments and stayed clear of possible gunfire. "We're going to help,

28

don't try to stop us. That's my mom!" "Let us do the Police work, you be here to hold her when we bring her out. That is what she will want. You need to be here for her to see and feel. Do not risk her seeing you get hurt. Please." He waved his hand horizontally in a 'that's final' gesture and joined Matt Brewer in the stealth approach of the cabin.

"We can't just sit here guys!" "Nope." In a huddle formation; left arms over the other's shoulders and each with a right hand in the center; quietly they recited each letter individually: "A-M-I-G-O-S" They began the trek to the cabin.

Cecelia sat in her father's overstuffed chair staring at Sara's non-moving body on the floor. The faint snapping sound of a twig outside the cabin diverted her attention to the south facing window. Though the woman on the floor was unable to hear her, Cecelia whispered in her direction "You'd better hope that was a deer out there or you're dead a little sooner than planned." Cece rose slowly from the chair and crawled toward the window out of sight. Turning her head back over her right shoulder, she had to be certain that Sara was still unconscious.

She heard footsteps. "Damn! How the hell did they find me?" Looking around the cabin trying to determine the whereabouts of the intruder, Cece did not notice the flutter of Sara's eyes and the quick movements in her hands as she regained consciousness. Without moving her head Sara took in the scene and began figuring what she would have to do in order to escape. Sara could hear the footsteps behind her just beyond the back door. She wanted to yell for help but knew her best odds were to have Cece remain thinking she was unconscious until it was too late for her captor to re-maneuver.

Kent hand signaled Matt to stand on the opposite side of the front door and he motioned to Nick and Bruce to cover the back door. The four men were quickly in place without a spoken word.

"Did you see that? Wow! It is like they have their own language. Only problem is maybe they don't know the window over here isn't boarded up like the rest." Brent was leaning down as he spoke. Michael stood to get a better assessment of the cabin and after just a moment turned back to Brent and Charles. "You thinkin' what I'm thinkin'?" "Yes, we are!" You get ready with the horses just in case she does get away, and I'll cover the window. This ends now." As the riders untied the horses and prepared to mount, Michael slipped towards the side window out of sight of the Detectives.

Cecelia heard the footsteps on the front porch and then followed the sound of another to the back door. "Ha! They went to the wrong side! Dumb asses... well little Missy, looks like I'm gonna have to shoot you and git out the south side. A little change of plan but it'll work. Just as long as you are dead, that's what counts!"

She had no idea that Sara heard every word and was preparing her return attack.

Unaware that Michael was crouched outside the window, Cecelia slowly reached her right arm up to the sill to push up the sash. Reluctant to open after years of closure, with a final thrust the pane gave way. He could hear her labored breathing as she pushed on the window. Michael was smiling as she opened the window. "Hmmm cool...that makes it easier for me, Thanks." His silence never broken.

Adrenalin raced within him as the anticipation of action mounted. Never before had he been so frightened yet exuberated at the same time. He could feel her on the other side of the cabin wall. Staring at the log wood siding with only his heartbeat interrupting the silence, he tried to anticipate her next move. He was ready to protect his mother and shoot Cecelia Lang if he needed to.

Kent burst through the front door with Matt a step behind him. "Halt! Stop right there!" Matt directed his attention to Sara. "Sir..." Cecelia had been readied with gun loaded and as Kent burst through the door, she fired a single shot towards Sara confident her aim was flawless. She did not turn back to insure she had hit her target, instead she leapt through the window where Michael waited for her. Both Detectives returned gunfire as she disappeared through the narrow window. Nick and Bruce burst through the back door; all four men looked at the window, looked at each other and then ran out the doors to follow Cecelia.

Sara groaned loud enough for them to hear her. "I'm alright... Get her..." "Are you hit?" "Yes, but not bad... get her..." "Oh Sara..." "Go!"

As Cecelia flung herself out of the window, Michael lunged at her intending to overtake her and hold her there for the Detectives. As soon as she realized he was there, she fired a second gun. The searing pain in his left arm fueled his anger yet when he grabbed for her, the strength to hold her was insufficient and she slipped his grasp. He fell to the ground as she ran for the woods.

"Get her guys!" Brent and Charles were in pursuit even before Michael had the words out.

Inside the cabin, Sara heard Michael's voice. "Michael..." "I'm here Mom!" "Michael..."

Regaining his footing, holding his left arm with his right, Michael ran to his mother. Falling to his knees when he reached her, he pulled her to him with his right arm and held her tightly to him. "It's over Mom, it's over." "You're hurt..." "But you are safe... that's what matters. Oh God, Mom..." "Just hold me" They remained together on the floor of the cabin unaware that Brent and Charles had roped Cecelia less than 50 yards from the cabin and were leading her; bound by their ropes to the Detectives.

"Well, would you look at that!" Bruce slapped his knee and shook his head. "I just don't ever recall when I saw such a thing! You boys done caught yourself a hell of a heifer this time!"

Cecelia tried to free herself from the restraints as they led her: Brent on the right and Charles on the left. "We got her for ya! What do you think of horse power now!?" "Mr. Hunter, Mr. Thomms, you directly disobeyed an order!" "Yes Sir, we know but…" "No 'buts'… you were told to stay put." "Yes…" "And it is sure a good thing you disobeyed me… this time. Don't make it a habit you hear me!?" "Yes Sir!" Brent and Charles 'high fived' in the air and then turned Cecelia around for Kent to put the handcuffs on her.

Michael and Sara emerged from the cabin clutching to each other. Sara limped with her injured ankle and ambled dizzily as the bullet aimed at her had slightly grazed her head above the left ear. Michael's arm bled through his shirt sleeve as he grasped his mother to help her walk. The setting sun silhouetting them against the evening sky as they made their way toward the others, they held tightly to each other, stopping momentarily as a hawk flew overhead. Both looking to the flight path, Michael embraced his mother. "Our Bridge to Heaven, Mom… our Bridge to Heaven." A slow tear rolled down the left side of Sara's face as she returned her attention to the men that had helped to save her. She smiled as she heard the echo of a low squawk in the distance.

The sight of mother and son bewitched the others to silence. The view of them in the sunset stopped all movement, Cecelia lowered her head and with a side to side bow, she too was awed at the true triumph. It was beyond the lifesaving and the criminal apprehension; it was family. Love and family. Her father had told her that "Goodness gets you nowhere in life, you have to take life in your own hands." Looking again at the approaching duo, she shook her head and said "You're wrong Pops, you're wrong. Goodness does win."

"What was that?" Kent grabbed Cece's arm and began leading her to the squad car. "Nothing. Just muttering." "You're gonna be doing a lot of that as there won't be anyone for you to talk to where you're going!"

"You have the right to remain silent, anything you say…" Kent's tone of voice as he recited her Miranda rights reflected his disgust of her intentions. "I know my 'Rights' officer Big Shot, or have you forgotten I was a Cop too until you people had to have that damn big city 'legal fleagle' brother of that bitch over there spoil a good thing for me. I had it made over there..." "Shut up Lang, I've heard all I want to out of your mouth. You are a disgrace to the Badge and there isn't a Cop anywhere to disagree with me."

Charles and Brent were off their horses and joining Michael and Sara at the ATV.

"Take me home boys, I want to go home." Brent leaned in to embrace her "Mrs. Barnes... I uh..." Sara reached her right hand to his cheek, "Brent, thank you. You three proved today you are more than the fun 'AMIGOS', you are men now and capable of handling yourselves. By the way, love the fancy roping you two did on Cece... pretty impressive there, boys!" Sara held her left hand out toward Charles. He took her hand with his right and wiped a tear from his cheek with his left. "We had to help. You are our Mom too. I know we were told not to, but it was you... we had to." "I know and I do truly thank you, all of you. I just want to go home."

"Mom, I think we need to go to the Hospital first." "We'll ride on back to the ranch and let everyone know." "Thanks Brent. Hey Bruce... you know how to drive one of these things?" Michael pointed at the ATV. "Sure do and time is a wastin' so let's get this show over... you dig?" "You dig???? You've been watching *Mod Squad* re runs again haven't you" Nick shoulder fisted the young man while holding back laughter. "You did good today Rookie, you did good." Bruce smiled and positioned himself on the ATV for the ride back to the Moore Ranch. "If he has any problems the real horsepower will come to his aid!" Charles fisted his chest twice. "Ain't that right ole Brent boy?!" "Shor nuf is... Chuckie!" Michael turned toward Sara, "Well, so much for the 'men' part!" Mother and son smiled at each other and then at Brent and Charles.

"Hold up! There are a couple horses in the shed. What are we going to do with them? One's got a saddle and one doesn't" While the men were talking Brent threw his reins at Charles and went to the shed. "Well, Matt it seems your introduction to ranch law just included a bit of saddle time. You do ride... Right?" "Yes, but..." "Not to worry Sir, my Lady here will 'pony' the 'packer', he can ride the saddle." Charles untied the spare lead rope from his saddle strings. "Pony? Packer?" Matt regretted his lack of 'Cowboy' yet again. "You got a lot of learning to do for this job my friend. He's going to lead the horse next to his that was used to carry equipment." "I don't get why it's called 'Pony'...." The men were unable to halt their laughter as Brent arrived with the horses.

Charles watched Brent leading the horses toward them, shaking his head side to side, with a chuckle he threw his hands in the air. "You are just a Cowboy's Cowboy now aren't ya! I can see by the way you handle them cayuses that the ranch life is gonna suit you well." Why, yes indeed Mr. Hunter, my love is the land! And Mary Shanks of course!" Holding the reins, preparing to mount, Brent leaned over to Charles and smirked as he spoke. "If I was your girlfriend I just might have to be jealous of how you love that horse!" "Well, it's just a good thing you're not my girlfriend now isn't it! Speaking of girlfriends, I'm thinkin' about Lady here bein' a girlfriend of that two-year old stud colt Michael's mom has been raising to take over as ranch stallion. My princess here is getting older... I need to think ahead. "Man, you and that horse... I just don't know!" Brent gathered the reins of his bridle and stood beside his gelding. "Benji my boy, we don't have all those problems now do we?"

"Mount up!" Sara spoke as loudly as she could as she watched the final moments of the nightmare fade into a memory.

The quartet of riders disappeared into the woods. The ambulance arrived for Sara and Michael while Kent placed his hand on Cecelia Lang's head and pushed her into the back seat of the Police vehicle.

Russell was at the hospital entrance when they arrived. Sara reached her hand to him as they brought her in on the gurney. "Oh Sara…" Slowly lifting her head when she heard his voice, with a 'knowing' of his being there beside her, she tried to open her eyes to smile for him; hoping to reassure him she was alright. "I'm fine, well… at least I will be. Michael and the boys…" Her head dropped back and as her eyes closed, "Help her! She's…… she's……" He laid his head softly on her bosom trying to hold back his tears as the EMT reached forward placing a hand on Russell's left shoulder, "She's just in shock and we have her medicated Mr. Barnes. Do not worry; we're taking good care of her. Michael should be coming in right behind us. He has a wound on his arm… the bullet went clear through we have to get him to the E.R. right away. Sara's head wound is not as bad as it looks. The scalp bleeds heavily, she was grazed by a gunshot but that is it for that. We do need to x ray her ankle and her jaw so sit tight in the waiting room, the doctor will be with you shortly. Russell lifted his head and stood straight up when the woman mentioned bullets. "What the hell happened out there? Bullets? I …" His words stopped when he saw Michael enter the turnabout in the wheelchair followed closely by Kent Harrison and Nick Borden.

"Russell, sit down, I'll explain everything. Nick, maybe you could get us some coffee?" "Good idea, be right back."

Kent replayed the details of the kidnapping and the capture for Russell. "We got her, she's in County lock up and you can sure as hell believe me, Blakeman won't let her out of his sight, not for a minute!

"I called Mark. He needed to know and I'm pretty sure he will be arriving shortly." Good call Russell, if anyone can get her the maximum sentence it's him. Oh, and I really wanted to tell you again how sorry I am that we had to be tough on you earlier, but do you understand now that she needed you here, safe…" "I do, but…" "I know." Kent reached out his right arm to shake Russell's hand but instead of the usual formality, as he leaned in, Russell embraced the younger man. "Thank you, you kept your word, did your job and brought my Sara back to me. I am forever indebted to you." "No debt ever Russell, my job goes beyond the daily law enforcement battles, my job is my heart and my life. Can't win them all, but the ones we do manage to get right are really right. I'm truly glad this is one we got right. Take care of her." Russell watched the young man walk to the door, he then leaned back on his heels, spun around and briskly walked to the waiting room-- only to pace the floor.

"Russell! How is she? Is she alright?" Recognizing the boisterous voice of Sara's brother Mark Bloom, Russell could feel the relief of no longer being alone while waiting for 'updates on the condition' of Sara and Michael. "Oh Mark, you made good time getting here!" "How is she? And Michael? What about Michael?" There was a falter in his voice as emotion took hold of his words. They were both shot, Sara has a head wound a dislocated jaw and a broken ankle. She's in surgery... Michael has a 'through and through' they called it in the arm. He's in the E.R. I haven't heard any more...Oh God, Mark this is just horrific. And all because of that damn Lang woman." "That 'damn Lang woman' is going away for keeps this time if I have my way... don't you worry Russell, I'm here now and this time I'm staying." "What do you mean you're staying?" "I'm moving to Brandon, seems my sister has taught me that family has to come first and well, since she's my only family left, I need to be here with her. Besides, I like this little town and there is need here for a good attorney guess that just makes it all the more the right place for me to be." Engaged in a tight 'man hug,' neither man noticed Linda Thomms entering the waiting room.

"Ahhh Guys... hate to interrupt all this but..." The men separated and turned to Linda. "Linda, so good you are here... um... how did you know already?" "Well, you know I have the Diner in town, and the Cops all hang out there... and..." "Say no more. Sara will be so happy that you are here." Mark nudged Russell's left side and gave him a glare of 'introduce me'. "Oh... ah... Linda .... this is Mark Bloom, Sara's brother, Mark, Linda Thomms." Linda smiled as she held her hand to Mark. "I remember you from the trial." "So nice to meet you, officially. I take it you are one of Sara's friends." "It's complicated, but yes. Lately we have been getting… well… back to friends." "It's a pleasure meeting you. Perhaps now that I am moving here, we will see more of each other." Russell could not help but notice the flush of Linda and Mark's cheeks as they spoke to each other with intense eye contact.

"Russell Barnes! Call for Russell Barnes!" The screech of the wall speaker startled the trio. A woman banged into the waiting room doors as she repeated the announcement. "Here! I'm Russell Barnes…" "Oh good…your wife is in recovery. The ankle surgery went well and the head wound is treated. The jaw has been reset. You can see her now." "What about us?" Mark abruptly interrupted the nurse." "Not yet, just the husband. I'll let you know when you can come back." Russell and the nurse disappeared behind the swinging doors. "Guess we just sit and wait." "Guess so. So… tell me about your Diner?"

Part 2
Transitions

Leaning against the barn corral panel, Sara smiled as she watched the mares with their colts coming in from the Red Pasture. The foal crop this year showed great promise of financial gain for the ranch. She had changed her mind regarding retiring 'Captain' the year Samuel died when it was necessary to geld Capp for Michael. Sara had planned on him being the new breeding stallion but just could not bring herself to take the colt from Michael. A decision she never regretted and Captain, now 28 years old remained the lead stallion until last breeding season when the 'Dodger' mare kicked out suddenly and injured his stifle. Word of Captain's final season brought numerous requests for outside breeding and pre-payments on colts he sired out of the ranch's broodmare stock.

Sara smiled widely as she inspected the progeny. She spoke softly to herself as the horses settled in the corral. "Ladies, you have again blessed this ranch with your foals. They are all so wonderful. Thank you."

A soft nicker from her beloved Jazzy diverted Sara's attention toward the barn.

Lost in her thoughts, she did not hear Russell approaching her. He realized he was undetected and when he stood behind her, he wrapped his arms around her waist. "Penny for your thoughts, my love..." "Did we do the right thing? Retiring him? Look at those babies... they are magnificent. Sometimes I wonder..." Turning her slowly, Russell held her close to him. "Yes, you made the right decision. As you stated, and very well at that if I do say so myself... and not just because I love you, you said, "Go out with a legacy of greatness and improve the generations forthcoming." My dear Sara, your knowledge and hard work has proven itself without fail. Each time someone rides a Moore Ranch bred horse they know that they are riding greatness. My goodness, you have ranch horses, barrel horses, Western Pleasure show horses, those that do that fancy footwork Dressage and even some that have made it on the race track. If that is not a Legacy of greatness… You did this. I am so proud of you… of this ranch. Every day I stand in amazement that I am a part of it with you. I love you so much." "That is it! You did it! Russell, you just named the next breeding stallion!" "Huh?" "Captain's Legacy" Sara kissed her husband with a fervor that aroused his awareness of the closeness of their bodies before he could quell his physical response.

"Russell…" She moved closer to him applying pressure with her loins to his. "Oh Lord, Sara…" "Here, let me help you with your situation…" "Sara…" Moving rhythmically against him, listening to his pleasure with each deep breath, she slowly placed her hand on the zipper of his jeans and opened the barrier between them. "Maybe we ought to take this to the barn…" "I think that is a good idea!" "Grab your crutches!" Sara grasped ahold of the crutches as Russell swept her in her arms to carry her to the barn. "To the loft my dear?" "To the loft".

****

"Hot brew! Any more for you?" Michael reached for the carafe and smiled as he looked around the table at his family and friends gathered to discuss the upcoming cattle drive from the North Grazing Lands at the end of October. "Ahhh our funny poet… alas he has found his 'calling'!" Michael arm fisted Brent as his remark was endorsed by the others as they held their coffee mugs up in the air as if in a 'toast' to Michael. "Ha… Ha…" Michael retorted. "Hee-hee better hope I don't spill it all over thee!!!!" In a motion of tilting the carafe over Brent's lap, Michael feigned tripping just as he reached him.

Gramp's deep voice broke the laughter as he read from the *Brandon Times*. "Hey, listen to this… Says here the trial of that damn Lang woman has concluded." "John! Watch your language! The children are here!" "Oh Mary, my dear, I am so sorry but perhaps you should notice they are not exactly children anymore!" At this the 'AMIGOS' of Michael, Brent and Charles each raised their coffee mugs and clanked them together. Smiling at her grandson, Mary Moore then turned to her husband, "Well, they'll always be children to me and you should just watch your language anyway!" "Yes, Ma'am." The laughter around the table was quickly revived. "Keep reading Gramp, but watch your language now, you don't want a whooping from Gram!" "Such a warning from our own Mr. Longfellow!" Brent slapped the table with his left hand as he grinned.

"Says here she's going away for 25 years to life but could be out in 18 if the Parole Board grants it on 'good behavior'. Oh, hell no... sorry Mary... she won't see the outside of that prison if I have anything to say about it!" "If you ask me, I highly doubt any judge is going to agree to that as she shot at Police Officers and held a woman hostage and had planned on killing her. Just don't see it happening!" "I hope you are right Mary, I hope you are right." "John, haven't you learned after all these years of marriage that I am always right!" "Actually, you pretty much are, that's why I keep you!" "Oh John!" "Whoa up there! If you old folks is gonna go getting' all mushy now, I'm outta here!" Charles waved his hand in front of his face and looked away as he spoke through his giggle.

"Here's the story about the Co-Op... wow... nice picture of Russell standing in front of that fancy feed mixer. That thing is huge and according to the article, the benefit to the Co-Op is pretty impressive as well. Good for him. He's been a real asset down there. Helping a lot of folks and getting a name for our little town. I sure am glad things worked out as they did." The man sitting at the head of the table, the patriarch of the Moore Ranch sighed significantly, as he concluded his sentence.

"Any room at the table for a 'hop-a-long'?" "Here, Mom, you take my seat." Michael stood and pulled the chair out for Sara to have ample room for her crutches when she sat. "I hope to be off these darn contraptions by the end of the day! Got a Doctor appointment and he just has to tell me good news. That is all there is to it. I have been walking on it a little and it is time to get back to life. We've got a Drive to plan!" "How about a wedding to attend first, then we can get to the planning of the Drive. And besides, you haven't ridden in months and Jazzy is loafing about as well…" "Loafing? Did you just say loafing?" "Didn't mean you, Mom… No… you have been far from loafing I know…" Sara smiled at her son as the others seated were silent, unsure if her reaction to his words was serious or not. When it was realized that she in fact returned her words in jest, everyone relaxed.

"Hey Mr. Poet man… how about getting your mom some coffee?" "You heard?" "Sure did! But I'm thinking perhaps you ought to rethink your vocation." "Speaking of that… The 'vocation' as you call it… I have actually been doing just that." Placing the filled coffee mug on the table for his mother, he turned to retrieve the extra chair from the corner of the kitchen, he swung the chair around so the back was up to the table, while waiting for the chatter to cease, he raised his right leg over the seat and sat down. "Young man… you have straddled that chair like you were mounting a horse!" Gramp moved his head side to side as he smiled at his grandson. "You are 'cowboy' through and through. Now… what's this about you having an announcement?" "You all know how involved I was in the investigation two years ago, and then the involvement in the apprehension of Cecelia Lang… well, I've been talking with Kent Harrison and Matt Brewer about the Police Academy. Even Nick Borden said he would put in a good recommendation for me. I want to protect the family I love and the people in the town that I love. This is my home and I want to know everyone is safe."

Sara placed her right hand on Michael's left, "Are you sure about this? What does Katy say?" "She wasn't real keen on the idea at first but as her dad is on the 'Force' she understands and I think she'll come around. I know Gramp, you wanted me to take control of the Rodeo stock, but Russell is here and Brent over there, he's been working with me for a couple years now and he could take over at any time and run the whole show." Brent pointed to his chest and shook his head to the left and then the right, "Me? You want me? Wow."

Before John was able to answer, Charles stood quickly. Thoughts around the table were that he was going to rebuff Michael's announcement. To their surprise, Charles had an announcement of his own.

"Well, seems like as good a time as any to declare my 'vocation' as well. I'm joining the Air Force." There was a renewed silence from those seated and he could see astonishment on the faces of his now very captive audience. "Yes, you heard me correctly. This cowboy wants to fly fighter jets. I'm going to Officer's Training and…" "Whoa… stop… The Air Force? Boot Camp? You know they wear laced up boots, right? And there ain't a horse anywheres near you, like ever!" Brent was nearly in tears at the thought of losing his friend to the military. "I know, but only for a little while…" Charles did not get the chance to finish when Brent stood up flailing his arms, he interrupted… "You…" he pointed at Michael. "You are going off to get shot at… and you…" Turning to Charles, "You are going off to do the shooting! Hell no! I'm staying right here on the ground… Not getting shot or doing the shooting! Yes, I'll keep the Rodeo going so when you two get your brains back there will be something for you to come home to. What are you guys thinking? We're the AMIGOS! We are Cowboys! We ride horses and motor bikes and four wheelers-- not squad cars and fighter jets!" Michael and Charles were soon at either side of Brent leading him back to his chair as the others took in the scene of the young men facing their first heart breaking challenge of growing up and finding their own places in the world. Sara and Mary exchanged the maternal glance of despair and understanding of what the boys were dealing with as Gramp lowered his head, closed his eyes and realized that they were truly men now and he had to let them make their own decisions and therefore their own mistakes as well. A slow tear fell from John Moore's left eye.

"I can't believe you didn't talk to me about this… you talked to your girlfriends and not me? Maybe they're on board with all this but not me! No way… not on board at all!" Brent remained confrontational with Michael and Charles as they helped him to sit back in his chair.

No one had heard the arrival of truck in the driveway.

"On board with what?" Katy burst through the back door of the ranch house, halting her words and stride as she gaped at the scene before her. "I... have... my... Maid of Honor... dress... anyone... want ah... to see...it?" She spoke slowly hoping someone; anyone would break in and let her know what she walked in to. In the ensuing silence, the door slammed behind her as she was locked in her stance at the sight of the tear on Gramp's cheek and Michael and Charles standing over Brent. "Oh God! What happened? Is someone hurt?" She ran toward Brent. "Brent? Someone say something!" A pleading glare at Michael illustrated her fear and need for an explanation. "You'd better sit down... You want anything to drink or..." "Just tell me what's going on"

"What's going on here, Katy, is that these two clowns have announced their intentions to get killed!" "What!!??" "What he means Katy, is that I told them of my wanting to go to the Police Academy and then Charles opens up and says he is going into the Air Force. Brent is just not too happy with us right now." "I can see that! Charles? The Air Force? What's Marge got to say about that? At least Michael will still be here." "Took her awhile, but she's ok. I can't ask her to wait for me but I sure hope that she does." "Well, good for you. When do you leave for Boot Camp?" "It's called Basic Training and not until I actually sign on the dotted line and then take my oath. I'll get my orders then. Not to worry, I'm told it will after your mom's wedding and maybe even after the Drive. Which would be good as I really want to go again this year... you know... ride out one more time before it will be a while before I even see a horse again."

"Yeah, I for one would like to know when you are going to see your brains again!" Brent swigged his coffee and slammed his mug on the table. Placing his right hand on the shoulder of one of his best friends, Michael leaned in and softly spoke. "Brent, it is ok to be upset... now... but you are going to have to accept our decisions and you will either choose to support us or not. I sure as hell hope that you do. We are forever the AMIGOS whether together or not. Our bond shall never falter and shall never fail us." Michael could see the wrinkle of a smile forming as Brent looked up from the table. "Seems our 'Longfellow' here has tried his hand at 'Emerson'!" Simultaneously all seated at the table raised their mugs and laughed.

"Let's talk about the wedding… change the subject… shall we?" "Good idea Mom, so… Katy… about that dress… Yes, I would like to see it. Anyone else?

"A cowgirl in a dress… boots too? Or are you actually going to try to walk in high heels? This I gotta see!" "If you must know Brent, I don't always wear boots anymore…" "What? You, Katy McGregor not wearing your boots? I don't believe it!" "I'll be right back boys so you can feast your eyes on the dress, and me of course!" Katy laughed as she walked through the kitchen to the den to change into the dress.

With an honest concern to his tone, Charles leaned over to Michael. "Vet school is changing her, better hope one of those big city Vet 'wannabes' doesn't change her mind about you and this lil ole ranch town!" Michael was quiet as he inwardly agreed with his friend.

Breaking the silence as he pushed Charles and Michael aside, Brent stood at the head of the table, leaned over placing both hands on the leather placemat before him. His eyes focused on Charles, "What about Lady? I suppose you will want me to take care of her… we all know how much you like that mare… I thought you wanted to breed her? If I recall you were all gung-ho on it… suppose you want me to take care of that too… ok… I can… with Mrs. Barnes' help I am quite certain your precious mare will have ready for you the great colt you are looking for." Brent turned from Charles and smiled at John Moore; "Gramp, you have my word I will keep the Rodeo going. As for you two…" He looked back at Michael and Charles, "You two have my support in your stupidities. We have always stood together and I will not be the one who breaks that. I do not like it, but I have to live with it. So, I will. I will keep everything here ready for when you both return to your senses. And to us… all of us. Okay, I'm done." He sat down just as Katy reentered the kitchen.

"Wow!" Charles again looked at Michael silently expressing his prior comment again. The first to speak, Gram had both her hands on her cheeks. "Oh my! Where is the young girl that danced with our Michael at the rodeo? The girl on the barrel horse? She is a beautiful woman now."

In his mind Michael remembered the Rodeo when he and Katy met and how he surprised everyone with his skills on the dance floor that night. The visions of their first kiss still so clear in his mind. He fell in love with a girl and before him now stood a woman. "I… ah… Oh Katy, you're beautiful."

Sara saw the fright in her son's expression, recognizing all too well what he was trying so desperately to conceal. "You know Katy, the Maid of Honor is not supposed to upstage the bride… I just don't know how you are going to not do so. The dress is as if it was made just for you. The sage color is perfect." "Thank you, Mrs. Barnes, it is pretty nice, huh!?" Katy twirled several times letting the long layered panels of the dress flow open around her. "I feel like a Princess!"

"You may be a Princess now, but you will be a Queen as you walk the aisle in the white gown to me." Michael's words halted Katy's spinning. "That is… of course… if you want to be married to Brandon's Police Chief… someday." "Someday be the Police Chief or someday be married?" "Someday the Police Chief, married soon, I hope. Katy, what I'm saying is, I, ah,… I want to marry you when you are ready and I hope that is soon." The audience of family and friends silently awaited her response, Gram placed her left hand on Gramp's right hand and her right hand on Sara's left. Katy cast a smile to each and then to Brent and Charles. "Yes, Michael, I will marry you. I have wanted to marry you from the day standing in line at the Rodeo. I want to finish Vet school and return home to Brandon and be the wife of Brandon's finest Policeman. I love you." Katy rushed to Michael as he engulfed her in his arms oblivious to the cheers of everyone else in the room.

Charles leaned over to Brent, in a hushed voice; "That's one way of keeping her from changing her mind!" "What are you talking about? We all knew they would get married". "Vet school... high heels... our Katy is a woman of the world now... he had to do something to keep her in Brandon!"

"What's all the hoopla about in here? Holy smokes Katy, that dress is gorgeous on you! Why are you crying Sara? Gram? Gramp? Someone tell me what's happening!" "Russell, Michael and Katy have plans to marry when she finishes Vet school." John Moore made the announcement in a 'matter of fact' tone as he stood. "Miss McGregor, I, for one, am most pleased with this. I think it is safe that I speak on behalf of the entire family... we always knew you two were meant to be together. This is just wonderful!" He lifted his coffee mug; "A toast! To the engagement of Michael and Katy!" The patriarch's face beamed with pride as he reached his right hand to his wife, helping her to rise then motioning for the others to do the same. "Here... here! To Michael and Katy!"

Sara felt the familiar unseen hand on her right shoulder. Placing her left hand upon the sensation, she smiled. A 'knowing' that Samuel was there and pleased with how Michael had become a good man. Within herself she stated, "Yes, my dearest Samuel, he is a good man." Russell recognized the 'far away' look on Sara's face. Walking to her; he reached for her and then turned to the others as he drew her to his side. "Michael, I know your father is proud of you. He is a part of this celebration with us. I am honored to be the man that is here with you to fill the void and be a 'presence of a father' in his absence for you. I love you as my own son and am so deeply proud of you for the man you have become; overcoming circumstances no young man need ever bear, you embraced the responsibilities and now stand before us an inspiration..." "Russell..." "Wait... hold your thoughts, I'm on a roll here... don't stop me now!" Everyone laughed at Russell's request to Michael. He was a man of few words until it was a topic of great importance to him. Out of respect, Michael ceased his talking to let Russell finish. "Miss McGregor... No finer a lady could we hope for Michael. Heck, I saw in you on that very first day at the Rodeo a true Cowgirl. You live the Cowgirl Code to the deepest part of you. I was impressed then and am impressed now with your values and your honesty of character. He is a bit of a challenge at times, but you are his love and if anyone knows the power of love, it is me... and this family. Thank you for all you are for Michael, for Sara, for your family but most of all, for yourself. A good woman about to marry a good man! Our families are truly blessed." "Amen!" The agreement of all again signified by a rising of coffee mugs.

"Mr. Barnes, I don't know what to say..." "You said 'yes'... you said everything you needed to!" Katy looked up to Michael and smiled. He took his eyes from hers and turned to Russell; "Russell, it is I who am the lucky one. Not only did you bring a life back to my mother..." Michael paused slightly, met Sara's eyes then refaced Russell. "You were the one that taught me that overcoming grief need not diminish it, but strengthen me as a person. You never tried to take my father's place. Your respect for him and for me, and for our family in that... is beyond measure. You have been a great father to me and I hope that... in the future..." He smiled as he looked at Katy, "I will carry the combination of both my fathers to our children." Turning back to Russell; "Thank You. I love you"

The tear cascading Russell's cheek fell uninhibited as he embraced Michael. "I love you, too." Through the 'welling' in Sara's eyes she could see the same in John and Mary's.

"My son is getting married... married!" She spoke the words slowly as she lowered herself to her chair. "Russell!?" Kneeling next to her, he placed his forehead on her left shoulder placing his left hand on her thigh and his right arm across her back, "Yes, my love, time does not wait in a bottle. The family is growing and is stronger today than yesterday but not as strong as tomorrow!" The corner of Sara's mouth wrinkled as she displayed her approving smile. "Where do you come up with your wisdoms!?" Russell raised his head to look into her eyes, he realized the attention of everyone was waiting his answer. "A fine philosopher by the name of Jim Croce. Okay, so I mixed a couple tunes together... his... and... well... I'm of the age to remember the band Spiral Staircase." Sara's smirk and approving glance incited laughter from everyone.

Reaching for Michael's left hand, Katy smiled as she caressed his ring finger. "First things first Mr. Moore..." "Yes, Mrs. Moore to be..." All the while smiling as he spoke. "My mother's wedding is just days away, we can start on ours after hers is over. Right now, I am going to take this lovely Princess gown off as I am sure that Brent and Charles are near ready to collapse from the sight of me in it..." She slowly spun again as she danced out of the room. Brent and Charles mocked fainting as she passed them. When Charles was certain the Katy would not hear him, he turned his back to the group as he stood in front of Michael. "Well, that's one way to insure she won't run off with a College Boy!" He then fisted Michael's right arm. Turning back to the table, Charles raised his mug for another toast. "The Amigos!!!!!" "A – M - I - G –O – S!" In unison the three friends put their right hands in together and boasted their cheer.

"Um... ahh... Are we going to talk about the October Cattle drive? All this big news has over shadowed the original intent of conversation this morning." There was no response to his statement. "Guess not, well maybe tomorrow. Mary... lets you and I go for a walk around the ranch, I need a little fresh air." She took his right hand as they passed through the kitchen to the back porch. Approaching the last step, she halted and with an adoring look to her husband; "Another chapter, huh? We have lived a good life here and there is so much more that the kids will 'live' now. I feel good that all is as it should be." The matriarch took the last step in silence as she and her husband walked toward the Red Pasture gate.

****

"What a great day for a wedding! The sun is shining and the temperature is actually above normal for a change! Callie is one lucky lady today!" Sara opened the cupboard and retrieved her favorite coffee mug. "Yes sir-ee! A great day for a wedding!" Alone in the kitchen; she spoke aloud. While pouring her coffee she fumbled through a whistling rendition of the wedding march tune. "Oh Callie, you so deserve your 'happily ever after'. You and Nick both do. And our Katy… she is just beside herself that she and her parents are finally going to be the family that they should always have been. I suppose it is too bad that your father isn't here, but on the other hand…" "My lovely bride, are you talking to yourself again? I might have to start worrying about your conversations…" Sara had not heard Russell enter the kitchen. When he enwrapped her with his arms, she could feel the warmth of his chest against her back. Placing her left hand on his left as he stroked her abdomen, he could not see her smile as she slowly moved her head side to side. "Oh Russell, I hope they have a love like ours for the rest of their lives." She placed the coffee mug on the counter as he turned her to face him. "Like ours? No. Like their own, yes." "I love you Mr. Barnes." "And I love you Mrs. Barnes." The passion still intense between them when they were in each other's company not forsaken by time or their age, they were lost in each other's gaze as they stood in the quiet kitchen. Cupping Sara's face in his hands, he leaned in to gently kiss her and just after that 'moment of hesitation', with a deep sigh, she felt him pulling her into the intended kiss with a fervor that could challenge any man half his age.

"Whoa there… Mom… In the kitchen? Really!?" Michael laughed as he walked toward the refrigerator. "I sure hope there's some of that fancy peach jam left for my toast. Do I have to separate you two?" Shaking her head and placing her right hand over her face; index finger over her nose, Sara giggled as she looked at Russell and then toward Michael. "You could always send us to our room!" "Mom!!!!"

"I've got to get to the Co-Op for a meeting; I'll be home by noon. Are we still leaving at one o'clock for the Church?" "Yes, Callie will be here late morning… she is shooting for around eleven to start getting ready. If you're here by noon then we will for sure get her to the Church on time." Russell leaned back on his heels, spun around and was heading out the back door all the while singing 'Get me to the Church on Time'. "Sing it for me 'Blue Eyes' sing it for me!" Sara waved her right arm over her head as he disappeared through the doorway.

*****

Knowing her mother was soon to follow her, Katy stood in waiting under the archway leading from the foyer to the aisle of the small Church. Her heart raced as she felt the power of God in the expanse of the nave. "Breathe Katy, breathe" she heard a whisper in her right ear. "Aunt Cassie, it's so beautiful. The scent of the flowers on the Altar and the Pews… gosh, it's just perfect!" "Just how your mother found a florist to coordinate the white and lavender with the exact sage hue of your dress… I know I'm impressed! Perhaps you should keep her in mind for your wedding" Placing her arms around her niece, Cassie rested her right cheek on Katy's shoulder and then with a slight squeeze told her "You will be the talk of the town when you and Michael get hitched." "Oh, Aunt Cassie!" Katy laughed as she responded. "You make it sound like we're going to be a team of Draft horses!" Both women chuckled loud enough to gain the attention of a few guests seated in the rows close to them. Katy tipped her head towards Cassie and while still laughing she spoke softly "One wedding at a time, ok… it's Mom's day today!" "Yes dear, it is. I will check on her while you stand here and imagine the next time." Katy turned her gaze back to the interior of the aging yet dramatically appointed hand carved woodwork around the stained-glass windows and the Altar that she had seen nearly every Sunday of her life yet now seeming to mesmerize her with new meaning. Katy bowed her head for Prayer-- "Dearest God, Lord of Lords, today I walk for my mother, soon I will be the one in white and it will be my wedding. Lord God, thank you for this day and the re uniting of my parents. May they forever be together here and with you in all Eternity. And, as for me, thank you for Michael…

I made a vow to love him always and with your help, it will be him and me next at the Altar. Lord, you have Blessed me with a family that loves me and stands by me and you have Blessed my mother in her reuniting with the love of her life. We may not truly understand all that has come before today, but today we know deep in our hearts that this is a ceremony not only of love, but of family as well. Thank You Lord God. Amen"

"That was beautiful" Katy did not realize that she had been speaking her Prayer aloud. Michael stood beside her on his way to his seat and placed his right arm behind her waist, leaned down and kissed her left cheek. "No need to blush, I think I'm the only one that heard you. I love you Katy McGregor, soon to be Moore." "I love you, too. You had better get your seat." "Yes ma'am." He proceeded forward to the third pew row. Placing his right hand on the wooden seatback, he turned to smile at Katy. Thoughts of their first meeting overtaking his emotions, he could feel the welling of tears in his eyes as he sat beside Charles. "Ah, Mountain Man… you okay?" "Yes, she's so beautiful and she loves me. I… I just…" "Say no more my friend, you and Katy have been connected since the day we stood in line at the rodeo. I guess 601 is your lucky number!" "That it is. That it is."

Marge Pelton entered the transept and took her seat at the piano thus quieting the attendees. Bemused by the sudden rising in unison of all those that had been seated, with bouquet in hand, Katy turned to her mother and smiled as Marge began Mendelssohn's Wedding March. "Ready Mom?" "I am more than ready!" Callie's smile and nod gave indication that is was time to proceed. "I love you, Mom!" "I love you too my sweet girl, now hoof it down that aisle so I can finally get married!" Not even trying to conceal their grinning, mother and daughter shared a moment of unspoken affection. Katy stepped toward the Pastor; proud of her mother for all the hardships she endured and through them all, she never lost her Faith. To herself she vowed to emulate her mother's strength.

"Get a few more chairs… I'm thinkin' since word got out your mother made her famous apple fritters there just might be a pretty good crowd here today to talk about the Drive. Hey, do you know if Brent and Charles' convinced both girls to help this year? Marge sure did surprise us at being a natural out there it would be great to have Mary join as well. Besides that, they're both pretty darn good to look at too!" "Gramp!" "Hey… truth is truth. I may be an old man but… I'm not dead and those two hooligans got themselves a couple real good fillies. Oh… and you too… of course. Katy is just the best!" "Good save Gramp, good save." "The chairs…" "Yes sir. I'll be right back." Retreating to the cellar stairwell, Michael mumbled to himself, "Hooligans got fillies… Where does he get this stuff?"

"First things first! Mrs. Barnes… We heard there would be fritters!" "Yes, Brent. You heard correctly." "Lord knows ole Brent boy here can't to any decidin' about anything on an empty stomach!" Charles raised his hands off the table and shook them toward Brent. "You got that right Charles… 'specially when it's apple fritters!" The laughter did not cease until Sara had placed the plate of fritters on the table with a dish of butter beside it. "There, now we can get some work done!" Gram smiled at the sight of the young men still boyish in their antics. "Imm a mimit Missses Moore… gotta fimish mah fribber." "Yes, I do believe that would be a good idea for you Brent. A good idea." Sara and Gram stood together leaned back on the kitchen cabinets. "Yes, Mary… no matter how old they get, they will always be the boys we love." "Ah herbrd thet Missus Barms!"

Michael laughed so hard at Brent's attempt to talk that he nearly coughed out his fritter himself. "Sara… better get these starving men something to drink." "Right away"

"Okay… now… for the details of the Drive. Sara, have you been keeping an eye on the weather forecast?" "Yes. We have a good window this year. A little early but we will just have to adjust." "What do you mean early?" Knowing John was a man set in his ways and the Drive had been ridden within the first two weeks of October for as long as she could remember him telling the stories, convincing him to change to ten days earlier was not going to go well. Sara returned to the table with six coffee cups; three held by the handles in each hand. "Help me, Michael, careful..." Rising from his seat, Brent offered to help Michael retrieve the cups and set them on the table. "Ok... now, we have coffee, where were we?" "You said some nonsense about riding early this year. I just don't..." Mary Moore placed her left hand on her husband's right, "Hush John, let her tell us why. You and I and everyone here knows that she is the best judge of the weather and conditions of the herd. I am quite sure she has thought about all of the factors before making her decision." "I know, but... okay Sara, what's the scoop that my dear wife seems to be beholding to your 'Cow*girl* Code' in backing you up over her adoring and wonderful husband of 55 years! Oh wow... Has it been that long? Seems like yesterday..." "John, your rambling..." "Yes dear. Sorry Sara. Go on." Mary leaned over and kissed John's blushing cheek.

"We have had rather a drought this year and the likelihood of the vegetation retaining nutrient levels necessary for the herd to have the energy levels needed for the..." "Ranch man terms girl, ranch man terms. You and your fancy education do at times make it hard to understand you. I know at your meetings and such that is all good, but here, just the simple folk want to hear simple talk." His biting words were felt by all seated around the table. Lowering her head and looking at the table, Sara moved her head side to side a couple times and sighed. He was not making this easy for her. Regaining her posture, she knew she would have to be mindful of his request. Looking into the eyes of the Patriarch she dearly loved, Sara smiled and continued.

"The lack of rainfall this year and the shallow snow pack from the easy winter last year didn't do the grazing lands any justice. I am afraid that the grasses will be depleted and the cattle won't have the body mass and endurance for the drive home to the ranch.

I just hope the cows were able to milk enough for the calves. I really think we need to get them off the grazing lands and back here for better, more consistent feed if we are to have those going to market by the middle of November ready. When I rode up that way a few weeks back, I could see the decline in the quality of the range grass. It is already starting to die off. As for the water resources up there, the Hobbs Spring line leading into the river is, or at least was at the time, still flowing. The Anglin Spring is dried up. The cattle are pretty much settled in just the other side of Hobbs Ridge through the Draw." A slow tear cascaded her cheek as she recalled the memory of Samuel dying in her arms at the river bed.

It was not un noticed by those around her.

"Mom, you okay? I didn't know you rode that far up. I..." 'I am ok. Just rememberin'. We can ride out the same trail I took through the Red Pasture. I made a new trail out past where the tree arch is up in the corner. We'll have to use the same road as always for the herd coming back in. We can do this in four days if all goes well, five if we have to slow them down. I counted 465 head including calves. We haven't lost but just a few and I'd like to keep it that way. I even saw the old Bossy cow still out there. I'm thinking if she makes the winter then come Spring she ought to stay right here and get pampered. She's earned that."

"Well, I think you are right. We should get them down here, the sooner the better." "Gramp! You mean that?" "Yes, I do. Sara knows her cattle as well as she knows her horses and if she says they need to come home, then by God, let's get them home!" Hugging her husband, Mary's smile was clear indication that she was yet again surprised by John. "You just don't ever cease to amaze me old man..." "Old? Not me!" With the mugs held high in the air, the group of friends and family clinked them together. "To this year's Drive!" "Here, here!"

"So, when are we leaving?" "We are leaving the twentieth of September, you John, will be making sure that Mary has her famous Pigs Knuckles and Sauerkraut ready when we get home!" "Mom!" "Mrs. Barnes!!" "Yeah... ooooo... Mrs. Barnes!" Mary laughed at the silly faces the boys made as they remarked their displeasure. "I suppose I could find something else for you hard working ranch hands!" "Gets them every time, doesn't Mary?!" "Sure does"

"Say, boys, where are those pretty girlfriends of yours? They both going to ride too, or are they going keep an old man company?" "Gramp!!"

Part 3
The Other Side of My Dreams

"Well, old girl… this may be your last Drive. I'm thinking that I ought to retire you." The mare stomped her left fore hoof and snorted. "Not retire, retire… just from the Drives silly girl." Jazzy lifted her nose three times as if she was communicating acceptance of Sara's explanation. "I do love you my friend…" Sara gently brushed the mare while in conversation with her companion of so many years. "When I look back…" Jazzy stomped her left hoof and gave a quick snort as she looked back to Sara. "Oh, too rough? Sorry. I try forgetting about the scars from *that* ride even though I never will, guess you have your own as well."

Moving around to face her horse, Sara placed her left hand under Jazzy's chin and with her right, she slowly rubbed the bridge of her beloved friend's nose. "I love your face markings, your wide blaze and funny sideways snip… always looks like you have a grin. I love you girl. Oh, what we have been through! You sure turned out to be a great ranch horse as well as competitor in the regional shows. Remember when we went to Carnon and blew them away that the Paint horse from a ranch could actually out execute the fancy Thoroughbred horses in the regional Dressage Event? I still remember the looks we got when we took our exit from the arena…" Another stomp from Jazzy. "I know, it's time to saddle up… you know your job… it's not that I'm procrastinating…"

Snort.

"Really, I'm not… just, it's tough thinking about this being your last Drive. That filly out in the lot with your same head markings… you do 'stamp' your babies… she's got some really big shoes to fill. But, as she is the only filly you seem to have produced for me, I'm thinking that it is your doing as well as God's that she is to be your replacement. Your colts are great, but you know how I like mares!"

Stomp. Snort.

"Geez... okay... You are only retiring from the Drives there little Miss Impatient... I told you, I'm still going to work with you here on the ranch." A soft nicker as she lowered her head and pushed into Sara showed Jazzy's acceptance of her 'semi-retirement'. Laughing aloud Sara walked toward the tack room.

Walking through the doorway, Sara placed her hand on Michael's saddle, still on the first rack. "Oh Sam, be with us again today. These mars in the leather may be worn through the years... but they will always be a reminder of your great love for us and the sacrifice you made. Gifting your saddle to Michael has... for me, always been a security that you will ride with him and protect him. Be with us again today, please." She again felt the familiar 'touch' on her right shoulder. Looking up, Sara smiled as she placed her left hand where she could 'feel' Sam. "Thank you."

Jazzy pulled on the cross ties and then pawed the aisle way floor mat. "Yes, dear, I'm on my way... you sure are ready to go aren't you. You do realize you are going to have to stand here while I tack up Buck, don't you? After this ride the two of you are going to enjoy living in the home pastures. I sure hope that will suit you!"

Stomp. Stomp. Nicker.

"Thought so."

The devil went down to Georgia was playing on the radio. "Fire on the mountain, run boys run..." Sara sang along to her favorite Charlie Daniels song as she saddled the mare.

***

Sitting in the chair at the desk in the study, watching the ornate hands of the Grandfather clock as they slowly moved to the top of the hour, Russell sat in awe as the hand carved horse head weights continued to move the chain. "Old clock… you stand so majestic. You are History. You are Family. You have chimed one hundred and ten Christmas mornings… been here for all the birthdays and anniversaries, heard so much laughter and stood strong through the tears and heart aches of this family. Oh, the stories you hold deeply hidden beneath those beautiful carvings. This family has been Blessed by generations of honorable heritage. I was not so lucky in my youth. But now, now I am a part of something I never dreamed could be for me. I still mourn the loss of Samuel even though I did not know him."

Seven robust chimes filled the room with sound.

Russell stood slowly as he continued speaking. While walking toward the clock, he was not aware that Sara had been entering the room. When she realized he was deep in Prayer, she held back and stood behind the wall to grant him his time.

Approaching the clock Russell continued speaking softly. "Lord, through the years I have learned what 'family' truly means. I am so deeply in love with my wife, Michael is a son to me… and John and Mary… thank you Lord for they are the parents of her deceased husband and they accept me. Took a little doing for John, and I know you helped in that…" Placing his hands gently on the filigreed inlays, slowing moving his fingers over the grooves he continued. "I thank you every day Lord… I thank you by being the best man I can for this family and I promise until my dying day that I will honor you and them with all that I am. And Lord, if I might ask… this Drive we're going on… please watch over Sara, I know that even after the passing of the years, she still relives that horror. If not for that… I would not have all that I do, but I would trade it all for her to not have had to go through that. Lord, you were watching over all three of us then, please watch over us all this week--- those on the Drive and those here at the ranch. Oh, and Jazzy… she's got some age on her now, and you know our Sara... she just has to ride her. Yeah, she's a good mare, but... please, don't let anything happen to her. Sara just couldn't... well... you know. Thanks, Lord. Amen"

Sara peeked around the corner when she heard Jazzy's name and watched him stepping back from the clock. Placing her right hand on her heart, to herself she spoke, "Oh Lord, he's a good man. Thank You." A small tear fell on her left cheek as she watched him dab his eyes with his right index finger. "Thank You" she spoke again with no volume. She could see he was going to turn around so she slipped back out of sight; retreating to the kitchen as he walked toward the doorway.

"You ready Sara? Sara?"

"In the kitchen!" Moving swiftly, Sara met him in the doorway and startled him with an unexpected embrace of great strength. "I love you." "Okay... I love you too... what was that for?" "For loving me... that's all." "What are you up to? I know that grin on your face... either you already did something, or you are about to! Which is it? Come on... you can tell me... Saaara...?" "Nope! Nada! Just wanted to tell you that I love you!" "I know better than to push it... speaking of 'pushing'... we'd best get to the barn and get the horses ready." "Already done!"

"I should have known." "Yup! You should have!" "Come here, I want another of those hugs from you!" "I think I could be persuaded to oblige that request!"

"Hey... really? In the kitchen? Now? We have a ride to get ready for!"

"Our horses are ready thanks to yours truly... but you still need to get saddled, so while you are out in the barn, I think I shall take the opportunity now to..." "Okay Mom... I get it... man, I hope that Katy and I are still pawing at each other when we are as old as you two!" "Did you just say 'pawing at each other'? When you are as *old* as we are, I should hope that you will still have..." "Ok... you aren't really old yet... carry on... I'll be in the barn." Michael shook his head, turned back and smiled at his mother as he walked through the back door of the kitchen. The day she married Russell Barnes she not only returned to herself, but she did so as well to him. He hoped she knew how deeply happy he was for her to have found love again. Michael recalled the day they rode to where Tonk died and they found his father's letter to Sara in the saddlebag still where it was left under the horse that she could not retrieve at that time. Michael shot a quick glace toward the sky as he departed the porch. "She did dad. She found love again just like you wanted her to." Looking back through the doorway he could see his mother snuggle in close to Russell's chest. Michael smiled as his arms surrounded her.

"Last to arrive as usual! At least I'm consistent!" "We would expect nothing less of you Charles." Sara waved her left hand in the air as she led Jazzy toward the group gathering at the center 'holding pen' gate. "Love you too, Mrs. Barnes!" "Remember you said that when you're out in those hills up there and you are up to your boot tops in cattle butts!" All those in hearing distance of the conversation between Sara and Charles soon were laughing. "Now I know why I love being a Cowboy!!! It's the cattle butts! Oh, those hefty haunches how they sway all back and forth... Oh, those cattle..." "We are soooo going to miss you when you take off for the Air Force, you know that don't you?" "I'm going to miss you all too. Are we ready?"

"Last 'check' before you ride out..." John walked to each rider to ensure that all the needed items on the saddles were accounted for; canteens, pocket knives, spare leather straps and snaps for repairs, hoof picks and most especially the two flashlights attached to each saddle. He had always teased Sara about her having them until the ride that Sam died and had it not been for the second flashlight acting as a beacon on top of the Ridge, she may not have been able to get back to the horse and mule. Since then, no one was allowed to ride at any time without two flashlights. It was not questioned, it was just done.

"Whoa... is that Jeb... *and* Pete? Brent asked with surprise in his tone. "Two packers[5]?"

"Brent boy, let's look at this, Mom and Russell need a tent... and believe me when I tell you they need their own tent... and then we have guys... and gals... so that means two more. So, in deciphering the panniers it was clear that more than one mule was going on this 'outing' with us. Besides... what if we meet a bear up there, *I* shoot it, and we have to bring it home? I'm not thinking any one of you rough riders are going to give up a horse!"

"A bear? No one said anything about bears, Marge... did anyone say anything about bears to you?"

"Get serious, he's just joshing... but sure got to you didn't he, Mary?"

"Now, who says you are going to be the one to shoot it!? I'm a far better shot than anyone!" "No way Mom, remember... I'm the one heading for the Police Academy..."

"You guys are serious... there is a chance we are going to be attacked by bears!"

Sara reached up to put her right hand on Mary's left leg as she was already in the saddle, "Mary, there is always a chance in meeting bears up there, but the likelihood that there will be a problem is very slim. Now the wolves..."

"That's it! I've heard enough, let's just get going... Brent, you best be ready to protect me!" "Absolutely my love, absolutely!"

Sara Stood beside Jazzy as Mary Moore approached her. "Sara, may God be with you all and bring you home safely." "Thank you. We'll

---

5   Packers: additional horses or mules for carrying gear in pack saddles designed with panniers for holding the 'stores'.

be home before you know we are gone." "Sara, I always feel you when you aren't here, if you need me, just think hard and I will know." "I love you." "I love you too"

Hank and Baron stood at attention waiting for 'the command'. "Mount up!"

Standing beside Buck, Russell watched as Sara mounted Jazzy. Smiling and tipping his hat to her when she was set in the saddle, he rocked back on his heels, turned and as he placed his left boot in the stirrup, he let out a heavy breath. "I absolutely never get tired of watching you mount that horse!"

"Mom! Tell him not to start that already... we got girlfriends here... and..." "And what? Are you afraid they're going to want you to be romantic too?" "Take a few lessons from this old man... I got the swaaaav-aa and the swaaaag-er" "Oh brother! Let's ride!"

John closed the holding pen gate as the eight riders were approaching the Red Pasture. Walking toward Mary, feeling the crisp wind that had arrived ahead of prediction, John reached for his wife. Pulling her close to him, feeling her slight tremble, he was unsure if it was the chill or a hidden fear that was the cause. "They will be fine. There is strength in numbers and they have that this year! She was right to ride earlier this year. They are good riders, know the land and know cattle. Marge helped them before and Mary will learn quickly. Everyone you see riding out can handle this." "Are you trying to convince me or yourself?" "Both. I admit, I get anxious too, when they leave... but we just trust in God and have Faith that they return quickly and safely. It's all we can do." Mary looked toward the sky... "Please God, watch over them."

In unison they both turned as the sound of a truck coming in the driveway severed the conversation.

"Looks like Mark and Linda. They have been seeing a lot of each other lately... hmmm." "Mary, you just stay out if it... keep your..." He didn't have a chance to finish his sentence when Mary raised her voice in greeting.

"Hi! You just missed them leave, Sara would have so liked to have seen you, did she know you were coming?" "I told her I would try to be here but not to wait. The real reason I, ah... *we* are here is to stay with you two and get the chores done and see to the barn and livestock while they are gone. We won't take 'no' for an answer and if you want, we can bunk out in..." "Nonsense... you will stay in the house with us, there is plenty of room."

***

"Where in tarnation did this wind come from? Good thing it isn't cold yet or we'd be sitting icicles!" "I'll keep you warm Katy... ride a little closer..."

The line of riders made their way to the far corner of the Red Pasture to the new trail Sara had cut through under the 'tree arch'. Sara and Russell rode the lead positions followed by Brent, Charles, Mary and Marge. Behind them, Katy and Michael held each other's hand while riding side by side. "Sure glad you boys offered to take first shift with the packers. I'm hoping that my trail will be accommodating... might have to make a few adjustments in the route so thanks again for leading the mules." "Not a problem Mrs. Barnes and by the end of this Drive Marge and Mary will be old pros at it too!" "Young pros thank you very much!" "Oh, and such beauties too!" "Charles, if you think that saved you... guess again. I can see by the expression on Marge's face you have some making up to do!" "Mrs. Barnes... now, *that* I am a pro at!" Glancing over to her husband, knowing he was chuckling to himself, Sara reached her right hand to his rein hand. The smile on his face told her all she needed to know... young love... young men... young dreams. He still felt all that and more with her and she adored him for it. "Too bad we have the kids, Ma... or..." "Copy that"

"Katy… look over to the left… see that 'hole' in the trees back there… that is the trail head to Hobbs Ridge. As far as I know anyway, Mom has not been back in there since the day I followed her and she found my father's saddlebags." "That's the day you shot the mountain lion, right?" "Yes." "Promise me you won't tell Mary up there that story, I don't think she could take it. Not after the panic about a bear!"

"Hey! Mountain Man!" Charles turned around in the saddle as he spoke. "Isn't that the trail you shot that Lion?"

"Lion? What Lion?"

"Ut oh…" "Double ut oh!"

"Charles, do you really need to bring that up now?" Brent tipped his head and glared over his sunglasses at Charles. Turning his head back to Mary, he nudged Benji beside Nugget. "Mary, don't let these guys scare you. I got my guns and there is no way I will let anything happen to you. But, if you want to go back, I will go with you. It will be like the one day Drive you were on-- un eventful. Just a nice casual, this time several day jaunt in the mountains and some snuggle time with your 'wonder boy'…"

"Only around the campfire… 'Wonder Boy'… separate tents remember?!"

"Yes, Mrs. Barnes." He turned around in the saddle so Michael could hear him, "How does she do that? She hears everything!" "She's my mom, that's how."

"I'm fine. Really." "You sure?" "Positive. I'm a 'Roper Girl' remember… we're fearless!" Both Marge and Mary raised their right arms with a fisted hand in the air and together exclaimed "YEAH!!" Charles, Brent, Michael and Katy followed their lead and raised their arms as well. "AMIGOS" The boys said together, "Roper Girls" from Marge and

Mary. "Barrel Babe" from Katy. "Hey, I had to call myself *something...* you all have a moniker! "All righty then... 'Barrel Babe' it is!"

Hank and Baron had been off the trail on the scent of an unknown animal; when everyone cheered the dogs lost concentration on their task and playfully ran back to the line of riders barking so as to be included in what they thought to be an opportunity to play. "There's my boys! Where you been? Keeping the varmints at bay are ya? Good boys!"

"What's that big grin on your face Russell? Enquiring minds want to know!"

"Sara, I do believe we are in for a very entertaining few days."

Still hand in hand, Sara and Russell led the riders toward the Trail Head. The grasses of the Red Pasture had turned brittle early this year from the drought conditions. Leaning over to grasp onto a handful of 'heads', and then watching them crumble in between her fingers, Sara was reassured that they were doing the right thing by bringing the herd home early. "Sure has been a lot of years since last I saw this pasture so dry. Wow!" "You took a chance with John, but you are right, and I think he knew it... it's just that he probably thinks he should have been the one to 'know the right thing', he's getting older and it's hard for him to accept." "You hit that nail on the head! You should have known him in his prime years... there's not a thing about ranching he doesn't know, hasn't done or didn't take part in on this ranch. He took it hard in his own way about the Drive that Sam died. He had planned on going with us, but the doctor told him 'no' after his gall bladder surgery. He sure put up a fight over that, if it wasn't for Mary and her putting her foot down, well... who knows... but never the less he hasn't been on a Drive since. Thank goodness we've had plenty of good help." Sara turned and smiled toward the riders behind them noticing they were all quiet and contentedly taking in the scenery and enjoying the ride together. Looking back at Russell, "They've got so much ahead of them... What are we going to do when they go their ways and follow their own paths?" "Let's not worry about that now, today is today and today we ride for the herd and we ride for the Moore Ranch." "For the Moore Ranch!" In unison the riders behind her raised their right hands "We are the riders of the Moore Ranch! To the herd!!!!"

Sara did not look back when she asked of the others, "Ready?" "Ready for what?" "We are off like a dirty shirt!" Katy tried to hear Michael's barely audible voice as his mother nudged Jazzy into a canter and then a hand gallop followed closely by Buck. Marge and Mary put the heals to their horses and were soon in pursuit. "Heee Yahhhh!" "Hang On! Nugget here really likes to run!" Wanting nothing to do with expending the extra energy, Jeb and Pete stubbornly resisted the quickened gait. "Now you know why you have the mules! Mom likes to play when she rides." Michael and Katy sped past Brent and Charles. "I see this, but wasn't it great to watch those wranglers in the saddles as they rode off?" "You are talking about the girls I hope!" Brent fisted Charles' left shoulder. "And yes… there is just something about a cowgirl wearing wranglers! How are we going to catch up if these darn mules don't get to hoofing it?"

Halting Jazzy and asking for a 'turn on the haunches'; Sara raised her right hand indicating to the others to 'hold up'. "Guess we best stop here and wait for the mule skinners to get here."

"Better late than never, our long-eared friends here are conservin' energy… we didn't want them to feel left out so we stayed with them." Brent leaned down to pat Pete's neck.

"The trail head is just up there by the tree arch. We have to go around to the left then cut back hard to the right. It's going be a little tough dallied to a mule… you guys think you can handle it?" "We got this Mrs. Barnes. You just lead the way and we'll be right behind you." "Speak for yourself Brent… Jeb here is a bit on the ornery side. Just how much packing has he done anyway?" "I'll take him if you want… he can be contrary. I only had him leading a few times and truthfully, I would have brought Annie but she still has that 'gravel' in her right front hoof. Jeb was elected without a vote." "I think I'd like to see if I can get him through this Michael if you don't mind. I kinda like the long eared fellow… we look alike don't you agree?" Jeb trotted up beside Charles as he pulled on the dally rope. "Yeah… screwy hair and untamed whiskers… that's us!!" "The question is who the bigger ass is?!!!" "Why Brent, I do believe you have left us to ponder the truth in that statement!"

"You boys done solving the world's problems? Can we get into the woods now?" "Yes, ma'am"

"Hang on! The real riding is about to begin!" "I don't like the sound of that, your mom can like ride anything and anywhere… she is amazing…" "That she is and she will lead us through on her own terms so just be ready." Charles and Brent exchanged a look of concern. This was a new trail and they had no idea what lay ahead for them. "If it were me, I'd let the dally rope loose… just in case." "Reassuring there partner, real reassuring…" "Just trying to help."

"Take it slow Brent… Pete's a tad hesitant at times, he might think he won't fit, but he will." "We got this Mrs. B… Ole Pete and I… we are a working unit! Come on, Boy! Here we go, stay behind me… watch that rock…" Thunk! "Oops! Hope there wasn't anything too fragile in that right pannier! Yo! Charles… it is a tight turn for the packs… hope your Jeb can handle it!" "Don't you worry about us…" Thunk. Thunk. "Okay… you can worry a little…"

"After you my dear…" Michael reined Capp to a halt to make room for Katy to ride through the arch before him. "Why thank you kind sir!" Capp nickered as if he was the gentleman saying 'You are welcome'. "I swear that horse of yours talks sometimes." "He does as a matter of fact… that he does. Good boy with good manners!" Michael put his hand on Capp's mane and ran his fingers through the long black hair.

"Everybody through?" "Yes Mom… your favorite drag riding son is right on line! Lead on!"

"The way through here is narrow and we'll be on the edge of the ridge for a short time, now's your chance to check your saddles because after this, well, it won't be possible to get off the trail." "Did you all hear her? Saddles tight?" "We are all good!!!"

The riders settled in line.

"How far have we gone, Mom?" "We are about three quarters of the way to Robb's Rock. We are making good time. Did you want to stop for lunch? The last flat area is just ahead." "Sounds like a plan"

"By the time we all get through here there is going to be a well-established trail. Good thing too, as it was a little difficult to find coming back when I was up here before. If we keep to the right and head north to north east, we should be about three miles closer to Robbs Rock than the Hobbs Ridge trail. The terrain is a bit better too and even with the two packers we will make way better time.

Riding behind Sara, Russell smiled as he spoke back to her. "It's a good thing you rode this out already. Do you think we'll make it in to the Pass by nightfall?" "Not sure. Guess that depends on what we find on the other side of this ridgeline." "Well, there is that cave up there of we need to use it... you think it is large enough to hold all of us?"

Sara's heart stopped for a brief moment. She lost her breath. *The cave.*

Tipping her head forward and with a light toss side to side ... a sigh heard only by her... The cave. How could she stay there again? How could she go in there with so many memories of the night she and Sam spent there... how could she not relive feeling so helpless as he intensely suffered both physically and emotionally from the injuries sustained when he and Tonk plummeted down Hobbs Ridge... how would she hold herself together in front of Michael and his friends, and most of all... Russell? That was the last night that Samuel was alive.

That was the last night she lay next to him sleeping... so long ago but still so much a part of her heart.

Russell had told her on numerous occasions that she has more 'Grit' than anyone he has ever known; this might be the time she was going to have to prove it to herself.

Cowgirl Code.

"Yes, there is a cave up there... it could be a bit cramped, but if I recall, it will fit us." As soon as she spoke, Russell realized the error of his suggestion. He knew it would be too hard for her to be in that cave. "We'll probably be well beyond by nightfall... we have the tents... there is plenty of area at the bottom of the bowl between the tilleys."

To herself she spoke. 'nice try, thank you, but....'

"Is that Robbs Rock up there? Isn't there that 'Haunted Pass' around here somewhere? I've heard some pretty horrible stories about that Pass." "Yes, Marge... though it is farther away than it looks, that is Robbs Rock, but don't worry, this ridge we are on... that 'Haunted Pass' as you call it is below us. You really can't tell but we are riding the top side of the 'wall' of the Pass. From the other topside you could see the old Indian carvings below us. If you ride the Hobb's Ridge trail you go through the Pass and can actually get to the carvings." "What about the ghosts?"

Sara tried to conceal her chuckle. "The ghosts? Well. I don't know of any actual real ghosts through there, but I will admit that the horses always sense something... or someone... when you ride through it. Maybe there are ghosts in there!" Brent could see the look of great concern on Mary's face as Marge and Sara talked of the Pass. "Mary... don't you fret none... the stories are just that... stories." "Brent, you ever rode through there?" "Well, no... but..." "Maybe we'll just have to change that for you!" "No thanks, Michael. I think not. I'm not sceered… but…. I just can't speak for Benji here…" "Riiiiiight!" "Oh, just ride wouldja?"

Riding the ridgeline, the riders were quiet. The scenery of vistas looking out through the great expanse of wilderness kept the attention of the riders and the maneuvering skills of the horses and mules. The footing was rocky and in places quite loose thus presenting the possibility of a slide or fall. At last reaching the far end of the trail Sara again halted in line but this time she could not turn her mare. Speaking loudly as the wind at that altitude was ever present, "Russell, tell Marge there behind you to 'keep it going'… we are going to start descending the end of the ridge… it's a bit tricky, I hope I can find my 'switch backs'… take it real slow especially with the mules."

"Okay… hey Marge keep it going… steep hill… go slow through the switch backs!"
The others all followed through with sending back the warning.

"Well, here goes!" "It can't be that bad… Sara, where'd you go?" Russell looked below him and could see the top of Sara's head. "Holy crap! Steep much? Buck old boy, don't let your legs fail us now!"

"Ahhhh… Noooo…" "Hang on Marge, let Winnie pick her way… you gotta trust her!" Raising her voice, Marge was quick to respond, "Easy for you to say! She's not a seasoned horse like Lady…" Keeping the two-horse length distance between riders, granting Charles full view of the situation, "Try this… 'set on your pockets'… tell her through your body you want her on her haunches and not the front end, hopefully she'll sit on her butt and level out a little for you!" Placing her legs a little forward of the cinch and only leaning her balance to her hips, she tried to body language maneuver the young mare to the haunch positioning. "It works!!!! Look at this!! She's doing it! Thanks Charles… you know your horses just like everyone says!" "That I do! That I do!"

Observing the 'lesson' between Marge and Charles, Brent shook his head, raised his eyebrows and smiled. "Too bad it isn't the infantry you want to join... they might even still have a horse hanging around... noooooo... you want to fly fighter jets!" Interjecting before Charles could respond Michael spoke up, "Not now Brent... not now. Let's just get down off the ridge and get the cattle home, right now we are cowboys... he saw the look in Katy's eyes and the expression on her face and then continued. "And cowgirls... doing a job. No one is a fighter pilot, a Police chief, a Vet, a rodeo man or the heiress to a ranch. We are all here for the job."

"You are right. C'mon, Jeb... we got work to do." Michael was puzzled by the tone in Brent's remark. Was he in agreement or did he feel chastised and slighted? "Brent..." "Not now Michael, not now." "Okay, but... okay."

Trying to turn in her saddle, hoping she could give Michael a reassuring glance proved detrimental to Chance's balance. As Katy twisted toward the left, knowing her balance would be slightly moved to the uphill side of the trail thus rendering any shift in Chance's balance to be grounded, she did not see the loose rock in the trail just in front of his right foreleg. Her movement in the saddle took his concentration off the trail for just the split second he needed to determine his footfall over the rock. Having no chance of recovery after stepping directly on the loose rock, as it rolled from his weight, he lost his balance and soon found himself stumbling to his knees. Amid the ensuing struggle to regain his balance, he was able to regain control of his haunches, at that point, still on his knees, with a slight hesitation, pulling his left leg up first and then his right, he let out a snort and walked on as if it had not happened.

"I wasn't going to tell you he had a hind over the edge... but, man, I know that was scary as hell from where you're at, but for me, looking at how he recovered himself... that was pretty awesome." "Awesome or not, I don't want to do it again..."

"Everybody down?" "Just waiting on Michael and Capp... they are at the last switch back now. Man, oh man Mrs. B. that was a heck of a hill! We got us some good trail ponies now!" "No weenies out here Charles... can't afford it." "And my Winnie ain't no weenie anymore!!! Whoo Hoo!" "What's everyone laughing at?" Michael rode to the group as they were jesting about Marge's young mare.

The trail opened to the stretch of range between Hobbs Ridge and the North Grazing lands. The horses were relaxing into a steady walk as the terrain leveled. "Let's give these guys a little break and let them graze. They sure deserve it after that mountain." "Good, I sure could use a bit of leg stretching myself." Sara and Russell dismounted their horses followed by the others. "Are we going to be here long enough to hobble?" "It's getting late; I'm thinking no more than thirty minutes. If you want to hobble, that is up to you." "I'm in!" "Me too!" Michael, Charles and Brent dismounted. Walking toward Katy, reaching his hand to her, "My dear, may I assist you?" Observing the reactions of Marge and Mary as Michael helped Katy dismount, Charles and Brent both decided to emulate their friend's courtesy.

"Well, would you look at that, chivalry is alive and well on the range!" Standing on the left side of Jazzy's head, Sara looked toward the group of young adults as she unsnapped the reins from the curb bit and tied a long line to the center chin ring of the halter part of the bridle. "That it is. Good stock those boys, good stock." Russell tied the long line in the same manner on Buck. "I sure do like these halter bridle combinations... glad you found them!" "Me too. Let's sit over there and get a little 'us' time... not going to have much after this for a while." "Great minds think alike my love; great minds think alike!"

"Look at those two over there... sitting there silhouetted by the sun... looks like they ought to be in a movie. The horses munching happily on either side of them sitting in the tall grass... if this isn't a 'Kodak Moment'..." "Just so happens I brought my camera with me... huhuh!" Oh Mary! You and that camera... get a good shot of them, please. This would make a great Christmas present." "Will do my best Michael. I've taken several shots already, but you are right, capturing them... together like this... well that will be..." "The photo,

Mary..." Mary knelt in the shade of the horses, focused the zoom lens and captured Sara and Russell looking at each other leaning in for a kiss. A quick reset and she was able to put to film the actual moment of the kiss. Lowering the camera, Mary smiled as she gazed upon the two people and their horses in the serenity of the flowing grasses in the setting sun. She felt Brent's hand on her shoulder, her response to those as spellbound at the sight while standing over her as she removed the zoom lens was simply-- "Wow." Charles was the first to find his words. "That right there... in the silhouette... is love."

Walking back from their respite, Sara and Russell remained hand in hand. Sara led Jazzy and Buck followed Russell. As they neared the group Sara raised her voice to gain the attention of the conversation. "It's time... get the hobbles off, we are burning daylight." "Oh, Mrs. B. you should see..." Marge pushed Mary just in time for her to not mention the photo. Understanding the glare of her sister's eyes she realized her mistake. "See what?" "You should... ah, see... how the setting sun bounces off your hair!" "Really? That's how you 'cover'... the sun bouncing off her hair...?" "My hair, huh, it's under my hat... now you have sparked my curiosity as to what you all were talking about..." "Let it go Mom... just let it go... it's a sister thing I guess." Smiling at her son, Sara put her left foot in the stirrup.

"Mount up!"

The dogs arrived from their wanderings as Russell turned on his heels and hopped up and onto Buck's back. He took great pride in still being able to mount cowboy style even in his aging years.

"Let's Ride!"

"What a sunset this evening! Those colors are fascinating... can't remember when last I saw such a diverse pattern to the clouds and last rays of the sun! It's stunning!" "A reflection of the beauty here on this ranch... it truly is God's Country. I just can't imagine a more befitting end to such a great day. I don't think we are going to make it to the bowl in time, you sure you are alright with the cave?" "I'm sure. It will be good to have a pleasant memory there, I shall never forget the past, but this is now... and now we need shelter, dinner and rest. We'll get to the herd tomorrow and then the real work begins."

"Send word back... we will be making camp in the cave tonight."

Prodding Capp forward to ride beside Katy, Michael reached his hand to hers. "Wow, I would have thought she would have pushed the daylight as far past the cave as she could. Katy... that was their last night together. Her and my father. And it was so... it was just awful for both of them. I just can't believe she would go back in there." "I can. Your mother... your mother is cut from a tough cloth. She is gentle and she is nurturing, but when needed... that woman is a rock. You know how Mr. Barnes is always saying she has 'grit'? He is right. She puts everyone else first despite how it affects her... that is who and what she is. A true and good woman." "Still, it has to be so hard..." "That's what makes her so... *her*. Go with it, be there if she needs you, but my guess is she has come to her own terms about it and really is okay." "I hope you are right!" "And you doubt me?" "Never... kiss me... the next Mrs. Moore to be!"

There was an uninhibited silence among the riders and stillness in the landscape around them as they rode the hillside toward the cave.

"Hang on a minute, I need to breathe." "Take your time, Sara."

"Okay, before we go in... the west wall is the best for the horses, there is... or was anyway, a couple points in the wall to tie a line for the horses. We will probably have to go around the back side as well."

"Boys, you three and the mules, you are with me. We will go up ahead and get the line up so we aren't scrambling in the sleeping area." "Thank you, Russ. That will be a big help." "Mr. B... you think we ought to tie here or..." "We'll hold your horses. Mary reached over for Brent to hand her his reins. "Thanks."

Russell led the trek ascending the last hundred yards to the mouth of the cave.

"Helllllllooooooo" Charles fisted Brent's right shoulder as he was trying to get an echo. "It's a cave goofball... not the Grand Canyon!" "That depends on how far back in the mountain it actually goes!" "Well, I'm not going and looking for mama bear way in the back thank you..." "Oh Lord, not more talk about bears..." "Boys, get the rope tied so the girls can come up." "Yes sir."

Russell's attention was soon on the marring in the stone floor that resembled the outline of a fire ring. Michael followed his gaze to see the mark. Lifting his stare from the floor he looked at Russell. In unison they spoke, "Get a tarp over that before she gets in here!" "Already on my way to the panniers!" Michael did not take the time to complete the sentence before he had turned and was retrieving the tarp from the left pannier on Pete. "What's the fuss?" Brent and Charles both looked at Russell. Russell looked at the floor marring. Brent and Charles followed his gaze and realizing the significance of the mark, they briskly walked to Michael to help him. "Good thing we came in first!" "If I know my mom, she had that planned." "She probably did."

"Come on in ladies, your abode awaits you!" The men walked to where the women and horses were waiting. "You girls go ahead, get settled in... I'll be right there..." "Here, hand me Jazzy and Buck... take your time sweetheart, take your time."

A statuesque figure, Sara stood there staring at the mouth of the cave while observing the conversation and energy of the family and friends as they made their way up the hill.

She heard the distant squeal of a Hawk.

"Okay, Sam. I can do this." Looking toward the faint sound of the familiar bird, in her mind she recalled him promising to bring her back here. "Oh, Sam..."

Another screech. This time gaining the attention of the hill climbers. Stopping and then looking back, they could see the back of Sara with her arms spread wide in the air, her head tipped back. They had no idea that at that moment she was recalling his words to her, "You did good Sara, you did good".

No one interrupted her. They just turned and continued to the cave.

Taking in a deep breath, to herself Sara concluded that this is the right thing to do and she was able to do it! Climbing up the hill, she stopped only once as she put her hands on the trees that she had tied the barrier to years before. "You've grown some since last I was here for an overnight." Reaching the cave opening, she turned and looked out into forest. "Dreams... memories... good and bad... we need them all. Thank you, Lord." Beside her and without her knowing, Russell gently placed his left arm around her waist. "You are some kind of good woman Mrs. Barnes!" "A good woman needs a good man... and you are a good man. I love you." Pulling her into an embrace, again a silhouette now in the cave mouth encircled by the walls of stone and with the near trees and treetops of those on the hill on either side of them, Mary captured the moment on film.

"Oh, my..." "What?" "Hank and Baron are sitting sentry just as Rex and Bandit did. Same spots. I like that." "Me too. Everyone settled in well, dinner was great. I must say listening to those hooligans try to tell each other how to tie the barrier knots was rather entertaining." Sara and Russell were the last to be sitting around the fire. "They are tuckered for sure. I hope they get good rest. It's going to be hard tomorrow." "The boys will be fine and Katy... Marge has helped on a drive before and Mary, she's pretty handy in a pinch despite how everyone teases her." "We have a good crew Sara, we can depend on them all. It's time we get some shut eye as well. After you..."

Slowly walking toward the double sleeping bag, memories began flooding Sara's mind. Russell took note of her faltering steps and walked ahead of her to get to the bag first. "I'll just warm that up for you a little…" He slipped into the wool lined camp bed and raised the side inviting her in with him.

"Sleep well, Sara. I love you." Rolling over into the fetal position, Sara quietly sobbed as she looked outside the cave into the darkness. Wrapping his arms around her, Russell wanted only to be with his wife, holding her in his arms for comfort; shielding her emotion from the others. A low whisper in her ear; "I love you, it is okay for you to miss Samuel. I know I have never had to 'compete' with him… you are my first real love… you know that… I am not your first love and I accept that and all that is needed of me to do so. He was a good man, and for you to love him and me… lets me know you think of me as a good man too."

Rolling her head back to look at him and raising her left hand to gently cup his face, she smiled. "You are a good man. I know no other that would understand as you do… you were sent to me for a reason and I truly believe Sam had a hand in it. I think he spoke with God when he knew he was in his final moments and…"

Russell leaned forward to engulf her in his arms. Speaking softly, he finished for her. "…And he spoke with God and God spoke to me, and through all of us you and I have made a life of love and family.

Again, the squeal of the Hawk. Sara and Russell both turned to peer out of the cave and in a flicker of moonlight watched as the trees swayed in the wind. In the distance they could barely make out the flight of the bird. A tear slowly fell from his left eye onto her cheek. "I've got her Sam… she is safe with me and I with her." "Oh, Russell, I do love you with all my heart. I'm actually glad we camped here; I now will have a good memory of these walls. And… thanks for covering up the mark of the fire pit." "You knew it was here didn't you?" "Truth? I was here when I scouted the new trail but couldn't take the pain after seeing the marring and left."

"Sleep, my love. We have a long ride tomorrow and I plan on surprising the kids with an ah-thehn-tic cowboy trail breakfast in the morning!" "Really? Where are all your pro-visions for this here cowboy breakfast?" "You are not the only clever packer!" A brief moment of giggles between them, Russell enwrapped her with his body as she rolled back over. "See you on the other side of dreams." "The other side of my dreams... I like that."

"John Moore!" "Uh oh! In here my bride... Mark and I are in the den. We are watching the *Golden Girls.*" "This 'golden girl' is ready for dinner and a little boot stompin'!" "Holy Moly Woman! You look great!" "Better than Blanche?" "Every day of the week my dear, everyday of the week!" "Where's Linda? Is she ready?" "Ready as I can get!" Both men stood as Mary entered the room. At the sight of Linda, Mark gasped and fell back onto the couch; he had difficulty regaining his stance. A final push and he was able to walk over to Linda. "Wow! I am the mostest luckiestest, my Lord, I can't even speak right... Linda, you take my breath away!" "Mrs. M, I believe you were right in suggesting I choose the red dress, Thanks!"

"We interrupt this program to issue a weather alert for the northern portion of the state..."

"Hold on... we need to hear this" All attention was on the television set. Mary reached her right hand to John. As he held her close, he could feel her begin to tremble. Leaning over, he kissed the top of her head. "It said the northern part, we're central... let's not get in a hurry to worry."

"...the atmospheric pressure has shifted and the cold air coming down from Canada will most likely meet with the warm air from the south..." "John... he said 'most likely'... that means they aren't sure!" "Hold on... let's listen to the rest of it." "...could mean the threat of thunderstorms in the lower regions and even a possible early winter storm in the higher altitude. Look for high winds in the overnight through early morning hours. There is…" "Oh John! What are we going to do?"

"Right now, we are going to the Holler for dinner and boot stompin' like we planned! We can't change the predictability of the weather and they will be fine. By now they are close to the herd… they will get to them early morning and be on their way home. Perhaps maybe a little wet, but they are going to be fine." "You promise?" "I promise." "Alright then… to the Holler we go!"

"Russell… you awake"

"Huhhh"

"Look outside"

"Before coffee?"

"Russell… Look outside!"

The alarm in her voice prompted him to full waking. Pushing himself up with his left arm in order better position himself to see over her, kissing her back as his mouth passed by her. "I think the kids are still sleeping…" "Not now, look outside!" "Okay… okay"

"Ah… when did that tree fall?" "Sometime during the night. Did you hear anything?" "No."

"Good morning!" "Katy, you are always so chipper in the morning… don't know how you do it!"

"Get used to it Mikey… you are going to have 'chipper' to deal with every morning, I just hope she can deal with you! Hey Brent boy… wake your butt up!" "Yeah… okay… hey… when did that tree fall?" Charles and Michael noticed that Brent was looking to the opening of the cave. "Well, that sure puts a twist on 'if a tree falls in the woods and no one is there to see it, does it make a sound? We were here and didn't hear it!"

Marge and Mary ducked under the tree as they re-entered the cave. Noticing the puzzled looks on the faces staring at them, Mary looked at Marge and then back at Sara. "Ah… we were just out taking care of business… believe it or not; the only tree down is that one there. It sure doesn't make sense; that was a big strong oak." "Nothing else… really?" "Really. It's like something is telling us not to go out there today… hmm kinda weird"

"About that fancy breakfast…" "On it!"

"Is the news on? Any more word on the weather?" "Nope. Not even any reports from up north. I'm guessing they once again misinformed us!" Knowing his wife would inquire at her first chance, John had the television on for the early morning seven o'clock news. "That makes me feel better. Any sign of Mark and Linda this morning?" "Not yet, but you get the aroma of your muffins wafting up the stairs and it won't be long!" "Turn that thing off and come and help me, think today I'll put strawberries and bananas in them." John quickly rose from his seat and while pressing the power control on the remote; "I still can't get over this 'remote' thing…" Shaking his head as he walked in the kitchen to assist Mary.

"Packing the panniers was a bit easier this time. You all set Sara?" "Ready when you are. And… to all you fine young strapping men… thanks for removing that tree!" "After that great big breakfast there was no way we were going to let Russell do manual labor! Why… he's been voted the camp cook! No offense to you Mrs. B… but man oh man can he put out good grub!" "Yeah, I'm just like Hop Sing… gotta keep my cowboys full of good vittles soze they can ride the range… wait for it… I hear the music… yup…" Russell waved his right arm from his waist toward the far side of the cave. Taking the cue, Brent, Charles and Michael started to recite the theme from 'Bonanza'. Through her laughter at watching the three friends mockingly get through the verses, Katy interjected, "Bet you can't tell me the actual title of the song?" "I can, but I want to see if any of the cowpokes over there know it." The boys finished their recitation, slapping their knees and laughing, Michael looked up, "Somehow Mom, I knew you would know it and as Gramp has me watch all the re runs with him, I know the name is 'Homestead'. I even know that Lorne Green and Michael Landon had a part in writing it! So there!" "Score for the AMIGOS!!!!" "The AMIGOS!!!!"

Russell turned to Sara, "It's going to be another entertaining day." "Never thought otherwise!"

"Let's ride."

"Mount up!"

Part 4
Lost and Found

Walking their horses side by side and keeping several horse lengths between themselves and the other riders, Sara pointed to the right as she spoke. "We are making good time. Ought to be to the Hobbs Spring head in less than an hour." "I sure do hope it hasn't dried up; I'm thinking it may be the best source of water for the herd." "Russell, you know this territory, are there any other routes we could take if it has? We are all going to need water by the time we get there." "With you saying the Anglin Spring is already dry... we just better hope that Hobbs isn't. There isn't much else out here."

"Hey Mom! You are the weather guru... what do you make of the cloud formations up there?" Sara slowed Jazzy to better able herself to answer. "Very unusual. The Stratocumulus and that higher layer of Altocumulus are indicative of some really unstable air up there. Looks like a Congestus..." "A what? English, Mom, you know, so us 'cowpokes' can understand?" "Okay... more simply put... the ground is pretty hot today, more so than I had expected. That being the case, the warm air rising is meeting with the cold air of the atmosphere enabling cloud formation. The tops of the clouds are positively charged whereas the bottom of the clouds are negatively charged. Remember your science class with magnets...anyway, the ground is positively charged and is attracted to the negative in the bottom of the cloud..."

"Um... Mrs. B... hate to interrupt but does that have something to do with lightning? Cuz I just saw it hit the ground over on the right!?

Russell had been looking at Sara as she explained the cloud formations answer and had not been aware of the lightning strike.

"Dry Lightning to the ground!"   "Means only one thing out here in the dry grasses… Fire!" "Dally those mules boys! Let's go!"

Across the parched ground eight horses with riders and two pack mules galloped toward the Hobbs Spring. Capp stumbled on a lone branch, he strategically regained his stride and soon was back in line. "Boys and girls… we're riding now!"

Approaching the Spring, Sara motioned to slow up by putting her right arm out behind her with her hand open. The exhilaration of the speed masked only by the anxiety of the reason for doing so, fueled the adrenaline of riders and mounts alike. The mules had followed the urgency with greater acceptance than expected.

Michael rode around the group toward the Spring head.

"Any water in the Spring line?" "Nope"

"You smell it?" "Yes… it's over the hill."   "So is the herd!"

"To the herd!"

Arriving at the summit of the line between the Hobbs Ridge valley and the North Grazing Lands, each rider took a place alongside the one arriving before, forming a line at the top; all the riders were aghast at the view that lay in front of them. What they saw now was not what had been anticipated just two hours earlier.   Hank and Baron arrived and took their place beside Michael.

"Lord, be with us"

"Me too, Lord… Keep us in your prayers"
"Shit!"

"Double shit"

"Make that triple"

The entire area to the north of the herd was ablaze. Flames were quickly approaching the cattle.

"There can't be four hundred yards between the herd and the fire line!

"They're getting restless!" In a sudden burst of noise, the bawling of cows for their calves had an urgency so severe it caused alarm enough to start a frenzied movement of the herd.

"We're going to have a stampede if we don't head them off... let the mules loose, tie their lines, we can't be burdened with them... we need everyone riding the herd! Hopefully they will follow and find us... if not, well, we're gonna be hungry! Michael, you take the south side with Charles and Katy... the cattle will be trying to head off to the Pass but we have to get them going west over to the Cramden Ranch! Trust me! I know the lay of the land over there, if we get them over there, we should be able to get out of the fire zone... this thing is going to ignite at any time into an inferno and will not care that we are here. The trees on this ridge are going to be match sticks! We have to get them over before that happens. From there we'll head south back toward Brandon. There's an old abandoned trail that used to... sure as hell hope it still does... come in just east of town."

"How do you know this?" Brent's questioning tone indicated the want for an answer.

"Don't ask, just trust me. I can tell you later. Brent, you and me we are 'drag'. But dragging isn't going to happen... we have to push and push hard to get them to up this ridge! Sara, you and Marge ride the north side and Mary... do you think you can ride Point? I need the strength on the sides and your Nugget seems to have the cattle's attention... I think they'll follow you best."

"Sure thing Mr. Barnes, we got this!" Leaning over to pat Nugget's neck, "Did you hear that big boy! He thinks you have the potential of being a good cow horse! Let's show em!"

"Best get your wild rags up over your nose... the dust and smoke are about to be in-tense!" Simultaneously, everyone pulled the cloth over their faces.

"Point rider first! GO!!!!"

"I'll pick up that Ace of Clubs and with that I have Rummy!" Triumphantly placing his 'hand' on the table, Mark smiled. "Yes, again he wins! I think I like this game!"

"I'll get more cheese and crackers, anyone need anything else to drink?" Linda stood to help Mary.

"We have company." "We do?" "Yes, John... I see a truck coming in the drive."

Standing slowly, John pushed the captain's chair behind him and then as he walked past Mary to the back door, he lovingly patted her buttocks. Her giggle satisfied him as to having made her happy.

"It's Kent Harrison and Nick Borden. I wonder what brings them out here so early in the afternoon."

"How are we going to tell them?"

"*We...*? Oh no... my daughter is up there with them too... you get this one."

"Thanks"

"Mr. Moore… hello… may we come in?" "Absolutely. Mary get some more cheese and crackers and a couple cups of coffee for our friends. Come in… have a seat."

"Mr. Moore, Sir… I'm sorry, but this isn't a social call. We came here to inform you that there is a wild fire up in the North Grazing lands."

"A… fire? The kids… the herd…" Nearly missing his seat as he fell back into his chair, John Moore spoke slowly. Linda reached to him to try to steady his balance and help him sit. Looking toward Kent, Mark was the first to speak again.

"So… what you are saying is that there is a wild fire going on up there… how? We haven't had any bad storms?"

"There were reports of dry lightning…"

"This can't be happening again."

"Mrs. Moore…" Nick walked to her, took her hands, helped her to her chair and continued. "We have smoke jumpers and choppers already on their way. There are Fire Districts from eight locations assisting us. We wanted you to hear it from us before you see it on the news. The media is going to sensationalize it for coverage, and well, we really think we've got it under control. I know your family… and mine… is up in that area. You have got to let us do our job; have we ever failed on our promises to you?"

"No, and Nick, I know you must be scared as well for your Katy, what can we do to help?"

"They are setting up for the Search and Rescue as well as the Fireman from other districts to meet at the Holler. The men are going to need food and good rest. Anything you want to bring for them will be greatly appreciated."

Linda lost her balance at the words 'Search and Rescue'. "You are telling us that our family and the herd are *in* the fire? *Search*... and *Rescue?* Are they in danger?" Mark put his arms around her and helped her to her seat. "Nick, please expound for clarification. These women and well, okay, men here need to know the truth."

"The truth is, we don't know where they are." Nick's voice lowered and faltered as he spoke.

Silence befell the entire group.

Ever the matriarch, Mary stood in defiance of her fright.

"Food, well there won't be any shortage on that for them! I just won't have it!"

John followed his wife's lead. "She's serious about that, Nick. And, we've got the old bunk house; it sleeps eight if it has to. All the bunks have a mattress, you want them or the men can stay here if they'd like."

"Might have to take you up on that, the Holler is only just so accommodating. Thanks. In the meantime, try not to get too excited over what the news reports say. Please"

"John, Mary, Linda... I'm going with them to help." "Thank you, Mark... please be careful, you are family too and well..." "Family sticks together..." "Yes, they do!"

Placing her hands on Mark's chest, Linda laid her head close to him. "Be careful. I'm proud of you." Mark placed his hands on either side of her head and gently pulled her away so he could look in her eyes. Softly she whispered before he spoke, "Come back to me..." "Every day for the rest of my life." Mary smiled as they kissed.

"Chopper one, this is Ground Control, you got eyes yet?

"Ground Control, this is Chopper One, we are just about to the... wow!"

"Chopper one? Come in ..."

"Ground Control... this thing is way larger than we thought! There are four ridge lines and valleys ablaze out here. We are most definitely going to need more back up!"

"Come back, chopper one... repeat please, repeat."

"Ground Control, there are four ridges on fire out here, did you say the Moore Ranch is out *here* driving cattle?"

"Copy that Chopper One"

"Ground Control, I'm not thinking they have a prayers chance of getting out of that hell down there."

"Chopper One, you don't know the Moore Ranch."

"Call in the Smoke Jumpers and the air units... we are going to need everyone!"

"They're turning!!!!" Sara's voice barely audible over the thundering hooves.

The stampede had begun. With flames on two sides of the herd now, the frenzy was unavoidable.

"Hold em back Mary... criss cross em... try to slow them down!"

"I'm trying..."

"You got the side line Marge? Mary needs help..."

"Go… I can hold the line"

"Mom's heading up… Charles, you and Katy keep the side… we gotta slow these cattle… the calves are falling back."

"Go… we got this"

"Hank! Baron! Hep hep!"

Michael joined Mary and Sara at the head of the herd. The ability to control the cattle depended on them being willing to follow the horses. At this point, one horse was not convincing enough to gain their attention. With Mary in the middle and Michael and Sara just back and on the outside of the point, slowly the three regained control of the speed at which the cattle moved. Together with the side lines they would control direction.

"I'm going after those calves Mr. B…"

"Don't push them too hard… they are already fatigued… we don't want to lose em so early in the game. Just get them turned back to follow"

Russell watched as Brent skillfully reined his horse over to the calves and with his voice and steady arm language, turned the calves back to the herd.

"That's some sure fine riding Brent! Good job!"

Waving his hand in recognition that he had heard Russell, Brent said aloud "Hear that Benji Boy! Whoo Hoo! Get along little doggies!"

"Katy… turn em …"

"Charles… help me! I…" Chance was at a full gallop, Katy had to keep her left leg hard into his side to keep him from trying to evade the cattle. "Push them over Chance… you gotta do it! We have to keep them straight just a little farther"

"I'm here, you're doing a great job!"

The flames had encircled the Valley. Russell had been right; the only way out was west then over the ridge and south. "Mary Moore… if you can hear me like you said you could… please hear me now… we are going over the ridge and down to the Cramden Ranch… if we can't get over the ridge then we're taking the top to the Pottery Rd… please Mary… pleeease!" Sara squeezed her eyes tightly and shuddered as she spoke. "Lord, this is really important… let her hear me, or feel me… or something!"

"The top News story of the day for the local areas of Brandon and Carnon is of course the wild fire raging over the Anglin Pass area…"

"Turn that up Mary… what are they saying?"

"…Fire Fighters on the ground and in the air from four states have come to combat what is said to be one of the largest fires in the central portion of the state in over a century. Here with us now is Brandon Police Chief Kent Harrison. Chief Harrison, can you tell us anything regarding the cause of such a wild blaze that has evidently burned beyond your control?"

"Good evening, I agreed to speak on behalf of the Fire Chief as he is busy on the Fire Line. My contact with him has been of a positive nature and that he has assured me that containment is at sixty five percent as of three hours ago."

"Three hours? How do you know if he has been able to hold to that containment level?"

"Actually, in truth I cannot answer that. I have been unable to reach him."

"Does this concern you? That you are no longer in contact with the Fire Chief heading this operation?"

Mary grabbed John's left arm as they stood in front of the television. "Oh no… if they can't talk with the Fire Chief how will they find Sara and…" "Remember what Kent said to us… the media is going to sensationalize this. Look at him… does he look worried? No. It's under control Mary. We have to keep holding on to Faith." "You are right. It's just…" "Listen, they mentioned the cattle drive…"

"Chief Harrison, I have been informed that there is a local ranch trying to push a drive of more than four hundred fifty cattle through the very area that you say is in flames? Has there been any sighting of the riders or the cattle?"

"No, not yet"

"How do you feel about the Helicopter pilot's remark and I quote- "I'm not thinking they have a prayers chance of getting out of that hell down there."

"At that I will quote the Ground Control officer! "Chopper One, you don't know the Moore Ranch."

"Is there a chance of them making it out of this?"

"Again, you don't know the Moore Ranch. They'll be found and they will get home. We have every possible man searching for them. We know the route they had planned and we have crews on the ground and in the air ready to assist. Now if you don't mind, I have work to do."

"Thank You for your time Chief Harrison. Stay tuned for more local news after this brief announcement from…"

"Turn it off… I don't want to hear any more and sure don't want to see anymore pictures of the burning forest. It just makes me sick to lose all those tress and wild life. I know in my heart that they will come home, it's every other living being that is perishing that saddens me." "I know Mary, but God will restore his forest in time." John turned the television off.

"John!!!!!" "What? Woman you scared me!" "John… they are looking in the wrong place!" "What do you mean? We told them the route the drive always takes." "What if they had to change course due to the fire, I think Sara… never mind what I think… where is the old topographical map of the Anglin Ridge and Pass?" "The old map… why the old map? That thing is ancient!" "Because I think there is an old road way back up in there, some folks say there used to be a Pottery back in the hills, they could be heading for that. The news coverage showed that area not completely engulfed in flames yet. John, do you think they would know about that?" "It's always worth a try. I'll get the map, you call Kent."

"We've got them turned toward the ridge… finally" Michael was near enough to Mary to yell over the cattle and be heard.

"Yeah… now to convince them to go up it!"

"Mary… move up… get over to your right… Michael… turn hard!!!"

Katy rode ahead of Charles as they worked the cattle to the right. Marge held her side with help from Brent behind her. Russell hooped and hollered the drag to keep the hesitation at bay from the weaker cattle.

Russell hoped that in their complete attention to their jobs, that no one else had noticed the close proximity of the fire. The intense heat behind him quickly closing the gap of survival for humans and animals was presenting a danger far greater than the stampede. Fear.

Fear in the humans that had to keep control of the situation. Fear in the animals both bovine and equine that the instinct of flight would overrule domestication. "Come on Lord… Give us just enough time to get to the Ridge… Please!"

"Where do you want me to go in?" Mary had no idea now what to do. Having only been on one other drive and never riding point, she was afraid of doing something wrong.

Actually, she was just afraid. They were in a Forest Fire with over 450 head of cattle. As they approached the tree line, she slowed Nugget to a trot to give her a chance to look at the possibilities.

"Pick an opening big enough for a large group… if a bunch go in the rest will follow!" Sara then said to herself, "I hope." She could hear in Mary's voice that she was losing her edge. If the herd would follow her, it just might give her a little reassurance she was doing a good job. Right now, it was hard to believe it was all going to turn out for the good, but keeping Hope and Faith was just about all they could do at this point. "You got this… good girl… yes… in there!"

Mary led the cattle toward the only opening she thought they might be willing to head into. Feeling the heat rising she looked behind her to see the flames just beyond Russell and moving fast. Turning to look in front of her panic started to take hold. "Oh God! The flames will consume this ridge with us on it!!!"

Sara had ridden beside her as Mary cried in anguish. "Not going to happen… not on my watch! We are all going to make it out of this… *all* of us! That includes the cattle! Get a grip girl… we need you!" "Yes Ma'am!" "That's what I want to hear! Now ride that ridge like your life depends on it… because today, it does!"

Sara swung around to ride back to help Russell and Brent get the last stragglers into line. Riding past Marge, she saw the same fright as Mary had. "Buck it up Girl… can't be losing you now!" She did not wait for a response. Riding quickly beyond Russell she motioned to Brent. "Head up the side... keep them moving forward! I'll ride the dirt for a while."

Sara slowed to position herself near Russell. "You know getting these cows over the logs and rocks is not going to be easy." Sara pulled her neckerchief down hoping to clear her lungs but soon realized her mistake. "Ugh, the smoke is as thick as the dust. At least once we are in the woods it will only be smoke, not that that is any consolation." She reset the wild rag over her nose and mouth.

Russell gazed at the ridge and shook his head. "Up won't be as bad as down... if they frenzy again then we face an awful lot of trampling, and if the kids don't get out of the way in time..." "Don't go there, don't you even think about it! No one is getting hurt out here!"

"Michael!!!!!!" Charles looked away from the herd just as a tree fell behind Michael. Seeing Capp bolt sideways, stumble and then regain himself, He could not help pleading for acknowledgment that his friend was alright. "I'm okay... just some fancy foot work!"

The flames had reached the tree line that they had just minutes before entered.

"You hear that?" "Sounds like a helicopter." "Smoke jumpers. Means the Air Patrol isn't far behind." "It also means this fire is bigger than we think. Russell, you do know how to get us out of here..." "Yes, I do. And I will. But, if when we get to the top and there is fire on the other side, we will have to ride the ridge to the old Pottery Road and into Brandon. From there, we'll have to decide what to do. "Take the cattle across the top of the ridge? You know we are going to lose some, and what if they run up there, the point won't have an escape?" "There won't be a point. Just for that reason. We just have to hope the cows are smart enough to just keep moving as we push them." I'm riding up to tell them the plan. See you at the top. I love you!" "I love you too."

Watching Sara ride to Marge, Russell held back his tears. He had no idea if his plan would work. "Don't cry now you fool, the mud running on your face will be a dead giveaway… that's what I'm afraid of… the dead part. Lord… if ever…" Buck bolted to the left as a tree ignited just a few yards away on his right. "Move cows… let's go! Whoop whoop!!"

Sara had been able to get to Marge, Brent and Mary to let them know before heading back down the sideline to Michael and Charles. Navigating the rocks and the trees that for decades had lain fallen was cumbersome at best and she was worried she would not reach them in time.

Snap!

Jazzy stepped on a 'Y' in a large branch still connected to a partially fallen tree. Sara could hear the breaking of the trunk and instinctively put her hands up and caught the tree as it continued to fall. Halting Jazzy with her voice and her seat, she stayed there holding up the tree. "Help!!!!!!"

"Hang on Mom! I'm coming!" "Time to remember our jumping lessons Capp!"

"Charles… over here…" Michael yelled through the woods over the sound of the flames and crackling forest all around them. "Mom needs help!"

"Don't suppose you could take this tree from me… I really don't need it right now."

"I can do that Mom!" "It does come in handy you being so tall, thank you. My arms are about shot now!" Michael maneuvered Capp as he ducked under the branch to have a good place to lift the branch over Sara's head. "Look out! Timber!" Tossing the large branch to ground and then turning to his mother and Charles.

"Mrs. B... Jazzy's kinda got her foot wedged in this 'Y'..." "Oh no... think... Michael, put that branch over here as a fulcrum... now, lift that up so maybe we can raise the log... easy... stand still Jazzy girl... this really wasn't a good time for this... so much for my idea... you try your way!"

Crack!

"That's one way of getting her out... the Mountain Man saves the day again!"

"Yes, Charles, I again am a hero! Even if it is to a horse!"

The adrenalin pumping in Michael lent him the strength to stomp on one side of the 'Y' and it broke under the weight of his foot.

"We got fire on the mountain! Going to have to run the ridge!" Mary had turned Nugget to face the cattle as they frantically ran towards her. She was first to have to hold them from trying to go over the other side. Sara, Marge and Brent joined her in holding what was now a corner.

Sara recalled singing the Charlie Daniels song as she tacked Jazzy. "Not funny Lord, not funny."

Charles and Michael held the left side as Russell pushed the last of the stragglers to the top line.

"Over the ridge top we go! Everyone in the back pushing!"

Overhead in what sounded like the distance, Sara heard a helicopter. "Thank you, Mary!" Sara smiled behind her wildrag knowing that Faith had brought them this far, and Faith would get them home.

"Bill... you see anything?"

"Pretty hard in all this smoke… geez… they got binoculars for night vision, for under water, zoom in, zoom out… we need to see in the day!"

"That would be thermal recognition…"

"Yeah, a lot of good that would do for us now, Wayne."

"You have a point."

"That Harrison fellow, how'd he know about these old roads way back in here?"

"He didn't, the old man Moore had some maps from his grandparents. Still not seeing anything down there on my side, how about you?"

"Wait a darn minute…"

"What?"

"His son's widow married the Barnes fellow… right?"

"Yeah"

"It was his pappy that the big rustling trial was all about. There really is a good chance he'll know that area!"

"Hang on, we're coming about!"

"Did you just say 'coming about'? Aye Aye, Skipper! The Mrs. still must be putting the kibosh on you getting that Sunfish sailboat!"

"Yeah, so for now I Guess being Skipper of this bird is going to have to do! Anything?"

"Smoke is still awful thick... can't see anyone making it out... let alone a herd of cattle."

"Well, as long as you are not smelling steak, I'm going to assume they are still on the hoof!"

"Hey... look... over to the right..."

"Ground Control this is Chopper One, do you read me?"

Chopper One, we read you."

"You are not going to believe this... we found the cattle drive and they are on the only ridge top not burning right now heading toward Brandon."

"Good to hear Chopper One, I'll send the good news to the family"

"Pacing the floor isn't going to make the phone ring Mary, come in the den and watch a movie with me. We still have these rental videos... here they are... *The Color Purple* looks good... we like Danny Glover and Whoopi Goldberg... oh... wait... this should do it... *Bull Durham*... you ladies all ooh and ahh over Kevin Costner!"

"John, why hasn't there been word yet from Kent if they changed the search area?" Mary slowly walked into the den from the kitchen. "Do you think we ought to go down there and find out? I do have some more casseroles ready for the Firemen."

"If it makes you feel better, sure we can go, but we aren't staying long! There are plenty of people there already and I sure don't want one of those damn... sorry, darn... reporters finding us and asking if 'we have a comment'. I just cannot face that."

"I'll get the casseroles out of the oven; they are still a little warm but not too warm to carry." Mary quickly turned and was at the oven door before John had the television turned off. "There's a good box at the bottom of the steps by the fruit cellar…" "On my way"

"There now, all snug in the towels inside the box… that should enable safe traveling for the Pyrex. It's not too heavy for you is it?"

"Not at all my dear… to the truck! Let's get this over with." "Oh John!"

"Get the keys Mary…" "Oh, yeah… they would help!"

Mary went back into the kitchen and retrieved the keys from the phone stand, turning back toward the doorway she saw John standing stock still.

"What is it John?" "Kent's standing in the sidewalk… just standing there… staring out toward the Red Pasture. Why would he be doing that?"

Kent Harrison stood looking toward the only way he knew that they could get the cattle home; the Hobbs Basin and then Hobbs Ridge. It was the only route to the Red Pasture that was not ablaze. He stood there contemplating the location of where Fire Chief Hudson wanted to send the Moore Ranch and how he would be able get the fire lines secured. He knew it was only a matter of time and the blaze would broach the Upper Red Pasture. The winds had shifted and the direction it had taken aimed directly at the Homestead. He had to stop it.

"Hey! Kent! Come on up on the porch… what are you looking at out there?"

"Mr. Moore, Mrs. Moore… Sir, I think you will need to set that box down."

John had an instant shiver and with unsteady hands set the box on the table between the two rocking chairs.

Mary threw her hands to her chest. "NOOOOO! Oh, No... Please... No..."

John reached for Mary, drawing her close to him. He looked in her eyes and then back to Kent Harrison.

Kent took a glance to the barns and then back to the two people standing before him that he had known since he was a child and to whom he respected and loved. He knew he was doing everything humanly possible to help in the situation, but was it enough to satiate their emotions?

"First off... if it had not been for the old map you gave us, we would never have been able to find them." He paused as he knew the outburst from Mary Moore was about to begin.

"OOOOO OHHHH John! John! Did you hear him!!! They found them! Thank you, God!!!! John, they found them!" She was jumping so hard she nearly lost her balance, as Kent leaned to save her from her fall, she hugged him and kissed both cheeks. "Oh my God! They are alive!" With a sudden stop of her jubilation, she turned back to Kent, "They are alive aren't they"

"Yes, they are alive. See why I had you put the box down!?"

"Always thinking ahead... you are a good man, Kent Harrison!"

"Tell us... where are they? Here... sit... tell us everything!"

"We radioed the Chopper to see if they had found any sign, then we told them of the old road. Transmission broke up a bit for a while and all we knew at that point was that they were over the North Grazing

Lands and hadn't seen anything significant. It was about ten minutes or so later that they radioed back and said they had sighted them…"

"Where are they?"

"On top of Anglin Ridge… fortunate for them it is the only ridge top over there not burning. The smoke jumpers and airplanes are having a heck of a time getting back fires and chemical dousing set down what with all this wind fueling the blaze. I gotta say, the heat down there has got to be nearly unbearable. I do have to warn you, the cattle may suffer irreversible dehydration, that we will have to deal with later, and if the horses hold out it will be just short of a miracle."

"We are good about miracles around here!"

"That you are… you proved that today when you thought of the old map."

"I had a little help"

Seeing Kent's puzzled look, John grinned back and said, "Don't ask… it's a woman to woman thing!" "Got it. Enough said."

"So, what is next? How are they getting home?" Mary placed her right hand on John's left as they sat in the rockers.

"When they get to the end of the ridge, they will meet up with a back fire that will open the way down into the basin. We have crews all around the basin hopefully they can hold back the fire so when they get that far, there should be plenty of room and time to rest the cattle, the horses and the riders. We have Choppers waiting that have water for the animals, food for the riders and there is enough grass still there for the animals to graze. I am sorry… there is no way to get relief riders in there… the fire surrounds the area at this point. The team of firefighters and jumpers from Carnon have spent hours prepping that basin to hold your drive for a rest. I can't tell you how we have had to…"

"Kent, you have once again proven the man you are… and those helping you are proof they know you are a man worthy of your station. This town, this county, and heck, this state are all behind you. As for me, I cannot express in words the gratitude we have for all you have done… not only for us, but for saving this town. This fire got a head start and you and Chief Hudson were right on it. Thank you… from my heart, thank you. You manage to get those provisions in to the riders and the cattle and I guarantee as a Moore, that they will get that herd home!'

Mary stood on shaking legs, regained her balance and took Kent Harrison into a tight embrace. "Thank you. To all of you that are helping."

As Mary released her hold, Kent spoke again. "As awful as this is, you must realize that had you waited even a day to get your herd, they would have all perished. The North Grazing Lands are now barren. The cattle would not have stood a chance. She was right to get them early but not for the reason she had thought. Now, we have to get them home. It will be a long hard ride for them and a treacherous wait for you, but please know, we are doing everything humanly possible to see that they get home. I won't lie to you, they will need all the Prayers we can send them. It is ugly up there."

"Kent?"

"Yes Mrs. Moore?"

"Will you be one of the men in the chopper that takes the water and food to them?"

"Absolutely! I need to know for myself so I can relay to you. We will have medical kits for the riders as well as the animals for any injuries that need immediate attention."

"Tell them we love them and are so proud."

"For sure, I will do that now I really do need to get back to town now. And John…"

"Yes?"

"Watch the horizon behind the Red Pasture… call if you even think you see smoke!"

"Yes, Kent."

"Well, I really do need to go… I will keep you updated, I promise."

"Good bye… Thank you"

Kent turned and stepped off the porch to walk to his truck.

"Oh! John! The casseroles!"

"Hey! Kent! Wait… take these for us… I really don't want to get found by the reporters…" "I understand… mmmm Mary… is this your famous tuna …."

"Sure is!" "I think maybe I'll hold that one out for the riders!" "Good idea! Thank you so much."

Holding the box, Kent made his way to his truck. John and Mary Moore stood side by side, his left arm behind her, her right arm behind him. Mary tipped her head to rest on his upper arm and then raised her left arm to his chest. "They are going to be fine. Thank you, Lord, and all the men and women helping to battle this blaze and to get our family home. Keep with them Lord… just a while longer… please. Amen."

Peering through smoke and while trying to navigate through the thick underbrush, Sara tried to get to Russell. He was on the other side of the ridge top and this particular area widened out; indicating they were getting toward the end slope. The noise from the breaking branches, falling trees and the bellers of the cattle masked the clamorous attempts of the horses and riders to push the herd to the end of the ridge.

Sara dodged a falling pine as she crossed to the left side of the ridge top.

"That was close! You and Jazzy alright?"

Breathless she did not answer his question; she had questions of her own.

"Any idea what is at the end of this ridge? What's the slope we are looking at? Are we going to get side lines or just push and Pray?"

"I'm fearing it's the latter, and I sure hope going down will be easier than it was getting up here!" "You and me both! I haven't seen any losses over the edge on the right… how about over here?" "By the Grace of God, I do think we are actually getting through this."

"Do you hear that?" "Yeah…" "They found us!… look Russ… I see the propellers coming up the right side of the ridge!" Her speech stopped as she turned to him, "Just how steep is this if they are rising straight up from below?" "It could get rough, we have to go down and to the left to pick up the old Pottery Rd. This side is far steeper than the face or the left…" Good to hear as the chance of getting through that stand of lit sticks does not show much promise! The left isn't much better – the smoke is starting to thicken… are you sure we can get to the Pottery Road?" "Sara… we don't have a choice that I can see." "Well I see a chopper and that is hope!"

The helicopter rose just above the trees and hovered over the riders. The horses were so exhausted that they were not intimidated by the noise. "I think they like the breeze of the propellers... it has to be cooling them down a little!" "It sure is me... so it has to be for them. Look at them... they don't mind the intrusion at all."

"Bill... the megaphone is behind my seat..." "Aye Aye, *Skipper*" "I'm flying this bird so you get to do the talking. Tell them what they need to know... there is a lot they don't at this point. Choose carefully, they have to keep all the edge they can. Good luck!"

"Russell Barnes! Can you hear me? Russell Barnes! Raise your hand to confirm!"

Russell raised his right arm and waved at the helicopter.

Sara and Russell exchanged a concerning look, then smiled as Sara raised her arm as well. Inwardly, Sara knew Mary had heard her.

"They found us... I don't know how, but they did!" "I know how." Russell put his hand to his mouth and sent a kiss to her as they held their hands together in the smoky air.

"You cannot get down the ridge to the left toward the old road. Confirm!"

His heart sank as Russell raised his arm.

"You will have to push them to the right *before* the face, there is a team holding back the fire. Confirm!"

Russell raised his arm. "How are we going to turn them with no point Russ?"
"We better hope they thought of that ahead of time, there is no way we are going to be able to get up to the front of this herd!"

"I'll go… I'll get as close to the front as I can… push them over as much as they will let me."

"Charles… it's too dangerous… you got a way better chance of being trampled than not if you do this."

"Someone has to… and that someone is me… and my Lady here. I promise, I'll back off it looks like we're in real danger." "Charles…" Charles and Lady turned back to the herd and rode the left side of the ridge top to get as close to the point as possible. "Oh, Russell…what if…" "No what ifs at this point. Right now, we have to just trust instinct." "Easy for you to say…"

"Russell Barnes!" Russell raised his arm again. You will have to push through a narrow egress through the burn… it will open to Hobbs Basin. Confirm!"

They raised their arms.

"In the basin we have an area for you to rest the cattle and yourselves. Confirm!"

They again raised their arms, still looking at each other each with unspoken concerns.

"Hold up in Hobb's Basin, we are going to drop jumpers to help you. Confirm!"

All the riders raised their arms. Brent was first to audibly react. "YEEE HAWWWW… git along little doggies… we are heading home!" All the young riders followed in the rejuvenation of spirit. Reaching his hand out to Sara, his gritty face no longer behind the wildrag, with a dismayed attempt of a smile he bent over to kiss her gloved hand. "We are still a long way from home, but they found us and we're not alone out here anymore." She leaned to him for a celebratory kiss.

Bill set the megaphone on the floor behind the seat. Wayne placed his right hand on the young man's shoulder. "Good job kid. Good job. I hope to God they can make it down that side and get the herd through a narrow burning alley. Look at them, they sure have tested themselves in this. I just can't imagine the strength they have… to make it this far…"

"Wayne! Look!" Bill had looked out the back windows and had a good view of the north east quadrant of the fire.

"It's heading for the Moore Ranch!"

"Chopper One to Ground Control… Come In!"

"Ground Control to Chopper One. Have you…" Wayne did not give the man time to finish his question.

"The fire… it's heading for the Moore Ranch… yes, we instructed Russell to hold up in the Basin, but the line is clear across the ridge over to their Red Pasture. Gonna need a lot more men over there fast!"

"Copy that Chopper One, and Wayne, …thanks. You and Bill just changed the outcome of this mess when you found them"

"Chopper One heading back to ground." Wayne banked the helicopter to the left and as it straightened out the two men 'high fived' in the cockpit. "Sail this bird home Skipper!"

Noticing the temperature increase after the fanning effect of the propellers had ceased, the truth of the situation was again before them. Charles had managed to get a good hold of the left side and was able to force the cattle over, Marge and Mary held the right hind ready in position for taking the right side down the slope. Katy and Michael positioned themselves for the left push down and Brent stayed back to help Russell and Sara nudge the stragglers. No one needed instruction.

Each individual took a role and worked it. They were working as a team even under such horrific conditions.

"We're almost to the drop off... going to have to push hard! Charles!!!!! Charles!!! Russell... Go! He just literally dropped off..." Michael and Russell dug their heals into the horses hoping for enough energy to get to Charles. Buck pushed a straggler calf out of his way and when doing so, knocked the calf down and stepped on his leg. The mournful cry was heard over the noise of the moving cattle. Mary had stayed back a bit and was able to get to the calf. "I've got this, you go..." She dismounted, picked the calf up, laid him across Nugget's withers and then joined him in the saddle. "Looks like you get preferred seating on the way home, I am going to tie you in place as I can't be worried about you falling off!"

"Charles? Yoo hoo... how many fingers am I holding up?" When Russell and Michael had reached Charles, he was lying on the ground, face up, his legs looked fine, but his right arm was positioned as to most likely be broken. Don't move yet... catch your breath. I'm sure the wind was knocked out of you and at this point... well, that wind aint worth nothin' more than blowin' smoke! Seriously, though, set still a minute, Lady is right here, she didn't leave you." "She'd never leave me... she loves me. What the heck..." "Don't try to move it... it's broken." "It doesn't feel broken... oh... ah... until I try to do that!" Russell joined them on the ground. "Here, wrap it tight like you would a horse leg..." "Ahhh... maybe Katy ought to do this! She's the Vet!" "Nonsense, I'm sure you've been taught a thing or two by your mother over the years... prove to her that you listened!" "Hey... good point!" Russell handed him his wild rag. "What are you going to use to cover your face now?" "My whiskers... you need that thing bound together." "Here..." Michael removed his as well. "We will double wrap you until those choppers come to help us. Maybe they will have a splint or something *EMT-ish*."

"That's the last of the stragglers... good to see you boys have rejoined the ride... new attire there Charles?"

"Mrs. B… just a minor setback… a little thing like a broken arm isn't going to stop this cowboy! Hey Mary… who's your friend… Brent's gonna get jealous! To the Point Lady! We're off!"

"Youth…" Sara shook her head back and forth several times, grinned and smiled. She was so proud of everyone. "Michael… looks like you wrapped it well." "Thanks Mom." Looking at Russell, Michael gave a little wink to acknowledge his being right.

"I see the narrow passage ahead!" "We're getting there! Hank! Baron! Here Boys? Has anyone seen the dogs?"

Michael and Sara both turned toward the ridge when they heard the barking.

"Oh, thank God! You boys are a little singed around the edges and I can only imagine the burns on your feet… we'll be with help soon. Perhaps you should ride up with us." "I'll get them mom… you stay put." Reaching down to lift Hank up to Sara, he could hear his friend whimper. "You boys have more than filled your call of duty… time for a little rest." He then placed Baron on Capp and re mounted.
Mother and son rode behind the herd with their trusted dogs held tightly to them as the cattle willingly walked through the open top tunnel of burning forest. Riding in beside Sara, Russell spoke, "I think they know they have to, there is no more disobedience in any of them."

There was silence among the riders through the walls of flames. About half way through the passage, a few of the Fire Fighters came out to watch the disheveled group of horsemen and women as they pushed the cattle past them. Russell stopped to talk with a group that motioned to him.

"They are ready for you up there. I already radioed them to let them know your location and approximate time of arrival to the basin. Man, you guys have had it rough… as soon as we get you secured in the basin then we are heading to the north end of the Moore Ranch while the other outfit stays in the basin with you. Rest, but don't take too long… a couple, maybe three hours tops… really… we… man, you look like hell Russell…" "I've been ridin' in it so I guess I ought to look the part! How close to the ranch is it? John and Mary are there…" "We've spoken with them; they are safe at this point. After you leave the basin, we won't have communication again, but we will keep our eyes on you in the air." "Thank you. I really mean it." "We know, and as odd as this sounds, our job is always burdened with tragedy, at least this time maybe not so much. Ride safe…"

Russell turned Buck back toward Sara and Mary. Rejoining them he recited what the Fireman had told him, he did however; choose not to repeat the part about the fire heading toward the Moore Ranch.

"Land Ho!!!" Charles dropped his reins and held his good arm high. "I sees land that ain't a burnin'!"

Marge looked over to her sister with absolute pride and adoration. "I'm going to want to take a picture of you and the calf… no one is going to believe it! I tell you what little sister; you sure showed me what you are made of through all this. I am really proud of you." "Truthfully, I'm pretty proud of myself! I had no idea the what exhilaration of 'Cowboy' really was until yesterday." "We are the Roper Girls! Together always!" "You got that right! And, yes, I would like a photo with my friend here. I'm hoping Sara will let me tend to him once we get back, I've gotten rather fond of the munchkin."

Michael turned Capp to ride back with Sara. 'Well, we have gotten this far, we've almost got it licked. A little rest, some water and food, this is good Mom, really, this is good. I know you are worn out but we're almost there." "Michael…" "Yes?" "We're in Hobbs Basin, which means to get back to the Red Pasture we have to go up and over Hobbs Ridge." "I know, but Mom… if there is any place in this journey from hell that there will be no doubt in my mind that we will be alright, it is Hobbs Ridge. *He* won't let anything happen to us there. I know it." "Thank you, Michael I hope you are right. There has been no sign of the hawk since the cave yesterday." "He's here Mom, don't worry.... he's here." Michael stood up in his saddle and ran his dirty, burned fingers over the marks in his saddle. "This saddle made it down that Ridge and you carried it back up... this time it's my turn."

"Oh! Russell... look... the cows are grazing and the helicopters have brought what they promised... I want a drink so bad... I don't care if it will be mud by the time it gets past my lips!" "Hold up... I'll get the dogs for you two and then you can get down." "Set them gently, their pads are excruciatingly sore."

"Sara?" "Oh my, Kent! How good to see you... you have no idea! Have you spoken with John and Mary? How are they? Do they know what is happening?"

"Slow down, Sara... here... I brought wash-ups for your faces and hands so you can enjoy your food and drinks." Kent handed several to Sara and Russell and then passed the rest to Michael to disperse to everyone else.

"You thought of everything."

"When you are ready, we'll talk. In the meantime, there is a crop duster plane going to come over with water to spray on the herd and you guys as well. There are some pretty sorry sights out there. You have to know that even if they make it home, they still may not survive the smoke inhalation, burns and wounds. I wouldn't be expecting any of the younger calves to... but then again, I've seen greater miracles come of your family; what's one more! Relax... we'll get to everyone with medical attention; I see Charles is at the EMT Chopper... what happened? No... you drink and eat... you can tell me later..."

Sara and Russell had their water bottles to their burned lips just as Kent spoke again. "One last thing... I brought one of Mary Moore's famous Tuna Noodle casseroles for you... she had sent several for the Fire Crew but that one I saved out for you guys."

"Did I hear Tuna Casserole? Where is it! I'm famished!" "Brent, you always are!"

"We better get our bowls before Charles gets back from the medical bird. He sure has been over there a long time."

One by one the group gathered together to eat and rest. There was no need to hobble the horses, they were heartily enjoying the actual grass under their feet and the chance to graze.

"Hi... I'm Bill... I was the one in the Chopper that spoke to you earlier today... you folks stay there, we've got salve for the cattle; those that will let us anyway... for the burns, if for no other reason than to ease a little of the pain. We'll check the horses too. Holy Moly... there ain't a one of you without cuts and burns and not a thing you are wearing isn't torn... wow... The water plane will be here soon." Bill shook his head side to side as he walked toward the cattle.

"When you kids are done, go ahead and rest a bit. You too, Sara, I'll watch the herd and help the men get their equipment loaded back in the choppers. Bill said they would wait to leave until we are out of view so as not to cause panic in the animals." "You need to rest too! Wake me in an hour and I'll take over so you can rest. I insist!" "Okay... since you inn-ssist. I'll have that talk with Kent Harrison while you are sleeping."

As Russell leaned forward to collect the bowls and cutlery to take to the choppers, he noticed that all six of the 'kids' were already asleep and Sara was not far behind them.

Walking toward Kent, Russell was relieved that by his talking to him now, perhaps he could keep Sara from knowing the information about the fire being close to the Moore Ranch.

"So, Kent... tell me... how bad is it? The Firemen in the egress said the burn is reaching the north end of the Red Pasture."

"Thank you, Matt! That is the best news you could give us. I'll tell Mary, we'll call the McGregor Ranch and let them know and the Pelton's as well. Keep us posted when you can!"

"Well… what did he say?" John had not reset the telephone receiver in the cradle before Mary was asking questions. "Easy there dear, everything is fine… more than fine! They got off the Anglin Ridge and are resting in Hobbs Basin. Matt Brewer said he spoke with Kent Harrison… the choppers are going to wait until the Drive heads back out to leave the basin. Matt spoke with Kent about an hour ago and he said they were going to stay and rest there for two maybe two and a half hours. The fire is still moving quickly but most of what was behind them is starting to burn down."

"Most of what is *behind* them…? What does that mean for between them and us?" "The crews are holding it back as best they can… we may be losing a part of the Red Pasture…" "What??" "Like I said, the crews are up there, they will keep it back so the herd can get through." "Where are they going to be able to come in at if the upper part of the Red Pasture is in a burn?" "They will have to come over this end of Hobbs Ridge to the lower section of the Pasture… don't look like that… I know… but she has to do it and she has Russell and everyone helping her this time. She will be fine." "I know, it's just so…" "No more of this talk, why don't you call the McGregor Ranch and let them know the drive should be here in a few hours. Matt said they are moving slow but should be here by sundown. You could call the Pelton's too. I'm going to get Mark and set the gates for their arrival. I am sure you and Linda have something to cook?"

Embracing his wife and then kissing the top of her head, he then whispered, "It's almost over." Mary sighed while tightly holding him.

"Yes, Callie… probably around sundown. They are resting in Hobbs Basin for a little while and then will come over the Ridge. Yes, they are all okay. Charles broke his arm but it hasn't deterred him they say. Oh, that would be great if you would call the Hunters. Thank you. Yes, see you soon. Oh, by all means… your blueberry pie is always a favorite! Uh Huh… okay… bye now."

Mary started to dial the Pelton Ranch when she heard John calling for her. She untied her apron, placing it on the chair back. As she was opening the screen door to the porch, she saw the truck and stock trailer arriving in the driveway.

"John… who do you suppose that is?" "Looks like Marge Pelton's truck… don't recognize the trailer."

Walking toward the truck as it came to a halt, John recognized Paul Pelton.

"We were just going to call you to let you know they should be here by sundown and to bring the trailer to haul your girls' horses home."

"Actually, I found your mules over by our place. Don't know how they made it that far over, but they did. Skittish fellows… wouldn't let me near them, but when I opened the back gate to the trailer and told them if they wanted to ride home instead of walk, they like understood and went right in. Trailer wasn't even hooked up yet! I would have taken the packs off but they just aren't too keen around strangers, I guess. Anyway, they are here, and if you don't mind, I'll hang around for the afternoon and help with whatever you need and then yes, I can haul the horses home in the stock trailer. Won't be the 'Taj Mahal' of Marge's Featherlite but somehow at this point I don't think they are going mind."

"You are more than welcome to stay. We can call Betty so she can come over too." "Thanks, she will be happy when they are home, it has not been easy for her as I know it hasn't been for Mary or any of us for that matter, just seems the women folk take things like this harder than us men." "No disrespect, but speak for yourself on that, as for me, well…" John looked at the ground as he stopped mid-sentence.

Quickly regaining his composure, John changed the subject. "Let's get these mules to the barn and get the packs off. Looks like they have a lot of burns and cuts we need to doctor before the others get here and need tending to as well. If I know our Sara, she'll make sure the animals are taken care of before she is so the more we can do ahead of her, the sooner she will get settled. You can park the rig over by the machine shed after we unload, I can take them both to the barn while you are parking." "That sounds good."

"Mr. Moore… you in the barn?" John recognized Matt Brewer's voice. "Back here un packing the mules."

"Oh, wow… when did they get here?" "I found them over by our place and loaded them up." Hidden on the far side of Pete, Paul startled Matt as he answered the question. "Oh! Hello Mr. Pelton! I didn't know you were here, my apologies. Seems there is a lot of un conventional travel going on. Kent has the dogs in the chopper with him; they just could not take any more heat on their feet, and several of the calves are going to get to fly to Doc Peterman's barn for now. He is going to be evaluating them and will let you know." "Thank you, Matt." "No problem… well, I'm heading back to town, please let me know when they are home. Everyone in town is Praying for them." "Will do. Please express our gratitude to everyone." "You bet… Mr. Moore… Uh… I have a load of stuff from the folks in town to help you when they get home; the Co-op sent over a ton of cattle feed and 300 pounds of horse feed, the hardware store has several garbage cans full of fencing supplies and that fancy new tack shop donated cases of medications and supplies. It's all in a trailer. I'll just leave it over by the bunk house. You can bring the trailer back to the station whenever you get to it"

John Moore sighed as he looked to the young Policeman. "This town, these people… I cannot express how I feel right now."

122

"No need, Mr. Moore… you are very welcome. I want to help here when you are ready for me, please… call. Good bye now."

"Sara… Sara, honey… wake up…" "Already…" "Yeah, we need to get the kids and keep the herd moving." "You haven't rested?" "No, I didn't have the heart to wake you… I'm alright. Just getting out of the saddle was a big help." "Did they doctor the horses and any cattle?" "The horses are patched with bag balm and a few of the cows too. You aren't going to believe this but they are going to take those few really young calves in the helicopters with them and straight to Doc's. Don't think they are going to make it, but at least now they have a better chance. Mary sure is taken with that little one she carried… if any of them make it, I hope he's one of those that do." "I don't see Hank or Baron?" "They are in the Chopper with Kent. Kent said he would have Bruce Netty get them to Doc to be checked out and then drive them out to the ranch. They are going to wait to take off until after we are out of the basin" "Well then, I guess it is time to climb Hobbs Ridge."

"Time to rise and shine… well, rise anyway, none of us are too shiny at this point! Get another drink before we go, the canteens are filled and on your saddles… you can thank me later… it's time to 'head 'em up and move 'em out!"

"Where's Hank and Baron?" "It seems Michael that they get to ride in a Chopper to go home!" "The smaller calves… they getting air lifted as well?" "That they are!" "No way??!!!" 'Yes… they are! They will be going to Doc's so he can get started on them." "Hey Mary… your little buddy is about to be all snuggly in a straw stall at Doc's… he gets to ride in the helicopter out of here!" "That makes me happy! I want him to live and carrying him was tough!" "If you hadn't put him up there with you, he would for sure have not made it. Mary… he's yours if you want him after we get him cleared from Doc." "Thank you, Mrs. B… thank you"

"Mount up!"

"We interrupt the regular broadcast…"

"Paul… you are closest… turn the radio up! I think it's about the fire…"

"You have a radio in the barn?" "Yeah… Sara says it keeps the animals calm… she spoils them, but she…" John abruptly stopped talking when the radio announcer continued.

"We interrupt this program to give you an update of the Brandon Range Fire and the plight of the small group of riders driving their herd back to the Moore Ranch. Here on the scene with me now is Police Chief Kent Harrison. Chief… please inform the listeners with the latest update on the status of the fire as well as that of the Barnes crew and cattle."

"Barry, I just flew back from Hobbs Basin where the cattle and riders have rested before climbing Hobbs Ridge and then over to the Red Pasture. The fire crews are tiring but have managed to keep the fire lines set to allow passage. It has been a fantastic joint effort of so many fire departments, citizens, emergency responders and rescue operators that have not only brought this fire under control, but through it all, eight riders and somewhere in the range of four hundred head of cattle have made it through."

"Are there injuries reported among the Fire Fighters?"

"We have pulled out only a half dozen men that through their gallantry succumbed to smoke inhalation. I do know that as of two hours ago all six of the Fire Fighters are well and waiting to go back on the line if needed."

"Where has the Fire Chief been? I have not been able to get a statement from him"

"Chief Hudson is right where he wants and needs to be... at this point he is helping to hold the fire line back in the Red Pasture."

"What about the riders and the cattle? You say you were in Hobbs Basin with them... how are they holding up? Did I see two dogs in the helicopter with you?"

"The riders are exhausted. They have pushed endurance limits that no one here or listening could possibly imagine. Their horses are injured and burned yet still work for them. They have carried the dogs and the young calves in the saddles with them and one rider has a broken arm. The calves have been lifted to Doctor Peterman's for evaluation. Russell, Sara and their family are determined... they are planning on arrival at the ranch by sundown this evening."

In the background of the radio broadcast the jubilation of the people present in the location could be heard through the speaker.

"I must ask though, Barry, that the public abstain from going to the ranch for the homecoming. The Moore's are extremely gratuitous to everyone for their support and help these last couple of days; however, they wish respect of their want for privacy at the time of the homecoming. The riders will need to rest and settle before any statements or festivities. I do hope you understand. I have been notified by the Carnon Veterinary Service that they are sending two Doctors to help with the herd and horses, there is one from Eastdale on her way and the 4-H clubs and the FFA chapters... even the Boy Scouts and the Girl Scouts have dozens of volunteers. We will be receiving the Veterinary assistance right away and the volunteer groups can call in the morning for scheduling. Thank you... I must get back now to the command post"

"Folks, we have confirmation that the fire is controlled and that the Moore Ranch Cattle Drive is almost home! Stay tuned to this station and your local television report at six and eleven. This is Barry Monroe... now back to your regularly scheduled programming."

"If all those people are going to be here, we had best tell the women to prepare a lot more food!"

"Russell?" "Yes?" "How bad is Charles' arm? Is it going to affect his Air Force dreams?" "Sara, we are about to push hundreds of cattle over one of the toughest ridges yet with flames at our behinds and you are thinking about the aspirations of a young man? You amaze me. No matter how bad a situation is for you, you always think of others first. He will be just fine. The Air Force will have him to contend with him if they change their mind. Right now, you need to worry about this hill and how we are going to keep from getting our asses singed!"

"I... just..." "No... you let him worry about that... you still have work to do... we need your head in *this* game right now. I don't mean to be curt, but come on... we are all tired and want this to be over, we need you to help make that happen."

"You are right. Bring everyone in; we need to set a plan for this trek over Hobbs."

Placing his right thumb and middle finger to his mouth, Russell skillfully whistled a loud signal for the riders to gather together in the back of the herd as they moved through the last area of semi level ground in the Basin before ascending the ridge.

"First and foremost, you have all... just...well, you have all amazed me. We could not have survived if it were not for all of us doing what we have done. You are so young and yet so seasoned at the same time. You need to know that Sara and I are so very proud of all of you and..."

Sara could see the welling in Russell's eyes.

"...And Russell and I love you all." "We love you too Mrs. B... Mr. B... we are almost home... all of us. A few injuries, but hey... the stories for the grandkids! Huh!?" Everyone laughed as they simultaneously looked at Michael and Katy. "Yeah, we can tell them how their 'Uncle Charles' dove over a cliff and broke his arm!" "And how Aunt Mary carried the calf in her lap…" "Okay… okay… enough fun, we need to set a plan for the ridge." "Always the 'trail boss'!" "Just you remember that!" Again, there was laughter. Russell sat back in the saddle taking in the scene of the tired and torn riders and horses. Even through it all, they found goodness and hope. Glancing his way, Sara could read his thoughts and mimicked his smile.

"God, Hope and Faith… mix in good family a few Prayers and you will prevail at every hardship and challenge." "You are so right, so right. Hope you saved a few Prayers for this ridge." "Big ones!"

"I'll ride Point again" Mary had already turned Nugget toward the ridge.

"Mr. and Mrs. Moore 'to be' will ride the left flank" Michael's smile for Katy as he reached for her hand was noticed by Sara; she in turn smiled at Russell silently relaying happiness for her son.

"Brent, you and Charles take the right flank. Marge, you can either ride drag with us or be up with Mary." "Mrs. B… I really want to be with Mary. I am so proud of her and want her to know that I will ride side by side with her through hell and back… literally." Marge took Mary's right hand in hers and placed in on her heart. "You are here, with me always. I love you." "I love you too." The sisters leaned out to each other for a quick, unsteady embrace.

"Mush!"

"Really… Brent? 'Mush'?" "Just emanating cool thoughts… you know… the Iditarod is in the snow… not the blazing heat of a forest fire!"

"Mush! It is"

Sara had hoped that as they approached the base of the ridge the temperature would decrease. To her chagrin it was just the opposite. She had planned to head up through the untimely dried Hobbs gulch at the north end, however as they approached the area, she could see the flames were too close to risk the time it would take to get the herd through. If they were in the walls and the fire took hold, there would be no escape.

"Russell, I'm going to ride up and let them know to turn south a little. We are going to have to go by way of Tonk's Ridge." "Sara..." "It's okay... we have to. That's all that is to be said on the subject." "Yes ma'am. I'll be here when you get back." "You always are! Come on Jazzy old girl... this is going to get a little tricky..."

The mare whinnied as she galloped toward Michael and Katy.

Riding the edge line and working several stragglers back into the main herd, then making her way slowly toward Michael, she could watch him as he and Katy worked together to keep the cattle moving. "Sam... if you can hear me... look at them... they work well together now... they will do so in their marriage... be proud." She hadn't heard the hawk nor had she felt the familiar touch on her shoulder since the cave, yet she hoped he would hear her.

There was no response.

"Can a mother ride beside her son for a while?" "Hey there, Mom... what brings you to our little niche in the herd?" "Need to move them off south a bit... the gulch has me worried with the flames so close. Push them towards Tonk's Ridge. Don't look like that... it has to be done. Michael... ride up to the girls to help them, you know the area. I'll stay here with Katy until you get back. Just get them heading the right way; when we get into the Red Pasture, I want them to lead us in. Those girls have proven to be fine horsewomen, fine cowgirls and most of all family. They have earned the lead to the ranch. I know we have all been integral in the whole debacle, but if you think about it, we all have been doing this for our lifetimes, they just signed on because of those two crazy friends of yours... they didn't have to, and yet they did."

"You are so right Mrs. Barnes. Go on Michael, I'll be here with your mom."

"I'll be back soon!"

"He rides well... looks good in the saddle, don't you think?" "He had a good teacher." Sara and Katy smiled at each other after they had both watched Michael ride away.

"Start pushing them over Katy... it's time. The smoke is getting closer; I don't want to get caught not being able to see the cattle while we are climbing that ridge. Where are the Fire Line guys... that burn is getting really close! Push them! Now!!!!" "I'm trying... they aren't wanting to go over..."

"Oh my God! Russell... Thank Goodness you are here... we need to get to Brent and Charles... they have to let the herd move toward them." "On my way!" Buck spun around and galloped to the back of the herd to ride around to Brent and Charles. "We are going over Tonk's ridge... gotta let them move over to the south!" "What!?" "The south... we have to move them south... fire... flames..." He did not wait for response as he turned back around to resume his position in the rear of the herd working both sides to keep momentum.

As the first of the herd began the climb, so did the blaze of the fire. Overhead an airplane designed for dousing forest fires veered to the north of them. Soon, Russell could see smoke jumpers exiting helicopters just over the ridge. To himself he thought, "They must be in the Red Pasture... the fire is that close... but what about over here... we are still a couple hours from the ranch!" The airplane took another swath. The cattle retaliated from the increase in smoke and started to panic.

"Keep heading them up! Watch that side line!" Michael could see the change in the temperament of the cattle and knew that if they did not get them settled that the result would be ruinous. "Brent! Over here! Help me with this side line! They are trying to head for the far ravine!" "On my way! Katy… you got this?" "Yea… I hope so…" "Me too… good luck!" Brent reined Benji to the left and was quickly in pursuit of the rouge cattle. "I'll help Brent" Charles had passed Michael before he had the sentence completed. "Mom? Where are you? I cannot see you in the smoke!"

"I'm pushing drag; Russell is up the right side behind Katy! You okay?" "Keep yelling… I can barely hear you!" "I'm riding drag… drop back a little… I just passed the…" "Oh! There you are! I see you now. Man, this smoke is getting tough. Do you know where Katy is? Is she alright?" "Why don't you go help her; she's holding the right-side point. Russell is up there somewhere… Marge and Mary are in lead point." "You okay back here by yourself?" "I got this… now go… I'll keep them moving forward, you keep them on course." "Will do! We are too close to home to lose them now!"

Michael did not see the expression of pride in his mother's smile as he rode toward Russell and Katy. "Lord, here I am again… in this same place… different reasons but just as prayerful. Be with us. Guide us over this ridge and through the draw. And, Lord, if the fire is spreading toward the ranch, please… please be with the Fire Crew as they diligently work to get us home safely. Please, Lord… Amen. Picking up the reins, Sara set deep in the saddle and with a slight leg pressure asked Jazzy to jog into the herd. "Here we go girl… we are almost there! I know I told you we would never ride Tonk's Ridge again… sorry… but we have to!" A slow tear fell on Sara's left cheek as Jazzy whinnied when they passed the ravine that took the life of their beloved Tonk.

"Marge! Where are you? I can't see you!" "Over here… on your left! I got stuck in a rocky spot and had to get off to get through it! How the hell the cows are going to through those rocks is beyond me! The guys better push them around!" "Good thing they know this ridge better than we do!" "Mary, I really am proud of you. Let's make the ranch proud and get this drive home... if I remember right, the opening to the Red Pasture isn't too far up on the right."

"Charles!!! Look out! There is a huge boulder right in front of you!" "Holy..." Charles had not seen the huge rock through the smoke, Lady veered to the right just as Brent yelled his warning to Charles. "Thanks for the warning... I do believe she just might have un saddled me... I was sure not ready for that maneuver!" Michael had arrived to help Brent and Charles keep the line moving toward the trail head. "No one and I mean no one ever falls off on this ridge... not ever again!" Raising his eyebrows as he looked at Charles, Brent silently conveyed acknowledgment of the words Michael spoke. In return, Charles nodded his understanding.

"We've got them up to the old trail! Not much farther now!" Katy blasted the announcement to the riders behind her as she and Russell arrived at the trail. "Katy... look! The cattle seem to know where they are now... see how they have settled and are moving better... I'm going to head back to Sara... I am sure Michael will be here with you soon. We did it! We are almost home. I want to make sure she..." "Go... I know... see you at the ranch!"

Russell turned Buck and retreated to where he knew he would find Sara.

Sara was stopped on the trail next to the tree she had carved the heart on. "Thank you. Thank you for helping us home." Her sore, bloodied fingers followed the outline of the faint mark now nearly unrecognizable on the tree. She watched Russell as he approached her. "Let's go home." "Right beside you my husband... right beside you." She slowly pulled her fingers from the tree.

"John... where do you think they are now? I see so much smoke up there!" "Mary, by my calculations I should think they are at least up the ridge by now. It won't be long." "Oh, John, I just want them home! I don't care if we never have a drive again, I …" Attempting to console the fright and discontent of his wife, John held out his right hand to her, "Mary, come with me outside, let's sit on the porch and keep an eye out for them. Why don't you bring your tea with you…" "Good idea." He helped her to the swing at the end of the porch and then sat beside her. "Here, now, from here we have a clear view of the Red Pasture." "Where are Mark and Linda?" "I do believe they are in the barn finishing the stalls."

"Well, Katy… looks like you are going to get to see the hole in the trees from the other side in just a few minutes!" "I waited a long time for this view!" "Hey Roper Girls… take this herd home!" The smoke was too thick for any of the others to see Marge and Mary raise their right arms as they together triumphantly shouted "Yeah!!!"

"John… I hear something!" John and Mary Moore rose from the porch swing and as he put his left arm behind her, she took a faltering step toward the railing.

Mark and Linda stood in the frame of the carriage doors on the gable end of the stall barn. "Hold me Mark…"

Mary walked to the post in the railing that led to the steps. Clinging to the carved wood she stared out past the gates and into the smoke. "Thank you, God! Thank you for getting them home."

"Mary, I don't hear anything! Are you sure?"

"Yes! I can feel them! I can feel them coming home!"

Mark and Linda turned to the scene on the porch and then back to the smoke. Mark held her tightly as her trembling increased. "The smoke is so thick… and… and… look how fast it is moving!" "Let's just hope that is because the cattle are pushing it!" "Sounds good to me even if that isn't the real reason!"

"There! Do you hear it?" Mary pointed to the left corner of the smoke line. With a renewed energy she quickly descended the steps, walked briskly to the fence line on the far side of the driveway and stood in waiting. John waved to Mark and Linda to stand with them.

Four members of the family stood in silence as they stared into the smoke.

"They are close! I can feel it in the ground!" Linda placed her left hand on Mary's shoulder. The two women exchanged a 'knowing' of each other's heart.

Silence.

Stillness.

Only a wall of smoke in their vision.

With a startling burst of suddenness, the first of the herd was through the smoke and in view. In just moments and with an equal surprise; Marge and Mary burst through the smoke on either side of the herd. Marge rode on the left and Mary on the right.

Mary Moore fell to her knees.

Her tears could no longer be detained. She wept openly as more and more of the cattle appeared through the smoke.

"Look! There... Brent.... oh God! Thank you for bringing my son home!"

Linda wiped the tears away as she wanted only to see him clearly as he rode toward them.

"I see Michael and Katy!"

"And… Charles!"

"Stay here… we will get the gates." Mark and Linda retreated to the barn area to open the side lot gates.

"The herd is home Mary. They did it. Look…" Gently John placed his hand on her cheek and moved her head so she could see the proof in his words standing in the pens. Holding her hand on his, softly she spoke. "Sara… where is Sara?" She rose to her feet and in unison they turned back to the Red Pasture just as Russell and Sara breached the smoke line.

"*Now* they are home."

Part 5
M Double RSC

"I read in the paper last night that the Forest Service will be coming back out to assess the re growth of the burn area. The article said something about the 'full turn of the seasons' and the supposition that the foliage and wild life has had time to re generate and repopulate. Personally, I think it is going to take longer, but … hey… they are the so-called experts! I sure hope the mountains have taken care of themselves up there. All those aerial views last year were just… so… so heart breaking." "John, do you think it will ever come back? That forest was so old… so grand…" "Mary, my love, in time all things 'become' again. It's God's way. He will see to the regrowth and the wildlife. Trust Him." "I know, but we have looked at those mountains for generations… the memories… we had so many rides together in our younger days." "I understand what you are saying Mary, I truly do. It is just not the same." John paused slightly; "Okay old woman, what is that grin for?" Tipping her head toward her lap, she spoke in a near whisper; "Just thinking of the Spring ride the year our Samuel was born… ah… nine months later…" Placing his right hand under her chin, he raised her face, "We did enjoy our times together." Leaning to his wife, John kissed her cheek then spoke again. "Brent should be in soon and as usual he will bring his appetite!" "I'm ready; I put an extra tray of muffins in the oven just for him!" "What about your adoring husband? I'm thinking he could use a couple himself!" "Always for you, my dear. Always for you." Mary smiled as she set the plate of muffins on the table next to the butter plate. Retrieving the carafe from the coffee pot, she refilled his mug. "This *Mr. Coffee* was a great gift last Mother's Day! I might just like perked a bit more but this new method sure beats the time of the percolator!"

Utilizing the floor mounted brush that had been to the left of the back-porch doorway for as long as he could recall, Brent scraped the dirt and debris from his boots before entering the laundry room. Satisfied in his endeavor he slowly opened the door. In a low tone he remarked, "Sure going to need that lava soap today, but man I just hate that stuff!"

He caught himself smiling at the 'wondrous find' Gram Moore had brought home from the Thanksgiving Church Altar Fund banquet. Gramp had cursed the tedious work and excessive time he spent refinishing the antique dry sink. His difficult labors resulted in a working fixture that added 'charm' as Gram called it to the décor of the homestead. He was hungry and in his anticipation of breakfast, he hurried as he scrubbed his hands with the abrasive soap that Gram said was the only way to really 'get the ranch off'. With the hand towel still purposefully engaged he walked into the kitchen.

Upon entrance of the kitchen he merged into the conversation he had listened to while in the laundry room.

"I couldn't agree more, Gram. On both counts! Gotta love getting the jolt of the java quickly! And… as far as the Forest Service fellas… that's why I volunteered to take the Rangers up there. Still got any coffee in the pot?" "She made apple muffins too!" "Gramp… you and I are the luckiest two guys on the planet… you do know that don't you!?" "Uh huh…" John Moore muffled his answer through a mouthful of muffin.

Placing a steaming mug on the table as Brent sat in the side chair, Mary smiled at the two men as they each extended their right arms for the plate of muffins. Not another word was spoken until the plate and the coffee mugs had been depleted of their offerings.

Satiated, the men leaned back in their chairs; each taking a deep breath.

"Well? How are the receipts from last week? Sure does seems to me like the attendance is down at the rodeos. Hope that is not a sign of the things to come."

"Actually, we are holding pretty steady Mr. Moore. Can't say that for a few of the other Stock owners though. As for the Moore Ranch Rodeo Stock Company, we are holding our own. We have good buckers and hearty animals. I made contact yesterday with Phil Anderson in Carnon for the Regional Rodeo they hold each year over the 4th of July. It's big... and if we get the commission it will mean that the other Rodeo committees will send scouts to evaluate our stock. My goal is to contract with the larger events, the Carnon deal would be a shoe in for them to employ the *M double R SC*."

"The what?"

"The M double R SC... the Moore Ranch Rodeo Stock Company. Here, I'll show you the logo I came up with for the letterhead." Brent retrieved from his left chest pocket a folded piece of paper with a capital M with two capital Rs back to back and the SC. The letters were arranged to form a cowboy riding a bucking bull.

"Clever... very clever! You think that up yourself?" "Sure did!" "I like it!"

Mary glanced at John as Brent spoke. She knew he'd had reservations when Michael turned the rodeo business over to Brent; allowing him the time needed to pursue his law enforcement career. The smile in her husband's eyes was all the proof she needed that he no longer doubted Michael's choice.

"Did you hear that, John! Brent has us lined up for the Big Time!" "Not just me Mrs. M., Russell said he would help me. This is kinda out of my league ... for now... but I'm learning and I know it will be monumental for the ranch to be the leading stock source for the circuit."

"No matter what we do around here... it is a team effort... a team of love." Mary had walked to the corner of the table between John and Brent. Placing her arms on each of their shoulders, she pulled them to her. "This is a good family. Now, has anyone heard from Sara or Russell this morning?" "They are at the Co-Op for an early meeting... something about that 'chain store' that wants to buy out the Co-Op. I'm thinking that is going to be one heated discussion that I am glad to not be a part of!"

"Mr. M... why don't you ride with me and the Rangers today? How long has it been since you were up in the hills anyway?" Stopping just shy of her mouth, Mary halted the movement of her coffee mug and seemed frozen in place as she raised her eyebrows over her eyeglasses awaiting his response.

"Ride?"

"In the Jeeps... oh did you think I meant horseback? Sorry. We are four *wheel* driving not four *hoof* driving... even I don't want to ride horseback up there... not yet anyway." "I suppose I would like a good 'tour of the grounds'... it has been years; more than I care to admit since I have seen the far corners of this ranch. Thank you, Brent for asking me. I really mean it. Mary... we are going to need a big lunch!" Rising from his chair, in a hearty gesture, John Moore smiled as he placed both fists on his chest. "Whoo hoo!"

Mary turned to Brent; mouthing the words "Thank you." The two smiled at each other.

"We'd best get ready they will be here in a few minutes." "Just give me a sec... I'll meet you in the driveway."

"Be careful up there, here is your lunch, enough for everyone. Enjoy your day with grandson number two... and John, don't give the Rangers too hard a time..."

"Off on an adventure!" As he walked off the porch, to herself she stated "Long overdue my love, long overdue. Lord, be with them today and please, give him peace with the ranch. He has blamed it for so much heart ache and pain, he needs to reconcile with his legacy. He needs to understand all that has happened here has been for your reason. Good and bad, for your reason. Please Lord, keep him in your arms. Amen."

"Oh! Wow! This means I have the whole day to just myself!!!" Mary laughed as she donned her apron in preparation for the kitchen clean up. "Whatever shall I do with *my* day?"

"Hello, Brent! Are we ready?" "Hang on a minute, Mr. Moore wants to ride with us." "Mr. Moore as in John Moore?" "That would be him... here he comes and laden with a *pic a nick* basket from Gram." Brent tried his best Yogi Bear voice as he spoke. "Better move some of the stuff in the back to make room." "On it!" Bill retreated to the Jeep to re arrange the equipment while Brent started the introductions.

"Gramp, this is..." "Wayne Leeds... I know... and that is Bill Turner at the Jeep. These were the guys in the helicopter during the fire. Good to see you again!" "You too, sir and I may add I am glad for the much better circumstances this time." "Amen to that."

Mary wiped her hands on the damp apron as she watched the scene in the driveway through the kitchen window. "Well, boys... they are on their way, sorry there wasn't room for you two. Guess that means you will just have to stay here and keep company with me today." Hank and Baron wiggled their haunches as she briskly scratched their backs.

"Order! I want order!" Paul Jennings slammed his gavel on the table in an attempt to quiet the disruptive nature the meeting had fallen prey to. "I want order in this room!"

"Silence!"

The large man threw his right hand to his chest and winced in pain, falling back into his chair.

The room was silent.

"Should have thought of that sooner!" Paul rose from his chair mocking his audience. "Now, let's get to the business at hand. We are here to discuss whether or not to sell out to The Farm Store or keep us as we are; a co-op for the ranchers who built this town and county. In an orderly fashion, we will hear from both sides. I mean it, we keep this civil... you all understand? I want to see a show of hands... those who will abide by the rules of order..." The men seated around the table grinned to each other as right hands were raised. "Good. Now, I introduce to you Henry Bloster. Representative of The Farm Store. Mr. Bloster..."

"Thank you, Mr. Jennings. Let me first say that I am not here to take your business away from you. We at The Farm Store want only to assimilate your Co-Op under our umbrella of legal academicism and with our vast resources we can push the growth of this business and this area into the next decade faster and with more potential for financial stability than you would be able to attain in the current form of organization and the processes of the obsolete and deteriorating framework that will with certainty restrain your ability for expansion. With our guidance, and a few small changes in managerial methods, this operation will be transformed from a local outlet to a regional hub of business transactions. The financial growth..."

Surprising all that sat in the meeting room; Don Harbor stood, placing both his hands on the table to steady his large frame. His interruption of the speaker jolted attention away from Henry Bloster transferring it to the man that seldom offered to vocalize his opinion.

"Excuse me, Sir... but you seem to have a fine repertoire of fancy legal mumbo jumbo kind of speech... and hey, if it works for you, then we can all applaud you. Believe me when I tell you, you are not fooling anyone here. If you think we are all just a bunch of 'ranch hicks' you have been seriously misled by wrong information. Everyone in this room is educated and your fancy talk of 'assimilation' and 'managerial methods' and all the other load of crap you are dishing out is just that... a load of crap. We know what you want to do... and that is take over, change the employee roster and then remove those of us that have founded this co-op and have generations of family that have not only participated in the everyday works of this organization, but have promoted this business as a family friendly and economy minded answer to the big business attitude of 'money first'. For your information, we have grown tremendously over the past decade due in part to the innovative forward thinking... yes, I can use fancy terminology too... of our members and clientele. We listen to what our customers want and how we can serve them better and more efficiently. Russell Barnes and his wife Sara have more than tripled the income from the smaller equine owner revenues and the larger ranches have supported our delivery service to where we have had to add three trucks and five more employees for the delivery service alone. This small little business as you put it is not as small as you want us to think and we know it. We are proud of what we have here and I for one think that it should remain in the capable hands of the contributors, the management and the employees just as it has for generations. We *are* forward thinking and I think you, Sir, should move your arse forward to the door!" Don waivered in his stance. "I need to sit..."

Holding Don's arm as he helped to lower the large man, Russell silently remarked to himself "Good thing we bought this oversized chair for you last Christmas!" Heard only by Don, Russell spoke softly; "Good speech there, big fella! Good speech!"

"Order!" Paul slammed the gavel on the table to no avail.

Jimmy Blane raised his right hand as he stood at the far end of the conference table. "My late father would have been appalled at this... this ... even the consideration of selling... to letting go of the heritage of the Co-Op, the *meaning* of the co-op, the *community* of the co-op... this is who we are! Maybe the big cities and bigger towns prefer the informalities of business, but we are still of the belief that family and community mean something. That is all I have to say." Jimmy sat hard in his seat and shook his head back and forth.

"Mr. Jennings…" Henry looked to Paul in hopes of his regaining control of the meeting. Paul smiled at the interloper and with a nod side to side confirmed his agreement with Don and Jimmy. He had no intention of further discussion.

"I can see that this group clearly does not respect the 'Rules of Order' for conducting a meeting! It saddens me that I have not been able to fully disclose our plans for this operation."

Russell had remained quiet throughout the banter, taking in the dynamic of opinions and recourse. Before rising, he leaned forward in the chair, looked at Henry and slowly stood to be eye to eye with him.

"Mr. Blosser, I think that by now you realize that we are a strong group of very dedicated people and though you will never openly admit it, I am quite certain that you agree that we will benefit more greatly by remaining as is than to 'assimilate under your umbrella'. Sir, with all due respect, it's not raining here, so we don't need your umbrella."

"Well said Mr. Barnes, well said. I will return to corporate and tell them I was unable to see the benefit of consolidation of the entities. Gentlemen, good day!"

Gathering his paperwork and stuffing the disheveled sheets back into his brief case, Henry looked at the men whose attention he realized he now had. "I know you probably won't believe me, but I'm glad this worked out this way. I grew up ranching myself and we had a similar Co-Op the other side of Eastdale. I know the importance… I really do. You men have held to your convictions when so many others have let go. I am proud of you. You should all be proud of yourselves."

Henry Bloster was through the doorway and down the hall toward the exit before anyone in the meeting room spoke.

"No need for a vote... meeting adjourned."

"I didn't know the trails up here were wide enough for anything other than a horse!" "The Fire fighters made a lot of these so-called roads when they were trying to navigate the fire line. When it was finally out, they came back up with equipment to help reestablish the trails in case of future needs. The Forest Service is starting to really push the safety issue and these trails are just a small part of the commitment to public awareness." "Yeah, now those pesky east coast 'think they want to be hunters' can get back in here and wreak havoc! I don't much like that potential too much!" "Mr. Moore, the Forest Service is working together with the local authorities to prevent unlawful hunting and trespassing on state, county and privately-owned land. You have our word we are doing our best to keep the poachers out." "I appreciate that Bill, thank you." "You have the largest acreage in the county here, is that right?" "I think so... Brent..." "Yes, Bill, they have the largest ranch. It runs from highway 9 down by town clear up to the county line and over to the McGregor Ranch and then to the river in the south. Don't ask me how many *actual* acres, I can't tell you... all I know is its big. There are grazing lands and mountain tillies up to several ridges. Folks around here don't need to know actual boundary lines; the ranches have been here for generations and we just know the general areas that border between. The Moore Ranch is the oldest established ranch and according to the first deed, the acreage count was 'somewhere around 62,000'. It's not real 'square' but close enough, guess back in those days it wasn't as important to have exact figures." John leaned forward to talk between the men in the front seat, "The Red Pasture is the smallest at about 1900 acres." "Impressive, and with you having Forest at the North and North West boundaries; I think we will be seeing a lot more of each other in the near future." "You are always welcome." "Thank you, Mr. Moore." "John, my name is John." "Yes Sir." "No, John." The men smiled at the familiarity of newfound friendships.

Parking the truck in the first space to the left of the handicap spot, Sara noticed a man hurriedly leaving the main entrance of the Co-Op. A last look in the rear-view mirror to verify her hair was neatly pulled into her braid, "Guess the meeting is over… missed another one… I'm sure I'll hear all about it! Later Reba… *Whoever's in New England* is going to have to wait for another day." Sara ejected the cassette from the dash and gently placed it in the glove box.

Russell met her at the entrance doors.

"Russ, I'm sorry I missed the meeting. The Landers' mare was down and I stayed to help Doc." "I am glad… not that the mare was down… how is she?" "Okay… but I think they are going to have to be careful, that bowed tendon just isn't pulling in like it ought to. Maybe Katy can look at it… she will be home for break this week end." "I'm sure she will. Anyway… the meeting… you won't believe this but Don stood up and gave that young man the what for and he took it! Then Jimmy, yeah… Jimmy stood up and it was all over by then. That poor guy from The Farm Store didn't stand a chance and he knew it. Actually, I think he was relieved. He's a ranch kid himself and well, he knows what his company is doing to the 'old ways' and I don't think he completely agrees with it, but it's his job." "I'm glad everyone stood together." "They did, literally, I'm telling you, and it was eye opening to say the least!"

"Can you get the afternoon off?" "What do you have in mind Mrs. Barnes?"

The familiar wink and grin on Sara's face was all Russell needed to see to know the answer to his question.

"That ridge up there… Brent, where does it lead to?" "Past Robbs Rock, but we have to go through Anglin Pass first. Hope you are ready for some pretty eerie vibes in there…" "Eerie vibes?" "I take it you don't know the history of that Pass and the snow slide off Robbs Ridge back in the forties." "That would be a negative on the information disclosure. Are you saying there was an avalanche?"

Wayne interjected into the conversation as he maneuvered the jeep through a rocky area just after the dried creek bed. "There is a box behind your seat Bill; it should have the seismic graphs of the area. I think there is a folder that has historical findings in it as well. It was a real active time underground around here and the research shows possible connections to geophysical activity over in Idaho."

Bill's eyes widened as he tipped his head while moving rapidly side to side yet changing position only slightly. "Idaho? Here? Connected?" "Could be... those layers of earth have a mind of their own and rumble even when no one is there to measure the information. We live in the rocks... you know, the *Rocky* Mountains... can you honestly tell me you have never wondered how much underground movement there truly is in this region? There has been a great increase in the geosciences documentation of the North West... California can't claim to be the only state that shakes!"

"So... about that Ridge..." "Mr. Moore better tell you." "John?"

"It was in '42. The wranglers were heading home and before they could all get through, the walls slid from the Ridge Line down and either trapped or killed most of the cattle and all of the men. The cattle that did get through were brought back to the ranch by the men that went to save them. There was no one left. It was..." "Say no more. I understand." "Son, I'm not sure you do. You see, it is believed the ghosts of the men and even the cattle are still there. You can hear them at dusk. You can feel them when you traverse the hallowed ground. Horses are nervous through there, riders are silenced. Brent may have called them 'eerie vibes' but they are far more impressive than that."

"Oh." Bill leaned back in the seat and stared out the window toward the Ridge.

"Buckle up cowboy! That's where we are headed next!" Wayne steered the jeep through the opening of the Pass, stopping abruptly and unseating the passengers.

"What was that for?" "Look!"

A large herd of Elk stood at the base of Ridge.

"Mother Nature has begun her healing."

"Not to bring up a sore subject but wasn't it just over that end of the ridge…" "Say no more, please. I just don't want to think about it." "I understand John, so sorry to have brought it up."

"Holy Moly! You're right… sorry, John, it's just creepy that so much has happened right here… so, really… do we still have to go through that Pass?" "Yup!" "Oh." "We are headed for the grazing lands to determine the regeneration rate. While we are there, we are to take a few samples of the ground and test the water in the creeks if there is any. Then we will do the same in the wooded areas. We need to determine if the Forest Service needs to intervene and plant trees and vegetation. One way or the other, this forest and these lands will return to their glory. We are here to determine just how that will happen."

"I think though, that we can all agree it was beneficial to have been contained to a surface and partial crown fire and not a complete ground" "A who? A what? Fancy names for a wild fire… fire is fire… and it's all bad!"

Understanding the tone of John's voice, Brent thought he needed to explain the terminology.

"Mr. M., what he meant was that the acres of the big old Lodgepole Pines were mainly in the 'crown' fire… just the tops took the brunt of their burn and the cones will have popped so the seeds are released. We should see new saplings up there. The rest was mostly a 'surface' fire and fortunately there is limited undergrowth and the branches are high on the trees and many were able to stay out of the flames. It was the smaller trees and areas of thick brush that caused the most problems for the fire fighters as well as for us when we were out there. There were a few areas of 'ground' fire but the crews working hit those with a vengeance to keep it from getting too out of control."

"Young man, I am impressed. You have taken quite an interest in this." "Actually, I overheard Charles talking with the Fire Chief the other day. That's how I knew all that." "Still, your interest was piqued enough to want to come out here with us. Good to know some of the young folk still care about the land." Wayne looked into the rearview mirror as he commended Brent.

"I agree that's great... but I still want to know-- do we really need to go through the Pass?" The quiver of Bill's voice was noticed and thoughtfully ignored.

"Mary? Are you here? We are back! At least I am anyway, Brent went with Bill and Wayne to the Ranger Station." "You will find me in the tub!" Mary's voice beckoned him from their rooms. "In the middle of the day?" John walked toward the door to their bedroom. "I had the day to myself and this is what I chose to do! Perhaps you would join me?" John entered the bathroom to see his wife submerged in a tub full of bubbles. "Bubbles, you want me to sit in bubbles?" "Don't knock it till you've tried it!" "If I were younger, I'd be knockin' something else!" "Oh John!" Mary giggled through her smile. "Come on, join me." "Okay, think maybe I will." He undressed quickly. Sliding down into the frothy warmth of the water, John realized instantly the rejuvenating effect of the lather. "Wow... you women really do know how to take a bath!"

"Tell me about the ride around the ranch today." Mary reached her hand to his as she asked him to share his thoughts and feelings. "Oh Mary... it was wonderful and it was horrible all at the same time. I told Bill about the slide through Anglin Pass, we saw the burned trees, the skeleton of a forest that they rode through, the barren lands that once held the waves of pasture grasses… I saw where Samuel died, my mind creating images that I could not erase. We took samples of ground and water there is so much more that needs done…"

"Tell me the good things now…"

John was motionless and silent for moments before he spoke again.

"The flight birds as well as the land birds have returned… we saw an elk herd… the wild flowers in the basin are making a grand attempt at replanting themselves. There were a few fish in the pools of Anglin Creek. The sky was bluer than I can ever remember. I stood on Hobbs Ridge and knew that through all of the destruction, through all the heartache, God was always present. Good and Bad. This ranch today stands tall in a reflection of our Faith in Him and His in us. The land was ravaged repeatedly yet we survived and are stronger for all the peril. I realize it could not be different that in the aftermath we lost a great many cattle to the fire damages of the Drive, but Sara and everyone made it. For each of the heartaches this ranch has endured, some good has always come of it. We are who we are because of all that we have had to withstand. Though much of what I saw today may have appeared as a destruction to some, it was all a construction to me. Every day I have lived and all that has happened in those days has led me to right now, to this moment. A happily married man with a family I cherish. I am this man, sitting in a lavender scented tub waving the bubbles as I look upon the woman that has stayed by my side through it all. I love you Mary Moore." "I love you too, John. We have a good life."

"Mr. and Mrs. M? You home?" When there was no reply, Brent picked up a pen and wrote a note on the scratch pad letting them know he would be in the pens sorting the cattle for inspection.

John slid a little lower in the tub and blew hard into the bubbles forcing them to fly off the surface and into Mary's face. Together they laughed as she continued the fun until they both splashed so hard that a great amount of water landed on the tile floor.

Brent looked back into the house as he approached the porch steps. "Hmm… I'm thinking that they are home… you go Gram and Gramps!"

Michael had pulled into the driveway and was parking beside the old wood shed as Brent descended the porch steps. Briskly walking toward the dust cloud left by the sudden braking of the old F150, Brent coughed jokingly as he started to speak. "Ahhhhh… that's a negatorie on approaching the ole homestead there cowpoke, it ah… seems the a-dults of age are revisitin' their youthful antics!" "Gram and Gramp? Hoo doggie! Guess we had best leave them to their 'afternoon delight'" "Skyrockets in flight!" "You know I never really liked that song… but I guess they do!!! Let's head down to the Holler and hear some real music. Maybe Charles will be there, he keeps telling me he has some high importance activity going on he wants to tell us about. Maybe he has made his decision…" "I know he wanted to 'serve' and I am proud of him really, but well, a little part of me is kinda glad he waited to sign papers until he knew his arm would heal from the unplanned plunge over the ridge during the Drive. I know that is mean of me, but it's the truth." "Don't worry, I'll never tell him you said that."

"Holy Geeze… the parking lot is packed! There is no way we are going to get in there now!" "That's okay guys, we got all we need right here!" Michael and Brent turned in unison to the left as they heard Charles' voice as he approached the truck. "We have a bit of celebrating to do and I would much rather do so with just my two best friends… out here… under the lights… and with this here bottle of JD"

"Do you see that Brent? *Black* label… he's brought us the good stuff!" "That's because I bring you good news!" Charles opened the bottle, slowly placed the rim of the bottle to his lips and swigged back. "Heyew! That's good!" He then handed it to Brent who in turn handed it to Michael. When all three had recovered from the 'knock' of the whiskey Charles took command of the conversation.

"Ok, here it is… Brent, you had better sit down. Hey, don't look like that, I see the corners of your eyes getting all shiny… you're afraid I'm going to tell you the Air Force awaits me… well, my friend, they will have to wait a bit longer." Whoo Hoo!!!!" Brent jumped off the tailgate of the truck, throwing his arms around Charles. He then stepped away, straightened his back, jutting his jaw left to right to crack his neck and then cleared his throat. "I mean…" "I know what you mean. It's ok." Brent leaned back against the tailgate. He did not care that his sigh of relief was audible.

"So… the next part of my announcement…" "There's more?" "Of course, Michael! You know when it comes to Charles, there is always 'more'!" "Can I speak …" "Oh yes, please do." Brent arm fisted Michael as to chastise him for interrupting Charles.

"I'm going to the Fireman Academy. I had to wait to make sure my arm was going to be a hundred percent and I was physically able to take the training. Remember on the Drive when I was at the EMT helicopter for so long?" "Yeah…" "Well, I learned a lot about what all those guys do and man, it really hit me and then on the rest of the Drive home, all those men out there for us… to save us… they put their own lives and their families… man, they risked it all for us! That impressed the hell out of me and I was so awed by how they worked together and, well, I guess I knew back then that I had finally found what I wanted to do with my life. I want to be a Fireman. I want to be a Forest Fireman. I want to protect my family, my town and the land." Turning to look Michael eye to eye, "I get it Mountain Man, I get it. Why you want to be on the Police Force. I get it." Michael and Charles 'man-hugged' as Brent stood next to them. "Hey, you may not be in fighter jets but you might get to jump out of planes and helicopters, not that jumping into fires is not dangerous, and it seems you want that 'danger' thing… so you still got that going for you, but… ain't nobody shootin' back at you so I am good with it!!!!"

Putting out his hand, the others did the same; A M I G O S their arms lifting with each letter so as to be fully raised by the sounding of the S. "That explains you talking with Chief Hudson the other day… I was wondering what that was all about! Hope you boys won't mind if I stay with the Rodeo Stock… just make sure I have one of those fancy scanner things so I know when I need to come and save your asses!"

"Copy that"

Part 6
Stills and Thrills

Standing at the arena rail, his left leg raised to rest on the first rung, grasping the top rail with both hands, Brent closed his eyes as he tilted his head back allowing the sun to warm his face with the last rays of the evening. After a few moments of pleasure, he opened his eyes as he reset his head to look out into the arena. Smiling as he moved his head from side to side, he was overcome by his thoughts. "Oh Lord God, thank you. You have Blessed me… and my family through some very trying times. And my mom… wow… sure didn't expect her and Mark. You did good on that one… I have never seen her so happy. I wouldn't mind if they got married… just letting you know that, and God, I'm kinda thinking about that myself. I want you to think about it too, okay? I need to know it is the right thing. I love her, I really do. She loves me too, and… well… my work with the Rodeo is taking off and she sure is working hard to get her photography thing going. I don't want to interfere in any way with those dreams and I guess that is why I haven't said anything yet. When the time is right God, will you help me?"

"I thought I'd find you out here!" Quickly and quietly so Mary would not hear him; "Amen, Lord" He kept his stare into the arena. "Hi! What brings you all the way out here this fine and wondrous evening?" Still approaching, Mary laughed her response to him. "Fine and wondrous… why yes, it is, may I join you?" "I would love you to." Standing beside him she placed her left arm under his right; with just enough pressure for a firm 'hold'. She too, looked out into the sand as a smile gave indication of her thoughts.

Turning toward the man beside her that she knew she now loved, she leaned into him and placed her right hand on his chest, she softly spoke: "It will be a great Rodeo, the weather looks good and the entries exceed those of last year, any reservations you may have are unfounded.

You have worked so hard and learned so much. Mr. Moore is so proud of you, as am I, and he… well, we all know you have turned the stock. Even the Rocky Mountain Stock Days Rodeo Committee has taken notice. They have had scouts at the last two events. That is all you Brent. All You. Don't ever doubt yourself. No one else does." In her moment of pause and without changing his line of sight, a slight smile and a low heheheh, he spoke; "Actually, I was thinking of the first time I saw you and your sister rope the tar out of that steer just over there…" Brent pointed to the left side of the arena in front of the roping chutes. "Seriously?" "Yup! You had the pink with white overlay blouse with the dark pink fringe across the yokes. Marge was opposite. Your pink saddle pads matched and so did your hats but your hatband was a little darker. Bet you didn't think I'd remember all that. "Brent Thomms, you, you… you amaze me. Kiss me…" "Yes ma'am! Drawing her to him he remembered their first kiss… and everyone since.

Leaning her head back and with only a slight pull away from his body, she placed both her hands on his chest. "I have news. Good news. Okay… great news!" Jumping backwards her arms now raising in the air, she twirled twice; halted only by the sudden restraint of Brent's arms. "Whoa there my little filly, you had best let loose of your news before you dizzy yourself!" "Yeah, I probably should do that… wow, guess it's been awhile since I've done that!" "If I recall it was your sister that took the ballet lessons not you…" Leaning over with her head low and both hands on her knees, "Funny, very funny! Whew! I won't do that again!" Mary stood upright, smiled and flipped her braid back over her right shoulder.

"I got the Show." "The Show… you mean you got the Photography Exhibit!!?" "Yes! I got the call from John Bynes right before I came to find you! I wanted you to be the first to know!" "Oh Mary, wow, that is great! We need to celebrate!" "Hold on there, 'Hoss'… I have to have written permission from all persons displayed in the photographs submitted to the gallery before I can include them in the show. So, I guess we need to get to the ranch…" Brent didn't grant her time to finish the sentence before he pulled her to him and as he lifted her off the ground; "You did it! You got the Show!!!!! Oh Mary, Congratulations. I know how much this means to you, this is sooooo good!" Silently his heart raced, "Thank you God! I'm taking this as my 'sign'!"

"Are you sure there has been enough time pass since the fire so that the wounds have healed and it will be alright to see it all again? That time was so difficult, and…" "My dear, it has been better than two years, I am sure they will all be just as excited as I am that you have the exhibit and, they will be proud of you as well. Come on, if we get moving now, we may even be in time for desert!" "I sure hope Gram has written down her recipes or there will be at least three men very disappointed later on in life!"

"Once again Mrs. Moore you have provided a meal of superior cookery!" John set himself deeper in his chair and placed both hands on the table next to his emptied dinner plate. "I am onest again a satiated man!" "And you are 'onest again' making up words!" "Hey! I'm old, I'm allowed, besides, how do you know if my words are or aren't really just words used loooong ago and that you kids don't know about? Huh! Maybe that's it!" "Okay Gramp, we will go with that. Charles, do you believe him?" "I'm going with yes acuz I be ashurred there is desert and I don't want to disagree and then not be able to have any!" "I am surrounded by comics!" "I remember when your comedy included warped poetry my friend, so don't be sniping about our neologism!" "Oh no… he's a bringing out the big words!!! Gram! Quick! Serve the desert before he really gets started!" She had the cream puffs on the table in one motion of her body. The laughter hastily ceased as Gram, Gramp, Charles and Michael savored the exemplar taste of Gram's homemade cream puffs. "Sure is too bad that Mom and Russell had to stay for a Co-Op meeting tonight." "Yeah, too bad… can I have another one?"

John watched as Gram placed her left hand on her temple; she began moving her fingertips in a circular motion massaging the apparent area of her current pain. "Why of course you can Charles, perhaps you could get the plate…" "Mary… are you having another one of those headaches? Do we need to call the doctor again? You know, the new one over in Carnon, you said you really liked ..." "Hush about calling any doctors, it's just a headache. No need to fret and over react. I'll just take a couple more Aspirin... it will go away when it is ready to. What will not go away however is these boys' appetite!" "Stubborn... you are just stubborn." "What was that?" "Aspirin, just need aspirin." John looked over to Michael who had his head tipped down concealing his laughter. Michael tilted slightly toward his grandfather mouthing his thoughts; "Not a good 'save' Gramp, not a good 'save'."

Charles decided it was up to him to get off the subject of Gram's headache. "When it comes to your dee-licious cream puffs Gram Moore... a man just can't have too many! You set right there, I will be more than obliged to retrieve the plate of greatness!" Charles pushed his chair back quickly; as he did so, he placed his right hand on Gram's chair. "While I am up, where might I find those Aspirin you wanted? Gotta take care of the cook!"

"Charles, do they have a class at the Fire Academy that teaches shmoozing?" Gramp laughed as he asked the question. Michael interjected before his friend had a chance to answer. "If they do, you should be the instructor!"

"Professor Shmooze... I like it! But you have to know, I am sincere when I say we have to take care of the cook!" He had placed both of his hands on Gram's shoulders and was now bending over to place his left cheek on her right. He kissed her gently just below her smiling eye. "I do love you Charles, you are a good boy... I mean *man*. The bottle of Bayer is in the cupboard over the range."

"Ahhh... Gram... I'm pretty sure you can ditch these St. Joseph baby aspirin... besides the warning against Reyes Syndrome, they are way out dated!" He retrieved the intended bottle of Bayer and as he closed the cupboard his attention was diverted toward the back of the house. "Looks like we have company coming! There are some really bright lights approaching rapidly!"

"At this time of night?" "My best guess, and we all know I am seldom wrong..." "Oh, yeah, if you say so!" "I do say so! I bet it is Brent... and I bet he is hoping for desert." "It is most likely Sara and Russell coming home. Charles, be a dear and get plates for them too, while you are up." "Anything for you, Gram."

"Professor Shmooze strikes again! Don't you agree Gramp?" "Michael, you best pay attention, you are going to be a married man soon. Shmoozing 101 over there is just the beginning!"

Brent knocked on the door as he opened it. "We are home! The last of the true cowboys around here and his picture taking and gallery showing cowgirl are here for a celebration!" Brent saw the cream puff on the table. "Bonus! Gram, how did you know? Mary, you are sooo right!" "I told him that if Gram does not have her recipes written down there are going to be three very disappointed man boys later in life." Michael stood, offered his chair to Mary and said "You do have a point Mary. Gram, are you going to let that happen to me, your favorite grandson?" "Or me, your favorite grandson number two" "Or me, the favorite number three?" At that point Brent and Michael were standing with Charles. The three young men leaned in to each other having their heads close; each tried to put a 'poor baby' look on their face in a plea for her affections. "Oh Mary Moore, what can you say to that? Look at them, better get those baby aspirin out of the trash bin!" "A recipe book... sounds like a great Christmas gift idea. Will keep that in mind."

"I believe I won the bet!"

"Hold on... Brent, did you say Mary has a Gallery Show?"

"Oh Mr. and Mrs. Moore... it's just so wonderful! John Bynes called me today to give me the news. I submitted a few of the shots I took on the cattle drive and he told me he would get back to me. I had nearly given up hope as it has been three months since I went to Eastdale to see him." "I remember when you went over there, but I had no idea why. Well, now we all know. Congratulations dear. You can count on everyone from the Moore Ranch to attend your opening night!" "Thank you, Mrs. Moore and actually I'm going to need more than your support at the exhibit... I need written permission from everyone that is in the photographs to use them in the show. Some new 'Invasion of Privacy' law that has made it necessary so no one can sue anyone for monetary gain from... oh, I can't remember everything Mr. Bynes said about it, all I know is that I need to have written consent from everyone. Some form named a 'Release for Use of Likeness' or something like that. I was also hoping to borrow the photo Michael had framed and given to his mom and Russell for Christmas; you know, the one of them sitting in the waning sun at the bottom of the last ridge before we got to the cave. It is a pretty awesome photo and I would really like to include it." "I just can't see any reason why you can't use it, but you will have to ask Sara."

"Ask Sara what?" "Oh my, we didn't hear you come in!" "If I didn't know better, I would think there were no watch dogs on this ranch! Where are they anyway? I have a few scraps from our dinner for them." Russell whistled his special call and both dogs were at his feet in moments. "Found them!" "Here you go guys..." Hank and Baron sat at Sara's feet; anxiously awaiting their tid bits" "Ok, that mystery is solved, now what is it that you need to ask me?"

"I have a photography exhibit and, well, I need everyone's permission that is in the photos before I can use them, and... I was hoping to include the one of you and Russell." Mary tipped her head and looked at Sara in hopes of her positive response. "Of course, you will have our permission and I am sure I can speak for everyone." All heads nodded in agreement. "As far as the photo in the living room... absolutely. I know you will take great care of it. Do you know when the show will be and where is it going to be held?"

"That's the other part of the good news! Mr. Bynes said that he had my photos with him when he stopped for gas and a man saw them on the seat and asked about them. Mr. Bynes told him about me and that I had enough for a whole show. Seems this guy is from Carnon and is some big wig for the Rocky Mountain Stock Days Rodeo and wants to do the exhibit during the Rodeo!"

"Holy Moly you didn't tell me that part!" Brent embraced her with fervor. By now everyone in the room was making their way to Mary for a congratulatory hug.

"Thank you everyone. I really do need to get home and see if Marge is there. I need her permission as well. My parents are in Jackson on a retreat. I'll try to call them later. Brent, will you come with me?" Michael noticed the enlarging of his friend's eyes as he looked upon the cream puffs; "I'll wrap a couple to go." "Thanks"

******

"Mr. Moore? Mr. John Moore?"

"Yes, this is he, and to whom am I speaking?"

"Mr. Moore, this is Alister McMadden of the Rocky Mountain Stock Days Rodeo."

"Well, Mr. McMadden, is it? What can I do for you today?"

"Sir, we need your help, actually we need your stock."

Taking in a deep breath, and after a long release of the breath, John responded.

"Our stock?"

"Yes Sir. For this year's Rodeo."

"In Carnon?" John shook his head back and forth as if in disbelief of the request being made of him. "Can you hold on a minute?"

"Sure."

"Brent, there is a fella on the phone named Alister something..."
"Alister McMadden? Holy cow! He is like..." "What he is like right
now is he is asking to use our stock at the big Rodeo." "Tell him we
will consider..." "You tell him, you are the one he needs to be talking
with... whatever you think is best I'm behind you all the way."

"Hello, Mr. McMadden?"

"Alister, please call me Alister."

"Alright, Alister, my name is Brent Thomms, just how can the
MdoubleRSC be of service to you?"

"It seems the Bolton Ranch stock herd has been plighted with Rumen
Acidosis[6] leaving us with the need for bucking stock and roping stock.
I am hoping you will be able to help us out in this dilemma. We will
pay you handsomely and of course, the housing of your animals is
secure and well maintained. I am quite sure you are familiar with our
reputation and frankly, you being a young stock company, this will be
quite a boost for you in the industry."

"Yes, it most certainly would, however I will make no obligatory
comments until I have received a contract and have my attorney
review it."

John Moore lifted his head in full attention to the conversation when
he heard the word 'Attorney'

"Mr. Thomms..."

"Brent"

---

6   Rumen Acidosis is a metabolic disease of cattle–lethargy, poor appetite,
     unexplained diarrhea, elevated fever and heart rate. Often in the acute stage
     leads to death.

"Brent, I will have the papers drawn up and sent by messenger tomorrow. Is the address I have for the Moore Ranch the correct destination?"

"Yes, it is. I look forward to reviewing the contract. Good day, Alister."

"And to you too, Brent"

Brent fell back into the Lazyboy recliner after he placed the receiver on the slim line phone that was on the small table between the two den chairs. John was sitting in the other recliner looking at Brent and shaking his head.

"Whew! *Alister…* who has a name like *Alister*! Good job on the legal thing… not sure where you learned all the fancy wordage, but it impressed me and I am quite sure Mr. *Alister* was not ready for it!"

"We need to call Mark."

****

Mary Moore was the first to speak as she and John stood next to Sara and Russell as they all gazed at the banner tied tightly between the entrance poles leading into the State Fairgrounds. "They did a great job on the logo, don't you think?" Without changing focus on the banner, Russell replied; "Brent came up with a great idea!" Unable to hold back tears, Sara stumbled through her words: "He did it, he really did it. He's made it to the big time and with our stock. Actually, Russell… your stock. You started all this craziness and through some real twists and turns in life, here we are standing in front of our banner at the biggest Rodeo of the year. Brent found himself in the work he does. All the boys have found themselves. Now the world will be watching us. There are television crews all over. I hope…" "Sara honey, please… stop talking. Let's get inside and wander around the vendors while we wait for the Rodeo to begin. Brent has Michael and Charles and they have hired a good crew and the Rodeo has the best pick up men and turnbacks[7] lined up. I myself am waiting for the Clowns…" "Didn't you just ask Sara to stop…" "Clowns… I have my own Clowns, let's go! I say we find Mary's photography showing first thing!" Sara, Russell and John simultaneously responded to Mary, "Yes ma'am!"

Mary's exhibit was set up in main 'Expo Center' of the Fairgrounds. The entry booth and Judges' quarters were on the left side of the doorway and Mary's photographs lined the right side and cornered to the back. A large 'A' frame style sign stood at the entrance announcing the 'Special Feature' at this year's Rodeo: *Fury of the Flames—Inside the Brandon Fire'. Photographs by Mary Shanks, with special Thanks to the men and women of the Moore Ranch whose courage and determination are depicted in the series.*

A small plaque at the bottom had written in calligraphy: Framing by Brandon Camera and Framing Company, easels donated for the show by The Brandon High School Photography Club

"Are you ready?" "Yes." "Ladies first." "After you, Mary."

The matriarch stepped to the first photo.

"Oh John… there we are at the Ranch… seeing them off. It is named *'Traditions of Hope'.* Isn't that lovely! I do recall just what a morning that was… the commotion…" "Yes, my love, we had no idea. You sure look pretty in your lavender sweater. I always love that sweater on you." Sara spoke next; "You know Russell… that will be you and me someday. She sure captured the light cresting on the house. Wow." "It's the most wonderful house my love." "You two have a long lifetime of memories yet to be made in that old homestead"

"Isn't that the Hobbs Ridge Trail head?" John asked the question to no one specifically as he looked at the second photograph. "Yes. And

---

7   Pick-up men are riders in the arena to release the bucking straps on the animal and assist the contestants with dismounting. Turnbacks are there to move the animal back to the return pen.

look, she named this one *'Tonk's Silent Honor'*. It is almost as if there is a shadow in the opening..." All four looked deep into the 'still shot', each seeing their own version of Tonk standing there. Simultaneously they moved to the next easel.

"I wish I could be here when Brent and Charles see themselves in this one! *'Young Muleskinners'*. Why the boys, the mules that is, look darn snappy all decked out in the panniers." "Brent and Charles look like they have a good handle on them." They did well with them and considering Jeb was basically green and Pete, well... Pete is Pete! Stubborn as a mule!"

As they approached the next photo, Mary slipped her left arm through John's folded right. Quickly glancing at the lengthy line of photographs then returning her attention to the one in front of her, Mary lifted her right hand up to touch the base of the stunning photo of the riders aptly named *'The Tree Arch'* approaching the entrance leading to the new trail. "Sara, I don't remember a trail in there..." "Remember... I had said at the table that I rode up there to scout out..." "Oh yes, I remember that now. What a beautiful arch. It is like the trees were groomed to grow that way. So similar on both sides and how they come together... I hate to ask; did it survive the fire?" Russell could see Sara's face as she looked down to the floor while an anguished sigh slowly ended. He answered Mary's question as he placed his right arm around Sara's waist. "Sadly, the entire top end of the Red Pasture took a beating from the fire." Mary placed her right hand on John's arm. "God will bring back His greatness. It may take a while, but He will." "That He will." John lifted his left hand; patted hers and leaned over to kiss her on the top of her head. "Let's keep moving, there are people behind us starting to come in" Russell noticed Sara's gaze kept returning to *'Tonk's Silent Honor'*. "You okay? If this is going to be too much, let me know." "I'm good. I am just amazed at her ability to really capture the scenery and ..."

A stranger approached them; "Just wait 'till you see the rest of them! This girl can shoot a frame! Hey... wait... aren't you the folks in these pictures? Holy Cow! You are!!!! Mabel! Come quick! These are the folks that are in the photos!" A stout woman approached from the far end of the building, "My apologies, he gets so excited sometimes! These are wonderful photographs and for the life of me I have no idea how any of you survived! I think now, after seeing these... people are going to understand more of what you all went through out there. It was truly by the Grace of God you made it."

"Thank you, this is the first we have seen the photos, so if you don't mind, we would like to keep moving." "Yes, yes of course. They truly are fabulous. Far more deserving of a bigger venue than this Rodeo. Good Day now." "Good day!"

'Atop the Haunted Pass' awaited their arrival. "I wonder how many people will actually know where this is... and what it stands for? "There aren't too many folks left around here that will know about 'The Slide', but for those that do, this photo of the notch of ground cut out of the top line where the earth slid to the farness below will be a reminder of the resulting wall that killed so many. She has no idea of the real impact of this one." John faltered in his speech as he spoke of the photo; catching himself nearly tearing twice as he paused repeatedly through his sentences.

Lifting her right arm to point toward the next frame, Sara gasped. "I really did not know that was so steep!" They were looking at *'Switch Back'*. "My goodness! She's looking at the top of your heads!" "That she is Mary, it was a bit snarky going down there. Only had one trip to speak of by any horse or mule." Pushing Russell's right upper arm with her right fist; giggling, Sara retorted; "Like I said, no weenies on my ride!"

"I bet Betty and Paul like this one... Mary does love her sister." "Step sister." John thought he was correcting her. "No, sister. She was just young girl when Paul married her mother, she loves Marge as nothing other than a true sister." "You are right Mary. That she does." Mary lightly slapped John's arm, "I like her title 'Sisterhood', no one will ever guess the background.

A large woman pushed into Sara, "I'm so sorry, there are people lining up to see these pictures and it's getting crowded in here." "No harm done, we will keep moving on." "Hey... you are..." "Yes, we are. Please don't make a scene of it. I would really appreciate it." "I understand." She turned to the young boy standing beside her; "Johnny, these are the people that were riding in the fire." The boy tapped Russell on his upper thigh; "Mister? I sure am glad you are okay. My Cub Scout troop all pitched in when the calves were at Dr. Peterman's." Russell squatted to be eye to eye with Johnny. "Thank you, Johnny. You helped those calves survive. We might have lost them if not for you and your friends." Sara touched Johnny's mother's shoulder; "We appreciate all you did for us, your support and most of all your Prayers." "Oh, Mrs. Barnes, we were all so worried..." "Please, call me Sara." "My name is Anna. My husband was on the fire line. He said you all took a real beating out there." "Please, thank him again for us." "Sure will. Johnny, let's let these folks finish looking at these nice photos." "Anna, please join us." "Are you sure?" "Absolutely." Mary and John Moore shared a smile of pride.

"This one is my son Michael." Sara tipped her head back to speak to Anna. "Why is it named 'Mountain of a Man'?" "His friends have nick named him Mountain Man because he is so tall and muscular. He has on many occasions proven his strengths in the time of need. He helped to save my life a few years back when I was kidnapped, and on the Drive, he was, well, a major force to be reckoned with, to say the least." Russell interjected during a pause in her words. "He was the last one off the switch back, just look at the severity of the wall behind him that we came down... wow. She did a great depth perception in this one!"

"Here's your picture Sara... I just love this of the two of you." "As do I and the name is so perfect; 'Silhouette of Love' we were so happy in those brief moments of respite" Five adults and a young boy stood in awe as they looked at the back lit figures of Sara and Russell as they each sat 'Indian style' in the tall grasses gently flowing in the breeze at the edge of the mountain meadow; Sara on the right and Russell on the left; heads tipped together. The side stance of Jazzy with her head next to Sara's leg was replicated in reverse for Buck next to Russell. The light from the waning sun positioned perfectly between them.

Anna spoke softly, "Such a moment of stillness, a moment of beauty, of love... and a moment of God. This is a work of wonderment. What perfect timing to get the light just right behind you. No words will ever be needed when looking at this photo. This picture does say a thousand words... and then some." "It hangs in our living room and we cherish it every day." Sara smiled at Russell as she responded to Anna.

"I can hear people grumbling, we don't want them to turn around and leave because we are holding up the line."

A voice from near to the first photo was heard above the crowd. Sara recognized Paul Pelton's boisterous outburst.

"Folks... please... be patient. To most of you these photos are illustrations of what took place just prior to, and then actually did happen during the fire. But... to the people standing at number nine, these depictions of the truth are reminders of the days they spent just trying to survive what you see in the pictures."

"Sara, I see my friend Margaret back farther in line, we are going to go back with her. It was sure nice to meet you." "You too, Anna. Perhaps we will meet up again soon." "I'd like that." Mother and son turned around to join her friend.

Through the heightened excitement of the crowd, Russell raised his hand to wave at Paul. Many of the attendees began to applaud. "Please, everyone, enjoy the exhibit. We will move along..." As Russell spoke, Sara moved on to the next display.

"That had to have been hard on you dear, you..." Sara touched Mary's arm, "Actually, I was ok with staying there. Truthfully, that night was healing as well as restful. The kids entertained us and we had a good time in there." Russell and John had joined the women as they smiled looking at '*Sitting Sentry*'. Hank and Baron positioned in the center of the cave mouth in the waning light of dusk.

"And here is part of that entertainment!" "Oh Mary, you should have heard them! The Cartwrights they are not! But they sure tried to sing the Bonanza theme!" She sure put the right name to this one; '*Singing Cowboys*' I will never in all my days forget that skit." "They started that because of your fine vittles if I do recall!"

Mary stared at the next photograph. "Wow! Not even when the tornado hit did I see anything like this. It is scary enough to look at, but to actually be there..." "I will admit when I saw it, I had no idea what it meant. Sara here had to enlighten us with her education and then we were concerned. It was not long after that the dry lightning struck. I'm surprised she got such a good shot of this, the lighting got really goofy and a bit eerie just before the strike." "Well, she did a fine job with '*Cloud of Anger*'.

"Whoa, let me help you Mary..." Russell caught Mary's arm just as her knees began to buckle. "Oh my Lord..." John tried to hold back his near choke as he stood transfixed on '*Lord, Help Us*'. Before them was the photo of the riders and dogs atop the hill overlooking the cattle below as the fire blazed close to the herd.

"We had no idea what lay ahead. Just, no idea."

The room fell silent.

"Please Mr. Barnes, tell us as we look at the pictures." "Sir, I really don't think I can." Russell had glanced at the remaining easels in preparation for Mary and John's reactions. "From what I can see, the photographs will tell you all you want to know."

A collage of all the riders with their wild rags on in various moments moving the cattle toward the first ridge: *'Hard Riding'*.

Mary had turned in her saddle just in time to capture the flames on the grassland at Russell's heals as they entered the tree line: *'Hot Seat'*.

The cattle charging toward her in a smoky haze: *'Running for their lives'*.

The propellers of the helicopter as they rose up the side of the ridge and into view: *'Found'*.

Sara leaned to Russell, "I was sooooo happy to see that bird…" "You and me both!"

As Mary led the cattle toward the egress, she had managed to get a full shot of both 'walls' burning and named the photo *'Walls of Fire'*. Next to that she had placed 3 photographs of the Fire Fighters standing along the edges as they slowly make their way toward the basin. It was only by the hard work of the men captured in each frame did they have a chance. The three photographs were arranged around the handwritten words: *'Our Heroes'*.

John remarked at *'Taking Paws';* "Oh those poor dogs… they really tried." "Yes, they did and I am quite certain they appreciated the horseback ride through the egress." Russell put his right arm around Sara's waist and whispered into her left ear; "This beautiful small waist of yours left plenty of room for your passenger!" "Shh…" Giggling she gently pushed his head away.

"Thank Goodness!!!! Marge got a shot of Mary carrying Phoenix… she sure took to that calf!" "I think Mary asked her to before she dismounted when we got to the basin. Marge was more than happy to have photographic proof her sister had joined the ranks of true cowgirls." "What a great title: *'Out of Harm's Way'*. Don't you think so John?" "Yes, my love, I do."

"Oh my! Mary must have awakened from our naptime to get this one." "That herd, the horses and all of us sure needed that rest." "She must have somehow blended several photos together to get the whole scene."

"If I may interrupt... Hello, my name is Doug Jones. I am out here visiting my niece. She knows I like photography shows so we came to see this one. These photographs are really good. This young woman has a keen talent. To remark to your wonderment as to the large scene, that would be using double exposures or perhaps if she was at the end of the film roll, there is sometimes an overlap in the images. Whatever happened, be it intended or luck, this piece is terrific." "Thank you, Mr. Jones we will be sure to tell her." "I hope to meet this young lady and tell her myself." "I am quite certain that can be arranged." "Here's my number, I'll be in town until Tuesday." "We will be sure to talk to you before then. Good day." "And to you as well."

"Well, he sure knew a lot about photography. I wonder who his niece is." The four remained fixed on 'Weary Travelers'. The extended frame included the cattle grazing, the horses standing together and the riders asleep in a circle. "She had to have walked quite a way despite her fatigue to do this. Wow. I had no idea. Russell, you stayed awake, did you see her leave?" "Must have been when I was talking with Kent."

Below the large frame a smaller photo of the twin engine plane dousing the herd had been place in the forefront of the setting. 'Relief'. Seeing Mary's fixated gaze, Russell spoke. "You have no idea the truth in that title. Not an animal one flinched or balked when that plane flew over. I think they all were both too tired to care and just happy for the cool down. It was a great idea to do that. It really was. If they had not... well, the herd and all of us would have not had the gusto for the rest of the push."

"Sara, honey... maybe you should pass this one." "Why would I want to do that John?" "Um..." "Step aside please I want to see all the photos."

Sara fell to her knees.

'*Mark of a True Heart*'

"Russell, help me up, I don't want to make a scene." Russell reached for her as she slowly rose. "All these years… that mark remains." Mary looked at Russell to see his reaction as Sara spoke of the carving she left on the day of Samuel's fall over the ridge. She placed her right hand on Russell's left arm in hopes to reassure him that Sara's love for him is strong enough to bear the hurt of that day. "It's okay Mary… it would be wrong of me to expect her to not 'feel' for your son. She will forever love him, and she should. I will never ask her not to." "Oh Russell…" His smile ended her comment before she finished.

"Here we go… this is the good part!" "Good part? And just how do surmise there was any 'good part' to this Drive?" "Mary, I'm telling you, this next one is going to make you smile!"

"Ooo…Ooo…" Mary nearly shook with joy as she looked upon '*Smoke Break*'. The photo in the top position in front of them was taken as Mary burst through the smoke line and saw the ranch and the families waiting for them. Below the photograph of the homestead were placed two pictures of the cattle appearing through the smoke with riders at their sides and below the herd, the appearance of Sara and Russell as they emerged through the smoke line symbolizing the end of the Drive.

Tears cascaded the cheeks of the onlookers. Each again relived the relief of those moments just as they had felt it on that day.

The last easel had a large print entitled '*Home*'. The herd resting in the pens, and riders dismounted next to the horses at the water trough beside the barn door.

Russell placed his left arm behind Sara, she had her left arm behind Mary, and Mary's left arm was behind John. As one, they sighed, smiled and with their right hands wiped the tears from their eyes.

"Gram, Gramp… Mr. and Mrs. Barnes… hi! I was told you were here; I wanted to wait until you saw the entire display before I talked with you. So… what do you think? I was kinda worried about a couple of them as I know how personal they are for you, but I just thought that they all belonged together and depicted the story as I thought that it should be told. I hope you don't mind."

"Mary, this is not only a fantastic showing of events but an honor to the Moore Ranch that you have done this. I would not have wanted you to change a thing. I cannot express to you how proud I am of you. You rode as a true cowgirl and you captured the heart and the spirit of the Drive. It's… it is… just amazing." Sara engulfed the young girl in her arms, holding tightly for many moments. Stepping back, Sara looked into Mary's eyes; "You can sure ride a horse young lady! You had to be using legs only to balance and steer so you could hold your camera! That is impressive!" "We learned that when we started roping together." "A true cowgirl, a true cowgirl."

"Okay… okay… our turn!" Sara stepped away to allow the others their time of praise.

"Thank you so much. I really do think it all came together well." "I am quite certain this will be the first of many exhibits for you. By the way, a man by the name of Doug Jones gave us his number; he wants to talk with you. He is in town until Tuesday. Oh, here it is…" Sara placed the card in Mary's hand. "I'll be sure to call him Mrs. Barnes. Thank you." The hope and anticipation in her voice was not unnoticed by the elders standing with her.

"Oh! I almost forgot… the bareback broncs are almost ready for the championship round and two of the pick-up men got hurt during the saddle broncs so I guess that two of the chute men are subbing for them." "Oh Lord! Do they know what to do? I mean really? Are they aware of the real duty they are about to uphold?" "Mr. Moore, the foreman of the crew assured Brent these guys have ridden before…"

"They better know what they are doing, that stock is tough and ready for thunder! Intimidation is just a part of their talents. I chose only the best, and Brent has done so as well." "Let's get in there and see what is happening." "You three go get the seats; I'm going down to the chutes to see if I can help the boys. If I know them, they will be ready to ride. I'll catch up to you in a bit." Russell leaned back on his heels, turned and headed toward the arena. "Well… you heard what he said, let's get our seats and pray for the best! After you, ladies."

****

"Well, well… look who we have here… you boys have sure done some growing up since your 8.92 ride in Brandon a few years back."

Michael and Charles abruptly stopped when they heard the boisterous voice of the man they knew only as *the* Judge Dewain. Aware that the large man was standing behind them, they turned in to each other trying to conceal their apprehension of the remaining conversation.

"At ease, boys. Or should I say men? It has been a few years. I take it you are still in the Rodeo game?" "Sir, I'm just stunned you remembered our time…" Charles had gathered his composure and spoke distinctly. "Mr. Hunter, I remember the good ones. And you two had a good one. I'm glad you are still competing." Michael reached his right hand out offering a handshake to a man he respected and was earnestly happy to see at the Rodeo. "Mr. Dewain, we are not competing today. Actually, we are here helping Brent Thomms with the rodeo stock." "Thomms… hmmm sounds familiar… oh I do remember his bull ride on the Big Bopper… the kid had velcro on his seat that day, very few cowboys get 8 seconds on that hog head. He got something to do with the stock you said? I heard there was a replacement string come in pretty last minute." "Yes sir, the other string had to pull out due to Rumen Acidosis and our stock was called in." "Your stock?" "The Moore Ranch bought the Barnes Rodeo Company and well, that was just the start. There's lots more but with all due respect sir, we really have to get to the chutes. A couple of the hired pick up men doubled as clowns in the bull riding and… long story short, the bulls had stronger wills than the clowns. They are okay… but will not be riding the rest of the event so, yes, Charles and I are ready to ride, if needed but as pick up men not competitors. It has been great seeing you again. The family is in the center section, third or fourth row, I'm sure they will have a seat for you if you would like to join them." "That's mighty kind of you Michael, I think just maybe I will find them. Thank you."

"Mrs. Barnes?" "Oh, my goodness! Katy!! You are here! What…?" "I took my exam early so I could be home for the big debut. I told my professors that I just had to be here. I had…" "Oh, Katy, we are so glad you are here. Michael will be thrilled. He and Charles are helping in the chutes and are on standby if needed to ride pick up. I see John coming, he stopped at the concession… you know how he is about his popcorn!"

"*Now* this rodeo is complete! The beautiful Katy McGregor is here!" Katy turned as John wrapped his arms around her. "Hello Mr. Moore. I'm so glad to be here." Mary had remained seated and now lifted her right hand to Katy. Taking the matriarch's gesture, Katy smiled. "My dear, have you seen Mary Shanks' photographs in the Expo-Center?" "No, not yet. I hear they are fantastic. I want to wait to see them when the six of us can go together." "That will be nice. Sara, Russell, John and I went just before coming in here. Prepare yourself, they are really something!"

"Excuse me, Michael said I would be welcomed to sit with you… my name is Martin Dewain. I judged at the Brandon Rodeo a few years back." Katy smiled as she greeted the newcomer. "I remember how you intimidated Michael and Charles when I found the loose wire and we had to pull the electric eye. They ended up with a good ride." "And I remember how you looked at the tall young cowboy…" "I'm going to marry that tall cowboy after I finish Vet school." "I knew that day you two were going to make a thing of it!" 'Hi, I'm Sara, Michael's mother, this is Mary Moore his grandmother and, on his way here… is John." "Gramp, just call me Gramp. Have a seat; Russell's is open, he is going to stay with the boys." "Russell? As in Russell Barnes?" "That would be the one! He's my husband now." "Barnes Rodeo -- Wes Grant-- okay… clear as mud…I'm just glad things worked out. Why don't we leave it at that." "Yeah, good idea. I believe the Bareback Broncs are about ready."

With both arms draped over the top rail of the arena; Russell perused the spectators as they assembled in usual form; filling the mid sections of seating first. His thoughts were consumed by remembrance of the first circuit venue of the Barnes Rodeo Company. Smiling, he turned his head toward the chutes and was awed by the precision Brent displayed as he coordinated the lineup of riders, horses and the pickup men. "You got this kiddo… I'm really proud of you." His words were spoken softly as he removed his arms from the rail, leaned back on his heels, turned and started to walk to the chutes.

"Good to have you here Mr. Barnes." "Thank you, Brent, anything I can do to help?" "You know the business better than anyone… oh man… I need to get to the back pen, seems there's a young mare back there causing havoc… keep an eye up here?" "Sure." "Thanks."

"Ladies and Gentlemen! Children of all ages! Welcome to the Rocky Mountain Stock Days Rodeo Bareback Bronc Riding! My name is Warren Nilles, our Judge today is Percy Hancock coming here from the great state of Idaho and this year we have the Moore Ranch prime bucking stock ready in the chutes to challenge our cowboys. Get ready for action! Our first rider is Jimmie Bonds from Carnon. He is in chute one getting ready to ride Frisco. And there's the nod!" The chute gate opened and with a sideways thrust the large gelding bolted into the air. The crowd cheered as the young cowboy raked the shoulders and held fast to his position on the horse. The buzzer sounded indicating a successful 8 second ride. Jimmie hopped off the back end of Frisco as

Ron and Craig loped to the horse to release the flank strap and push him back to the pens.

As the applause ebbed, the announcer declared a score of 38 for Jimmie and 42 for Frisco for a combined score of 80. The crowd again applauded the first ride of the event. "That my friends... is how it is done! A fine ride Jimmie! In the chutes we have Tom Young riding Kieke with Bob Hentin and Bert on deck followed by Harlon Myers and Wanda. Okay folks I see the hat nod... Holy cow! Look at that belly full of bedsprings! That young man hit the ground before he even got to the third buck! That broncs name means *baby* in Hawaiian, well... he sure *lei-ed* out Tom! That's a no score for Mr. Young."

The horse was still bucking as Craig released the strap. "If these two are any indication of the quality of stock this guy has... we are sure in for a good afternoon!" "You got that right, Ron." Kieke continued bucking as he entered the return pen.

"And it's Bob Hentin and Bert... Wow! What a shoulder mark! Look at that horse twist and jump!" The buzzer indicated a successful ride. "These horses know their job! Judges... the score please..." A young boy handed Warren the Judge's card. 40 for the cowboy and 43 for the bronc. Total 83! These good horses are ideal for good scores if you can ride them! We have a mare in the chute—look out boys!"

As the chute opened, Wanda stood with all four feet nearly in the same spot; head tucked in low to the ground. The crowd fell silent as the horse snorted boisterously. Harlon Myers knew at that moment this was going to be either a no buck DQ or a full throttle rage of 'mare mad'. He had no time to think about the choices.

John Moore leaned over to Martin; "I love this horse... she hasn't been ridden yet... wait for it!"

The mare burst into a frenzy before actually leaving the chute. Jumping out of her confinement, her front legs flashed to the right as she twisted her hind legs to the left. In an instant she had her hind legs nearly straight in the air as her body thrust to the left. The snorting and bellers more intense with each rake to her shoulders. The crowd cheered the young man as he held to the horse. Wanda rapidly continued her skillful maneuvers. Determined to outwit the rider, it was as if she knew the timing and how to unseat him. Her high buck and kick to the right was more than Harlon was prepared for, as she thrust out backwards, she tucked close in with the front; Harlon's free hand slapped the croup of the powerful mare and as the buzzer rang, the crowd sighed for the young man that survived the mare yet would not get scored.

"Wow! What a ride! You may not have received a score young man, but I just got word from the stock company, you are the first to actually stay with her!"

Harlon had dismounted abruptly from the horse and was waving his hat to the crowd as he returned to the pens. Brent walked to the disappointed cowboy; as he approached, he reached out his hand. "What's that for, Mr. Thomms? I didn't get…" "Didn't get, what? A score? Hell Fire kid! You rode that bitch! There is no, and I mean no, other person alive that can say that!" Brent fisted Harlon's left shoulder as he again extended his hand. "Hoo-ey! You got a career ahead of you … you keep ridin' like that!" "Thank you, Mr. Thomms." Brent leaned in, tipped his head, looked side to side then back at Harlon. "A word to the wise… she'll remember you… you ever pull her again, prepare for the rematch of your life!"

While Brent and Harlon talked by the Crows Nest, two riders had tied scores of 78 and three riders bucked off before the buzzer.

"John, you have fine stock out there. Hasn't been a score under 40 yet for any of your buckers. And… that mare! Whew! She took a 48 in my book! After this gig, I think your young men are going to be very busy! I haven't seen the likes of this in a long time! *This* is Rodeo!" John said nothing as Mary glanced to him in time to see the corners of his mouth raise. He looked to her and winked.

"I think we can all agree; this string of horses has been as much a surprise for the cowboys as it has been for the spectators! I don't know just where the M double RSC has been hiding out, but I can pretty much say in confidence they won't be in hiding much longer! In the chute now is Pete Woodron from Eastdale. A relatively young cowboy in this event; he has pulled Poncho, a stout Appy gelding with a cropped ear. Can this be the winning ride? He'll have to beat 80…"

The gate flung open as Pete gave his nod. The first buck set his balance off to the right as the powerful horse blew hard as he thrust sideways. The tit[8] of his glove held tight as he regained his center. The horse twisted and jumped with each buck and seemed to propel sideways after landing.

"Get ready Craig… this fella is going to need us!" "I do think you are right on that! We best get into position and pray he don't go gettin' hung up!"

In the holding area Michael and Charles watched as the young cowboy strained to ride out the horse. "Charles, what do you think?" "Not looking like Poncho's going to get rode out today!"

As Charles finished his reply, the crowd gasped in unison. Michael and Charles' attention now focused on the commotion in the center of the arena. "Shit! He's hung up!"

"You got em Craig?" "Trying, this cayuse is a clever one! I'll try to get him cornered, you get the flank strap[9]!"

Still bucking, with cowboy hanging off his left side, hand stuck in the hold, Poncho flung wildly in circles. Each time Craig reached for the flank strap the horse bolted sideways. Ron could not convince the

---

8   Tit of the glove: a 'hook' to help hold the hand in place

9   Flank Strap: tightened strap to the rear of the horse's belly that initiates the 'buck'

frenzied horse to straighten; if Pete had any chance of getting to his feet long enough to try to get back over the horse to loosen the tit on his glove, he needed the horse to be at least slightly aligned.

A woman standing on the rail screamed. "Noooooooo!" Sara leapt from her seat to get to the woman before she screamed again. "Don't scream! It only scares the horse more! Believe me!" "Oh, my Lord! Sara? Sara Moore? Is that you?" "It's Sara Barnes now." "I haven't seen you since that night years ago at the Holler. I'm Sancha Woodran I was there with Linda…"

Another gasp from the crowd.

Sancha's body language prompted Sara to touch her shoulder. "Don't. It will make Craig and Ron's job harder." Sancha turned in to Sara and fell her head on Sara's shoulder. "He's my baby brother and all I have left." "They are going to get him safe…" "Please…"

"Mount up Charles, we're going in!" "Not without me!" Brent passed them at a run as they each grabbed the horn of their saddles and swung their body in an upward motion. They were not yet seated nor did they have their boots in the stirrups as they cued the horses into a full run toward the center of the arena.

"Circle around him boys! Don't give him an out!" Brent rode to the right to join with Craig and Ron as Michael and Charles closed the circle on the left. "Keep moving in a circle… get the flank strap if you can! Pete? You still with us?" "Dammit… get me the hellouta here!" "I'll take that as a yes." Moments seemed an eternity to the young man trying desperately to evade the flailing legs while unsuccessfully getting his chest back over the horse.

Michael could see the fatigue quickly feeding fear as Pete tried diligently to regain his footing.

"I have no idea what you are going to think Poncho, but the hell with trying it this way!"

Positioning the head of his mount in front of Poncho, without hesitation Michael pushed off from the forks of his saddle, with one boot in the seat; stood and then launched himself onto Poncho's head. Scout stayed in formation as the others closed in on Poncho. Michael wrestled the large horse with a new-found adrenalin fueled strength until at last the gelding slowed his furious twisting.

"Stay with him 'Mountain Man'... you got him now!"

Charles released the flank strap as Brent reached over to push the tit through the grip. Craig and Ron had dismounted and were there to catch Pete as he was released from the horse. "You okay?" "I'm alive... that's a good thing! Thank you."

The crowd cheered as Poncho ran to the return pen. The five men that came to his aide were all standing beside him as Pete rose up, looked around to locate Sancha and waved his hat to her indicating he was alright.

Sancha placed her hands on her heart, "Thank you, Jesus!"

Six men walked back to the chutes. Five leading horses and one thankful for those there with him to have done their jobs for a man they did not know. As they approached the chutes, Pete turned back to face the spectators; lifting his hat off his head and with both arms stretched upward he smiled and yelled; "Thank you God! I love Rodeo!"

Every seated person stood and all in attendance applauded the young cowboy and the fast reactions of the pick-up men.

Russell had assembled the medical team and had them in the west end entrance by the concession stand.

Martin turned to John; "Sir, I knew those boys would become good men. That was impressive. Rodeo may be trying to change with the times, but the true spirit of the cowboy will forever hold steadfast." Mary leaned forward to present herself slightly in front of her husband and Martin Dewain. "They come from good stock!" The three were laughing as Sara returned to her seat. "Okay... do I want to know?" The question remained unanswered as Judge Hancock spoke over the loud speakers: "Pete Woodron's preliminary check from the EMT on the grounds is a few bruised ribs and a banged shoulder. Nothing broken, nothing serious. Back to you Warren... on with the Rodeo!"

"In chute number three getting set is Andy Wilson, riding Lefty; a five year old palomino... there's the nod!"

******

Sitting at the large desk in the office, Russell held the morning edition of the *Brandon Times*; his stare fixed on the front-page article announcing the MdoubleRSC's nomination for the honored title of 'Regional Bucking Horse Stock Company of the Year'. Setting the paper on the blotter protecting the desktop, his left hand reclaimed a hold on the now cooled cup of coffee. His gaze shifted to the right side of the desk; stacked neatly were numerous requests yet to be answered regarding hiring the Mdouble RSC for Rodeos across the Rocky Mountain Region. "There sure were a lot of naysayers said it couldn't be done-- at least not rightly if a man only had horses, calves and steers in their stock company. Well, maybe that's so, but this here cowboy wants nothing to do with the woes of bulls. My heart has always been with the horses... and it seems they have done us proud!" Placing his right hand on the top letter; "Yup... this is proof... we are now in the game! Someday... and soon... maybe, just maybe we'll nominate one of horses to the National Finals in Vegas. Wanda, yeah, that mare is a real champ, she could be the one... I can see it now..." Russell waved his hand in the air while smiling at the imaginary sight of the big mare bucking. "And the crowd goes wild!!! Really? Barnes... you're losing it!" Laughing at himself, he shook his head. "In due time, in due time.

Won't be easy... there isn't anything easy in the rodeo business!" He swigged the last of his coffee.

"Mr. B... you got a minute?" "Absolutely! For you, my young paragon I have all the time in the world!" "Do you remember that fella Jones, Doug I think his first name is... anyway, after the Rodeo we all went to Mary's exhibit and he was there waiting for her. Seems he is some big shot with a magazine in New York." "New York?!" "Yeah. New York." Brent looked at the floor, sighed and spoke again slowly as he returned his focus on Russell.

"He offered her a job."

"A job? As in... New York?!" "Yes, Sir" "What did she... I mean, did she ..." "No, she hasn't given him an answer. He told her she had two weeks to think about it. He went back that Tuesday but said he'd be returning on the 16th... that is the day after tomorrow and he wants her answer. Mr. B., I'm scared shitless she is going to want to go but I'm just as scared if she doesn't." "You, young man, are in a 'catch 22', that you are." "I know. She is really a good photographer, and she sure has a passion for the entire process. You should see the dark room her dad built for her in their cellar; it is amazing to sit there and watch those prints come to life right before your eyes! I really am proud of her and want her to pursue her dreams and aspirations because I know she can do it and anyone that hires her will be glad they did... but what if there isn't room for a Rodeo Cowboy in her life anymore? I love her and want to be with her but..." "But on the other hand, if she doesn't go, you are afraid she will end up resenting you for holding her here... I get it. Have you heard the phrase 'If you love something, let it go... if it comes back to you then it was meant to be'? This could have relevance for you. Let her know how you feel and let her know you love her enough to let her go if that is what she wants to do. Be supportive and be reassuring. You will have to accept the outcome either way. I don't envy you this one. This is a tough lesson in life and 'growing into our own' as my father would say." "Yeah... it just hurts that I might lose her to some fancy smancy city boy and that she might actually want to trade the mountains and ranch life and stay in the concrete jungle." "Then even though it will hurt, you will know that by your being supportive of her decision, you helped her on her journey to success. She will know in her heart you sacrificed for her and she will always remember that." "Guess it's time I go talk to her. Thanks Mr. B." "I'm proud of you Brent. It is a hard thing sometimes to let your heart take the fall so someone else can have joy. That… that is what love does. Let me know how it goes." "Will do"

Resting both arms just past the wrists on the desk edge with hands curled inward, Russell watched as Brent left the room with his head tipped forward walking through the doorway. "Lord, please… please give that young man the strength and the courage to get through this. Lord, he needs you now as I did *then*." Russell sat back in the chair, his thoughts drifting back to the time he spent in the County Jail wondering if Sara would come back after he told her to not get involved; he was trying to protect her. He had let her go… and despite his pleading with her, she had come back to him. Now young Brent faced Mary most likely accepting Jones' offer and leaving her life here for a job in New York. "You certainly have grown into a brave girl Miss Shanks" he spoke softly as he stood slowly pushing the right side drawer closed as he withdrew from the desk; looked through the now empty doorway, "We have your back Brent. It will be alright. One way or the other, we are family and family sticks together."

Part 7
Just Do!

"**R**ussell... the phone is for you! I'll wait for you to pick up the extension in the office! Then I'm heading out to the barn for a ride." "Ok, care if I join you after the call?" "Sounds good."

"Hello, Russell Barnes here, how can I help you?"

"Mr. Barnes, this is Scott Prampt from Sweeten, could we set up a time to speak with you and your wife Sara in regards to a proposal of mutually beneficial financial means..." "Slow down Scott, you haven't told me who you are yet, I won't be agreeing to anything until you are a bit more forthright." "Understood Mr. Barnes. I represent the Prampt Ranch Cutter Racing Team and we've been researching the versatility of the get from that Paint stallion of yours and would like to come over to your place and look to purchase for this year's circuit." "Now that I understand! Let me write your name and number down and Sara and I will discuss it on our ride this morning and I'll get back to you." "Fair enough." Russell wrote the information on the desk pad and quickly removed himself from the office stopping just long enough in the kitchen to retrieve the last two muffins from the counter and then empty the coffee carafe into a thermos. "Must have pro-visions! Thank you, Gram!" He needed less than six steps to be through the back doorway and hustling to the barn in anticipation of the cool autumn morning ride in the mountains with Sara.

Approaching the barn doors, Russell reached down and scruffed the foreheads of Hank and Baron. "Just wouldn't be a ride without you guys, now would it! I had best get to saddlin' or I'm going to be the one left behind!" Looking down the aisle way, both the horses stood in the cross-ties. Sara smiled as she turned her attention from currying Cotton's left haunch to the stomp of Manny's right fore hoof on the

189

rubber matting. "He's a bit on the anxious side today… just how many times have you ridden him?" "This ride today will make four. But if it's any comfort, today is going to be the first time out of the round pen!" "And that is supposed to be a comfort?" "Shhhhurrrre!" "Never a dull moment married to a cowboy!" Sara laughed as she returned to her task. "Mudballs on legs, I'm tellin' ya it's like they knew I was going to catch 'em up this morning! I think we should re name Manny 'Pig Pen'. Russell… Russell are you listening to me?"

Russell stood beside the large gelding and stroked his neck on the left side. "Don't listen to her champ! We can do this. A good cow horse is a good cow horse and you come from fine stock! Three days of education under saddle is all you need… right?" "He's a 'Captain colt'… good minded and handy with himself. I have no doubt he is ready to hit the trail." "Did you hear that Manny? She believes in you just as much as I do… I think… and considering she has loads of hours on Cotton already, I'm thinkin' we really need to bring on our 'A' game today"

Snort. Stomp.

"Mount up!"

Having just passed through the Red Pasture gate, Sara reached her left hand to touch Russell's right arm, "We are being watched by two very jealous old horses back in the side barn yard." "I am quite certain we are. Buck just can't seem to understand the arthritis in his knees and Jazzy, well, that girl will never accept you on another horse even if it is her daughter. You two were glued to each other for nearly two decades." "That fire left her with upper respiratory airway constrictions that she just never will get over. I hate seeing her struggle to breathe these days. Katy says she's working on a team that is dedicating themselves to respiration and allergen issues, sure hope they can come up with… well… any kind of relief! I offered Jazzy as a test subject if they need her." "We have good mounts now, with some fine tuning and plenty of wet saddle pads I'm quite certain they will be for us what we need. There will never be another Jazzy or another Buck, and that is how it should be. We don't 'replace' a horse, we simply start again with another." "You are so right; I like how you said that. When Prairie Wind died, I never thought I could have a 'right horse' like that again. When Jazzy was young she was a real handful but so willing... and as the years passed, she was the 'right horse' again for me. I have been fortunate to have had the right horses at the right times throughout my life. Now it is time for Jazzy's Cotton Top to make her mother proud and be with me for many years to come. Time will tell." He reached his right hand sideways palm side up 'asking' for her to reach to him. She did so with a smile. "I'll never figure out where that unruly white bush of a mane came from on your mare." "Me neither, Jazzy has such beautiful long tresses. It did however make it easy to name her!" Both riders laughed as they turned to looked forward as they rode hand in hand toward the upper east corner of the Red Pasture.

"About that phone call... seems a man by the name of Prampt..." "Scott Prampt?!" "That would be correct." Russell turned his head sideways lifting his eyebrows and with a slight squint while looking at his wife, wondering to himself how Sara knew of the man and also why the elation in her voice when he mentioned Scott's name. "Seems he wants to meet with us as they are interested in the Captain's bloodlines for adding to their Cutter Teams." "Holy cow Russell! The Prampts! They are like the reigning champions 5 years running! This is huge for our bloodline! The first of the Captain's Legacy colts are two-year olds now. When does he want to meet?" "Why Mrs. Barnes, I had no idea you are so interested in the Cutter races!" "I saw a documentary on them on the Public Television station a few months ago. The Prampt ranch was featured and how they have contributed to the popularity of the sport while keeping it traditional. It really looks interesting and believe it or not, they race the teams in the snow!" "The snow?" "Yes. The cutters have runners. They talked about how in the 1920's over in Star Valley ..." "Star Valley? Wyoming?" "Yes, cool huh!" "Okay, okay, I can see you took interest, I'll call him when we get back." "Oh Russell, this could be really good for our ranch! I'm surprised he'd be interested in Paint horses, most of the racers are Quarter Horses or Thoroughbreds or a cross between them." Sara looked to the ground and then around them as she finished her sentence. Letting loose of their hand hold she placed hers on the saddle horn to steady herself as she stood in the stirrups allowing her to twist at the waist and turn her upper body enabling her to see behind them. Still looking backward with a concerned tone, she spoke again. "Hey, have you seen the dogs?"

"Actually, no. Not since the Red Pasture gate." Without prompting, Sara and Russell simultaneously whistled for the dogs. "Hank! Baron! Where are you guys?" Noticing the pleading tone to her voice, "They are fine; I'm sure, no need to fret. Those boys are just out enjoying a good romp in the hill country chasing the ground varmints." Satisfied the dogs were not behind them Sara turned back in the seat to face forward. "I'm sure you are right. Still, I wish I had seen when they took off so I knew where they were headed."

Russell felt Manny's back raise and his step quicken as Sara whistled for the dogs a second time. "Easy there big fella, no worries today… remember? Ah, Sara, if my hunch is correct, those dogs are on their way back here and…" Sara turned toward Russell and noticed the frame of the big gelding telling her he was about to blow, "Hang on Russell!"

"This ain't gonna be no crow hop! Hanta Yo! Manny grabbed the bit in his teeth, plunged his head downward and with a snort threw his haunches up and then kicked out while twisting his body. Landing front feet on the ground first, when the back feet were secured in position, he raised his head and stood on his hind legs. "Lean into him!" "I'm getting there!" Russell raised his arms and plunged his chest and upper body weight against Manny's neck. The horse was nearly straight in posture and Russell knew the only way to keep him from falling over backwards was to push him with his body. "Damn it Manny! Enough of this shit! Get your feet back where they belong! NOW!!!!" The gelding dropped back to the ground; breathing hard and quivering.

"Nice riding there, Cowboy!" "Thanks. All in a day's ride… all in a day's ride." "First time off the ranch, yup! What better way to scare the hell out of your wife than to take a green horn out for a spin!" "He was just playing his part helping me strut my stuff to you… show you I still have what it takes to take your breath away! We had this all planned!" "Riiiiiight… that was a pretty good display of sunfishing; maybe you should consider him for the stock. Seriously, are you okay?" "Sure am little missy… are them thar hounds present and accounted for?" "They are here, they were smart enough to heed your warning and stayed out of the way while you and that bronc demonstrated your acting skills."

"Shall we ride on, Mrs. Barnes?" "The key word in that would be *on*… *On* your horse, hooves *on* the ground…" "*On* my way! Can that filly catch my boy?" "Are you really thinking of… oh geez, Cotton, he was serious… a nice lope will suffice. We'll pick him up off the ground when we catch up. Holy cow, he's moving out!" To her surprise, while cueing for a lope, the young mare sprinted into a hand gallop and was soon in pursuit at a full run. It was merely moments until she reached Russell and then sped past him. "Whoa! Just where did that bolt of lightning come from? Slow down Sara! Sara?"

"Easy girl! Sara sat deep in the seat, changed from neck reining to direct reining and pulled the right rein out slightly to direct the mare in a large circle. She continued a steady tension on the rein to tighten the circling until at last the mare settled into trot, then walk and then halt. "Whew! I don't know where that came from! Don't expect a repeat anytime soon!"

"If you aren't real set on that horse yet, maybe Prampt ought to think about her! Sara, that mare has speed. Needs refined, but speed!" "Yeah… but do we have anything to match her? They race teams." "Well, I guess that would be up to him to find out. I know you are keen on her being Jazzy's daughter, but at least think about it." "I… uhh… yeah… okay. Holy Cow! Did you see her? She can really run! It was like she was flying!" "You kinda liked it, huh?" "Now that I have survived it, yes… it really was cool! But I think we'll keep it to a dull walk for a while. Let's head into the woods up here on the right. The view from the point should be peaked in the autumn colors." "Seems the dogs knew to head to the trail. I hope they are done with their shenanigans as well. After you, my love." Hank, followed by Baron led the riders through the trail head.

"Wow! There sure has been damage up here. I had no idea the storms had been this bad." "The re-growth obviously is not rooted near as well as the giant Ponderosa's that withstood the fire. You would have thought the carbon and nitrogen levels in the soil would have been a healthy start for the saplings." "Lord knows, Sara... I'm no Forest Ranger but maybe there was too much 'above the ground' growth and not enough attention paid to the 'under the ground' growth" "Makes good sense to me Raaanger Russell! It does pose the question of just how solid of ground are we riding on if it can't help hold the trees in place... what about us? There are a lot of boulders up this way that used to have trees and roots and..." "Sara, we are fine. What's got you worrying so much?" "For starters, my love, um... we are both riding green horses and we've already had a fine demonstration from Manny of his 'frog walking' skills, and I'm just not thinking that Cotton is ready to play boss mare quite yet. This needs to be a courage building ride not the opposite. Russell... just what is behind that grin of yours?" "You always say 'no weenies' on your rides... perhaps in the past you may have meant riders, but I can see now it means horses as well. Neither of these two have any experience and yet they are willing, for the most part, to do as we want. We are going to be fine. Besides, if I get thrown and you have to ride back to the ranch, I know I won't be waiting long!" "Russell!" "I've made my point... lead on" "You heard him girl, lead on!"

"How about we give the horses a break and stop for lunch?" Sara had been scouting for an amiable place in the woods for resting the horses and themselves as well. "Sounds good to me. I grabbed a couple muffins on the way out the door and filled the coffee thermos." As she began to reply, Sara tapped the leather of the left flap of her father's saddlebag. "You just enjoy those... both these saddlebags are brimming with all kinds of picnic delights so I guess now I won't have to share since you brought muffins" Sara teasingly smiled at Russell as they tied the horses in separate tree crotches. "Mrs. Barnes..." "Yes, Mr. Barnes..." "I'll share my muffins if you'll share your picnic!" "Oh Mr. Barnes, I think I just might want to share more than your muffins…"

Sara had a blanket on the ground and as she began placing the food in the upper left corner Russell approached her, slowly brushing her hair to the left side of her back and over her shoulder to expose the nape of her neck. Leaning forward he slowly began kissing the muscles that now as she tipped her head were exposed and offered to him. He could hear her take a long breath in and sigh as she exhaled… "Oh… Russ…" Placing his right hand on her waist so he touched the underside of her breasts as he silently asked her to turn to him; his passion aroused as they faced one another, he drew her to him; right hand now under her buttocks he lightly snapped his hand so as to position her against his loin. He held her tight to him as he swelled in their closeness. The strength of his left arm lowered her to the blanket. Their eyes fixed to each other, she reached to his belt with knowing fingers pushed the left side to unhook the tongue on the right and release the hold…

The stratum of the forest floor as their pallet; each with a passion long held in reserve, the fervency of their coquetry left them spent and satiated. Moments passed as they lay side by side feeling the warmth of the sun on their moist bodies, holding hands while looking to the sky; exhilarated by their lovemaking.

"Russell…" "Yes?" Sara quickly mounted her husband; her upper body tipped to lightly touch his chest with her breasts. While doing so, her hair brushed his face, with one motion she flipped it away in time to see his smile. "Love me again…" "Forever my Sara, forever."

"Mr. B… Mrs. B.? Anyone home?" Brent waited to hear a response. "Hmm guess not, and an empty muffin plate… don't that just beat all!" "You gotta get here before ten in the morning if you expect there to still be muffins!" "Oh… hi… Gram, ah, good morning, well actually afternoon. Have you seen Mr. or Mrs. Barnes?" "Sit down, Brent. I just happen to have a piece of leftover pie in the Frigidaire." Fisting both his hands and with arms bent at the elbows, Brent drew them in a downward motion. With a slight twist of his torso he jubilantly expressed his good fortune. "Yes!" Mary Moore smiled as she peeked sideways over the top of the lower door of the refrigerator. To herself she spoke: "They will always be my boys. I don't care how old they get to be. Thank you, God for Blessing this family" Retrieving a fork from the top drawer she placed both on the table. "A glass of milk?" "Oh Gram, you know me so well!" Again, to herself; "That I do. That I do."

"So, what brings you to needing Russell or Sara this morning? I thought you had all decided to take the weekend off... if that is even possible, which I know better than to think it is..." "Charles just got word he is in line for a permanent position with the Brandon Fire Department and to top that off he got accepted in a program for Forestry Emergency Management! This is like huge for him! We have to have a party!" "You boys and your parties... but yes, you are right, this does call for a celebration. I am so proud of all of you." "Mmm, this pie is great! Thanks. Any idea when they will be back?" "I saw them ride out on Cotton and Manny just after nine this morning." "Manny? Gram, he hasn't been out of the pen yet and Mr. B. has only been on his back I think maybe three times... and sure, Mrs. B. has ridden Cotton quite a bit, but to say she's broke enough to go out there... wow..." "Promise me if they are not back by two you will go looking for them?" "Absolutely Gram! For you, your wish is my command" Brent stood, bowed at the waist and waved his right arm in front of him. "You know what, I could use a good ride today, think I will fetch up whoever will come in and head out." "Thank you. It will ease this old woman's mind." "I have to find them first... I suppose they have the dogs..." "That they do." "Well, time to put my 'Curley' on!" "Curley?" "Yeah, Gram... you know... Curley... Custer's Crow scout..." "Custer's? We all know how that turned out... perhaps you could refer to your Boy Scout handbook!" "You have a good point there! Off I go! Wish me luck!" Mary did not have time to respond before the back-porch door slammed behind Brent as he jumped over the steps heading towards the horse barn. "Lord God, keep your eyes on that boy!"

"Mount up!"

Hank and Baron sat at attention on the trail as Sara stepped Cotton over a log. "Good girl. Your old lady here needs a little boost getting back on". "You didn't need any boost 'mounting' a few minutes ago!" The toe of Sara's boot slipped out of the stirrup at Russell's remark. "You okay there… having a little difficulty? Careful not to fall off that log!" Sara patted Cotton's neck, "He thinks he's a comedian, he's just jealous. Manny over there won't half step over a log like you do to help him." As if she understood, Cotton bopped her muzzle in the air a couple times and nickered as Sara settled into the saddle and placed her boots in the stirrups. "I don't know just how it is you do that, you just talk and they respond. You truly are a horsewoman." "I let them into my heart and they know it. Tally Ho!"

Jubilantly the two dogs launched themselves into a trot and with noses down, followed the trail toward the overlook.

Hearing the familiar nicker as he stepped through the carriage doors of the horse barn, Brent smiled. He, Charles and Michael had won the Senior Shop Class Project when they presented the renovation of the barn walls with newly constructed doorways having Dutch style doors leading out to private pens for three of the five stalls on each side of the barn. The end stalls and the middle stalls had the doorways and the dividers between all the stalls were fabricated to be removable enabling enlargement of two stalls into one or three into one if needed for foaling or medical purposes. The original foaling barn providing eight oversized stalls had become insufficient as the breeding program expanded with the demand for Captain's Legacy sons and daughters. Now that the weaning of this year's foal crop was completed and the mares and foals were in separate pastures, the riding horses enjoyed the new stalls with turn out.

"Hey there old fella!" Benji stomped the floor mat and nickered again. "Okay, you are not *that* old! Seems the others are enjoying time under their 'cabanas'. Goofy Gram… calling the lean-to structures cabanas! That's what you get when the old folks come back from their one and only beach vacation and see what happened in their absence. At least we kept Mrs. Barnes from calling them paddocks… they are corral pens for God's sake! We are in the west… the mountains… not some fancy smancy Jumper *stable* back east! Nothin' against them English style riders, nope nothing at all… just sayin' they got their ways and we got ours." Brent slipped the halter over the horse's ears and snapped the throat latch. "You my boy are about to reprise your mountain skills!"

Stomp. Nicker.

Astride his friend of many years and adventures too numerous to count, Brent healed the gelding into jog in the direction of the Red Pasture gate. "I sure do wish we had the dogs."

"Suppose those hounds are still ahead of us?" "Not thinking they have much choice in the matter; this trail is getting narrow and it's steep up on the right and steep down on the left. Just have to get around this bend and the lookout should be pretty close." "How long has it been since you were up here Sara?" "Spring, last year." "Last year… not this year?" "That is what I said, why?" "Well, for starters that really big tree fallen across the trail up yonder a ways might not have been there when you were…"

Russell's sentence was stopped as the pleading bark repeated numerous times until fading away… only to be replaced by the screech of the remaining dog on the trail.

"Hank! Baron!" Another imploring bark in high volume… "We're coming!" Riders with heals into horses swiftly and carefully maneuvered the terrain of the trail to reach the site of Baron staring over the edge whimpering.

For just a fleeting moment Sara could not stop herself from the anguish… silently, as she halted Cotton and was dismounting even before the mare had stopped, to herself she thought "Not again Lord, not again." Before the thought was completed, she was peering over the edge searching for signs of Hank. "There! Over there... he's down the side a couple hundred feet in the rocks. His tail is wagging! He hears me! Hank... hang in there, buddy!" Sara turned back toward Russell assuming he had dismounted and they would go down the side together to rescue the dog. To her surprise-- and fright-- as she turned, she realized Russell and Manny had already leapt over the edge and were descending the hill. "Russell! What are you doing? The rocks! It's too rough for the horse!" She knew her words were falling on un concerned ears. In a lower tone as she stood trembling, she finished what she wanted to say. "His legs, he... he's so young and inexperienced... your life... God, help us... please!" Watching her husband below her traverse the trap laden terrain she held back her tears.

For the first time since the cattle drive through the fire she saw the shadow of a hawk. Looking up in time to see the bird fly overhead; at the moment it squealed. Sara placed her right hand to her heart. "Thank You!"

Russell heard the call of the hawk. "Hank, you are going to be okay. You have a lot of people looking out for you. I'm almost there, just a few more rocks to get around..." Manny placed his left forefoot on an unsecured rock and as his weight rotated the top of it, it rolled out from underneath him. Losing his balance, he fell sideways and slipped down the hillside while trying to regain his foot hold. The horse's attempts to regain his footing created an avalanche of the dislodged shallow rock bed.

"Russell!" Sara's scream echoed through the walls of the ridges.

Russell heard the guttural grunt from the horse as he fell against a tree and finally was able to get enough of a foot hold to stop the fall.

'Shit!" He took in a deep breath. "Whew..." Shaking his neck as if he understood the man astride him, Manny lowered his head to inspect his left fetlock. "You okay? Guess we ought to both take inventory after that, huh?" Russell leaned forward and stroked Manny's shoulder. Satisfied the two of them were relatively unscathed from their additional decent of the hillside, Russell perused the entwined fallen timber and the massive rocks consuming what he thought to be at least the distance of an additional hundred feet or so added from their fall now separating them from the boulder where Hank lay.

Cotton whinnied. Baron barked. With her left hand cupped over her mouth and cheeks, Sara, with great difficulty stood steadfast; ready to dash over the hill if he needed her, but willing to remain atop for him as well. "They are going to be fine." Remaining instance, her right hand reached up to the horse's neck as her left reached down to pat the dog. Each voiced their anguish again.

"Sara… we are okay… Manny can do this! He has to! He's about to get his first lesson in self-preservation! Have trust Sara! Have trust! You stay there!" Russell's tone was of determination, Sara realized this was out of her hands. She had to let the man and the horse be one. In a tone too low for Russell to hear, and as tears welled in her eyes, Sara looked at the sight below her. "But he's so young…"

She watched every move of man and horse below her.

Startled, Sara turned toward the sound of rapidly approaching hoof beats. Brent reined Benji into a sliding stop and was in aim of the edge. "Brent… wait!" "What?" "He's got this. If he needs us…" "Mrs. B… how could he not need us… look at the situation down there!" "Just wait. Brent, I'm going to tell you something… something about the spirit of a man, the spirit of cowboy. Of *that* cowboy down there risking his life for a dog. Risking breaking my heart… for a dog. The true heart of a man is in his willingness to do what fears him the most. To put aside his own self for those he loves. A man is a creature that continuously self proves his worth through his actions and his reactions. That young horse has no business being on that hill. It is his misfortune… but in truth, is his great fortune that he is being guided into an early maturity by a situation he had no option of participating in. That man has told that horse he trusts him. That man has asked that horse to 'just do' so they both survive. I watched that horse take a mis step and in his un- educated response, he learned the meaning of 'just do' so… he did. Russell is a man of honor, a man to be trusted and despite his upbringing, boundless Faith. His commitment to each fuels him to 'Just do' despite consequences to himself"

"But…" "No 'but'… he said they are fine. Until proven elsewise, we stay put. Right now, there is no panic down there. Let's not create one. Manny seems to be holding his own and so does Russell."

Placing his right arm over Sara's shoulders, Brent held the reins of both horses in his left hand as Baron moved to her right side.

"Well my friend, we seem to be in a rather interesting predicament here. Perhaps we ought to do this separately…" Russell had planned on dismounting enabling them each to 'pick their way' back up the hillside. Manny set his hind feet securely on the small area of actual earthen dirt and then launched himself onto the large rock in front of them. "…okay, or not… what the hell was that?" No sooner had he spoken and the horse was bounding to another ledge of stone jutting between several fallen trees. "Take a breather… please! Or at least let me!"

Snort.

Breathing heavily, Manny concentrated on the remaining path he intended to follow. Realizing he was not going to have a say in the decision making, Russell set deep in the saddle and 'gave Manny his head'.

"Easy there, big fella… just a little more… pick your way… one foot at a time… there you go… you got it…" Hank lay on his left side across the top of a boulder. "Wag your tail buddy so Sara can see you are okay… she really needs that right now… actually, so do I… so please?" Lifting his head Hank tipped it back toward the hilltop and wagged his tail. "Look at that! I can talk to the animals too! I'm the next Dr. Doolittle… well, maybe not. Okay there, Hank… just how are we going to get back up this face?" Slowly the dog pulled himself to a standing position, yet only on three paws. Reaching down to his left front paw he whimpered and then started licking the toenail area. "Let's take a look at that shall we?

Think you can stand here for a few minutes and rest?" Voicing a low nicker as Russell dismounted; Manny pushed him with his nose toward the dog.

"Yup, I'm going to be keeping this horse!"

Another low nicker.

Gently Russell handled the paw; he slowly removed the intrusive twig lodged between two toes. "Well, that certainly wasn't enough to hold you down here, what else is there… let's look…" Hank whimpered as Russell ran his hands over the right ribcage area. "Ahh… let's take a look at that…" A quick glance back at Manny to assure him of his courage; "Good boy, just keep right there. Hang tight we'll be ready to go in a few minutes." Russell shook his head as Manny bopped his muzzle several times. Turning his attention back to the dog, "Dr. Doolittle here to save the young pup from certain despair and peril."

"How's it going down there?" "Removed a twig from his paw… think he might have some bruised ribs but other than that not too bad!" "Are you okay?" "We are good. Be up soon!"

Turning on the rock, Hank walked off the side and toward Manny. "Well… I take it that's our cue. I'm thinking we ought to follow him. Are you ready Manny?" A quick snort indicated the horse approved of the departure instructions. "Okay then, let's go!"

"Mrs. B… you are so right about him. He is a man like no other. You know…" "I know, he's a father to you, and Brent, you are a son to him. He loves you. As do I." "Did you see how Manny jumped on those rocks! It's like he's part mountain goat or something. I've never seen a horse do that before!" "Well, it's not generally recommended trail procedure but I will say it was quite impressive. I guess he wasn't thinking of the possible consequences either"

"Like the lashing I'll get from my wife for risking my neck against her wish…" Sara flung her arms around Russell as he dismounted and before he could finish his sentence. Baron ran to Hank as he and Russell stepped onto the trail. "Howdy Brent! When did you get here… why did you get here?" "You were a bit contained when I arrived… um… Gram was worried about you being on young horses coming up here. Wait till she finds out about Manny jumping rocks like a mountain goat! Hey… he's a Manny goat! Sorry Mr. B., I couldn't resist. I won't repeat that."

Manny stomped his right front hoof repeatedly. Sara put her right hand on Russell's chest halting him from speaking. "No worries about the horses. Manny grew up in record time today."

"We'll need a chainsaw up here to work on that tree before we can get to the look-out." Russell pointed up the trail to where the very sizable trunk angled downward over the trail. "I'm pretty sure Hank would prefer a retreat to the ranch." "I agree Brent." Sara reached to retrieve Cotton's reins from him and then turned to dash a smile toward Russell.

"Mount up!"

Part 8
Decisions

"We will only be gone a couple days; just long enough to get over there, check out the landscape of the ranch, see how the ranch is run, and maybe get a little education on this Cutter Racing thing. Sara is really excited about this, we have enough to do with the Co-Op, the beef cattle herd, the Rodeo and her breeding program, just why she thinks she wants to get involved with more is beyond me."

"Russell, you ought to know by now that everything 'horse' excites her, she really is the definition of hippophile. Besides, if you think about it, you may have fueled this adventure along just a tad!" "Oh? How so?" "Was it not you that told her on your ride to the Look-out that Cotton had speed?" "Well, yes, but that is Cotton…" "And Cotton is one of many in the young herd with similar lineage and they all have Captain's Legacy blood in their veins. I think Sara is just seeking ways to keep options open for financial opportunities in a very fickle market. Horses have fads and she wants to keep ahead of the rest." "Well, I'll be! Did you hear her Russell!? Mary Moore… just where in tarnation did you come up with all of that?" "I pay attention to what is important to her. I hear her half of phone conversations and she has confided in me. She is a smart businesswoman as well as horsewoman. She has to be in this day and age to compete with all the men out there that think a ranch woman belongs solely at the ranch."

Russell met eye contact with John and with no hesitation on either man's part, simultaneously they spoke; "Not that ranch woman!"

"All set! I sure am looking forward to our trek to the infamous Star Valley. There is lore that in the walls of the draws through Swift Creek there are caves that housed the likes of the lawless men during the winters when the west was still known as wild. Seems the protection of the north and south passes helped to give refuge from the bounty hunters. Just how much truth there is to all that I do not know, but it is sure fun to try to imagine!"

I certainly don't want to disappoint you but the directions he gave me don't take us all the way to that area. Something about a Diamond Flat... I thought we might stop south of Jackson for tonight and head over to the Prampt ranch first thing in the morning. I found a nice little hide-a-way cabin on the road heading toward the North Pass, and... just in case we want it again after our visit, I secured a second night." Sara leaned forward to embrace Russell. "I love you, you think of everything! Mary, be not worried if we tarry in our return." Sara tipped her head and winked as Mary smiled. "Just call please, if you are going to stay longer." "That... we will do."

Pulling back from Russell, Sara released her hold from her husband and placed her arms around Mary. Resting her head on Mary's shoulder she whispered, "We will be fine and you have Brent here if you need anything." "He's a lost puppy without his Mary. I am sure he will be here keeping his mind off her absence." "Good luck with that!" As the chortle between the women subsided, with raised eyebrows, Russell and John looked at each other and then smiled. "Nope! Not me!" "Me either!" Sara turned around, "Whaaaaaat?"

"Stop the truck Russ." "I know. Whenever you leave the ranch for more than just a local type outing, you need your moment." "I adore looking at the house through the arch. The iron emblem sets directly above the roof when you stand off set of the left side support. This is our home. I have to tell it I will return. I will always return." "Take all the time you need." Leaving the truck door ajar, Sara walked toward the upright Lodgepole Pine, her gaze toward the east followed the upward slope of the land. "Mary is on the porch waving!" Russell leaned over to the passenger side; "How can you know? We're too far away to actually see!" "I know"

"I believe that you do. I really do." Sara returned to the truck. "Okay, I'm ready now. To the Prampt Ranch!" "Okay to stop in Alpine first or do you want to wake the man in the middle of the night?" "You do have a point, if you don't mind; yes, we should stop in Alpine." "Alpine Away!!!"

"Hope you don't mind, I just have to stop and get out to really look at them!" "Mind? I want to too!" Russell slowed the truck, applied the four-way flashers and then parked on the side of the road. Sara opened her door as he turned the ignition off. "Wow!" Russell stood next to her as they both gaped in awe at the sight of the Sweeten Elk herd. "There are hundreds, maybe a thousand..." "I've heard stories... but to see it!" Both bodies fell back against the truck bed.

"Camera... get the camera!" "Way ahead of you!" Russell focused the telephoto lens and snapped a photograph. "Now, to figure out this wide-angle thing Mary tried to teach me...there! Got it!" Click. Click. Click. "Alriiight! Now, Sara you go over there so I can get the herd behind you!" "I'm not getting too close to those bulls!" "Humor me... I just want to get a shot of them behind you... waaayyy behind you." "How about you set the timer on the camera and we both get in the picture!" "Good idea!" Russell set the timer mode and then stood beside Sara for a photographic memory of a lifetime. "You will have to show Mary..." Sara stopped mid sentence. Not yet used to Mary having taken the job in New York, she found herself referring to her as if she was still in Brandon. Russell placed his arms around Sara; he knew she was feeling the absence of a 'daughter' she loved dearly. "We'll get double prints and send her one." "Thank you, Russell."

"Do you hear what I hear?" "I do and it sure isn't the Christmas Carol! Here he comes and he's not alone!" Sara and Russell turned their faces toward the sound of running hooves and bugling bulls "Truck!" "This time I'm ahead of you!" Sara jumped in her side, slammed the door shut and reached over to open the driver's door from the inside and pushed it outward. "I have always loved that you do that for me, this time I am really happy you have that courtesy about you!"

Thump! Whap!

"Oh boy!" "Hang on, I'm going to have to push through them or they will up turn this dually!" "Be careful! I'm quite certain the Elk have the law on their side around here!" "Oh, probably, but ..."

Thump Whap!

"Go... just go... they can ask questions later!" Sara looked in the side mirror and could see the damage to the side of the truck. "So... how do we explain this to the insurance guy?" "That, my dear, we will deal with when we get home... what are we going to tell Prampt? These are his homeland treasures!"

"Oh crap."

Approaching the grandiose wrought iron gates between rock pillars, Russell slowed the truck and looked at Sara. "Now *those* are impressive!" "Yeah! How do they know we are here? I don't see anyone?" The gates opened. Russell tipped his chin looked over his sunglasses at Sara; "They know." Proceeding cautiously, Russell and Sara looked side to side at the expanse of the Prampt Ranch spanning the acreage bisected by the roadway.

"Don't suppose you can call this their *driveway*, we've already been two miles. This is spectacular. This ranch runs from one side of the valley to the other!" "You know what Russ? It is spectacular... and pretty much flat. I'll take the rugged mountain sides any day!" "That's my girl!" "Look! Over to your left... that must be the ranch house."

Supported by the hand carved railing alongside the staircase with custom wrought iron risers that duplicated the Cutter racing images that were displayed on the massive entrance gates, a man of staunch stature descended the steps.

"Impressive again!"

"Yeah!"

"Well, hey there folks! So glad you could make it to my little piece of Heaven here on Earth! My 'Diamond Flat' as I have it referred to between mountains... even have the tourists driving through here to Yellowstone thinking it is a town all its own! Say... you have a little trouble on your way over here with the Elk? Now, don't look like that, I've seen it many times... folks want to take pictures... and well, before you know it the old bull has them cowering in their cars. Don't ever recall him taking on a big dually before; you sure must have pissed him off! Or... he was jealous of that pretty girl sitting over there! Hi! My name is Prampt... Scott Prampt." "Hello, I am Barnes, Russell Barnes and my wife Sara." "That would be Barnes, Sara Barnes. Hey, if you guys can do the whole name game thing so can I!"

Russell and Sara waited for Scott's reaction before joining him in the ensuing laughter. "You two are going to fit right in around here! Let's get something to drink and then take a tour. What's your pleasure? We have whiskey, wine and water... no beer. I just can't have the abomination on the place; if a man is going to drink, he needs to drink whiskey, for a lady we offer her a choice of wines should whiskey be not of her liking and, well, the water is just courtesy for young folks and the livestock." Again, he bellowed in laughter. "Water is fine." "Same here." "Elizabeth... please get our guests their water. Thank you." The blond haired and blue eyed young girl turned and ran back up the steps and into the house. "My granddaughter... her parents were killed two years ago in an accident on the Snarl River. She doesn't speak much, but she is my little girl's girl and will forever have a home here. My wife passed before Elizabeth was born so to her, I am her everything. Mom, dad, grandpa... the whole works."

Sara and Russell looked at each other and with a silent 'knowing' understood that they both now had a new respect and honor for the man standing in front of them.

"Hope you like Jeeps! This here is my little get-about toy. They didn't name it a Wrangler for nothing! Sara, you can ride up front here with me and Russell, you are in charge of making sure that little red box doesn't fall out the back!" "Red box? Fall out?" "There is a gizmo inside that if in an unlikely situation I don't return when Elizabeth thinks I should have, she calls the sheriff and they do whatever it is they do and they know where I am." "I'll be sure to keep my eye on it." Placing her left leg over the raised rim on the floorboard of the vehicle, Sara reached for the grab bar over her head and hopped into the front seat. Russell entered the rear area head first with his legs following. "You folks better buckle in… no doors and no roof… and no speed limit on my own ground!" Sara turned her head back to insure Russell was securely fastened. They shared a smile to each other as Scott suddenly accelerated rapidly through the lower gears. Sara turned around to face forward and regained her hold on the grab bar. Russell had a grip on the roll over bars on either side of the jeep and held his boots tightly around the 'little red box'. He had no intention of it getting separated from the vehicle; he was not so sure of the human inhabitants as they were thrown sided to side and lifted from their seats often as the jeep sped across the rough terrain.

"Hang on my new friends! We'll be at the track in no time!" Speaking loudly to be heard over the engine and the wind created by the openness of the jeep, Russell leaned forward. "You sure have a large spread here!" "About twenty five hundred acres give or take a few. I've been buying ranches that have been going under for a few years now. The Cutter Racing is just my hobby of sorts. The real money is in the alfalfa hay we raise here and ship to California, Arizona and Nevada. I'll expand out further if I acquire more ground but I won't push anyone to sell. I pay above market value and always give the option to stay in the house and have a little of the ground for their families if they want. I sure don't need the homesteads but they do. It works out rather well. I have even hired a good many of the folks that didn't leave the valley all together to either work my main ranch or to stay on and work the ground I paid them for. I may be an outsider in a lot of ways, but I respect the heart of a rancher."

Sara interjected as Scott paused, "So I take it no cattle?" "A few... maybe a hundred. A man's gotta eat!" Russell leaned back against the rear cushion. "Alfalfa, huh... grows here well I take it?" "It thrives here. We bale at night. The days are terribly dry; need a little moisture to keep the leaves from separating. We actually have a lot of dairy cows for the Cheese Factory. You can't leave here before you taste our Valley Cheese! Look hard to your left... the track is over there down the way. We'll head to the barns and the arena. I'm sure you will want to see the operation at the core."

"Mr. Prampt..." "Scott. Please." "Scott, I really want to thank you for inviting us here... and for your interest in our bloodline." The jeep plunged down an embankment; Scott surged the vehicle to climb the other side. Sara threw her arms in the air as if riding a roller coaster. "Whewee!" Russell noticed the creases at the corner of Scott's eyes and the broadening of his smile as he looked sideways at Sara. "The pleasure is definitely all mine." "And Sara is all mine" Russell spoke softly to himself.

Scott had been slowing the Wrangler as they approached the barn area. "You may not know this, but I have an own son of Captain and two daughters. Not on my race roster, but as my ranch mounts. Their mind set is amazing and the endurance is remarkable. I inherited the mares with a ranch I bought a few years back. It didn't take long to understand the remorse that man's wife had at losing those mares. The old gelding was at a production sale in Denver." "So, you knew the horses were bred up north and looked into us?" "Hadn't actually done all that until I met up with Martin Dewain, we have been friends a long time... he told me about your ranch, the boys and the Rodeo Company and then went on to praising your horse breeding operation. I'll be honest, the Paint horse thing kinda threw me but he insisted I look into it. So, I did. I researched and found a lot of other owners of your line and have decided I need to put aside the fancy pajamas and really look into these horses of yours. Who knows maybe I'll start a trend!

Tossing her head side to side and grinning as she lifted her right leg over the floor guard, Sara exclaimed; "I must say… that's the first time I have heard someone describe the color patterns of a Paint horse as 'fancy pajamas'" "Here, let me help you out of the Jeep." "I'm here Scott, I'll help my wife." Russell had exited the back and was attentively standing to the side of Sara holding out his arm for her to take hold of. Sara had thought about replying that she didn't need help, but the tone of Russell's voice alarmed her. Looking at him over her sunglasses with her eyes she mutely asked him for an explanation. He whispered quickly as she passed in front of him "Later. I'll tell you later"

The trio walked through winding graveled pathways between corral pens to reach the main horse barn. Sara noticed that only one of the pens was occupied. A lone brown mare stood lethargically in the corner as they approached. "Is she sick?" "No, I've had her vetted, she was so poor at the auction barn I just couldn't leave her there. Doc says it will be a while for a full recovery. What in the hell I'm going to do with a Rocky is beyond me." "A Rocky?" "Yes, come to find out she's some fancy gaited breed. I guess they show them and trail ride with them. They are tough buggers I'll give 'em that." "Gaited? Like a Missouri Fox Trotter?" "I guess similar. The actual name is a Rocky Mountain; I have no experience with the gaited breeds. I'm a true stock horse man. Except for my runners. I brought a few Standardbred horses in from a track back east in Cleveland. Already broke for my purpose and they run consistent. And… they are used to running in the cold." "Cleveland? Ohio?" Russell joined the conversation as they neared the gable end of the barn. "I want to win. So, I buy winners. Most run Quarter Horses and Thoroughbreds. My Standardbreds are holding their own. A quarter mile on the snow and ice is tough for any horse. I do have a couple teams of Thoroughbreds; I like the long legs and stride length. I run them when I know Sanderson is running teams."

"A little friendly competition?" "Sara, my dear, there is nothing friendly about it. Me and that no good Ed Sanderson have been rivals since grade school. And then when he stole my 'steady' girl Jane in the tenth grade by lying about my family, the feud was borne. I waited for Jane to realize her mistake and leave him. Him being rich and all, she saw the benefits for herself to stand by him and his accusations. It did not take long for Louise to... oh you folks don't want the whole sordid tale. The ending of the story is that he claims I stole Louise from him in retaliation but in truth, she was a far better woman than Jane and we realized we were much better suited. We married four months after graduation. It is her photo you see in the ranch house. Jane left Ed a month after the wedding. Ed never could let go of it no matter how many years ago it was and seems to be continually trying to prove himself a better man than I no matter the situation. I have to admit, I have done my fair share of dirty deeds towards him over the years as well. It is just what we do. Everyone in town just accepts it and looks forward to the next challenge. Truth be told, I probably could like the guy, but he does some pretty underhanded stuff and I just can't condone it. Now, where were we? Oh, yes... the racing classes... we do have a circuit here for state bred horses only... that's where your horses will run, but we have open events as well."

Sara looked at Russell and mouthed the words "our horses". He returned in the same manner; "Yeah, this guy means business!" They smiled at each other as Scott continued his spiel regarding the operation of his Cutter Racing Program. "You will like the track, it is just beyond the hedgerow. We run straight, we run hard and we run fast. If we're lucky Ben will have a team out there training."

Sara heard a low nicker from the sullen mare in the pen. Slowing her pace, she drifted behind unnoticed by the boisterous one sided conversation of the men now several paces beyond her. "What are you trying to tell me girl?" The mare perked her ears at the sound of Sara's voice. Another low nicker. "You are so right... you do not belong here." Glancing toward the distancing men, Sara noticed a lone man stealthily leaving the tractor shed and making his way to the hay barn. Taking note of the appearance and body language of the ranch hand, she thought to herself; "hmmm... that looks a bit suspicious..." Turning back toward the mare she bid her farewell; "I have to go, I will try to see you again before we leave." The mare lowered her head and closed her eyes. Kneeling beside the pen panel, Sara reached her arm through as the muzzle met her hand. "I ... I... oh Lord, please. Please bring peace back to this fractured soul..."

While still kneeling, Sara glanced back at the hay barn door just in time to see the man turn in the doorway and look around as if checking to see if he had been noticed.

"Sara?" "Right here!" "Uh huh... you are a bit winded... perhaps from a sprint to get back here from talking with a lonely brown mare?" "I'm sorry..." "No, you are not. I kept Prampt busy and moving forward for you. I just knew you could not pass that pen and not 'talk' with her." Sara placed her left arm inside Russell's right arm and put her right hand on his shoulder as she leaned in to speak lowly. "Thank you. I think I may have seen..." He tapped her arm with his left hand. "I love you, now pay attention... we are almost at the track."

"Over there..." Scott pointed to an area just off to the left. "We will have a good look at the track there."

Standing behind the dilapidated snow fence, Russell placed his right arm around Sara's waist. Their attention transfixed on the team of speeding bay geldings, neither had noticed the arrival of the young man standing beside Scott. "25.83" "They're going to have do better than that on the snow if they plan on winning. How are the blacks doing?" "Bob has them ready... should be any minute... here they come!"

Sara could feel the adrenalin rush as the team came racing toward her. "Oh Russell, this is just so exciting!" Noticing Scott's reaction to Sara's excitement, Russell tightened his hold on her waist.

"24.42" "Now that's a better time! Sara, Russell, this is Ben Zander. He's been training my horses for, well, years now." Relieved that Ben was not the man she had seen at the hay barn, Sara smiled at the display of enthusiasm as he spoke. "Hello Mr. and Mrs. Barnes. Scott told me you were coming by today to look at the operation. And, yes, I've been here for years… twelve actually. I started with my late father when I was still a young teenager. I love the horses and I love the racing. We have a great program here and from what I understand we may be adding a splash of color to the track." "Please, Sara and Russell. Now that we see how this all works, I am quite confident we have just the 'flash' to add to your 'dash'!" The jaunty guffaw of the young man immediately produced the same throughout the foursome. "I think we have our new ranch slogan! Come on, I'll show you the trophy room. Thanks Ben, I'll catch up with you later. Flash in our dash…"

"Gram? Gram? Are you Home? I received a letter from Mary today!" "Be right there!"

Mary Moore entered the kitchen with her arms laden with bed linens. "Geez Gram, let me have those." "Help me fold?" "For you, you bet!" Each picked up the ends of a blanket and began the ritual of folding.

"I received a letter from New York today… sure doesn't seem like she's been gone four months already." "You miss her, I can tell. Have you told her?" "I want to, I just don't know how to tell her and not sound like I don't support her doing this. I just…" Mary placed her right hand on his chest. "You want her to be happy, just had thought it would be here in Brandon." "Yeah, but times are changing and she is part of a whole new 'way' for women. Her talent was recognized and she was presented an opportunity that even girls in the east that have grown up there only dream of. Here, hand me your end of the blanket, I'll finish it and then read you the letter."

Brent,

First off, I want you to know how much I miss you.

To say I feel like I fit in around here, well, at this point I admit I am struggling with that. The big city life is so different. It

217

took a long time, but finally I have found a nice apartment and am rooming with two other girls that hope to make their mark on Broadway. Can you believe it? Broadway! Sometimes it all seems so unreal to me. They are helping me adjust to the city ways and I think I may have helped them a little to understand rural life which they need for the roles they are auditioning for in a Playhouse production titled 'Westward'. Truthfully, a musical embodying a family moving west in the 1880's doesn't seem right! I watch them rehearse and let me tell you, I am surely going to have to see the end result! While they run their lines, I take photos and am working on my digital videography pretending I am a director. It's loads of fun. Maybe someday I might try it for real.

My job working for Mr. Jones is grueling yet so exciting! He has me traveling to locations all over New York City and Long Island, I have been to Rochester and Syracuse in upstate New York, Boston Massachusetts, Bar Harbor Maine, Killington Vermont, Philadelphia Pennsylvania and next week we are headed to Atlanta Georgia! I have been able to learn about so many places and have seen things I only read about in books. It truly is remarkable! The trip to Rochester involved a day at Eastman Kodak! For me anyway, it was a photographer's dream come true! When we get back from Atlanta, Mr. Jones has enrolled me in a class at UNY for photography editing and color adjustment.

I really feel like I have found 'me'. I know you really didn't want me to leave Brandon. I could see it in your eyes and hear it in your voice. Brent, you believed in me enough to support me. That is by far the most endearing thing anyone has ever done for me. I do deeply love you. You are such a good man. You broke your own heart for me. Please do not ever doubt that I know what you have done, and do not ever think I will ever forget your sacrifice. Though my daily life now consists of city sounds, subway tokens and street lights,

I dream at night of the lowing of the cattle, the rides in your dually and the stars in the open sky.

All my love,

Mary

Brent set the letter on the table. Gram reached her right hand and placed it over his left. "You did the right thing Brent. She is making *her* mark her own way. She knows she has you to thank for giving her the courage to try." She patted his hand three times and rose from her chair. "I just... just wish her 'mark' had been here with me." Gram stood beside him, placed her right hand under his chin and turned his head toward her; "You love her, you let her go... she will return to you. Maybe not soon, but she will. I know it. Have patience. Have Faith." He stood up to embrace her. "Thanks Gram. I hope so."

Gram crossed her hands over her bosom and pulled them to her heart as she watched the back of his lowered head and slumped shoulders reveal the truth of his downtrodden reaction to the letter as he slowly left the kitchen and walked toward the back door. A low sigh, closing her eyes and pausing before reopening them, with her lips held tightly together she spoke softly. "Lord... that is a fine young man. And, well, he really loves that girl Mary. I know in my heart you have a plan for them, but Lord, please don't make him wait too long. He just isn't whole without her. This may be one of those times where you will either pick him up... or teach him how to fly. Either way, I'm here to help if you need me."

The sudden slam of the door behind him knocked Brent out of his stupor. Standing at the top step with his left arm wrapped around the porch post, he lifted the letter to his heart. Gazing at the ranch before him; the afternoon sun peeking through thin cirrus clouds shone in distinct rays over the Red Pasture gate. "I have to let you go. How could you ever want to come back now? Oh Mary... you are out of my league" He walked off the porch; *'She's like the Wind'* sung by Patrick Swayze in the forefront of his thoughts.

Gram stood behind the screen door unable to keep the tears from her eyes.

"Well I suppose we ought to be heading back; Elizabeth most likely has supper started! Have you seen what you came here for? Any questions?" "You have a fine operation here. The horses are so well cared for. Now I see why Sara is so wanting to get involved the sport. Scott, I do believe you have prompted this cowboy to expand his horizons." "Prampt prompts again!" Sara glanced at Russell as Scott laughed at his own remark.

They could see Elizabeth leaning on the porch post as they approached the ranch house. "Made it back all safe and sound I see. Did Grandpa keep you in the jeep? He gets a little wild out there sometimes." "Oh… he tried a trick or two, but we kept our grip on the bars." "I'm quite certain you did Mrs. Barnes! Mrs. Barnes, would you mind helping me with something in the kitchen?" "I would be glad to! Lead the way."

"Now that the girls are doing woman things, let's you and I have us some *man* time. What do you say?" "Ahh, ok…" "Tell me straight Russell, do you think your horses are capable of fitting what I need? I mean… we both know women are over exaggerators when it comes to horses…" "Whoa there, with all due respect Scott, what your opinion is of women… is just that … your opinion. I do agree that there are those that may think more with their hearts, and for the horse's sake it is usually a good thing, and for my business, well, I actually depend on it, but what you are asking me regarding Sara… I need to tell you that you are way off. When it comes to the breeding program, the training, the ranch horses and even the rodeo stock, she is the decision maker. There isn't anyone that compares with her knowledge, skill and honesty when it comes to the horses. If she says we have what you need, then we have what you need. But you will have to decide for yourself. Why do you think we came here before you coming to see our horses? She isn't going to get involved with someone on any level until she is certain that the bloodline will be respected for what it is and if that means we take a road trip for a few days to satisfy her requirements, well then that is what we do. My wife may be small framed, but be assured, she is a formidable horsewoman."

With a startled look on his face, Scott leaned back and then slapped Russell's right shoulder. "So, what exactly do *you* do at the ranch? Seems you let your wife …" "Sir, again with all due respect, do not finish your statement. It is obvious we have different opinions as to women's roles on the ranch so I think it best that we agree to disagree for the sake of your probable further involvements with the Moore Ranch." "Yes, that's right, the *Moore* Ranch… not the Barnes… I did my homework; I know about your father. I know how you came to marry Sara." "And I know how your wife died. I don't hold that against you, I should hope you will not take your apparent infatuation with my wife and twist the information you think you have about me and allude to any wrong doing. I can assure you, you will forfeit any hopes of business with Sara if you do. So, *man to man* do we have an agreement?" "Yes, I believe we do." "Good, shall we check on supper?"

"A fine meal Elizabeth. So fine, that you just set yourself in a comfy chair in the den and chat with Sara, your grandfather and I are going to do the dishes." "We are going to what?" "We are going to show our appreciation for the hard work put in making this meal!" "This is an outrage, men don't…" "Yes, men do." Sara spoke over her shoulder at Scott as she followed Elizabeth to the den.

"Can I ask you something Elizabeth?" "Sure Mrs. Barnes…" "Do you have a ranch hand that is probably six foot three or four, pretty stout and sports a mustache?" "Not that I know of, why?" "When I was chatting with the brown mare in the pen today, I saw a man like that down by the hay barn and he just seemed out of place." "I'd say all our guys are like retired jockeys or something. There are a couple 'hands' that hire on during hay season that aren't on the payroll full time. For the most part, Grandad shies away from the big men around the horses for weight control in the carts and chariots. If you ask me, and don't tell him I said this, but him being a big man, Grandad I mean, I think he feels formidable around them and they respect him more." "Really?" "Yeah, all but Ben, Grandad thinks of him like the son he never had." "I caught that, but this other man…" "Come to think about it, Grandad just bought the Haynes ranch, maybe he hired on their men. He does that." "Yes, I heard that about him. I'm sure you are right."

To ensure that she was heard, Sara raised her voice and giggled a little as she remarked: "It's pretty quiet in the kitchen…" Elizabeth winked at Sara. "Imagine that… no broken dishes!" "I heard that!" "I love you too Grandad!"

"Seriously, this Cribbage board is like a work of art! You really hand carved all this? You have been holding out on us Gramp Moore! The detail work of the horses and cattle along the edges is fantastic!" "Took a piece from the barn you boys tossed during your fancy renovation for the base and then it just worked itself out on the rest. The horseshoe nails for the pegs was Gram's idea. Can we get back to discussing your wanting to host a Rodeo here at the ranch?" Brent set the Cribbage board back on the small table by the west window of the office.

Entering through the opened double pocket doors holding a mug of coffee in each hand, Gram smiled as she raised the mugs in the air. "A fine idea! I can hear it… years from now… cowboys and cowgirls will be hoping to qualify for the finals at the M double R SC… they will come in from states across the country…" "Slow down old woman, we are just thinking a small amateur type Rodeo for the locals to start." "Oh, well, in that case, still a good idea, better run it by Russell. Hey, I bet the Co-op could be your first sponsor!" "Thanks for the coffee dear, any news on when Sara and Russell will be home from Prampt's?" "She said on the phone last night they would be leaving by six this morning. I will hold dinner until one o'clock hoping they will be in by then. And, yes, I told Michael and Charles of the time change." "Gramp… how does she know what I am thinking?" "She's a woman.

They have a trickery about them." "I heard that!" Mary had returned to the kitchen. "They have a keen sense of hearing too… sometimes a good thing… sometimes not!" "I heard that too!" John Moore shook his head and looked over his glasses at Brent. The younger man smiled.

"Did someone say we're gonna host a rodeo? Wait 'till Mountain Man hears that!" Charles emerged rapidly through the doorway, took notice of who was sitting where and chose the high back arm chair next to the grandfather clock to settle into.

"Hears what?" "About time you showed up *Remington Steele,* we got a lot to discuss before your mom and Mr. B. get home." "I just don't see the correlation of me and Brosnan. Yeah, we both fight crime but surely you will agree I am muuuch better looking!" Michael laughed as he leaned over to kiss his grandfather's forehead and then rolled to the left side of him to the open seat on the sofa. Charles looked at Brent, "Oh Lord, he wants to be Magnum!" "Not in your dreams would I have a 'stache like that! Katy would never kiss me!"

"It seems you boys have a bit of brainstorming to do before you approach Russell with your ideas. Better have enough truth and facts to back you up. I am sure you… how do you kids say it?... 'catch my drift'?" "Ah… Gramp, maybe kids in the '60's…" "We understand Mr. Moore. I have worked hard on this and will have them interject their thoughts and opinions before presenting the venture to Mr. B." "Well, alright then. I shall leave you young aspiring minds to your business and I shall attend my bride on the side porch in wait of the travelers."

Russell stopped the truck under the arch. Reaching for Sara's left hand, he drew it to his heart. "We are home my love. We are home." They both looked above them to the Ranch emblem atop the arch. "Russell, you could not possibly know how happy I am right at this moment." "I have a pretty good idea." Each leaned to the other with eyes held captivated; Sara touched his cheek with her right hand. "Thank you for loving me." She drew him into a deep kiss.

"Let's get to the house. If we are lucky the dinner Mary prepared is still hot!"

"Look who made it just in time for vittles!" "You know it is said that timing is everything!" "Set your satchels down and pull up a chair. Supper is hot, drinks are cold and we want to hear all about your trip." "Thanks Mary, dinner smells great!" "And then after dinner the men will retire to the office for a brief meeting of the minds." "Oh?" "Sara, the boys have an idea… a good one too, I might add that they want to discuss with Russell." "Well, okay then! But now I'm starved!"

"Tell us about the Prampt Ranch…"

"Granddad…?" "Yes, Elizabeth…" "Do we have a six foot four tall ranch hand?"

Part 9
Big Day

S tanding beside Charles, Brent stood transfixed on the sight of the newly constructed rodeo grounds on the acreage to the west of the machinery shed. "There sure were times when I didn't think this day would get here." "Twelve months. Twelve months and look out there..." Charles waved his right hand chest high across their line of sight. "Just look at that Crow's Nest... top of the line P.A. system, how you swindled the deal on the timers I will never fathom; that was pretty sweet... and the stock pens... donated! Donated just for having their logo on a banner! I'm telling you, people believe in you! Tomorrow there will be rigs arriving with hopefuls of all ages excited to be at the first MDouble RSC Rodeo. You did it Brent. You really did it." "*We* did this. Me, you, Michael, Mr. Moore and Russell." "Perhaps we supplied some of the muscle, but this concept, this creation... that's all you. You took a dream and made it reality. This is *you*. Michael actually got hired on to the Brandon Police Force and me, well next week I take the final exam for the Emergency Flight Rescue so I can get with the Forest Firefighters Squad. We love the ranch life but you, you totally *live* the ranch life. Way to go, man! Way to go."

"I knew you would figure out a way to fly something!" "Sure did and what a rush! Took Marge up in the bird last Tuesday; she gets it now." Brent turned to look at Charles. "I'm happy you and Marge worked everything out. You have her, Michael has Katy, and me..." "Stop right there. You have no idea what or who is in your future. I know you miss her. It's been a whole lotta months since she left and she has not even come back for a visit. If she had, I would know. She's a city girl now. The right one will come along when she is supposed to. You just have to be patient and wait. Too much is going right for you now. Maybe you just needed to get this part situated before adding a girl to your life. Think of it this way... the girl for you is going to have to be a rock solid ranch girl. You have proven who you are so you know who she needs to be. No question on that. If she can't handle your life, then she's not right for you. On to the next…"

"You have an odd way of saying the right thing. You do realize that?"

"Absolutely… the truth…"

Both lifted right hands for a 'high five' and turned back to the arena.

"We best hit the hay, tomorrow is going to be a busy day!"

"Prampt don't know nothin' does he?" "Hell no! He's so caught up in this little Rodeo gig over there… and something about bringing a couple Paints back for a team. What a joke… Paints on a cutter course? Can't wait to see him laughed off the track!" "You're sure…" "I'm sure." "I'll call Ben."

"Elizabeth… are you about ready? We need to get on the road if we are to make it over there by sundown." "I was out in the pen with the brown mare. Did I ever tell you how much Mrs. Barnes liked that mare? I saw her out the window darn near on her knees patting the bridge of the mare's nose and could tell she was in deep conversation with her. I've been spending time with her for weeks I really think it is helping her." "What would help me would be to be rid of her! A horse here needs to work for their keep and that mare is not! I never should have agreed to take her out of that sale barn." "That's an awful thing to say Granddad. Just an awful thing to say." Holding back her emotion to her grandfather's words, Elizabeth quickened her pace to get to the truck. The disappointment she felt in her grandfather was foreign to her and she was unsure of how to handle it. "Young lady, you are old enough now to learn what is what on a ranch. Get in the truck and let's get on the road to the Moore Ranch. You still happy to be going with?" "Yes, Granddad." Noticing the four horse stock trailer hooked to the F350, Elizabeth glanced at the trailer and then at her grandfather. "Trailer?" "Yes, what if we decide to buy while we are there? We'll need a way to get them home, right!" "I suppose…" "Then let's hit the trail!" Putting the large truck in gear and moving toward the driveway, Elizabeth heard a thump and felt movement in the trailer. "Granddad?"

She had turned her head to look at him with a questioning and curious tone to her voice. "That would be the brown mare." "Oh! I love you grandad!" "I know." He turned his head, smiled and reached his hand to cover hers on the bench seat just behind the gear shifter. "What you said before..." "Is true. For me. For my ranch. But not for all ranches. I have a feeling that Mrs. Barnes will be very happy with my offering and perhaps that will soften her statutes a bit for me to sway her into business. There are many levels to the ranch business and you will soon learn there are ways to work them all."

"I think I have a pretty good teacher." He squeezed her hand.

"Big day today. The start of a new era at the Moore Ranch. Are you ready?" "Yes, sir!" "Russell giving a speech?" "Of course! You know him and his 'oratory skills'!" John Moore man hugged Brent and then slapped his back. "I hope you know how proud of you I am." "Thank you, sir."

"I heard your mom and Mark are back from their honeymoon..." "She called last night and said they will be here for the opening." "Good. Good."

Russell ascended the stairs to the Crow's Nest and then turned and looked out over the arena. "Mrs. Harrison, I thank you for doing this for us. Just didn't seem right to not have you here." "This sure is a fancy set up... that boy knew what he was doing when he put this together!" "Only the best for the M Double RSC Mrs. Harrison, only the best!" "Don't you think by now you could call me by my first name Russell?" "It's a respect thing ma'am." "Fine, sure, but after all these years... please... call me Ann." Russell turned to his left to have full eye contact with the woman seated before the microphone. "Ann." "Short for Annabel, Ann will do. Don't make me regret telling you!" "Never from me shall the name Annabel be known" "Good. So, is it time?" "I do believe it is." She pushed the green tab on the sound board. "Attention on the grounds! The Rodeo will begin in fifteen minutes. Could we please have all contestants to the main arena area and spectators to their seats for the Opening Ceremony at that time. Thank You."

"Good afternoon everyone. My name is Russell Barnes. I am the Livestock Superintendent and Steward of the MDouble RSC Rodeo. On behalf of the Moore Ranch I would like to introduce to you Brent Thomms." Brent arrived at the top of the steps precisely in time to wave to the crowd of an estimated three hundred. "As some of you may know, Brent was raised here in Brandon and has been a lifelong member of the Moore family. His dedication and commitment to the Ranchers Association combined with acute knowledge of the Rodeo Circuit birthed the foundation of the MDouble RSC. The Moore Ranch Rodeo Stock Company is proud to present to you our fine stock of bucking horses, roping steers and calves. We have brought in the mutton busting herd from the McGregor ranch for the youngsters and Bucking Bulls from the Crason Stock Company to fill the roster of exciting events. Our Rodeo is based on the promise of tradition combined with technology and the accuracy of both. Our Judge today is Mr. Martin Dewain. Will you all please stand for the National Anthem to be sung by Marge Pelton followed by the Cowboy's Prayer lead by my wife Sara."

Transfixed on the crowd, Marge took her stance at the microphone preset to her height. Brent looked over to her and smiled. "You got this. Go for it. Let them all hear your voice." She reached her hands to the black metal housing, clasping them around the shaft. Taking in a deep breath, gazed again at the crowd; "O, say can you see by the dawn's early light..." Ann Harrison was taken aback in admiration of Marge's vocal talent as the young girl sang *The Star Spangled Banner* with her heart.

As Marge retreated from the microphone, Sara moved the switch to off before exclaiming her admiration of Marge's voice. "Those lungs are going to take you places young lady... wow!" Turning back to gaze upon the bleachers filled to capacity with cheering participants, their friends and families and many local and non local townspeople supporting the Moore Ranch, Sara took a deep breath.

"My name is Sara Barnes, my late husband Samuel Moore and his parents back to their grandparents founded his ranch during a time of great change in our nation and faced the challenges of the west when few survived. It is with great pride and love that we are here today to continue the traditions of the generations in *all* our families. I will now recite *The Cowboy's Prayer* by Clem McSpadden." Clearing her throat, she needed not to read from notes; this poem she knew in her heart: "Our gracious and heavenly Father, we pause in the midst of this festive occasion, mindful of the many blessings you have bestowed upon us. As cowboys, Lord, we don't ask for any special favors. We ask only that you will let us compete in this arena as in the arena of life.

We don't ask that we never break a barrier, draw around a chute-fighting horse, or draw a steer that just won't lay. We don't even ask for all daylight runs.

We only ask that you help us to compete in life as honest as the horses we ride and in a manner as clean and pure as the wind that blows across this great land of ours.

Help us, Lord, to live our lives in such a manner that when we make that last inevitable ride to the country up there, where the grass grows lush, green and stirrup high, and the water runs cool, clear and deep, that you, as our last Judge, will tell us that our entry fees are paid. Amen."

In one voice those listening spoke "Amen"

Russell paused for the moment of silence that followed and then in a boisterous voice spoke into the microphone. "Let the Rodeo begin!" "Oh Russell... listen to them... listen to the crowd! This is just so wonderful! Look! Over to the chutes... is that Harlon?" "I think so, by God he's back and if he draws right, maybe he'll get a re ride on Wanda!

Think I'll go down and see what he's been up to." "Mind if I stay up here with you Mrs. Harrison?" "Don't mind at all, it'll be nice to have the company. Between you and me, Harlon drew Poncho not Wanda. Either way, that young man has a chance at a really good ride and score for his point earnings." "That he does. I think we agree that Harlon is a rising star in the Bronc Riding events." "You able to scribe a bit up here for me?" "Sure. Let's do this!"

"Do you have a minute Mrs. Barnes?" Sara turned toward the familiar voice of Scott Prampt. "Mr. Prampt, what a surprise! And Elizabeth!" Sara reached out to embrace the young woman and was stunned at the fervor of the returned gesture. "What brings you back to the ranch?" "I heard you were putting on a shindig over here and just had to come see for myself." Sara glanced over to Mrs. Harrison just as she spoke "Go. Sara, I'll be fine up here. You see to your friend and show him how we do things in this part of the state." "If you are sure you don't need me…" "Been doing this since those boys were in diapers, think I can manage." "Thanks. I'll be back as soon as I can." "Do you still have that Paint mare I looked at a few months back?" "Yes." "I'd like to look at her again while I'm here." "I do hate to miss the mutton busting. We can go to the horse barn after the buckaroos ride the wool." "I'll agree to that"

Sara, Elizabeth and Scott quickly descended the stairs and headed toward the chutes where the sheep were loaded and the youngsters prepared for event.

"Prampt gone?" "Yup." "How long?" "Long enough." "I still wonder if that woman saw anything when she was here." "Hell no, she was too busy bein' a horse hugger. Stupid cayuse anyway! No place around here for that sorta…" "That's enough Adam, we have our instructions and we best not let the boss think we be slackin!" "Well I sure would like to be slappin' with that bitch of his if you get my drift!" "Leave Raven alone. She has a job in all this just like we do." "Lucky son of a bitch Prampt…" "There ain't nothing lucky about getting tangled up with

Raven, believe me he will never see it coming. Todd?" "Yeah?" "You got the trucks ready?" "Yes sir. We meet at the bridge as planned." "Good. Let's get this done quickly and quietly."

"Oh, Elizabeth I am so happy you came over with your granddad this time. You can see our ranch and how it works and a Rodeo too! Have you ever thought of competing?" "Girls only ride the Barrel races, right?" "Girls can rope too, just ask..." "Just ask me, Marge Pelton! My sister and I roped together for years!" "Wow I didn't know..." "Stick with me and you will see the *real* Rodeo!" The smile on his granddaughter's face was all the elder needed for reassurance her accompanying him was timely.

Sara leaned over to Scott and nudged him in the left arm with her right shoulder. "She is in good hands with Marge, you need not worry." "I know, it's just..." "She is growing up and needs to know what is out in this big world, granddad... let her go." He was silenced by his lifetime of shielding her from what now seemed unavoidable. "She is going to grow up anyway isn't she?" "Yes, she is and the best you can do for her is know who and what her influences will be along the way."

"Thanks Granddad!" The two young women thrust into a run toward the chutes.

"Attention on the grounds! Attention on the grounds! Would the owner of a red F-350 with gold graphics hooked to a Stidham trailer please come to the concession stand... your horse has decided she would like another snow cone and Frankie wants paid for the first one before offering her another!" Mrs. Harrison's raspy voice added to the humor of her announcement.

"Ummmm, that would be me..." "You brought a horse with you?" "I *had* planned on surprising you, no... to be truthful I brought her here hoping to sway your decision on the paint mare and a match if you have one." Sara shook her head and smiled. "Did you bring the brown mare?" "That I did and I have been corrected several times by my granddaughter that the proper term for her color is chocolate." "And she is eating snow cones..." "That she is." "Didn't tie her too good, did ya?" Sara was so excited at the thought that the mare was at the ranch she could not help herself the continued teasing of Scott Prampt. "Nope, suppose not. Best go pay the bar bill on the lassie." Stepping in front of Scott, Sara turned slightly to look back at him. "This one is on the house!"

Their arrival was met with cheers and laughter from the crowd that had gathered to see the horse licking the snow cone held by the Mutton Busting Champion six year old Timmy Alden.
"Hey there young man, I sure do thank you for the help in seein' to my mare's well being! That is mighty 'cowboy' of you." "No problem mister, I mean sir. She was carryin' on something awful in the trailer and then all the sudden the door opened and there she stood. Just looking at me. Why, I didn't know what to do acuz weren't no one around. I looked for a rope... thought maybe she'd been tied to a knot as my pa used to say but I seen that she wasn't..." The young boy had the full attention of his audience as he relayed his tale. Timmy could see the fixation so he decided he would keep it as long as he could. Smiling as he spoke, he continued. So, I pulled a string from a hay bale and tied a knot all myself!" He waited for the response of the onlookers. Pleased with the cheers and applause he walked to the horse, put his hand out and she lowered her head for him to reach her. "Awwwwww" "That's just so darling!" "What a kind mare." "Timmy, it seems she likes you!" Sara placed her right hand on the left shoulder of the boy, glanced toward her right then back to Timmy; "It does appear that way Joan now doesn't it!" The beam of delight on the young boy's face radiated over the crowd.

"Young man, give the man his horse and stop this foolishness." The elated frame of the child slumped to submission at the harsh sound of his mother's voice. "Yes, ma'am." While looking at the ground he handed the string to Scott and walked over to his mother and stood behind her.

As they walked away, he turned around and silently said good bye to the horse that had briefly taken him from his despair and he was happy.

"Sara, what was that all about?" "We've been watching the family pretty close. Peg, Timmy's mom has had a really hard time dealing with her husband Roy's death last year. He was hunting over in Oregon and was shot by a member of his hunting party. It was awful. Timmy's older sister Royann has had to take up the slack on the ranch." "Didn't I hear a Roy something announced earlier?" "Yes, that was Royann, she took the Barrel Racing trophy buckle today. Great little rider with a lot of guts. Good thing too because her mother forbid her to ride today and well, we see how that went. Perhaps that is the background to Peg's foul mood taken out on poor little Timmy."

"So, where's this Frankie fellow? It seems I owe him an apology and a…" "No apology and Mrs. Barnes here says the Rodeo will take care of it. Just never saw a horse likin' grape snow cones… now that is a first!" "You're Frankie?" "That is correct, short for Francine and am I to assume then you are the owner of this gentle soul?" Interjecting Sara stated, "Perhaps not for long though."

"Suppose I could see that Paint mare?" "I have others you may be interested in as well. You do know that Cotton is a daughter of my Jazzy and will be hard to let go of, lucky for you Jazzy is in foal again. There is a gelding out there… he's a tad bit smaller but every bit as fast as Cotton and believe it or not they are marked quite similarly." "You have perked my interest Sara! Lead on."

The trio of man, woman and horse left the rodeo grounds towards the private barn area of the ranch.

"The MdoubleRSC would like to thank all participants and sponsors for a fine turn out at our debut Rodeo! Please come back and join us in October when we will be hosting the Brandon Fair Round up Rodeo. Yes, folks the Moore Ranch has been selected for this year's jamboree. We look forward to seeing you here. Would the contestants from today's events please gather in the center pen for a group photo. Thank you all and safe travels home!" Mrs. Harrison turned the microphone off and placed it in the black wooden case. "Well, Russell, it's official… your first Rodeo was a success and no injuries. Congratulations. You have certainly become an important member of our community and I for one would like to tell you that I am proud of the man you have become despite the cards you were dealt as a youngster." Thank you, Ann. Coming from you that means a great deal. I know you had your doubts." "That was a long time ago Russell. A long time ago. Shall we see if there is anything left in the concession stand?" "After you… be careful on the steps."

"Sara, I am pleased with the two you have paired for me. I thank you again for the opportunity to campaign your Cotton mare and what is the gelding's name?" "His name is Captain's Crown… got that from the pattern of his 'medicine hat' looking more like a crown. When he was a colt it really stood out." "Cotton and Crown… that will be easy on the entry forms. I should probably check on Elizabeth as it is getting late and we have a long drive." "You are more than welcome to stay at the ranch tonight and head out in the morning if you would like." "Your kindness is much appreciated. I will call home and let them know, I have a phone in the truck. "A phone in your truck?" "Yes, some newfangled fancy thing I hope I can figure out how to use it." "That's a new one on me… anyway last I saw the girls they were over by the chutes. I'm going to get the Rocky Mountain mare settled in and take a few minutes with Cotton. See you at the house later. Glad you are going to stay."

Walking in the direction of the main arena Scott was unaware of the woman stealthily approaching his right side from behind.

"I'm sorry, I couldn't help overhearing that you have a phone in your truck, I know how they work if you need some help." Scott turned his head and with great pleasure smiled at the woman standing with him. "Hello, my name is Scott Prampt and you are?" "My friends call me Raven"

Brent opened the carriage doors of the horse barn; "Mrs. Barnes? Are you in here?" "Sure am! Come see the new addition to the ranch!" "I heard there was some horse dealin' going on over here." He stood in the doorway of the last stall on the right. "Wow... never quite seen that color before... not a liver chestnut, not a brown... just what is that color and with an almost flaxen mane and a tad bit in the tail..." "She is a Rocky Mountain by breed and her color is chocolate." "This the horse you saw at Prampt's place when you were over there isn't it?" "Yes. She's just the sweetest... just look at her kind eye. She's had a bit of a rough go but from here on she's going to be just fine. I am going to have to learn about gaited horses..." "Gaited? Ah... explain please" Brent moved his arms and legs trying to simulate the right legs together and then left legs together description. Sara smiled at the humorous attempt to interpret her explanation.

"Is there anybody in here? Please! I'm looking for my cousin Timmy... I was told he might be here with a brown mare!" Sara and Brent simultaneously turned to see the person behind them distraughtly asking in an unfamiliar voice. As Sara turned, she could see the expression on Brent's face as he took in his first sight of Becky Burnell. To herself she spoke, "Oh boy... who is this girl that has Brent so mesmerized?"

"Forgive me my manners, are you Mrs. Barnes? My name is Becky. Becky Burnell. Timmy is my cousin..." She had already turned her attention to Brent as he held out his hand to her and her speech was halted. "Hello, Becky. Becky Burnell. My name is Brent Thomms, and yes this is Sara Barnes. You say you are looking for your cousin Timmy?" Sheepishly she answered "Yes." "Then I feel it is my duty as management of the Rodeo to assist you in your quest. That is if you would be so kind as to let me, that is."

Sara shook her head, smiled and turned back to the mare. Running her left hand along the underside of the muscular neck, Sara grinned as she tipped her head toward the mare's face and leaned in close to the horse. "Think he's got this?" Snort. "Yup, me too." Pulling the 'Bank

Robber's knot' off the tie ring, Sara then removed the halter and closed the stall door.

"Mrs. B...." "Go... If I see him, I will tell him you are looking for him. And Brent..." "Yes?" "Be sure to give our new friend here the grand tour of the ranch. I'm sure Gram has something special in the kitchen for after the Rodeo." Standing behind Becky, he was about to place his right arm behind her back hoping to rest his hand on her waist, instead he turned back to Sara and mouthed; "Thank you." He then crossed his arms over his chest, smiled "Yes!" as he exited the door in pursuit of Becky. Reaching her with his arm extended, he gently placed his hand on her back, "Let's find your cousin." Her smile to him rendered him momentarily speechless.

Sara turned back to the stall at the low nicker of the mare. "And now for you my new friend, it seems a naming is of the essence. I'll give this some thought. Right now, the other horses are at the gate patiently waiting to come in for the night and meet you on their way to their stalls."

Having completed the evening barn routine Sara returned to the entry booth to help in the final tallies of the entries. Russell sipped a cup of coffee as he raised his head to greet her. "We did good for a debut. We did good. I'm pleased." Sara looked out onto the grounds with satisfaction.

"Russell, who is that man over there? He looks familiar..." Placing his right arm behind her, he stood beside her as he answered. "He and a buddy were here chasing the cowgirls and well, let's just say they did not have the luck our boys had a few years back!" "We haven't had the dance yet; their luck may change!" "Oh Mrs. Barnes you are forever the romantic aren't you!?" "That I am and speaking of that, have you seen Brent?" "Not in a while, do you need me to page him?" "Oh no.... do not do that! He'd never forgive us!" "What are you talking about Sara?" "Becky Burnell" "Becky who?" "Walk with me back to the house, I'll tell you all about it."

"Did you get them in that rattle trap trailer?" "Yeah, but it was close, he came back around. Good thing Raven was on point, she got him all kinds of flustered over a car phone or something." "So you hid 'em good?" "Yeah. Hope he don't find 'em before the cutter race or we will be 'winging it' getting him trapped in public." "Leave that to me." "I'm cool with that!"

Part 10
Skylines and Drivelines

Halting his stride to stand centered in the doorway, Brent peered into the office of the ranch house. Russell looked up from the ledger when he heard the labored sigh, placed the pencil down and closed the book. "Well... out with it! There is something heavy on your mind. Might just as well get it off your chest." Brent quickly crossed the room and sat in the leather chair beside the large desk. "Sir, I think I want to go to New York to see Mary." Taken aback by Brent's proclamation Russell paused before engaging in the conversation.

"New York, huh? This wouldn't have anything to do with Becky now would it?"

"I suppose a bit, yes. It's just... well... I feel like it is wrong of me to think about another woman when I'm still in love with Mary." Russell felt as well as heard the anguish and frustration in Brent's tone. "Young man, please, stop right there. You torture yourself for naught. Mary has been gone a long time and, in that time, she has not once come back to visit nor has she given you cause to think she will return let alone to stay. She is your first love. I get that. I really do, but not always is the first one the one that carries you. Sometimes it is..." "Mr. B., I don't mean to interrupt you, but I know I need to do this. I need to know face to face. If I don't do this, then I cannot move on." "It seems to me you had your mind made up before you came in here." "Yes, sir I did. I leave the day after tomorrow." Russell placed his right hand on Brent's left shoulder, "Do you need a ride to the airport? I would be happy to take you." "That would be great, thank you. My flight leaves at noon." "With the time changes, hmmm... you'll be getting in quite late, that's a big airport... and the return time?" "Friday at four p.m." "What about once you get there?" "Already have that taken care of Mr. B. Scott Prampt used his connections and set me up with rides and hotels

243

for while I'm there." "I had no idea he had 'connections' in New York." "To tell you the truth I had overheard him talking at the Rodeo when he bought Cotton and Crown to a couple fellas about business in New York so I called him for suggestions. He sure surprised me when two days later he called back with all the information." "That man is just full of surprises, isn't he?" Russell's tone was not un noticed by Brent.

"We'll be back in a couple days, Mara. We have to be, need to get Brent from the airport! Thank goodness the weather is not calling for snow storms while he is in New York! Enjoy a couple days off." Sara wrapped her arms around the mare's neck as Mara pulled her close with her head.

"You sure have bonded with her..." "Oh! I didn't hear you come in the barn." "Russell is waiting for you at the truck. Here... I packed plenty of goodies for your trip." Mary handed the familiar traveling satchel to Sara. "I do like watching you with the horses. It brings a peace to me." "Thank you, Mary. That is kind of you to say. You know, I named her Mara because it is a variant of Mary and you are the heart of my life. She has the kindness about her and, well... I just knew it to be the right name for her." "Oh, Sara... how I do love you. I hope you have a great trip and don't worry about the ranch. Just have fun watching Cotton and Crown in their first Cutter Race!"

"Marrrrrryyyy... this does not have the weight of your usual cookies and muffins..." "Nope! The doctor says we need to eat more fruits and vegetables, then he said something about cholesterol and lost me but I heeded his advice and you have 2 whole wheat muffins and lots of carrot and celery sticks." "I think Russell would rather you had packed pig's knuckles and sauerkraut!" Both women laughed at the reference to their answer when the boys were young and would insist on knowing what was for supper even early in the day. "Not to fret my dear, there are some of those 'fun size' chocolate bars he likes... and yes, I can see by your face you question me, yes I broke into the Christmas candy stash you thought you hid." "Mary Moore, I love you!" "I love you too, now skedaddle on out to that truck and get going."

Sara wrapped her arms around Mary and as she pulled her close, she was taken aback at the definition of her upper spine and the curvature in her posture that she had not felt before. "Mary... are you okay?" "Yes dear, why?" "You, your, I mean, oh nothing... thanks for the goodies... see you the day after tomorrow and no pigs knuckles for supper okay?" "Okay, have a great time!"

Russell held the truck door open awaiting her arrival. Bending at the waist he offered her his hand, "My Lady..." "Why thank you kind Sir." Russell retrieved the satchel and placed it on the back seat as Sara took her spot in the middle of the bench. As Russell closed the passenger side door Sara leaned to the driver's door and opened it from the inside. While he walked around the front of the truck, she glanced back to Mary standing on the porch. She didn't want Russell to know of her concern so to herself she murmured "All this talk about doctors... Mary Moore, you are keeping something from me and I am going to find out what when I get home!"

Mary leaned on the rail post as the truck backed in the turnaround before heading out the driveway. "Oh, Sara I won't be able to hide this from you much longer."

Brent stood before the impressively large glass doors of the office building situated on the corners of two bustling New York City streets. Oblivious to the commotion of rushing people and traffic, standing mesmerized he took in a deep breath as he reached for the vertical door handle.

"May I help you sir?" Startled out of his trance, Brent looked at the man before him. "I, ahh..." "First time in New York I surmise?" The man's appraisal of him being clearly defined in his tone of voice. "Yes." "My name is Joseph, I am the doorman at The D J Agency. I would be glad to assist you in achieving your destination within the structure." Widening his eyes and lifting his eyebrows, Brent turned to the uniformed man; "Whoa… those are some fancy words to say you can help me find someone." "To whom is it that you seek?"

His inward voice questioned 'Who I seek? Are you kidding me? I can play along I guess.'

"I *seek* Mary Shanks." "Ahhh, Miss Shanks, she is located on the sixth floor. Through the lobby to the second elevator—elevator B—to the sixth floor. Straight out the elevator to the first hall on the right, her office is the third door on the left. Hettie, the floor receptionist will be happy to assist you. Good day, sir." Without change of facial expression, Joseph extended his right arm across the heavy glass of the door and with the length of his arm pulled the door toward him and signaled for Brent to enter the building.

Brent noticed the numerous photographs displayed on the lobby walls. Though he knew himself to be an outlander and unfamiliar with the mores of the city, and despite the feeling he had that to alter from his directed route to the elevator would be met with disapproval, he fulfilled his need to explore the stained wood expanse of the wall to his right and search the descriptions to see if there was one credited to Mary. *The Lower Gorge of the Great Genesee.* 'Photograph of the Genesee River, Rochester New York'. Brent set back on the heels of his boots. "Wow! Look at that! You did say in your letter you were excited to visit Rochester!" Brent was about to touch her name plate with his right fingertips when he heard foot steps behind him.

"Young man, excuse me, do you need assistance?" "No, I just wanted to see if she had a picture on your wall." 'These *photographs* are all representatives of our staff and their accomplishments. Who is it that you are here to see?" "Not to worry, Joe the doorman got me directions. I've got this." "See that you do." The staunch man retreated behind a half wall and descended a staircase. A slow pace to the elevator allowed Brent time to look at the other photographs neatly displayed on the stark white wall on the left side of the lobby as he approached the elevator area. "I'm not liking their idea of décor at all… does not make sense to me!"

Standing in front of elevator B he could see by the number display above the doors that the car was making its way downward. Just to be certain it was called to the ground floor Brent pushed the 'up' arrow. With each stop on the upper level floors, he could hear the turbulent conversations and vocal tones of hurried and inconsiderate passengers. Before the doors had fully opened to the ground floor, Brent was pushed aside by the rush of men and women oblivious to his presence in waiting. He held his hand on the doors to prevent them from closing in order for him to have time to get in. As the elevator door closed, Brent shook his head. "Holy shit, these people need to relax!"

When he reached the sixth floor the doors opened to a frenzy of men and women hurrying from room to room before him.

"Are you Hettie?" "Why, yes I am Cowboy! How can I help you?" "I'm looking for Mary Shanks"

A young man abruptly stopped when Brent mentioned Mary. "I am her assistant, follow me." Hettie motioned for Brent to follow. "If you don't catch up you will lose him!"

"Hi, my name is Brent." "Hi. I'm Calvin. Miss Shanks will be furious if I'm not there with her diet cola when she comes out of her meeting. Hurry up… "

Mary emerged from behind a large wooden door laughing with a co-worker and looking at documents still in her hand. Taken aback at her short haircut and curt demeanor, Brent gasped when her right arm flung out to her side in an assuming position; Calvin held out the soda for her to retrieve as she passed him. Calvin then held his right arm against Brent's chest holding him back from leaning in. "Calvin… I…" "No… first rule around here… never interrupt them when they are in conversation. Mary never took her attention away from the conversation she was heavily engrossed in; she did not know Brent was there.

"That's Mike. Mike Hendon, her project manager..." Calvin abruptly stopped mid sentence and turned to Brent. "Oh, my, you... you are the cowboy she spoke of when she first got here aren't you?" Unable to speak, Brent tipped his head. "Oh boy, oh boy... this is not good, not good at all... my God, I'm living a Hallmark moment here... Brent, buddy, oh man, look at her... she is in her element. She is good. Really good. Actually, she just got another promotion. Mr. Jones has big plans for her which means me too! You coming here, well... can't you see now... you are her past... her future is here, in New York. She's... she's not a cowgirl anymore."

As he wiped a tear from his cheek he spoke softly, "No, she is not." Brent lowered his head, turned slowly and walked to the elevator.

Calvin stopped at Hettie's desk as Brent turned in the elevator to face them. The door closed. Placing his left hand on the woman's shoulder, Calvin sighed.

"You okay Calvin?"

"I've never actually watched a heart break before."

"Attention on the grounds! The first race will begin in thirty minutes."

"That's our cue! Oh, Russell... this is so exciting! I wonder if Elizabeth is here?" "I wouldn't miss a chance to see you!" Sara spun around at the familiar voice. "I'm so glad you are here... where's my hug?" "Okay, okay, you two, enough. Elizabeth, are you needed with the horses or might you be able to sit with us?" "Sit? Oh no, there is no sitting at this track. Folks stand along the fence to watch. I came to get you guys to have you join us down by the lineup." "Really? Oh, wow, Russell did you hear that? We get to be right in the real action!" "Granddad wouldn't have it any other way. Mrs. Barnes, that team you sold him is incredible. When word got out he had a team of Paints the snarky remarks began to fly. Granddad brushed them all off. He only trained when no one was around so today he can show all the naysayers how foolish they have been. He said he is going make sure that today's race is one for the books and that no one will forget it." "I knew Cotton and Crown were a good pair!"

"Not just a good pair; they are a great pair!" The ebullient voice of Scott Prampt was intentionally raised for the benefit of those gathering in the area that had previously offered snide remarks regarding the Paint horses. Russell offered his hand to Scott as he approached. Scott heartily accepted and then placed his left hand on Russell's upper right arm. "These two are going to make history today, I just know it! Follow me, I want you to meet the driver, his name is Bob McClew. Good man. Been with me nearly a year now. Solid driver. Best of all, he really likes the horses and they like him."

Sara joined the conversation, "Do you know the team they are running against?" Russell added "I hope not..." Scott stopped him from completing his question. "No, Sanderson isn't even here. Lot of talk about that, he'd been talking big about the races today and then didn't even show up! To our good fortune we pulled a good draw. Henry Ross is driving the team from the Fork Valley Ranch. His team will spark the rivalry from the first stride. We need to hurry so you can see Cotton and Crown before they run."

"Mrs. Barnes?" "Katy?" Simultaneously they wrapped arms around the other. Sara was the first to pull back. "My goodness, look at you! You are here! Why are you here? I mean it is so good to see you, I had no idea..." "I am here on a school project. You know I am specializing in limb injuries and the racing commission has asked the students in my major to participate in a study of the long-term effects racing on the snow has regarding leg joint and muscle injuries and concussion to hoof analysis." "Oh...kay....." Russell thought it best to interject so as to create a reason to get to the horses. "You are here for school, great.

It is great to see you, where is my hug? I think someone should do a study on the human factor of standing in the cold to participate! Now, let's get to the horses… they race soon."

With Katy in the middle, the trio walked with arms behind and holding the others toward the line-up area. "Don't worry Mrs. B, I'm still working on the respiratory team. We are making headway on deep airway issues and have hopes to get a transportable Bronchoscope prototyped for the equine industry." "There is no doubt in my mind you are devoted to your studies. I hope you know how proud of you we all are." "Thanks, it's good to hear once in a while, the hours are overwhelming and the physical toll is excruciating at times but I know it is all worth it and I know this is what I want to do… and, of course… marry Michael!" Sara and Russell tightened their hold on Katy as they approached the line-up area.

"Well?" "Don't worry. I got this. Whoo doggie! Look at that pretty little filly over there with Prampt, now there's a bucking I could go for!" That's his granddaughter stupid…" "No, the other one…" The heavy slap on his back halted his sentence. "What'd you do that for?" "Focus lover boy. Girls like that will only cause trouble. Besides, I thought you had your heart set on Raven." "That bitch has actually started taking to that old geezer, can you just imagine… wanting an old guy like that when yours truly is right here waiting on her?" "You didn't seriously just ask that question." Slap! "We have instructions and we'd best get to it."

"I thought they pulled the cutter with runners[10]?" Russell asked abruptly while they watched the precision of the crew as they hitched Cotton and Crown to a chariot. Scott leaned to him to answer his question. "Not enough snow yet so we run on the dirt track with the chariots. Speeds

---

10 A 'Cutter' is the driver carrier. In the snow the Cutters have runners similar to wide skis to slide over the snow. Wheeled cutters are used when not racing on the snow. The driver stands behind a shield thus resembling a chariot.

are faster and the horses have better footing." "Just who came up with the idea of racing in the snow and the cold anyway? Isn't it hard on the horses as well as the humans? Doesn't the track pack down to ice after a couple heats? How do you maintain control of the cutters on that?" "Don't have time to answer all your questions... here it is in a nutshell... remember Ben Hur... yeah, the big chariot scene... this racing has been going on for centuries. Here in Wyoming early last century racing wagons with the work horses was a way to pass the time in the long winters. Pretty soon the light horses were brought to town for faster races. By mid century the All-American Cutter Racing Association was formed and the sport has continued growing ever since. Tradition keeps it in the winter but there are times when conditions are such that the chariots are used instead of the cutters with runners. Like today..." "Got it, thanks."

"They look great Scott!" Cotton nickered when Sara spoke. "Hey girl! Looking all fancy in your racing gear. You too, Crown!" Sara traced the black threaded Prampt brand across the forehead on the mare's red silk blinder hood. "The padding of the collars... it is like it molds right to their shoulders. And what technique in the stich work. Scott, these are really impressive!" "Would you believe me if I told you they are the work of one Miss Elizabeth Martin?" Sara turned quickly to insure Elizabeth could see her delight. "You have a talent young lady, a real talent!" Sara followed the matching color patterned hames through the girth rings to the chariot. "My goodness even the girth and the lines match[11]. This is serious business!" "That it is and no finer a turn out than from the Prampt Ranch! Our team of Paint horses in their finery will for sure make the cover of the Association Newsletter this year!"

Running her hand down the muscular haunch of the mare she dearly loved, Sara held her arm out for Russell. Abiding her wish, he approached her. "She was such a strong willed filly. Remember the ride

---

11   The collar of the harness is custom fitted to the neck set of the horse. The hames are wooden or metal strips along each side of the animal(s)the girth around the belly behind the front leg holds the surcingle with the rings that hold the hames. The lines are the length of leather held by the driver that extend to the bridle of the horse(s). Blinders cover the eyes at an angle to inhibit distractions from the side vision.

with Manny to the ridge? Look at her now! She is all grown up and a race horse! A Cutter Race horse!" Sara turned back to the mare. "I am so very proud of you. Both of you! Run like the wind and make Jazzy and Captain proud!" She had a hand placed on each of the horse's foreheads. Kissing first Cotton's muzzle and then Crown's in a voice for only the horses to hear; "Lord, please be with these horses and all the horses here today. And be with Bob and the other drivers... may the races be run safely and fairly and be their celebration of the sport and of you, our Lord God. Amen"

"It is time to start making our way to the gates. Why don't you folks go on up the fence a bit so you can see the power out of the gates and will have a better view at the finish line. We'll see you in the winner's area. And Sara, thanks for the prayer." Scott motioned to an open area on the fence line for them to stand. "Mrs. B., I'm going to head over to the holding area. I see a couple of my class mates over there and we need to detail our findings." "See you later?" "You bet!"

"Excuse me sir... my name is Gary Black. I'm with the newspaper, may I take a photograph of your team before you race?" "Absolutely young man, make sure my granddaughter gets in the photo with me!" Scott stood proud next to Elizabeth at the horses' heads. Bob McClew was positioned in the chariot holding the reins.

Henry Ross positioned his team at the start line. "That is a fine turn out Mr. Prampt! A fine turnout. They are sure an unusual sight for a cutter race, but wow are they ever something!"

"Thank you, Henry... now the two of you run a good race!" Shaking the hands of both drivers, he and Elizabeth then walked between the teams to depart from the track. "Hey! Henry!" "Yes Bob?" "Beth wanted me to invite you to dinner Friday..." "Sounds great! I do miss good home cooking!" "You know my Beth..." "This isn't a setup is it? And, yes, I know your Beth!" "Not that I am aware, but I suppose you ought to be ready just in case!" The men laughed as they positioned their teams at the starting gate entrance.

"Shall we take our spot on the fence?" "Snow fence, would never have guessed the use of snow fence for the barrier between spectators and the teams. This is looking a bit worn and weathered. Sara, if we are going to participate in this, and if Scott races at this facility, I think we ought to look into a more suitable type of fencing for here. What do you think?" "I think that is a wonderful idea and a great way to show our support. We just have to make sure we provide properly sanctioned materials. These associations have rules and regulations just like our Rodeos have." "Point well made. I will do some research and get with Scott before I make any decisions."

Russell leaned in to Sara; "Isn't that the guy you saw at our Rodeo over there hovering around Katy?" "Yes, I do think it is and that tall man, he could be the ranch hand at Prampts I saw when we were there. I don't like the way he is looking at Katy." "Katy can handle herself, this *is* Katy..." "You are right... but the tall man, I didn't see him at the Rodeo and Elizabeth said they didn't have a tall ranch hand."

"Oh Shit!"

"What?"

"*Both* teams are wearing red and black!"

"Ah... you...didn't?

"I ... oh shit!"

"They're bringing the starting gate! I wish the Fork Valley team was on the far side so I could see Cotton and Crown better." Sara turned her attention back to the track. "This track is only set up for two teams racing. I read some tracks race three teams. The gates are sure different than at the Thoroughbred track." The expertise of each driver secured the teams in the stalls of the gate. With a sudden burst the gates opened and the two teams charged through to the open raceway. Side by side they pulled forward. "Scott was right, they are well matched speed wise." "Oh, Russell, look at them… It's like Cotton and Crown are just, they are in their glory! Look at them use their haunches! The other team is right there… wow, you can see the competition in all the horses! This is so exciting!" Russell caught a glimpse of the right hame splitting on the Fork Valley team's harness. "Look out! Sara…" Russell urgently pulled her back from the fence.

The Fork Valley team thrust forward; rapidly approaching them, without warning the grey gelding bolted sideways to the left as the broken hame pierced his right side. Blood from the wound streamed across the ribcage of the frightened horse. The grunt of pain as he thrust himself into the air caused the black gelding to pull back putting too great a pressure on the breast bar and it snapped in two. The horses were no longer side by side; Henry Ross had lost all hope of bringing them back under control. Riders and men on foot were desperately in pursuit of the panicked horses. Having been in the lead position if the race, Bob McClew began reining in Cotton and Crown in an effort to give rescue riders room to regain control of the runaways. He did not know the hame was lodged in the ribcage of the right horse. Crying out their fears, spectators retreated from the fence line in avoidance of the blood splatter.

A final act of desperation to rid himself of the harness, the grey gelding roared a whiney of pain and crashed through the black gelding and into Cotton and Crown. The impact ejected both drivers and intertwined the lines of the harnesses.

Five men on horseback formed a wall stopping the horses. Katy ran out to Cotton and Crown for assessment while the others of her class attended the Fork Valley team while waiting for the equine ambulance. Two stewards of the race diligently tried to untangle the lines and chariots while three sheriff deputies held the crowd in order to allow the Track Veterinarian access to the horses.

Pushing her way through the crowd now reassembled tightly to the fence, Elizabeth ran to Sara and Russell. "Come with me, Granddad needs you. I need you... please!" The trio turned back through the horde of anxious bystanders to get to the team and help Scott.

"The horses..." "They are fine. Cotton has a laceration on her shoulder from the impact and several small abrasions as she took the direct hit, Crown must have jerked pretty hard too, he got his left leg outside the trace[12] and it is heavily bruised. No broken skin luckily, still, an x-ray of the hock will have to be done to rule out damage to the joint. A few stiches for Cotton. They are lucky. The Fork Valley team did not fare as well. The grey has been sedated and transported to the Clinic. I really hope he makes it. The black, oh man, he will most likely lose his right eye; when the grey ran into him, the blinder was crushed against his head and consequently severed the eye." Katy lowered her eyes and sighed. "What a horrible accident."

Scott shook his head, "I for one am very glad that you are here Katy, I am sure this is not what you had in mind, but will be a definite add to your research." Sara placed her left hand on Scott's shoulder. "Scott, this was an accident. All precautions are taken to prevent this from happening. Yes, horses have their own mind, but this, what happened here, is such a rarity. The horses will heal and be back racing in no time." "Oh, my dear Sara, you are right, but it goes beyond 'the next race'... it's..."

"Your version of 'Cowboy Code'" Russell spoke softly. The men met eyes, sharing an unspoken understanding between them.

Bob McClew opened his eyes. He was face down on the track looking toward the mountains on the east side. Acute pain deep in his left side made it hard for him to breathe. Spitting dirt out of his mouth he rose slowly to his knees and then one leg at a time tried to stand.

---

12   The trace in a harness is the strap or chain that transfers the pull of the horse(s) from the hames to the vehicle

Pausing to catch his breath in his ineffectual attempt to stand upright, with his hands on his thighs and still bent at the waist, he quickly wiped dirt from his eyes with his left hand, turned his head toward the pandemonium and looked on the track.

Henry Ross lay motionless.

"Noooooooo!"

The outcry drew the attention of the crowd from the horses to the drivers.

Unable to fully stand upright, Bob did as best he could to reach Henry. Each step a painful reminder of his injuries. His left leg dragged the ground as he pulled closer to Henry. A few weeks ago, he did not know Henry, and now this… when he stood next to the fallen man, Bob dropped to his knees; absent of thought to his own injuries, next to his friend and then laid across his body and wept.

"Over here! Brent!" The familiar voice found him through the sea of strangers. "Oh Mom! Am I ever glad to see you! I was expecting Mr. Barnes." "I asked if I could be the one to get you, basically for selfish motherly reasons, but as it turns out, there were complications at the Cutter Race. I'll explain later." The flow of passengers split around the mother and son as they embraced in the arrival gate area. She could feel his heartbeat. Pulling back, she placed her right hand over his heart. "What do you want to do?" "I want to go home with you. I can't face the ranch right now, I just can't." "Okay."

Trying to keep up with Brent, Linda felt a tightness in her chest; her heart ached for her son as he briskly walked slightly ahead of her through the main terminal toward the parking lot.

To herself she spoke "Oh my son, you went to New York for resolution… what happened? You haven't even mentioned her name…" "I'm sorry mom." "Me too. I didn't realize you would hear me." Brent slowed his pace and put his left arm over his mother's shoulders to assist her through the turn-style and then opened the large glass door for her. "Ahhh fresh air!" "Hope you don't mind a walk… I sure as heck wasn't going to park your baby where she might get scratched! Try to find row H3."

"My truck! I love my truck! You just cannot imagine the horrors of that city! I gave up trying to get cabs anywhere. I walked… but not far. Why those people think raw fish is a topping for like everything is beyond me! And order a cup of black coffee… you would think I was from another planet. Guess my hat and boots gave that one away… And oh, the night I ordered beef ribs, the waiter looked at me like I had two heads, so me being me said… those two heads you are looking at are actually connected to the horns on the bull I hope the ribs are from… yeah, I was escorted out of the restaurant. I found a hot dog guy on the street. Nasty dog but nice guy and we had a laugh at each other's accents. I'm telling you I never once saw the moon because the buildings were too tall and the lights are so bright that I couldn't see the stars. Nope, the city life is not for me! I want the open range and a mountain or two within view as the moon rises and the stars shine! Damn it's good to be home!"

She was glad he had started to relax.

"You want to talk about her?"

"Not yet."

"Okay."

"Is the newspaper here yet?" "Well, good morning to you too!" Placing a steaming cup of coffee on the table at John's right hand, he reached to hers, "I am sorry my love…" "You are forgiven, now why the urgency for today's edition?" "It seems that driver, Henry Ross, I heard he was an undercover big wig agent working a case." Mary sat in the chair next to John. "A what?" "An agent working a case and now he is dead. This is big." "Oh, my… whatever could an agent have to do with a Cutter race?" "Is there a cup of that for me? Good morning Mary, John… Sara is still sleeping, we got in late last night." Russell leaned over to kiss Mary on the cheek. Through a muffled chortle Mary spoke to Russell. "Your call was garbled; will you tell us what really happened before we read what the reporters think they know?"

"Better put on another pot of coffee!"

Russell sat in the captain's chair opposite of John. "Okay, but you are truly going to be shocked." Russell took a sip of his coffee as Mary and John exchanged a hurried look of concern.

"Yes, Henry Ross is, I mean was, oh man…" He looked down at his coffee mug and sighed. "…an undercover agent for the government. He was working a gun smuggling case…" "Gun smuggling?" "Let him talk Mary…" Looking at Mary, Russell continued. "I can only tell you what I overheard the Deputies saying when we were on the track. But the crazy thing is that they took Scott Prampt into custody due to finding stolen guns hidden in his horse trailer." "What!!?" "Yes, John, it appears he may have been involved. If you ask me, I don't believe it. I am not a true fan of the man, but smuggling… no. I just do not see that." "Me either…" "Worst part was they cuffed him right there on the track. Good thing Ben Zander was there, Scott had told me that Ben hadn't planned on attending the race but at the last minute decided to. Scott is fortunate to have a man he trusts to look over his ranch while all this gets sorted out." "How did Sara take to all this?" "Mary, this might be a good time to tell you that we brought Elizabeth home with us last night. She is really upset and Sara wanted to…" "Say no more, that young lady is always welcome here!"

Part 11
Fitting In and Working Out

Walking past the receptions desk of the Police Station, Michael placed his right hand on the hallway door to open it. He walked briskly to the far end in pursuit of the familiar voices.

"Well, Rookie… are we supposed to call you *McCloud* now?" Michael stood in the breakroom doorway smiling at the men before him. Men he had looked up to and admired for many years. Kent Harrison, now Chief Harrison; Nick Border the department's lead Detective and Matt Brewer, developer and head of the new Forensics Lab. His taut stance interrupted when Bruce Netty slapped his back while passing him on his way to take the fourth chair at the table. "Nice to see you *'Rookie'*, sure am glad it's you now!" Michael straightened his back and took in a deep breath; "Proud to be, Proud to be."

"Grab a chair, we have work to do."

Raising his hand, Bruce spoke as Michael spun a chair from the wall to the table. "Just how is it that the Brandon PD is involved with the smuggling situation? Aren't we a bit out of jurisdiction?"

Kent bit his lower lip and looked at Michael. "This is going to be hard for you and I have my doubts as to whether or not to have you assigned to the case, but… here goes…" Kent took in a long breath, stood and then slowly walked around the table. As he did so he tapped the left shoulder of each man and slowly began the briefing that in his heart he knew would be difficult for each of his men to hear and more difficult for them to separate home, family, friends and the job. "Men, we are involved because Prampt has had dealings with the Moore Ranch and had connections with Brent Thomms; regarding communication with Thomms directly just prior to his trip to New York City …" He shook his head and then looked at Michael. "… And Katy McGregor was seen talking with…"

The force of Michael's push from the table as he stood upset the paperwork, pens were thrown to the floor and three cans of soda spilled.

"And *THAT*… L.E.O. Moore, is why I have concerns! Sit your ass down or you *will* be removed from this case! You are dangerously infringing on being too closely tied anyway so *do not* give me just cause to put you back on patrol! Do I need to repeat myself?" "No, Sir." "Good. Sit." Nick placed his right hand on Michael's wrist, tightened his fingers slightly, nodded his chin with a turn and said to Michael "We do our job… and none of that will matter."

Though not pleased with the interruption, Kent granted Nick the opportunity to reassure Michael. He began again, "Your work on the Hammonds case was stellar, really impressive for such a young officer. Your intuition played a key part in apprehending the true perpetrator. We were chasing the wrong guy, you chased with your damn gut about the evidence and got the right man! Really good work. So here you are, this is not an easy day on the job. These kinds of cases make or break a cop. Michael, do you understand that certain parts of this investigation you are going to have to stand down on? I mean it, you can be involved but only in what you are instructed. We do need you, but you have to let us make the decisions. The big thing here is the 'gag' we have to put on you… you absolutely cannot speak a word to anyone in the family or your friends… you must put your oath first! And I will tell you right now they are really going to pressure you. Beyond your comprehension, they will try to twist words and get information from you. No one is a suspect at this point but they are all going to feel like they are and will want your assurance… believe me, I know how hard this will be for you. I have made my decision and you will have to accept it. If you want to remain on this case you will have to move off the ranch and reside here in the station for the duration. The guard apartment will be readied for you by tomorrow. You have tonight to gather your things, let your family know and report at 0600."

"Yes Sir. Thank you, Sir!"

"You are going to be a good cop, I'm just doing my job... seeing to you getting there."

"Thank you, Sir."

"You and Netty are free to go."

When it was confirmed that Michael and Bruce were out of earshot; Matt spoke first; "You think he can do it?

"Truthfully, yeah, I do. He really has it in him. This is when he is either going to find it or not but my bets are that he will. All of us here are going to have to step up to make sure he doesn't screw up. Netty is good, don't get me wrong on that, but Moore..." After first looking to Kent for nonverbal approval, Nick interjected the flow of Kent's response. "Matt, Kent said it right, Michael has that inner intuition and he knows when and when not to act on it. He's going to help on this without even realizing it!" All three men guffawed at Nick's observation. "Oh, he's going to know it alright! That young man is paving the way for himself, I don't think he's going to let the opportunity go by to prove he's got what it takes. He set his goal and he's going to achieve it." "That he has Matt, that he has." "Look out my friends, we may be training a future Police Chief!" "And that friend of his... the Hunter kid... he's making marks at the Fire Department. I bet he makes a run for Fire Chief." "At least we know the town will be in good hands when we retire."

"Right now, we have to worry about solving this case. I am sure not liking what I hear about Prampt's connections with New York. Either of you guys ever hear of a thug named Jimmy Veltone?" "Veltone, as in the Harbor Incident?" "Yes." "Holy shit, Kent, what are we up against here?" "I wish I knew. I do know that Prampt made a phone call to one of Veltone's known associates three months ago and that has a lot of people worried. So worried, that the Feds sent in Henry Ross undercover to look into Prampt." "Oh." "Yeah, and now he is dead." "You really think Prampt had anything to do with it?" "That's our job to figure out." The three men sat in their chairs, arms on the table and looked down at the grainy surface, let out a long breath and sighed.

"Mornin' everyone! It's a fine day now isn't it!?" Brent spoke loudly toward the kitchen. Stunned by the exuberance in Brent's tone; John, Mary, Sara and Elizabeth smiled at one another as he washed his hands at the dry sink in the entryway. Unaware that Elizabeth was there, as he came into the kitchen, he halted his stride when he saw her. "And just who is this fine beauty sitting there with you Mrs. B?" "This is Elizabeth. Elizabeth Martin. Scott Prampt's granddaughter." Brent quickly walked to position himself to Elizabeth's right. "Pleased to meet you Miss Elizabeth Martin! And for what do we owe the pleasure of your company?" Mary leaned over the table and reached her right hand out to Elizabeth. "This would be Brent. Is he always this 'charming?'... no. And I for one am most curious as to the origin of his current demeanor!"

"Pleased to meet you as well, Brent. Though I am surprised I haven't seen you sooner. I came back with Sara and Russell after the fiasco at the Cutter race." "So, you have been here over a week? My apologies for not being aware." "Okay, enough of all this... Brent, what in tarnation has you in this mood?" "Mr. Moore, you are looking at the man that is going teach a fine English style horsewoman the finery of a western saddle and the open trail! Yuppers... this here cowboy is taking Becky Burnell to the Red Pasture and maybe even down that ridge to the meadow." Sara and Mary exchanged broad smiles. "Not without muffins!" "I knew you would come through Gram Moore!"

"I'm done with chores, I got me stores now I'm a headed out... a good day to the fine folks of the Rancho del Moores!"

In unison all four stood and raced to the doorway to take in the view of Brent kicking his heals as he leaped and jumped his way to the barn

His twist in the air startled John "Oh boy… I think he has it bad." Sara turned to him; "Ya think!?"

"Well there Mr. Ruff, looks like you drew the short straw! No fast riding today, we are going to mosey through the meadow!" Brent snapped the right cross-tie to the halter and then the left. "Yup, us boys are going to share the day with two very special girls. Sara suggested Pippi for Becky to ride. I tend to agree with that, how about you?"

Snort. Stomp.

Walking toward Pippi's stall, Brent was singing a Keith Whitley song, *"The smile on your face lets me know that you need me. There's a truth in your eyes sayin' you'll never leave me. The touch of your hand says you'll catch me if ever I fall. You say it best when you say nothing at all…"*

"And he's a singing cowboy as well!" Brent did not know that Becky had entered the barn and was standing at Ruff's head combing her fingers through his forelock. "What's his name?" "Ruff. Actually, Ruff Rider but we just call him Ruff. He's a great cow horse. And this here will be your mount for the day, meet Pippi. Sara thought that since you are used to riding a horse with a longer stride and Pip being a little taller and longer legged, you would be more comfortable. She has a great jog and Sara likes to do her dressage on this mare and yes, she likes to jump too." "Sounds perfect! I didn't know there was much English riding out here. I look forward to talking with Sara about her schooling." "Schooling? I don't think she went to school for…" "No, silly… schooling, as in her riding practices and techniques with the horses themselves." "Oh, yeah, I am sure she would love to converse with you regarding that!" Brent turned to the tack room to retrieve the brushes; to himself he whispered "Converse with you regarding that… seriously Brent boy, get a grip!".

Laden with brushes, combs and hoof picks, he returned to Becky and the horses. "You could finish the song… I enjoyed hearing you sing!"

"Here, let us get the gate for you girls!" Brent maneuvered Ruff through the movements of opening and then closing the gate. "This… this is the Red Pasture." He waved his arm side to side as if opening an imaginary door. "This pasture leads in many directions and has a story all its own to tell. Today we are going to ride to the high corner, I want to take you to a meadow that sits at the bottom of a ridge… you will be awed at the backdrop. The mountains here are really something." "This is the biggest pasture I have ever seen! Back home there are a few stables out in the country with ten or so acres for pastures, but this… how big is this?" "Exact, don't know but I do know it takes about an hour to get to the trail head and at close to three miles per hour average walk, guess that makes it three miles or so to the other side of the pasture. I do know the pasture is about a mile wide, so… ready for a little math lesson… a square mile is one *section*, a section is 640 acres, so if it is about 3 miles to the other end…" "Then it is approximately 3 sections or 1920 acres! Wow!" "You sure came up with that answer quick…" "I like math, not that I let on about it, don't want to be classified a nerd at school." "I did hear Gramp mention 1900 as a fairly accurate acreage when the State Rangers where here after the fire. Don't rightly think it needs an accurate acreage count." "I suppose not. Big is big! Is the ground safe for cantering? No ground hog holes?" "Lead on! Just saying you might want to hold onto the horn…" Pippy galloped away as he spoke the last of the sentence.

"She's gonna fit right in around here! Guess I was wrong… we are going to play today! Let's get a move on Ruff!"

"Oh, gee, glad you could join us!" Brent reined back to ride beside Becky. "I see you and Pip have hit it off!" "She's great." Becky reached down to pat the mare's neck. "She's great… but…" "But I miss my warmblood Magnum." "Warmblood?" "He's an American, I can't afford a Hanoverian or a Trakehner… he's a Shire crossed with a thoroughbred. Cold blood and hot blood hence the warm blood. Anyway, he and I are really bonded." "Isn't a Shire like a draft horse breed? The drafts around here are mostly Percheron or Belgian but to be honest with you, they aren't ridden, they are work horses." "Shires are a working class as well, but are showier and more animated. They are actually suitable for riding as well. Nobody thought he turn out to be much of anything so I took him on and he sure surprised everyone! We've had scores in the low seventies at the Dressage Shows and he is really coming along in the Cross Country Eventing." "Not that I understand any of that, but why don't you have him shipped out here?" "I, well, I got into some trouble and my mother sent me here to stay with my aunt for the summer. The biggest punishment was not being able to ride Magnum. I suppose she thought if I got away from the influences…" "I am glad you are here." Brent reached his left hand out to her, she placed her right hand in his. "Ummm how do I steer with just one hand?" "We use neck reining… you lay the rein on the neck and the horse moves in that direction. If you need to, put a little opposing leg pressure so she is pushed in the direction you want." "Wow… we use leg cues as well… similar, yet worlds apart." "Only if you let it be." Her smile answered his thoughts.

"Holy Shit! Are we going down that cliff!?"

"Aren't you glad you have forks in the front of your saddle and a horn to hold onto?" "Ahhhh yes!" Brent reined Ruff to a halt. "We don't have to go down if you don't want to." Becky turned to him and smiled. "Oooh hell yes I want to go down that! You would not have put me on a horse that couldn't do it… what's my first move?" As Brent maneuvered to her right he smiled. "You surprise Miss Burnell, you really do." "Oh? And how is that Mr. Thomms?" "You got guts girl. Gotta give you that!" Looking into his eyes she softly spoke, "I trust you."

Brent met her as he pulled her towards him, he knew this was the right moment… they shared their first kiss.

"You okay back there?" "Leaning back, legs to the front just like you told me!" "Not too tight on the horn?" "Oh… noooooo." Becky hoped he would not turn around see her tight hold on the saddle horn. "First switchback, lean into the hill!" "Aye aye, Captain!" Brent looked over to her as he made the bend. "You are a natural at this." "I'll let you know about that when we are off the side of this mountain!" "Relax, you are doing great. Three more switches and we'll be down." "Uh huh."

Brent dismounted when he reached the base of the trail and waited for Becky. "Ride on over her little lady and let me help you down from your mount."

"Turn to your right... look ..."

Standing beside Pippi with her right hand on the mare's mane, in a heightened voice Becky blurted "We rode down *that!... I rode a horse down that!*"

"That you did." "Now turn around and look to the meadow."

"Oh wow! Hey isn't this the place that the picture in the living room..." "Yes." "This is beautiful"

"So are you."

Dipping her head, Becky quickly turned away from Brent.

"I'm sorry..."

No response.

"Okay, I'm not sorry. I do think you are beautiful. You are smart, you are courageous, you think with your heart more than your head, but your head does think pretty good..." She had turned back to him as he stammered through his words. Placing her fingers over his lips she stopped him. "It's okay... I like you too." They turned back to the meadow view, he reached his left hand to her right and in the silent moment of touch, the understanding of change was felt for them both.

The sight of the meadow before them and with the horses grazing just a few feet away, Becky hesitated before she broke the stillness of the moment. Sara had told her of Brent's heartbreak with Mary, knowing her time in Brandon was finite and she would be leaving soon she had to keep them from making a mistake they could not return from.

"About those muffins! I have heard Mary Moore is famous around these parts." "In the saddlebags… be right back!" As Brent retrieved the square plasticware protecting the muffins from his right saddlebag, he looked over Ruff at Becky as she stood in the sunlight. He leaned into the horse's neck to speak lowly, "Damn, I don't want her to go back, I want her to stay. I know she is a little younger, but there is just something…" "Brent?" "Yes, on my way…" "That sign over there…" "Sign?" He was walking back to her. "Yes, over there… is this place named for someone named Wegasar?" "Oh…" He sniggered. "Actually, beyond that end of the meadow heads into the State land. Wegasar Gap is on the other side of the next ridge. There is an old road through there the Indians used in the 1800's. The word wegasar loosely and I might add, it is still debated, is the Indian word for gap." "So, you could say it really means Gap gap." This time it was Becky that laughed aloud. "What tribe of Indian was around here?" "The Shoshone mostly, but many traveled through. This was pretty rough territory to survive in 'back in the day' just a few strong willed white men and women survived the winters and gained hold of the land. John Moore's family was the first to homestead the area."

"It's pushing three, we should probably start heading back to the ranch." "You sit right here, I'll get the horses." "Thank you Brent, I want to look at this view as long as I can and remember it always."

"Up? now we have to go up…" Becky checked the breast collar and spoke lowly to Pippi. "We got this." Brent watched in amusement as Becky and the mare seemed to understand each other. "Ruff, I'm a goner!" Snort. Stomp. Ruff shook his head towards Becky to direct Brent's attention to the ridge. "Holy crap! She's up and going!" Without using a stirrup, he swung into the saddle as Ruff moved off in a jog. "Hold on there, Cowgirl… wait for me." "Okay if I take the lead heading up?" "By all means… I'll be suited just fine to watch those wranglers work in the saddle!" "You just make sure I'm doing what I am supposed to be doing to keep these wranglers in the saddle!" "Yes ma'am!"

The Sunday edition of the Brandon Times remained un read on the kitchen table between the lazy-susan that set on Mary's favorite table doily and the placemat in front of the captain's chair closest to the kitchen counter.

John Moore glanced at the headline as he walked past the table to the coffee maker. '*Prampt Probe Leads to Smuggling Charge*'. He pushed the paper to the center of the table, upsetting the salt and pepper shakers on the lazy-susan. "Damn fool…" "Hey Gramp!" "Oh! Michael, didn't hear you come in. How's the case going?" "You know I can't divulge information…" "I know, it's just we miss you around here and Gram is always asking for you and your mother…"

"I get it Gramp… but I still can't talk about it."

"But we can and you can listen." Russell entered the kitchen and held out his arms to embrace Michael. "You can listen to us and use what you hear for whatever it is that you think you might need. Your mother and I were there. Harrison questioned us about Henry Ross and what we knew about him. Then there were of course the dealings with some fella named Veltone in New York… and did Brent ever mention that name, and…"

"Take a breath Russell. Get some coffee. Let's go over this again…"

"Detective Borden, can I speak to you in private?" Placing his left arm over Michael's shoulder Nick impelled Michael toward Interrogation Room A. "Close the door…" "Really? What is up?" "Is the microphone off?" "Geez, kid…" "I'm serious. I need you to be open minded about this. I think…" "Stop right there. Are you having second thoughts about being on the Prampt case? Because if you are…" "No… what would make you think that? No… I have a gut feeling…" I like your gut… we did good by it before, what's your 'spidey sense' telling you now?"

"What if Henry wasn't the target? What if *Prampt* was?"

"Go on."

"This past Sunday I had breakfast at the ranch, Russell mentioned a broken hame on the Fork Valley harness. Said it sure looked too clean a cut to be a random break."

"That still doesn't take the attention off Henry and on to Prampt." "Didn't you see?"

"See what?"

"In the photos…both teams had the same colors. What if whoever cut that hame meant to cut Prampts?"

"You are really reaching here, kid."

"Listen to me, Russell had a lot to say and I think it takes merit in the case. I really do."

"Okay, I'm all ears. What have you got?"

"You sure the microphones are off?"

"Yes."

"What's Borden and Moore doing in I room A?" "Flip the switch." "Na… let them have their little pow wow, we need to get over to the

Prampt Ranch. I finally got the go ahead from the Valley Sheriff to investigate my leads over there. Those two can stay here and keep an eye on things. Bruce, you and I are heading out for the truth. Leave them a message with my mother that we have gone." "Yes sir."

"Who the hell is coming in the road?" "Quick, get these crates covered in the hay mow. They need to find them here but not just yet."

"So just what is it you think we are going to find Chief?" "There has to be a link, some sort of connection to Veltone... too many signs point to him and Prampt working together on this. Somewhere there is a record of either guy knowing that Ross was a Fed. Barnes said there were a couple fellas hanging around Prampt and his crew that nobody knew anything about. Could have been Veltone's guys, check and see if you can find employee records around here and find that Ben Zander—I need to talk with him. While you are doing that, I'm going to look for records of shipments of anything in and out of here. Guns can be hidden easily." "Like in a hay wagon, like the one over there?" "Yes, as a matter of fact. Good catch. We'll start there. Okay, then... meet back here in an hour." "Yes, sir."

"Visiting hours are over. Sorry, Miss Raven." "Sargent Blakeman, please just a few more minutes?" "Okay, but five and that's it." She tossed her hair back over her shoulder and winked at him.

"Scott, honey, I heard that they are really trying to pin this horrible whole thing on you! I just can't seem to understand how?" "There is a lot of evidence against me. It's not true, but whoever is doing this is good. Really good. I just hate what it is doing to Elizabeth. She is young and the papers are saying such terrible things about me. She has never known me to be anything other than her granddad and now... now she thinks I could be a monster. That is the greatest crime here.

The worst ever, for a young girl to lose her faith in…" Raven reached to his tied hands, placed hers over his and pressed them to the table. "How could she ever lose Faith in you, and you can't be sure she even believes what they are saying about you. From what I hear, she is at the Moore ranch and with Sara Barnes keeping her busy…" "You are right. My sweet Raven, whatever I did to catch the eye of a woman like you I will never know. Sometimes I think that this isn't true as well but then I look at you and hope with my heart that it is."

Feelings of remorse welled inside the woman holding the hands of the restrained man.

"Time to go Raven." She stood, turned back to Scott as Sargent Blakeman held him in the doorway leading back to his cell. "I'll be back soon, I promise." She exited the room and looked down the corridor and then leaned back against the wall. Looking to the ceiling a tear cascaded her left cheek. "What am I doing? He really is a good man… and Elizabeth…he loves her so much. My God, what have I done?" She let out a long sigh as she walked toward the next door. "Well, I sure as hell know what I am going to do now!"

Mrs. Harrison sat at the newly renovated receptions desk in the main lobby of the Police Station. She was reading the note from Bruce stating that he and Kent were on their way to Prampt's Ranch as Raven approached. "Excuse me, I don't mean to interrupt…" "Can I help you?" Raven glanced at the note. "Yes, I need to speak with someone regarding Scott Prampt. I have new information." "Well it seems the Chief is out of the office right now, Detective Borden is here, will he do?" "Yes, that will be fine"

"Detective Borden, please come to the front desk. There is a woman here by the name of Raven. Says she has information regarding the Prampt case." The raspy voice came through the speaker on his desk. "Be right there" Nick passed the breakroom and noticed Michael at the vending machine; he quickly leaned in the doorway, "My office, now! Raven is here and wants to talk."

"Hello, Miss…" "Walken, Raven Walken." "Please, come with me to my office. Mrs. Harrison, hold *all* my calls"

"Sara dear, the phone is for you. Do you want to take it in the den?" "The news will be on shortly, I'll pick up the extension in the office." Sara rose from the Lazy-boy, folded the lap blanket and placed it over the arm of the chair before leaving the den to enter the office. Mary waited to hear Sara on the line before replacing the receiver.

"John, it sure sounded like Katy on the phone. I hope everything is alright." "Not to worry Mary, you know how close those two are, Katy probably just needs some advice about school or something." "I am sure you are right. I for one will be happy when that girl graduates and returns home where she belongs." "I suppose getting to plan a wedding has nothing to do with that right!" "Oh, John!" "Don't 'Oh John' me, I know you better than you think I do!" Mary lifted her shoulders as she giggled. He leaned toward her, "I shall kiss my bride before retiring to the den but… between you and me, I'm looking forward to it too!"

Sara sat in the large chair with the back tipped toward the wall. One hand on the desk blotter; lifting it as she always did when sitting there to see the deep scratch mark Samuel inflicted upon the polished wood when he was ten years old. Replacing the concealment, she reached for the phone.

"Hello, Sara Barnes here."

"Mrs. B.? It's Katy. We need to talk. Do you have time?"

"For you absolutely, is everything alright?"

"I don't think so."

"What?"

"I figured out who those guys were that pestered me at the race."

"I'm listening…"

"Okay… here goes. When Detective Harrison questioned me about those two guys at the track, they wanted to know how I knew them, where they were from, did they go to school with me, did they work for Scott, did they work for Fork Valley, were they with the racing association… there were so many questions. All I could tell them was that I had never seen them before. Ever. Like they aren't from around here or school. So of course, Detective Harrison assumed they were from Prampt's place. And then I remembered you telling me that when you were over there that one time and saw Mara the first time, that you had asked Elizabeth if there were any tall ranch hands and she said no. So, I got to looking into who actually works at Prampt's ranch…"

"Slow down, Katy… I really think you need to be telling Michael all this not me."

"You really think so? You don't think he will get upset?"

"He'd be more upset if you didn't. You could have information he needs. Information he can work off of."

"Okay, is he there?"

"No, he is still staying at the station."

"Okay, I'll call him there. Good night Mrs. B."

"Good night Katy, and Katy…"

"Yes?"

"You are doing the right thing."

"Thanks, I hope so. Goodnight."

Sara replaced the receiver and stared at the telephone unaware John stood in the doorway. Pushing the chair back from the desk in her peripheral vision she saw the patriarch. "John, this is getting far more intrusive to our family and community than we could have imagined." "It will be resolved soon Sara, Michael will see to it. Harrison and Borden are great Policemen and now they have our boy to help them. Take comfort in that." "Thank you, John. You are right. Have you heard from Russ this evening?" "He's probably still at the Co-op." "Look at the time… isn't *'Walker'* about to start? I know how you like that Texas Ranger!" Leaving the office, she turned and looked at the phone. To herself she thought "Be careful Katy."

"Have you heard from Raven?"

"Nope."

"Does Ben know?"

"Nope."

"Shit!"

'Yup."

"Bruce, you did some real good work here. We have evidence of stash in the hay barns as well as the transport of goods inside the hay wagons and shipping trucks. Good cover if you ask me, with all the exportation of alfalfa hay from this valley it's really a smart move." "But who helped him and what's the connection with Veltone?" "Veltone is probably receiving the shipments through a middleman. We need to find the dockets for these trucks and then we'll know where the exchange is taking place. My guess is somewhere in Indiana or Ohio. Big truck traffic states, easy to blend in. See what you can find on that." "I have the freight logs and Bill of Lading records." "That will do. Again, good job. I sure wish Ben had been here to talk to. I left a message for him to call me at the station. I know he's busy keeping this ranch running. Prampt's lucky to have a trusted employee like Ben Zander. Let's head home and go over those books with a fine-tooth comb. Maybe when Ben calls, he might give some insight into what we find. I want this case wrapped up." "How do we tie Prampt to Ross?" "I'm thinking more now like that is Veltone, Prampt just isn't that kinda guy. Smuggle guns, okay, kill a man… no. I don't think he has the constitution do that. I just wish I knew what Veltone has on him to get him involved in the first place."

"Ya think they saw us?"

"No way."

"We gotta tell Ben them guys from Brandon were here."

"Where's the truck?"

"Still hooked to the trailer."

"No time to unhook, let's go."

Bruce looked out the passenger window as they turned left onto the highway at the end of the ranch road. His eyes caught movement and he focused on the sight in the mirror.

"Chief Harrison?"

"Yes?"

"Isn't that Prampt's trailer heading south out of the ranch road?"

Kent's attention was transferred to the mirror on his side of the truck. "It sure is… hang on!"

The truck slid into the sharp U-turn before regaining hold of the lane.

"May we join you?" Becky walked across the stall fronts on the left side of the barn stopping at Pippi's door. "Hey girl, miss me?" "She could use a ride… you are welcome, in fact I insist. Please… I want to check on the north herd today and company would be wonderful." "I would like that, thank you."

"Same saddle?" "Yes, and add a pad, we could be out all day." "Will we be going through the Red Pasture again? It is so beautiful!" "Yes, and I'm going to take you to a different trailhead than you rode with Brent. I think it only right that you get to see more of the ranch he loves so much." "He does talk about it a lot. Sometimes it's hard to realize that he just works here the way he goes on and on." "Oh, my sweet girl, your perception of his words and actions betray you. Brent *is* family. He may not be 'blood' but that matters not. He stayed with us for several years when he was young and worked this ranch with Michael and his father Samuel. Those boys were seldom apart. And now, look at all he has accomplished with the Rodeo Stock and even the horses. He is family and he is a part of this ranch. If he boasts about it, he has every right to do so, though he is not a vaunting man."

"We ready?"

"Yes!"

"Mount up!"

Hank and Baron barked their delight in being included in the outing.

"You and Brent have been spending lot of time together this summer, how is it going to be when you have to leave?" "That is really why I wanted to ride with you today, I want to talk about... about how I want to stay here. In Brandon. With my aunt. I think she will go for it. I am pretty sure I can convince my mother that staying here away from the 'bad influences' as she called them, is the best option for me to stay clean and out of trouble. I will need a place for Magnum and my aunt lives in town. I was hoping there would be room for him at your ranch."

"First things first, you need to talk with your mother. We can go from there. I don't see an issue on our end, but... she is your mother and you need to respect her even though you are of age enough to make your own decisions. I am sure if you wanted to, you could pick up your classes at the Community College in Carnon." "Thank you so much! I will call her tonight." "Have you mentioned any of this to Brent?" "No, not yet, I wanted to talk with you first."

Both women heard the howl.

"What was that?"

"Wolf."

"Is that bad?"

"Well... it is the wrong time of day for them to be out..." Sara reached to the scabbard and withdrew her rifle.

"Okay, ah... Annie Oakley... what are you going to do with that?"

"Scare a wolf... or two." Sara heard the fright in Becky's voice. "Rather it be a wolf than a mountain lion... my odds have always been better with the wolves."

"What do I do?"

"Stay calm, ride your horse, and keep an eye on the dogs."

"Oooo, yeah, the dogs… Hank! Baron! Heal!"

"Look… off to the left… there they go…"

"They are gorgeous! I have never seen an actual live wolf, wow… what a stunning creature! Are they all that color pattern?"

"We have mostly grays in this area but there are also red coated and a black one was spotted a couple years back. The re-introduction into the forests has led to some bad feelings among the ranchers and the government. We do lose a few head each year to them, that is true, but I agree with you, they are magnificent."

"Here is our trailhead, go on in, I'll follow you." "How long will we be in the woods? Didn't you say you wanted to check on a herd today?" "They are in the 'bowl' between the ridges. You'll see." "I have sooooo much to learn!" Sara smiled while looking at the back of the young woman from the eastern part of the county 'getting her feet wet' in the ways of the west.

"Take a right at that dead trunk ahead. There is a short trail to the edge of the ridge."

"Edge?" "We aren't going down… not yet anyway. I just want you to see the view."

Becky took a deep breath as Pippi stopped at the opening in the trees. There was space only for them to take in the grandeur of mountain scenery.

"I… I have no words."

"You aren't supposed to."

"Well, Pip, looks like you are going to have to put it in reverse here. There doesn't seem to be much turning room out here on the edge." A lift of the reins and a little smooch from Becky as she cued the mare to back and she was beside Sara in just a few strides. "You ride well. I'm impressed. Time to head back to the trail and get to the herd."

Becky leaned over Pippi's neck, "Did you hear that? She said I ride well!"

Slowing Mara so Becky and Pippi could walk at her right side, Sara draped the reins over the mare's neck, lifted and opened her arms. "This is what is called a 'Tilley'" "A hat?" "A what?" "A hat... you know, the canvas kinda like hat... sort of like what Indiana Jones wears..."

Though she tried hard, Sara was unable to prevent her reaction to Becky's response. It took a few minutes for her to compose herself.

"Whaaaat? Tilley hats are the rage back home..." "My dear, here, Tilleys are the forest's fingers off a ridge into the bowl. Most are much rockier than this and un ridable, this one happens to not be as severe as the others around this bowl. Good grief, I do apologize for my outburst, but you really got me on that one!"

"I have so much to learn!"

"You up for a lesson on brands? I know there are much more modern ways to keep herd identification but there is something to be said for the old-school, tried and true art of branding. Brent purchased cattle from several ranch sales last year so we actually have a few here without the Moore Ranch brand. Let's ride over and I will explain the ways to read a brand."

Grazing at the edge of the small pond in the center of the bowl, the herd was untroubled as the women on horseback approached.

Remaining abreast, Sara pointed to the left side of the herd. "See that black steer..." "The one with the big letter A on his hip?" "Yes, that one. He and a few others came from the Rocking A Ranch the other side of Eastdale. Notice the half circle facing up... that means a 'Rocking' brand so if you put a letter or a figure of sorts in it you have the *Rocking* whatever. If the half circle is above the letter or figure then it is a 'Swinging' brand." "I get it, if it was over the A, then it would be the *Swinging A*." "That's right. Now, if that A were on its side then it is 'Lazy'. In the case of that A, if it were on its side with the top of the A on the left, then it would be read as *The Left Lazy A*, or if the top were to the right, then it would be read as *The Right Lazy A*. Have you seen the brand for the Famous King Ranch?" "It's a W with like wings or something at the top, right?" "Well, something like that, when the wings as you call them are short, then it is a 'Flying' brand, when they are longer it is a 'Running' Brand." "Running?" "Oh yes, and you will like these... imagine a mark like a foot at the bottom of that A over there... if the 'feet' are pointed backward, or to the left, then it is a 'Dragging' brand..." "Let me guess, if they point forward then it's a *Pulling* brand?" "Well, no, sorry. It would be a *Walking* brand." "There are so many ranches out here and throughout the west, how can they be kept from repeats?" "Each state has a brand inspection division with many brand inspectors keeping track of old brands as well as new ones. With so many people moving out here now and wanting to be 'all cowboy' and such, the inspectors are kept pretty busy. Russell attends the state meeting every year to keep up on the new brands and where they are located. The ranchers look out for each other as cattle rustling though glorified in the movies as a thing of the 'old days', it is still very much a threat to the modern ranch." "But, if the brands are registered with specific owners and then you buy cattle like Brent did, what about the brand?" "The steers Brent purchased were branded and then ear tagged for sale. The ear tag number was then transferred with the steer. We have the documentation for each of the transfers as does the brand inspector that completed the transfer." "That brown one to the right of Mr. A, is that the Moore Ranch brand?" "That big beautiful -M- in a sideways diamond... yes, it is! Samuel's great great grandfather established this operation in 1837 and was the first in this area of the territory to stake ground. The brand was registered in 1840." "Samuel, he was your first husband, right? Brent told me what happened. I am so sorry." "Thank you. He was a good man and a fine cowboy. I have been Blessed by the Lord with the men that have been beside me. Now, I don't know about you, but I sure could go for one of Gram's muffins and a drink before we head back." "In my saddlebags!"

"Hello Berta" Michael returned from the diner on Broad Street to the apartment at the Police Station. "The place looks great. Thanks for doing such a good job." "A tidy office makes for better thinking!" "If you say so." "Any idea when you will get to go home Officer Moore?" "Please, Michael, call me Michael and no, we have to wrap this case up first. I sure do hope it is soon, I miss Gram's cooking and listening to mom sing while she does the dishes." "And I am sure they miss you too. It'll be soon I am sure. And then it will be me missing having you to talk to while I am cleaning." "Aww Berta…" His tall frame engulfed her in his embrace. "I'll see you tomorrow, got a lot of notes to go over tonight." "Make sure you sit on the Davenport when you do?" "The what?" "The Davenport… the sofa silly… that relic is an authentic A. H. Davenport and Company piece from Boston! The story goes it was originally in one of Boston's High Society Country Club's smoking rooms! How it ended up here is the big mystery, but low and behold it did and it sure is fine piece. An awful lot of great men have sat on it while they conducted business. Seems right you should too!" "I suppose it does at that! My work is on the table, but for you Berta, I will transfer to the *Davenport*."

As he opened the apartment door, the phone began ringing.

"Hi, Michael, it's Katy… do you have time to talk?"

"Hello to the most wonderful Gram!" Unaware Michael had entered the kitchen, Mary Moore was stupefied by the sudden break in her concentration of the daily crossword puzzle in the newspaper. "Geez, Gram, I didn't mean to scare you!" "Oh, Michael, it is so good to see you! Are you coming home to stay?" "No, not yet. I hope soon. Is Mom around?" "No, she and Elizabeth went in to town, they will probably be gone most of the day. Today is the spay and neuter clinic at Doc Peterman's and they are helping with that." "Well, I was hoping to take a ride to the North Grazing Land today. There's just got to be a colt out there in the pen that needs a good ride!" "Oh, Lord, please don't make me have to worry about you, maybe you could take one of the broke ones… for me, please!?" "I shall see if Miss Pippi Longstocking is out there, that mare should ease your mind!" He embraced her as she tried to reply her agreement. "Becky had a nice ride on her a while back…" "Becky? As in Becky Burnell?" Michael stepped back from his grandmother. "That would be correct. She and your mother had a lovely ride together." "Gram…" "Yes?" "Brent kinda likes her, doesn't he?" Gram smiled. "I take that smile as a yes. I am glad he has someone. His heart broke after Mary left and then the trip to New York City… that about did him in. This girl has brought him back to life. But, doesn't she have to leave soon and go back east?" "Funny you should ask, when you are in the barn you are going to see a very large horse in the end stall. Brent paid to have her Warmblood shipped out here. Seems as though she plans on becoming a resident of the west." "*Brent* paid the shipping cost?" "Yes, he did. I was told it was not a good conversation regarding her staying here. Becky argued extensively with her mother. You have to give that girl credit, she spoke with her Alcohol Anonymous sponsor prior to talking with her mother. They have a new one set up for her here…" "Whoa… stop right there, Gram… Becky is in A.A.?" "It was news to us too… that look you have right now, yup… that was the same look your Grandfather had!"

"Well, you know what… that makes me even happier for Brent." Mary Moore had a quizzical grin as her grandson spoke. "You look stunned Gram!" "A little I guess…" "Brent never really liked drinking anyway, so it won't be a problem for him that way, and I'd say it speaks volumes for him that he doesn't judge her for it because obviously she got into some big trouble over it, and if she had the wherewithal to know to keep in contact with her sponsor then she is keeping with respect for the program. I commend her for her commitment. Shows she really wants to better herself." "Spoken like a friend more than a Police Officer." Gram smiled. Michael tucked his chin and then raised his fisted right arm with a burst; "And all is right for the Amigo's once again! Yeehaw!"

Returning to the kitchen sink, with her back to Michael, Gram spoke softly. "Any particular reason you want to ride out to the North today?"

Michael walked to stand at her right side.

"I need to talk with him"

"I understand." She placed her head on his forearm.

Pippi willingly galloped across the open grasses. Pleased with his choice of mounts, Michael rode in silence along the trail to Anglin Pass. He and the large mare fit well together in frame of bodies as well as minds. Arriving at the Pass entrance he transitioned her to a walk, as he did so, he reached down to pat her neck. "Miss Pippi, I do believe we have made it here in record time! Have you ever been through here before? Have they told you about old Hobb and the slide?"

The mare bolted sideways to the left.

"I shall take that as a 'no', no you have not been through here. Settle down sweetheart, we walk through quietly so not to upset the 'inhabitants'. Easy girl, you will be fine." The mare did not release the hunch in her back or the elevated position of her head. "Okay, we'll try this Mom's way... she says it is good to talk with a nerved horse in a low tone to keep their attention on you and not what is worrying them... here goes."

Pippi lunged forward; Michael sat deep in the saddle and applied an easy pressure on the bit. She reluctantly responded to his instruction though would not give up her wariness to the surroundings.

"Are you done now?" He placed his right hand on her neck. "We've got a while in here, let's talk. You know that girl Becky... she's brought her ginormous gelding here… he's huge! Have you seen him? Oh, of course you have. I bet you think he's pretty much something! Well, it appears as if our boy Brent thinks Becky is something too… I'm so happy for him. He needs a good woman and after Mary… anyway, now that Brent is back on track, hey there, what was that little hop? No, that is not a horse eating rock… get a grip… Miss Pip! No, Longfellow will not return… Have you met Charles? He has your sister. She's not as tall as you are but your markings are similar. Thank goodness he found the Air Patrol Squad. He sure loves flying things. This jumping into fires and all that he does is pretty awesome. Yeah, we all hated that breaking his arm during the cattle drive prevented his entry in the Air Force, but it ended well for him and everyone; he still can fly just now stays closer to home. You settling down there a little? Hey, did you know Katy and I are getting married? When… you ask… well that all hinges on her graduation and internship but as soon as possible! I really wish my dad could be there… we are heading to a special place where I can talk with him."

Reaching the end of the Pass he turned the mare back to look at where they had been. "See, just a Pass."

Snort.

Stomp.

"Okay, a Pass that is beleaguered, but still… you did good. Guess this talking thing really works but this stays between you and me… okay?"

She did not wait for him to cue her back to the trail.

"I guess this means you want to get to the river bottom!"

To Michael's delight Pippi had not objected to the hobbles; he sat on an old fallen log watching her contentedly grazing on the scrub grass next to the river. Retrieving a small spiral notepad from his left breast pocket, he flipped through the pages as he read his notes.

When he had read the last page, he slowly closed the note pad and let out a deep sigh.

"Dad... I need your help." Gazing upwards, he continued. "What am I missing?"

In the distance he heard the familiar hoarse kee-eeeee-ar of a hawk.

Part 12
Unveiling the Truth

"Hello..."

"Mom?"

Realizing the caller, Sara turned back toward the kitchen table.

"Oh! Hi Michael, it is so good to hear your voice!"

"Yours too... listen, is Russell there?"

"Yes, do you need to speak with him? Is this about Scott?"

Entering the kitchen and hearing her grandfather's name, Elizabeth halted in mid stride. "Granddad? What about Granddad?"

"I heard Elizabeth in the back ground, I need you and Russell to bring her to the station."

Sara placed the receiver on her left upper chest as she looked at Elizabeth and then Russell.

"He wants us to take Elizabeth to the station." "Now?" Russell reached for Elizabeth's hand. Sara noticed the angst of the young girl. "Yes. Elizabeth, honey, are you up for it?" "Yes."

Placing the receiver back to her ear, "We are on our way."

"Thanks Mom. Tell her not to worry."

"Will do. See you soon."

Elizabeth reached down to first pat Hank on the signature white border collie blaze and then she smiled as she smoothed the cowlick on Baron's neck. "See you later boys, time for me to go to town!" Hank quickly rose to his feet, followed by Baron; both nearly tripping her in the rush to the door leading to the back porch.

John exclaimed boisterously "Those dogs sure love that child. They are going to miss her!" After placing a kiss on her husband's cheek, Mary smiled as she remarked, "To be gone, for her, would be a good thing, that would mean she was back home again, but you are right, the dogs will miss her and frankly so will I. I love having a young girl in the house. What a difference from having the boys!"

"She's at the dually, looks like we're taking the big truck! Let's hope we'll need it for four passengers on the way home!" Russell opened the porch door for Sara. "I'm pretty sure she's banking on that." Sara looked back at Mary as she walked passed Russell. "We will be back as soon as we can." "Will you let Michael know I'm putting on a pork roast for tonight… maybe he could join us…" "Your roast… he'll be here!"

Russell stopped the truck under the arch. "Why are you stopping Mr. Barnes?" Russell and Sara locked eyes. Each telling the other without words, the understanding between. "Elizabeth, look back at the ranch house…" Pulling her knees up so she could twist around and the kneel on the seat to look out the rear window, Elizabeth saw John and Mary waving at her. She waved back. "Do you think they can see me waving?" "They don't need to *see* you honey, they can *feel* you." "I can feel them too."

She continued to wave as the truck proceeded forward until the ranch house and the elder Moores were no longer visible. Russell looked in the rearview mirror as Elizabeth resumed her sitting position on the bench seat and put his right hand over Sara's left. He knew her thoughts as she tipped her head down.

Arriving at the Police Station, Russell drove through the parking lot in search of an adequately sized space for their F350. Choosing the end space on the outside row, as he backed the truck into position all three passengers sat in silence. "Glad they have spots to accommodate us!" When there was no response, he looked first at Sara and then Elizabeth; both were staring, transfixed at the single story building that held the currently esoteric information regarding her grandfather.

"Are you ready Elizabeth?"

"I really hope this means Granddad is coming home."

"I really hope it does too." Sara looked back at Elizabeth as she unfastened the seatbelt.

Russell walked around the front of the truck to open the door for Sara, he lowered his head and spoke in a low tone; "What if he isn't... what if..." Placing her right fingertips over his mouth to halt his words, "Michael said to tell her not to worry, I am taking that as a really good sign." "You are right, we have to think positive. And right now, we had best catch up to a very anxious young lady!"

Elizabeth stood beside the flag pole looking up watching the banner wave in the wind.

"Sara, please... let me..." Returning only a smile to her husband, he knew she agreed.

"She's a fine flag, isn't she?" Russell now stood beside Elizabeth with his left arm across her shoulders. "That flag represents so much... the truth and honor of our great nation... the fight it took to achieve that truth and honor, and the duty of all citizens to uphold it." He placed himself in front of the young girl and placed her hands in his. "And today, that truth and honor will come to light. This fine group of men have worked very hard to uncover the truth and if you ask me, there are no better people than them to do it. Elizabeth, I cannot tell you just what they have called us here today for, and I can not tell you what the outcome of all this will be, but what I can tell you is that no matter what… you have us. Sara, me, Gram, Gramp, Michael… everyone at the Moore Ranch. We love you and we will take care of you."

Elizabeth stood straight and took in a deep breath. "Thank you, that means the world to me. And so does that flag up there. I believe in the truth and honor you speak of. I have to hold on to that." "I am so proud of you. Shall we see what it is that Michael wants to tell us?" "I'm ready; a little nervous, but ready."

Russell opened the large newly installed glass doors that lead into the lobby. In pursuit of approaching the receptions desk before Sara and Elizabeth, he quickened his stride. Sara walked with her left arm over Elizabeth's shoulders in an attempt to quiet her trembling. As they stood at the desk, Sara pulled her in close and whispered "Think positive. You and I both know your grandad could not have done all those things." "I know and you know but…" "And Michael knows… remember that." The embrace between Sara and Elizabeth caught the attention of Sargent Blakeman as he emerged from the door that lead to the holding cells. "Young lady, I have gotten to know your grandfather and I want to tell you, he talked about you every day. He loves you so much." "Thank you."

While Sargent Blakeman talked with Sara and Elizabeth, Russell approached the receptions desk. "Hello, Mrs. Harrison, we are here to see Michael. He called…" "Yes, please… follow me to Chief Harrison's office. Everyone is in there." "Everyone?"

Russell turned his attention to the trio standing to the right of him, "Girls… they are ready for us." Sara and Elizabeth followed Russell and Mrs. Harrison down the corridor to Chief Harrison's office. Leaving the lobby, Sargent Blakeman paused to look at the now closed door leading to Kent Harrison's office; "I sure as hell hope they realize how lucky they are. Those Moore's… they just don't give up! That Michael… he's a tenacious one just like his mother."

Scott stood in the doorway to Kent's office as they approached. "Granddad!" Elizabeth ran to the outstretched arms of her beloved grandfather. Sara placed her hand on Russell's arm and pulled back hoping to stop him. "Look... Scott is wearing his own clothes! Oh Russell, he is wearing his own clothes!"

Michael met them in the hallway. "We have a lot to tell you. We thought it best that Elizabeth and you two, get the truth before the press gets ahold of it. I asked the Chief for this favor and he agreed. Shall we join them..." Michael motioned with his arm for his mother to enter the room followed by Russell.

"Oh, Scott..." Sara reveled at the sight of him with Elizabeth.

"I am sure that Mr. Prampt would like nothing more than to get back home to his ranch, so let's get this wrapped up. Michael, before we start, did you get that warrant?" "All taken care of Chief." "Good, Mr. Prampt, you need a new foreman."

"I do? Why?"

"Here goes..."

"Everyone, please... have a seat, this may take a while." "Thank you, Nick, I mean Detective Borden..." "Russell... today, after all that has transpired, Nick is fine!" Russel pulled back a chair from the table for Sara and then took the seat to her left; Elizabeth took the seat to her right and Scott settled beside his granddaughter.

Chief Harrison sat on the corner of his desk; his right foot on the floor and his left leg hiked onto the desk at his knee. He reached to the left behind him and retrieved an envelope. He then stood and leaned forward, setting the envelope on the table in front of Scott Prampt.

Scott looked first at the envelope and then at Kent Harrison. He began to reach for it. "What the..."

Michael placed his hand on the envelope preventing Scott from retrieving it. "Mr. Prampt, before you open that, let us explain. Please."

Bewildered at the cessation of his action, Scott drew back his hand. "Okay…"

Kent was again perched on the corner of his desk. "First off… Scott, are you okay with Elizabeth being here? Keep in mind that much of what we are going to disclose here may be very disheartening and at best leave her disenchanted with those she had trusted. Are you okay with Elizabeth being here?"

"Granddad, I want to know the truth."

"Yes, Chief Harrison, I am okay with her being here."

Accepting Scott's approval, Kent continued.

"Once the Brandon Police Department became involved in the case, we questioned numerous witnesses that had been in attendance at the race track as well as ranch hands and business associates of the Prampt Ranch, the Moore Ranch and even followed leads to persons in several other states on this case. We all know the allegations against Scott the day of the race. The stash of Assault rifles in the horse trailer he owns lead to his arrest for gunrunning. The fact that the same type of weapon that was involved in the current Federal investigation of smuggling and that serial numbers of the guns matched those on the list were recovered from the trailer, there was no choice but to arrest him. The County Sheriff had been working on the case for months and had an acute knowledge of what they were looking at. To them, the arrest seemed like the break they were looking for. As you know, he was remanded to the County Jail with Bail denied. The charge against Scott in the Ross homicide was later added when evidence was found that Scott had knowledge of Ross being a Federal Agent working undercover…"

"Yes, I knew… I was sworn to secrecy…"

Sara, Russell and Elizabeth gasped.

"Granddad... you knew?"

"Yes." Dropping his head, he continued. "Eight months ago, I was approached by an Agent named Keith Miller. They were tracing leads to the Valley area of gun running. I thought at the time I had put their questions to rest but then I got another visit from Miller stating that they were placing an agent named Henry Ross in the Valley. I had no idea he was put in as a cutter driver, and really was surprised when I saw he was driving for the Fork Valley Ranch. I hosted a late summer bar-b-que inviting Fork Valley and a couple other ranches. I was sure happy when Bob and Henry picked up a friendship. Even though I could never tell him, I was glad to know Bob had taken favor to Henry. It was hard pretending I didn't know him. It was really hard keeping it from everyone but it was the Feds..."

Nick placed his right hand on Scott's left shoulder. "We do understand the predicament you were in, but, Scott... we really could have used that information sooner than we discovered it for ourselves... err... actually, Michael found out. Go on Chief..."

"Because at that time it was not known of your collaboration with the Feds; and with the weapons found in your trailer, it presented enough evidence for the County Sheriff to charge you with the gun running."

"And then when Henry died..."

"At first we didn't link the two of you together, then an anonymous tip came in to us and not the County stating that you were overheard behind the gates talking with an unknown other party about your suspicions and that 'something needed done to remove the problem' as soon as possible. That lead us to start looking at the possibility you had a play in the wreck on the race track. It was a good cover as horses are un predictable and that sort of situation, well, who would suspect foul play...foul horses yes, but foul play... no. Until Ross died."

"It all seems circumstantial Kent."

"Yes Russell, it does. But it was enough to make the arrest. The Brandon Police department was brought in to the case by the County Sheriff when it became known that Katy McGreggor had been seen talking with the same man that Scott had been with behind the gate and that the very unusual pair of Paint horses coincidentally turned out in the same colors as the Fork Valley Ranch team were from the Moore Ranch to which Katy is engaged Michael Moore, and to add to all that, Sara and Russell had been seen frequenting the Prampt Ranch. Not to mention Scott's contact named Veltone in New York that Brent met with. Are you starting to see the blurred lines yet?

"Again, circumstantial…"

"Michael, would you like to proceed?"

Sara looked at her son with enlarged eyes and a questioning tip of her head.

"The day that Chief Harrison and Officer Netty went to the Prampt Ranch, Raven Walken came to visit Scott…"

"I remember that day…" He smiled.

Michael continued; "When her time with Scott was finished, she asked if she gave us, Detective Borden and myself… if she gave us information regarding the case would she get some kind of a deal… Detective Borden asked her if she thought what she had to say might be incriminating, perhaps she should have an attorney present. She declined the attorney. She said she wanted the truth to be known as far as the innocence of Scott Prampt."

"Raven? Raven had something to do with this?" With his right arm bent at the elbow on the table, Scott supported his forehead with his hand. "How could I have been so stupid… of course… why else would a woman like that take an interest in me? I'm an idiot!"

Nick spoke to Scott before Michael continued; "Don't be too quick to say that… she came forward because she does have feelings for you. Yes, at first her part of the plan was unscrupulous, but in the end, she realized you didn't deserve what was happening to you and came forward at her own expense. The Judge is going to look favorably on her actions. You should too."

Elizabeth put her arms around him, "It's okay, Granddad."

"While we were talking with Raven, Chief Harrison and Officer Netty had driven over to the Prampt Ranch. They located several concealed stashes and transportation logs implicating Scott…"

"What?"

"Easy, Scott… let me go on, please. The name Veltone kept appearing in the records. On their way out of the Prampt Ranch, they noticed an unknown truck and a horse trailer matching the description of Scott's leaving the ranch and heading in the opposite direction. Deciding to pursue the trailer, they turned around and followed it to the Sanderson Ranch…"

"No good Sanderson… I should have known! I wondered why he wasn't racing that day…"

"Take it easy Granddad, let him finish." Elizabeth was soft in her words to him.

"When I was home at the ranch for breakfast one day, Mom and Russell started recanting the events at the track, taking in what they told me and what Katy had told me later about the strange men that approached her right before the race was to start, I started putting it together that these just might be the same men. It stood out because

Katy's description of them and Russell's recant of the young men at the rodeo and them not having the luck with the cowgirls that we had as teenagers... I called Kent on the radio and described the men to him and asked if they had been seen at the Prampt Ranch. He said they had not been there but they did have eyes on them at the Sanderson Ranch. Chief Harrison then asked me to question Scott about a man named Veltone..."

"Yeah...Jimmy. Good guy. Helped me with getting Brent set up in New York to see his girl. I've known him for years."

Michael dismissed the interruption.

"It was a short inquiry. Scott, you provided incriminating information that I found too easily against you. At that point my gut told me this was all a set up, you were very skillfully being framed not only in the gun smuggling, but in the death of Henry Ross. Scott, you really didn't know him. He's not a 'good guy' as you put it. Actually, the Feds have been looking for him for quite a long time. Thanks to you and the information you gave me, they have him in custody. So, back to the Sanderson Ranch... Chief Harrison and Officer Netty decided they should take a look around so they waited for the Sheriff to bring them the search warrant and then waited for the same unknown truck to leave. They went to the main house and informed the housekeeper they had a warrant and wanted to look around. Fortunately, there was no objection. Confident that they were there alone they went to the barn and proceeded to look around. They again found numerous concealed stashes of fire arms and transport log books. But this time it was evident that the ones found at Scotts were fabricated. Entries were dated similar but actual lading reports had the Sanderson address. This was proof that the log books had been planted at the Prampt ranch to frame him; as well as the guns. Though still speculation, more evidence was needed. Then Bruce found a saw with black and red painted sawdust in the teeth. Chief Harrison went back to the unit and called me to ask me again what Russell had said about the hames. When I told him they were painted red and black and that he was certain that they had been tampered with, perhaps even cut, Chief said he thought he could now back up that statement and disconnected the call. When Chief Harrison and Bruce returned to the station, they had with them numerous log books, weapons, note pads, the saw and a file with the name Veltone on it."

"I'll take it from here Michael"

"Yes sir."

"Officer Netty and I returned to the Prampt Ranch for one last look around before returning to the station. Michael and Nick had asked Raven if she would agree to recording her session. She did. When Bruce and I returned from Sanderson's we took the hame, both sets of books, a bloodied shirt and other items of interest to Matt Brewer so he could run all of it through the forensics lab and then we listened to the recording. I called Michael back in, asked him to go over Katy's statement and that of his mother's and Russell's. We went over the depositions from everyone including Scott and Bob McClew. Seems our Miss Raven Walken is actually the step daughter of Jimmy Veltone. And the two thugs working for him are the Markum brothers Adam and Todd. Sara, I believe it was Adam that you saw at Scott's place when you questioned Elizabeth about a tall ranch hand. He stands six foot four inches tall. We found a triple extra-large shirt hidden in the hay barn linking him to having been there. Matt confirmed it was Adam's by DNA found on it. Raven told us that when Ed Sanderson had found out Scott knew Jimmy, he thought the well-known feud between them would be a great cover up. Jimmy wasn't keen on using Scott, Ed convinced him he wanted in on his operation, he could supply an impenetrable cover and with Raven's help, they could make the sale to his buyers and get away with it. Jimmy then convinced Raven to play her part with promises of a healthy bank account. What he didn't bank on was that she would really fall for the guy and would clear her conscious. She gave up names and locations of numerous members of Veltone's operation, said she had overheard the Markums talking about cutting the wrong team's hame. Sanderson wanted Scott's team out of the race, not Fork Valley. She even told us where the trucking hubs are located and the drop points. Seems the woman knew how to get information with extreme discreteness."

Scott scoffed, "Seems she was discreet about a lot of things…" Russell stopped him from speaking on. "Seems to me Scott, she came clean for you. Perhaps you should bear that in mind." "I suppose you are right. She did."

Placing his right hand on the envelope still on the table, Michael turned his head to Scott.
"One more thing, your manager Ben Zander…"

Scott looked at Michael, "No… not Ben, I've known him since he was a young teenager… I trust him…"

"Scott, his true identity is not Benjamin Zander…"

Scott tore the end of the envelope and quickly removed the paper inside.

"Oh, dear God… Van Sanderson. Ed's nephew! I trusted him. Even asked him to take over the Ranch while all this was being sorted out. He… he… right under my nose… I trusted him!"

Kent stood beside the table. "Ed Sanderson and the Markum brothers are in custody. We have a warrant out for Van Sanderson. We are pretty sure we are closing in on him. Scott, now you know why we told you that you need a new ranch manager."

Part 13
Reride

"Well, well… aren't you in a good mood this morning!" "Yes Mary, I am. It is a beautiful day today and I have been out in the foaling pens all morning playing with the colts." "You do love the babies… foal or calf, you are right out there with them. Oh, there is a letter for you from Elizabeth on the table." Sara rushed past Mary to retrieve the letter.

Dear Sara:

Thank you again for all you and your family did for us. You may know by now that Granddad has hired your brother as our Ranch attorney and also for my new business of 'E M Harness Designs'; believe it or not I already have 2 customers!

Granddad is slowly getting back to himself. It really took a lot out of him being in jail and then having been betrayed so by Ben or I should correctly say Van. Raven has been a big influence on him. Yes, you read correctly I said Raven. I have doubts about her but he is smitten so I guess I will have to be the one to keep an eye on her as his vision is blurred looking through the roses in his glasses. Truthfully though, she is good for him and I do like her. She has connections in New York for fabrics I need—don't think I am using her for them, okay, maybe a little. I miss you terribly, but at least with her here I have someone to talk to when Granddad is busy.

This ought to paint a wild picture in your mind-- she is even learning to ride! Actually, I think he has been having her ride one of the horses he got with a ranch acquisition that originally came from your herd. The best though was the jeep. You would have laughed if you could have seen her face when Granddad took her for a ride in the jeep!

Well, I just wanted to send a quick hello and let you know we are getting back to normal around here. I hope you will come and visit us sometime.

Love always,

Elizabeth

After reading it to herself, she read the letter aloud to Mary.

"I know you miss her dear, frankly so do I. But isn't it good to know she is back home with her Granddad on their own ranch?" "Yes, it is Mary, but I do miss having her here. Look over there, I think Hank and Baron know we are talking about her." Both dogs held their heads up with their ears perked as Sara and Mary spoke. "She spent a lot of time with them, I am sure they feel the loss as well." They lowered their heads and sighed loudly. "You seem pensive my dear, does her writing about Raven upset you? I know how close the two of you had become." "I am so proud that she has started her business. The turn out on Cotton and Crown was remarkable. We even heard comments in the crowd as to how stunning they looked. And, truthfully, I am glad she has another woman there with her. Always being around the ranch hands is no way for her to learn how to grow as a woman... I do so hope that she and Scott... and yes... Raven will come to the Rodeo. I will make a point to call them with an invitation. This is big... we are hosting the Regional Finals this year. Wow!" "Wow?" "They just grow up... they all grow up... Michael is with the Police Force, Charles is a hot shot Fireman, and Brent... my goodness what he has accomplished with the Rodeo! The boys have taken on lives of their own!" "Yes, they have. And we know we have done our job well when we know they are happy. Every young person you have loved is happy. You are a good woman Sara Moore Barnes." "I have you Mary to be my influence, my teacher, my confidant, and my beloved mother." Sara reached for both of Mary's hands, took them in her own and squeezed tightly as she spoke to her. Each smiled.

Russell, John and Brent entered the room and looked upon the women. Russell was the first to speak. "Girl time?" Sara uttered "Letter from Elizabeth." Brent started to question "Are we in time for..." John interrupted, "Boy, you need to learn this now... you see two women with welled up eyes holding hands and smiling... you let them have their moment. They will explain when and if they want." "But isn't it time for..." "Not until they are ready. It's just a fact of life with a woman... you need to be willing to wait for her on her terms in times like this." "Well said John." "Thank you, Russell." "Is this *all* women or just the older ones?" At that remark John and Russell had great difficulty holding in their laughter until Mary and Sara laughed hysterically. "Geeze... what did I say?"

"Miss Shanks... Miss Shanks..." Calvin pushed himself hurriedly through the multitude of employees rushing toward the elevator at the end of the workday. "Miss Shanks!" Numerous heads turned at the urgency of his voice. Just as she stepped into the elevator car, she heard him. "Please, Miss Shanks!"

"You best find out what he wants, don't be too long or you'll miss the bus." "Why did he wait until now? Two more steps and I would have been out of here!" "Just luck for him, not you though." "I'll call you later. We still on for Clareys tonight?" "See you at seven!" Mary retreated from the elevator, waved good bye to her friend Cindy and then maneuvered her way against the rush of the crowd waiting impatiently for the elevator to return.

"What is it Calvin?" "It's Mr. Jones. He wants to see us right away." "Now? It's quitting time... you know the weekend..."

The gruff voice of Doug Jones halted her from continuing her complaint. "Change your plans whatever they are for the weekend. The two of you are heading on assignment."

Mary and Calvin synchronously turned around to face their employer.

"I'm sorry... about what I was saying..." "No need, I know this is short notice. I need my best team for this. And you two are it. And the bonus is that you... Mary, you have experience with this sort of shoot." "I..." "Let me continue..." Mary bowed her head acknowledging the chastisement. "You are both aware of the whole 'cowboy craze' thing happening... the movies, the television, the boots and skin-tight jeans... even rodeo stars are turning into politicians! I don't get it, but you Miss Shanks, you have lived it and there is a need for us to mark our territory of the profit margins so you my little cowgirl and your sidekick here are going to do just that. You are headed to the town of Brandon where I may add, I first saw your work, to photograph the big Regional Rodeo Finals. Something called the MdoubleRSC..."

"That's not a *thing*, that's a *who* or more appropriately a *what* and what it is... is a Rodeo Stock Company. And you are not seriously asking me to do this?" "Yes I am. You know those people, you are more likely to really get behind the scenes and get the real photographs of the real Rodeo life. You did it once when you were on that fiery Drive, you can do it again." "But..." "No 'buts' you two are going. You leave on the Nine o'clock flight out tonight. There will be a car at the airport waiting for you. Your hotel rooms are already booked, wasn't easy with all the hub bub around this Rodeo but I did manage two rooms at the Brandon Lodge. I imagine you know how to get there Miss Shanks." "Yes, sir. But if it is all the same to you, if I am going to go back again after all this time, I would like to stay at the family ranch. I am sure Calvin can stay as well. My folks will be very entertained by the total city boy! And who knows, maybe we'll even get him on a horse!" "Fine, whatever will make you happy, now go and bring me back the same quality of work you did on that cattle drive. I am really counting on you two. This means a cover story for you and national recognition.

I am sure I do not have to tell you the impact your careers will have…" "No, you do not! Thank you for the opportunity to do this! Miss Shanks and I won't let you down!" Calvin turned to Mary, "You were in a cattle drive? With real cows and horses?" "Yes." "I knew you lived on a ranch but I …"

"Calvin, come in to my office, let me show you what our girl here has done…"

The door to the stairwell closed behind her. Mary couldn't decide if she was enraged or excited. She had not been back to Brandon at all since her leaving. She was saddened by the waning communication with Brent but understood the distance between them was becoming more than miles, it was lifestyle and responsibilities as well. She loved her life in New York. The excitement of the city, her new friends, the fulfillment of her career… but all that came with a price. Brent. She stopped on the landing between the third and the second floor, leaned back against the wall and sighed. "What do I say to him? How will he react to my being there? Oh, God, he is a true cowboy… does he even still love me?"

"Mr. Jones?" "Yes, Calvin" "I didn't tell her, or you even, that she had a visitor some time ago…" "A visitor? What sort of *visitor*? Should I be concerned?" He recalled her hesitancy to leave Brent Thomms when he asked her to work for him. "The young man she was in love with when she first came here." Calvin cowered backward from the larger man as he spoke. "Brent Thomms came to New York? And you never told her?" "No sir. He almost got passed me but I…" "I thank you for that young man, I really do, but now with her going back there, she is most definitely going to find out he was here. We can't risk her ire that will most definitely be aimed at you while you are there." "But, sir, if he mentions he was there he will tell her it was me that kept him back." "You have to tell her. She is a professional, she will handle this with her usual grace and patience. Well, I really hope she does… you didn't know her when she was with him, I did. I suggest you wait until you are in the air to ensure she gets to Brandon. After that, you have your work cut out for you. Now, let me show you these photographs."

———

Marge entered the bedroom and saw Mary sitting on the bed looking at the photo album from the Rodeo when they met Brent and Charles.

"Marge…" "I know what you are going to ask me…"

Mary closed the album and set it to her left side on the comforter.

"You know, some days I think about all that I left behind, this ranch, the cowgirl life… but then I see my photographs in magazines and all the traveling I do, I really love it Marge, I really do."

"We have a copy of every one of your articles. Dad keeps them on display in the living room. He and your mom are so proud of you. So am I. You found what you were meant to be."

"But I broke his heart."

"Yes, you did. But he is resilient and look at what he has built. With the help of the Barnes' and the Moore's he has really made a mark in the Stock business. Did you know the first year they were nominated for the Regional Bucking Horse Stock Company of the Year they won… unanimously! Each year since then they have reclaimed the title and helped the town of Brandon become an economic influence in the state from the revenue of the Rodeo. Even had to create a new department downtown for the Tourism Bureau. Brandon is on the map now and not just for the Rodeo."

"Marge, you know I am so proud of him. I know you do. And, I know you know I tried to keep tabs on him for a while…"

"How could you not, you two were in love…"

"Calvin told me on the plane that Brent came to New York." "I was wondering if you knew…" "I, I wish I had known at the time. His absence of writing has been a worry for quite a while. I guess I just figured the distance thing… but this is Brent… loyal Brent. Now I understand. He thought I didn't want… or need him anymore. He was wrong… I just don't know what I am going to say to him…" "Knowing Brent, he will know exactly what to say." "I am sure you are right."

She knew it was not her place to tell Mary about Becky.

"So, what is up with Calvin?" "Oh my God! We have *got* to get him on a horse! Paybacks for not telling me about Brent's being in New York! The people at work will bust a gut!"

The girls fell back against the pillows laughing as they mimicked Calvin riding.

"Seriously, Mary… wait up!" "If you had worn the boots I put out for you, you wouldn't care where you were stepping!" She could hear the snickers of the crowd as they pushed their way to the Crow's Nest.

"Isn't that Mary Shanks?"

"I think you are right! What's she doing here?"

"She shows up now?"

The last comment she heard caught her attention. A quick look to see who had spoken it revealed Penny Harbin. Their eyes met with a coldness. Penny had taken every advantage point to let it be known that Mary was a step daughter to Paul Pelton. Mary never understood why the animosity was so vehement, and still after the years of her absence, Penny was compelled to continue with it.

Mary decided that now was the time to have the reason revealed.

"Penny, honestly, I have no idea why you are so angry towards me. All through school you were a bully to me and now, after all this time... time when I don't even live here anymore... I don't get it. What was done that was so wrong, so many years ago that you just can't let it go?"

The confrontation between the women halted numerous passersby. Mary noticed two of their classmates snickering secrets to others to heighten their curiosity.

Penny stood shocked at the stance of Mary before her. Molly and Amy turned to look at her with the same question reflected in their eyes.

Hoping to hold onto the grander stance, Penny took in a deep breath, let it out with a snarled sigh. She straightened both her arms and opened them across Molly and Amy with a pushing back motion as she walked three steps to Mary and stood before her. "He was supposed to be *my* step father not yours! Your mother weaseled her way into a party that he was hosting for my mother's birthday... yes, that's right... he and my mother were quite the item for a long time. It was just assumed that at the party he was going to propose... but then your mother showed up! I remember it clearly. She wore white go-go boots and a yellow angel dress like she was a *Bond Girl*... well one look at her and Paul Pelton turned into 007... my mother left that party in tears. I will never forgive your mother for that night and that goes for you too."

"Your indignation has consumed you for many years. I was in no way ever a part in the primary cause of your fury. Yet you assigned the punishment upon me in our youth and it harbors in you still. This rancor... my goodness Penny, we are grown women now! How long are you going to hold onto this?"

Amy and Molly walked around Penny and stood with Mary.

Keeping eye contact with Mary, Penny stepped back from her nemesis. Realizing the truth in Mary's words, she felt abashed for her actions.

"You talk in big city girl words… but you are right. It really never had anything to do with you. I was mad. Mad at my mother for not trying harder. It was selfish on my part. The Pelton's had so much money and a big ranch. I hated that you got to have what I wanted. I am sorry, Mary. I really am." "Thank you. Friends?" "Sure. By the way, who's the guy with you? He is definitely out of place at a Rodeo!" All four giggled. "That's Calvin, my assistant. And you are right he's never been out of the city. I best get to finding him we have work to do. We are doing a feature on the Rodeo. Maybe I'll see you later." Mary turned and was in pursuit of Calvin before Penny had a chance to say good bye.

"You should have told her about Becky."
"Oh, hell no! That's my last hoorah for her! Karma… it's a bitchy thing."

"I see you and the equipment survived without me!" "Who was that? You two didn't look much like you were having a 'gee it's been so long since I've seen you' kind of reunion talk." "It was long overdue but untrustworthy." "Girls… you are just toooooo complicated. Where to now?"

"The chutes. We can get shots of the cowboys as they ready for their rides." "Ride on! Partner!" "Calvin, stop." Mary shook her head. "Yes, boss…"

Sitting at the table against the back wall of the Crows Nest; Russell, Sara, Mrs. Harrison and Brent perused the entries for the upcoming afternoon events.

"Well I'll be! Harlon Myers worked his way up the scores and made it to the Regionals! Good for him!" Brent slapped the table as he complimented the cowboy. "Isn't he the kid that rode Wanda but got D-Qed?" "Yes sir… he would be!" "She's here, today isn't she?" "That she is… man, wouldn't it be just great if he drew her again! I told him if he ever drew her again to look out… she'd remember him."

"Then maybe he ought to not draw her…" "Oh Mom, where's that competitive spirit? You know what a scored ride on her could do for him! And think of the crowd participation!" "But what if he doesn't ride her, then he will feel…" "Mrs. Harrison, he is a tough young man and a good cowboy, Brent is right, either way it would be a good show!" "It's just not the same as when your boys were competing…" Charles stepped off the top stair and engulfed the aging woman from behind in his arms. "You *do* miss the AMIGOS!" "Mr. Hunter!" "And you thought I would miss this? Oh, contraire my best friend's boss' mother… I have been employed as a pick-up man, actually I volunteered for this glorious event and with Michael riding as well, my dear Mrs. Harrison, you shall again be in the presence of the infamous AMIGOS!" "And here I thought our boys had grown up!"

Michael entered the room as Mrs. Harrison guffawed. Jubilantly he added to the conversation, "You know, it has been said that growing old may be mandatory, but growing up… that is optional!" "Not for you Mountain Man… you had no option!" Charles fisted Michael's chest and tipped his head back to look up at his friend. The three young men gathered together in the center of the room, placed right hands together; "A M I G O S !"

Mrs. Harrison placed her right hand on her heart and smiled.

"You alright Miss Shanks?" Mary stopped and stood transfixed looking into the arena. Without waiver of stance she replied to his question. "Oh, Calvin… if you could only know my life growing up here. It was… well… what seems like a movie set to some, it was my life…" "I know… I saw the photographs in Mr. Jones' office. You know he really is proud of you." Removing her stare into the arena she looked around the crowd and the grounds. "I did love the ranch life. I thought I would never live any other way and then I started taking photographs and became entranced in the depiction of sight and sound together in one frame and with no audible words could speak with a greater volume…" "You do have a gift Miss Shanks." After the fire, I was consumed with telling the story through photographs and when I was awarded the

314

showing, well I was… I knew that was my 'path'. But there was Brent. The love of my life. He supported my dreams though I know it broke his heart to do so. Look around, this … this would have been my life. My life with Brent. And I would have been happy… but he knew. He knew. The cost for each of us was so high. The cost was our love and our future." She turned to face Calvin. "When you told me he had come to New York, I was furious with you for intervening. You acted selfishly. But selfishly because you didn't want me to doubt my decision and impair my judgement on the project. In the end you did the wrong thing but for the right reasons… I guess. What I am trying to say…" "Miss Shanks, you will say this in your photographs…" "You are right, and now you need to get names of the people we have photographed and release permissions… and I need to find Brent."

"Oh, no…"

Memories of the first rodeo when she met Brent and she and Marge were dubbed the Roper girls… the Wes Grant trial… Sara's kidnapping… the cattle drive… swirled in her mind as she endeavored to make her way through the horde of spectators and competitors to find Brent. As she approached the storage shed at the entrance to the holding pens, she heard his voice.

She heard a second voice. A female voice she did not recognize.

She leaned back on the wall of the shed, bent forward at the waist and with her hands on her knees; closed her eyes. "You can't stop now girl…" She stood upright and took a step around the front corner of the shed as Brent passionately kissed Becky Burnell. Shocked, Mary retreated to her former stance on the side wall. "Oh God… please don't let him have seen me!" Tears welled in her eyes until they could no longer be held.

She felt a light touch on her shoulder as she started to wipe away the involuntary tears. "No need for that Mary…" She raised her head and rushed into Sara's welcoming embrace.

Sara held her while she sobbed. "Let's find a good place to talk, shall we?" "Yes, I would like that."

They found themselves on the far end of the holding pens sitting on a table beside the spare parking lot entry booth.

"You need to know that he went to New York…" "I do know. Calvin told me on the plane."

"Then you know he never stopped loving you." Mary sighed from her heart, "Yeah…" "When he came back from that trip, the first few days he spoke nary a word. His face illustrated everything he could not bring himself to say. Truthfully, it was heartbreaking for all of us too as you were family, let me rephrase that, you are family. We just always thought…" "I did too." "It took a while and a lot of prodding from Michael and Charles to push Brent passed his sullenness." "Can I ask when he met her?" "This may surprise you, but… her mother Andrea sent her here for the summer to live with her aunt… Peg Alden. She was looking for Timmy Alden in the barns after a rodeo when she and Brent first met." "Sent her here…? From where?" "This may really hit a craw… but the truth is the truth… New York." The sheer torment on the young girls face prompted Sara to continue. "Upstate somewhere… not the city. She had her horse shipped… actually Brent had her horse shipped here. He is at our ranch." "She is from New York… she has a horse… it is here, and at your ranch. I take it by that kiss I just saw the end of summer intentions are past…" "Yes Mary, they are. She has transferred her credits from the College back home to Carnon. And to answer the question I see on your face; yes, he is happy." "I guess that is the most important thing. I never stopped loving him…" "It would seem that the tables have now turned, he had to let you go though it broke his heart so you could pursue your life, now you have to let go of him. I love you Mary, you know that…" "Yes, I do." "Be honest… your life and his life…" "You are right. I do love him, I love what we were, but what we are now… is different." Sara placed her left hand on Mary's right. The women stood. "Oh, Mrs. Barnes…" Sara held her as she cried briefly. "Make sure she treats him well." "On that you have my word. I think the loud speaker just called for Harlon Myers on deck... you really need to see this kid ride... he'd be a great asset to your article. We better hurry."

Brent leaned over the chute 4 gate as Harlan stood on the platform waiting. "Good to see you again kid!" "Oh! Hi Mr. Thomms. I've worked really hard... listened to you, went to several of Mr. Barnes' seminars, even did a few clinics with top riders. I've been preparin' for my re-ride! And looks like today is the day!" "Looks like it... best of rides to you cowboy! Best of rides!" The mare bolted forward, hunched her back and kicked the rear wall of the chute. Brent looked at Harlon and was pleased to see challenge in his eyes and not fear. Brent walked to chute 3 to recheck the gate pins and latch. He could see three young cowboys approach Harlon. "Aint you the fella that rode her but no scored?" "Yes, not that I like that known." "Why wouldn't you want that known? You be the only one to do it score or not! Me and the boys here, we watch that video over and over so we can ride like you!"

Brent smiled.

As Michael approached, "Listen to that..." He motioned with his head to Harlon. "That ought to make his day!" "Yeah... but think about it... he has pressure now to ride that bitch..."

"And now folks the ride you have all been waiting for! The long awaited and most anticipated re match of Harlon Myers and the famed bucking mare Wanda! Folks, we have waited years for this day! You may recall that a young Harlon Myers was the first... and still the only cowboy to remain astride Wanda at the buzzer. His misfortune of croup contact ended in a no score but whoo doggie! What a ride! Today he hopes to end her reign as the 'Un-rideable Wanda. Hold onto your seats ladies and gentlemen..."

As if she knew her title depended on this ride, Wanda started rocking front to back in the chute. "Ah... that don't look good Mr. Myers..." "You can't let the horse intimidate you... plus, this way I know where her head is at… you learn to read the behavior in the chutes and apply it to the ride."

Wanda sprang into the air, hurled her hind legs back into the chute. The clatter silenced the crowd. She had their attention.

Harlon adjusted his glove, stepped side to side, shook his arms and took a deep breath. This was the moment he had been waiting for. His career depended on this ride. Their last ride played over in his mind. He was ready.

Wanda was ready too.

Snort.

Stomp.

Harlon positioned himself over the mare. She turned her head ever so slightly and at the moment he tipped his hat, she did not wait for the chute gate to open.

She threw herself against the chute gate as it opened, spun to the right almost crashing back into the chute. She actually backed away from the chute while thrusting to the right so as not to fall into it. The sudden lunge into the air and twist back to the left with haunches straight up… Harlon nearly missed his shoulder rake. The crowd gasped. Tucking her head, she thrust her hindquarters as high above her shoulders as she could without falling forward, she twisted back to the right and kicked out. She could not unseat him. The snorts and the guttural groans intensified as she tried harder to throw him. Another lunge to the right as she bucked, and then to the left, malevolently she tried to disengage herself from man expertly raking her shoulders and seemingly knowing her next maneuver. Opting to change her signature move of the right thrust to a left, she hunched her back as she kicked her haunches as high up and far out as she could; this is where the cowboys that made it this far would slap her hip and be disqualified. A final grunt and she was in the air.

She did not feel the touch of his hand on her haunch.

The eight second buzzer sounded. The crowd stood with ovation. Hands clapping, whistles and shouts for the young man and his triumph. Harlon dismounted in a daze. He knew not how he got to the ground, he just knew that he rode the mare.

"Congratulations to Harlon Myers! Folks... okay folks... lets quiet down to get the judges scores..."

"The scores are in... Score for the horse is 49..." The crowd cheered. "Score for Harlon Myers...43! That's a combined score of 92! Folks, I think history has been made here today!"
Harlon dropped to his knees, took his hat off, placed it before him on the ground, crossed his arms on his chest and first tipped his head forward to look low and then threw it back as he opened his arms. "Thank you, Lord for your protection and your guidance!"

The crowd joined him with their applause.

"Hold on a minute everyone! Please, quiet... I have an announcement!" The crowd remained standing. "With today's remarkable ride Harlon Myers has now qualified for the National Finals! Yes, folks one of Brandon's own is going to ride at the National Finals Rodeo in Las Vegas! Let's give our cowboy a hand!"

Harlon held his hands up; "Wait... please wait. Thank you everyone for your enthusiasm. I am thrilled to have ranked for the NFR, but I have to say something..." He turned to the Crows nest. "In the Crows Nest stand two men that encouraged me and taught me the meaning of a dedicated cowboy. With their help and the love of the Lord, I have realized a great achievement. I thank Brent Thomms and Russell Barnes with all my heart." Cheers from the crowd. "And... and I would not be the cowboy I am today if it were not for the great, and I do mean great twelve hundred pounds of 'mare mad' named Wanda!"

Michael lead the mare to the center of the arena to stand with Harlon. He placed the palm of his right hand on the bridge of her nose and leaned in to whisper "You are truly a fine mare. I am sure that we will see you in the Bucking Horse Hall of Fame real soon." She lifted her head and whinnied.

Calvin leaned over to Mary; Shit girl… this is raw… really raw." "You have to live it to understand it." "Actually, Mary, I think it's possible that everyone has a little cowboy in their heart, it's just we don't know really how to find it, until something like this." "You may be right Calvin. You may be right."

Part 14
It's all about the Love

"Mrs. Moore, do you think that there will be another one of those Drives like Mary photographed and I hear so much about? My goodness, even the students and professors at school talk about the famed *Fire Drive*. When they found out that I live over this way everyone asked me questions that I really could not fully answer. Brent told me some about it, but... well... I don't push it due to that being when he was with Mary Shanks and all. I know this ranch is one of the founding ranches of the area and what happens around here is big news."

Mary Moore placed the plate she had rinsed in the drying rack. "Big news for the busy bodies that's all! Sometimes I wish we could just be left alone, but I know that won't happen. Mr. Moore and I come from a different time; a time when family business stayed in the family. But now, these 'new' days, with everyone travelling so much more, and gee... did you ever think there would be telephones for our trucks? And that fancy computer in the office? I see the benefits for the business, I do. But all these newfangled things... just seem so complicated to me.

"Oh, Mrs. Moore, you should see all the technology at school, it is so exciting! Professor Borth said that someday we might even have hand held computers!" "Oh, hog wash... there is no way that anything like that monstrosity in the office is ever going to be so small as to fit in your hand!"

Gram Moore put the dishes away as Becky dried them.

"I sure am glad Timmy came with you today Becky and I am certain your aunt Peg is relieved to have you there to stay with him while she is in treatment. I know it must be difficult for you with your classes and working at the Co-op. By the way, how is that going?"

"Mrs. Moore, it is just so great. Mr. Barnes now has me doing all the buying of the Boots, Hats and Tack for the Equine and Ranch Wear division. I thought Mrs. Barnes did that…" "She did." Gram paused momentarily then continued. "I overheard her and Russell one evening talking about it, she said she had been waiting for the chance to spend more time at home with the ranch equine breeding program and with you and your aptitude for the business, she encouraged Russell to give you the opportunity to prove yourself. I am thrilled you have risen to the challenge. Makes an old woman happy as a sapling to see how life grows the trees!" "Um… I don't…" Becky began expressing her confusion as John Moore entered the kitchen. "Fret not Miss Becky, you will find the matriarch of this family is full of quips. Personally, I think she makes them up as she pleases. But they are cute and I love them… and her." He had been walking toward her as he spoke. Wrapping his arms around her, he kissed her forehead. "Never quit quipping my dear, never quit quipping!"

Still looping the holder around her pony tail, Sara pranced into the kitchen. "Anyone been to the post box yet today?" "You are sure happy…" "The magazine that Mary's article is in should be delivered today!" "Since when do we get a magazine from New York?" Sara kiddingly tapped John on the back. "Since Brandon's finest photographer moved there! Not paying a lot of attention to the postal periodicals these days?" "I guess not, I feel the punishment for my lack of 'observationary' skills shall be the task of walking to the mail box."

"Did I hear John's voice?" "Yes, Russell you did. He is going to the post box… Mary's article is in this month's 'J' magazine. I sure am looking forward to seeing her photographs and reading the article. She was so excited the day she called… she has the cover story!" Smiling at his wife, Russell reflected her ardor. "That does not surprise me… the talent she has with a lens, she was bound to have the cover story sooner or later." Sara poured a cup of coffee for herself and one for Russell. "For you…" He kissed her cheek, "Thank you, my love."

Michael came into the kitchen from the back room.

"Gram... is that the aroma of nearly... I'd say they have four more minutes to bake maple buns blessing the internals of my nasal passages?" "Hello to you my favorite grandson... and yes, you are correct the buns will be done soon. If you would, please get the table ready?" "On it!" Michael leaned in to whisper in his grandmother's ear; "Do I get the first bun if I do?" She giggled as she turned to him; "Of course!" "Then I'm in double time!"

Closing the top drawer of the office desk that now housed the computer keyboard, Brent leaned back in the chair. Looking around the room at the generations of history before him, a sense of calm enveloped him. He could hear Becky's laugh in the kitchen with Gram Moore.

"Lord, thank you for the Blessings in my life. You have held me through hardships and you have released me in valor. Thank you for Becky. You have gifted me the woman that completes me. I will honor her and you... I promise."

"Sure smells good in here!" "Brent! You finally get your head out of those ledgers?" "Ledgers? You haven't heard... Mr. Moore, I believe you should be the one to tell him..." John sat upright in the captain's chair and puffed his chest. With a little wiggle in his torso he grinned as he made his proclamation. "Michael, we have evolved in to the age of home computers! Got a nifty one in the office that has all kinds of programs for the business. Sure has been a big help for Brent. Me, I just play solitaire and oh, yeah, this POGO place..." "Gramp... are you playing *games* on the computer?" Michael placed his right arm over the shoulders of his grandfather. John looked up at Michael, "They are not *games,* they are mind activities!"

Mary laughed aloud.

Opening the back door, Charles heard the laughter as he and Marge entered the back room.

"Sounds like we are just in time for a breakfast party!" Marge positioned their boots on the mat by the coat rack. "I do believe we are!" "Not without me!" Marge turned and when she saw Katy, the two girls tipped back and then embraced. "Oh, my goodness! Katy! I didn't know you were in town!" "It's a surprise."

"Ooooey! I smell maple buns!" Lifting his head and raising his nose upward, Charles took in the scent of the freshly baked sweet rolls.

"Look who is here!" Marge delighted in Charles' allowing of her to make the announcement.
"Katy! This is wonderful... we are all here, oh my..." "I know, Gram... more chairs. Charles and I will be right back; Mountain man probably wants to kiss his bride to be!" "You got that right Brent!" Michael picked Katy up and then twirled in circles as he kissed her.

"Hear ye, hear ye! I come bearing the awaited arrival!" John placed the brown paper wrapped publication on the table.

Ten sets of eyes stared at the concealing parchment-like covering in the center of the table.

Nine of the persons wondered how Becky felt about the attention being given to Brent's former flame.

Becky could see the concern of those sitting around the table. She knew it was for her to relieve them of their worries.

"I'm fine, really. I met her... remember? She is a part of who Brent is, and I thank her for that. She is talented and she is a part of this 'family'... please, I want to see it as much as you do."

Placing his left arm over her shoulders and his right hand on hers, Brent pulled himself closer to Becky. She placed her left hand on his; squeezing it affectionately.

Sara opened the casing, "Oh! Look! Harlan and Wanda are on the cover!" Russell read the headline on the lower right corner; "It's all about the Love." Sara leafed through the first two pages to the table of contents. "Page twelve... here it is!" "The pictures... we want to see the pictures; we can read the article later when we have time." "Okay, Mary..."

"It's all about the Love"

An in depth look at the heart of the cowboy and the ranch life of the Contemporary American West. Photography by Mary Shanks with sincere appreciation to the men and women of the Mdouble RSC and her home town of Brandon for the inspiration to write this story.

"The angles... how did she get that? That horse bucked so fast, how did she get it to seem like it stayed still just for her?" "Becky, remember the photographs of the fire? She can make the camera do whatever she wants." "She sure can Brent. These are amazing!"

Sara turned the pages eight times before the final photograph, the one of Harlon with his hand on Wanda's head.

"You guys go ahead and have your maple buns, I'm going to go in the den and read the article." Pushing her chair back from the table, Sara stood and then walked to the solitude of the adjoining room.
Mary leaned against the left side of the pocket doors to the den. "Care if I join you?" Sara looked upon the frail figure in the doorway. "By all means, that would be lovely." Mary slowly made her way to the sofa and then settled on the middle cushion beside Sara. "Sara, before we read the article, I need to tell you something."

"I know something is wrong Mary, I've known for some time, I have waited for you..." "I know you have. I have seen it in your eyes for weeks. A poker face you have not. I want to tell you that the worst of it is over." "The worst of what, Mary? I have been so worried. Ever since we went to the Cutter Race... you were so thin then and always, well...

just not you." Mary took Sara's hands in her own and slightly tightened her grip. "At first the doctor thought I had Rheumatoid Arthritis, that was about the time of the race." "Oh, Mary... no!" "But then..." She paused before continuing. "But then a visiting doctor from Carnon suggested we test for Lyme Disease." "Lyme? But that's an eastern and mid west occurrence." "Yes, primarily, but the upswing in travel and the climate changes are shifting the locales for a lot of insect borne bacteria and viruses. Because of my symptoms and that we live where we do, my doctor here in Brandon was certain it was Rheumatoid Arthritis. But as you know, my symptoms prevailed through rigorous attempts for relief through many medications. The headaches worsened and became more frequent, the joint pain was soon barely relieved; then one day when I was at an appointment this Dr. Sawyer from Carnon was visiting Dr. Leonard and he suggested testing for the Lyme bacteria. Sure enough the test came back positive. Keep in mind it has now been several weeks and the bacteria has gained a strong hold in my system. The course of action we took was a ten week term of Rocephin[13]. It was during that time that I lost so much weight. I just didn't want to eat and if I did, the nausea was horrendous." "I remember... you just always said you had a touch of the flu." "It was a plausible cover up. When the Rocephin was done, I felt better but that was short lived. I am now on Amoxicillin[14] for thirty days and that will hopefully keep the disease at bay long enough for my body to rid itself of the bacteria." "And if it doesn't?" "Then I will go back on the Rocephin. I might even have to go to Carnon General Hospital where Dr. Sawyer practices. But that is the worst case scenario. I do feel better, let us hope and pray that the Amoxicillin will do the trick and all will be good really soon." "Oh my God, Mary... you have been through so much, why didn't you tell me? How much does John know?" "I swore him to secrecy. Until I knew one way or the other how this was going to turn out, I did not want to burden you." "But I could have gone with you for the treatments..." "My dear, you have so much on your plate I did not want to add more.

---

13 Rocephin: is a cephalosporin antibiotic used to treat bacterial infections.

14 Amoxicillin: a penicillin antibiotic that fights bacteria.

I was, I am… fine. John did accompany me once we knew what we were actually dealing with."

Sara bowed her head. "Oh, my dear Sara, don't… don't be upset." Gently lifting Sara's chin with her left hand, Mary wiped the tear on her cheek with her right finger tips. "I am going to be just fine. I will admit there for a while it was up for debate, but I am going to be fine."

Sara held Mary in her arms with the fervor of a lost child having found its mother. "I love you so much, I can't bear it that you are sick. Please, please promise me that you will not hide this or any other from me, please." "I promise, now, let's get to Mary's cover story."

"Mom? Are you and Gram about done in there? It seems Brent and Charles are chompin' at the bit about something in here!"

Sara and Mary had finished reading the article and were taking in the heartfelt confessions of a young girl living the ranch life and growing into a woman through the ethics and mores known as the Cowboy Code. She explained how it was to be a part of a community and to honor the unspoken 'known' ways. Her photographs of the cowboys and cowgirls both young and old illustrated the complete dedication to a beloved lifestyle and respectful way of life. She wrote from her heart as her heart knew firsthand what the photographs meant. Her understanding of the strife and triumphs came through in every paragraph. The quotes from the contestants solidified all that she penned. And the final photograph, the one of Harlon and Wanda; she had written what he had spoken at that moment. He spoke of his love for Rodeo, his love for horses and his commitment to both. He praised a great horse before accepting it for himself, he revered his family and he exalted the Lord-- True 'Cowboy Code.'

"We certainly wouldn't want them to break any teeth!" Sara jokingly replied her son's question. Brent and Charles stood from there chairs and held them out for Mary and Sara.

Brent smiled at his lifelong friend, "Ready?" "Yup, just as we planned." "Okay, here goes." Brent offered his hand to Becky as Charles did the same to Marge. The girls looked at each other silently asking if the other knew what was going on.

"Michael…"

Charles had prerecorded the music portion only of Amy Grant's song *Every Heartbeat.* Just prior to Michael pressing the play button on the recorder he handed each of his best friends a long stemmed red rose.

Brent and Charles each held the rose as their microphone while they sang selected words to the song in unison to Becky and Marge.

Hear me speak what's on my mind
Let me give this testimony
To reaffirm that you will find
That you are my one and only
No exception to this rule
I'm simple but I'm no fool
I've got a witness happy to say
Every hour, every day
Every heartbeat bears your name
Loud and clear they stake my claim
My red blood runs true blue
And every heartbeat belongs to you
Oh, oh, oh, oh
Yeah, sure maybe I'm on the edge
But I love you baby and like I said
I'm here to tell you
I'm here to stay
Every hour, every day

When they were finished and the music was trailing off, Brent and Charles each bent down on one knee, opened a velvet covered ring box and proposed marriage.

Sara was the first to stand and cheer, then Russell. Katy helped Gram Moore to stand and Michael assisted his grandfather.

Becky and Marge simultaneously burst into tears and said "Yes!!!"

"Oh Goodness! Brent… does your mom know? I have to call her…" "Slow down, Mrs. B… she knows. She wanted to be here but she and Mark are at a legal convention in Denver." Brent turned to Becky, "She was pulling for you to say yes Becky, she loves you and is really happy that you will be her daughter in law. But I have to tell you, she'll be removing that 'in law' part right away!" "Fine by me, I love her, too"

Sara turned her attention to Marge. "And your family?"   Before he could answer Paul and Betty Pelton arrived to join in the celebration.

"Mom? Dad? Did you know about this?"   "As a matter of fact, yes. Charles came to the ranch a couple weeks ago and in true gentlemanly manner asked for your hand. I whole heartedly gave permission. We watched the whole thing from the back room. Charles blocked the door open so when we came in you would not know. We had to be here but we knew if we came in that you would question why we were here and we did not want to jeopardize their intentions." "Oh, my sweet little girl, I am the happiest mother in the world right now!" Embracing her daughter, Betty reached her arm out to Charles.

"I think we need more than coffee for this!"   John Moore started toward the den when Timmy flung the door open and threw himself into the middle of the adults.

"Come quick! Hurry! It's Mara… somethings wrong… she is down in her stall and won't get up! She's making horrible noises! Call a Vet! She's reeaaly sick!"

"Consider the Vet called young master Tim, Dr. Katy at your service. Take me to the patient!"

"Hurry Dr. Katy! Hurry!" Timmy grabbed her hand and hastily pulled her through the doorway to the back room and soon the sound of the back door slamming filled the room.

Sara did not have time to apprise Katy of Mara's condition.

"Oh, Dr. Katy, I just didn't know what to do! I, I... really love Mara and so does Mrs. Barnes! You have to fix her! She just *has* to be alright!

"What stall is she in Timmy?"

"Hurry, down on the end, the right side, Hurry Dr. Katy!"

Katy had her right hand on the latch of the stall as she looked in at the mare.

Sara had reached her and was standing beside her. Katy smiled at Sara. Softly Sara spoke, "He didn't give me a chance to explain"

"Timmy, come here..." Katy opened the stall door. "Come see a miracle."

"Is she okay"

"She's more than okay... she's a new mother!"

"A mommy!? Can I go in Mrs. Barnes? Can I, can I?"

"I'll go in with you, we'll stay off to the side so we don't upset Mara."

They knelt in the straw beside the hay feeder.

Timmy turned to Sara slowly, "When's he gonna stand up? I want to see him stand! How soon before he nurses? He is all wet, should we dry him off? I'll get towels if you want me to!"

Katy walked to Mara to check her vital signs and to congratulate her on her colt. Hearing the questions he asked to Sara, Katy giggled as she addressed Timmy.

"So many questions from you Timmy, all will be answered... right now you have to give him a few minutes, he did just endure being born."

Sara pulled the young boy to her so they knelt together just as the colt made his first attempt to stand.

The others had joined them in the barn. Russell, Becky, Brent, Charles, Marge and Michael stood in the aisleway crowding the front stall wall. Gramp held Gram in front of him in the doorway. Mary looked at her husband, "John, it doesn't matter how many times I see this, it is a Blessing from God that amazes me." She looked back at the mare and colt. Sara smiled at her mother in law as their eyes met. John replied, "It's all about the Love. She sure said it right."

The colt stood on wobbly legs and attempted his first snort. Timmy laughed.
"Go ahead, stay low... go slow..." Sara waved her hand in permission.

Timmy knelt in the straw at the colt's shoulder.
The colt reached his head around and tickled Timmy's cheek with the inquisitive movement of his soft muzzle.

Mara whinnied. The colt uttered his first whinny.

Sara stood and reached through the stall front to Russell. He took her hand.

"Look around us... look at this family, these friends that are family, this life, this ranch, the hopes and the aspirations, the young hearts eagerly striving for growth. Russell..."

"I know Sara, I know."

Everyone remained transfixed on the young boy rubbing the colt. Each onlooker held the representation differently yet all the conclusions were the same.

It's all about the Love.

CPSIA information can be obtained
at www.ICGtesting.com
Printed in the USA
FFHW012321080619
52907525-58498FF